THIS QUEST IS BROKEN!

J.P. Valentine

To the community of authors who've been mentors, supporters, and above all, friends.

Chapter 1

The Questing Stones

Eve flicked her status screen open and shut, the hideous blue boxes flashing in and out of vision at a blistering pace.

"Evelia Greene, don't think I don't see you! Any more of that flickering and you'll give yourself a seizure. Remember what happened to Mr. Potts."

Eve rolled her eyes. "*Everything* gives Mr. Potts a seizure." Still, she heeded her mother's words, ceasing the mindless blinking as the queue moved ever-so-slightly forward.

Seizure-inducing or otherwise, now of all times the girl had every right to indulge her nervous tic. Today would, after all, be the first time in years the unsightly status page would actually *change*. Eve could only hope it'd be for the better.

The woman harrumphed as she checked to make sure Eve's eyes didn't continue the telltale blue twinkling, but otherwise didn't chastise her further.

Martha Greene looked every bit the spitting image of her daughter. She had the same prominent cheekbones, the same lightly-freckled pale skin, and the same shoulder-length dead-straight hair which a poet might call 'chestnut' but any reasonable human being would call 'brown.' Effectively, she looked the same as every *other* resident of Nowherested.

Eve brushed a chestnut lock behind her ear as the family ahead of them in line took another step towards their shared destination. The Questing Stones loomed.

Nobody quite knew how or why the half-dozen misshapen granite monoliths traveled across the kingdom of Leshk, only that they refused to move while anyone was looking. A number of cities throughout history had tried to keep the Stones in place by hiring lookouts to monitor them at all times, but such attempts always failed when local adventurers began receiving quests to murder the watchers.

Eve cared little about such mysteries. What mattered to her, and indeed all the villagers in the isolated farming community, was that the magical boulders made their way to Nowherested precisely once every nine years, eleven months, twenty-two days, and six hours, give or take twenty minutes. The Questing Stones were nothing if not punctual.

She'd been a girl of seven when last the Stones had visited, far too young to embrace their power. Some might've thought her unlucky to be forced to wait so long before discovering her life's quest, but Eve rarely resented the fact. Mostly she pitied Wesley Rollund, unfortunate enough to reach nineteen and still bear the useless *Child* class. Wes more than anyone deserved to celebrate this day.

If she stood on her toes and craned her neck, Eve could just spot Wes's own chestnut mop towering above the rest of the line. Though technically still a child, already the boy stood taller than any man in the village. He'd make a fearsome *Warrior* should the Stones so choose.

2

As the queue inched ever forward, Eve's thoughts turned to her own quest. Just like every other youth throughout the kingdom, she'd spent her fair share of lazy afternoons daydreaming about the endless possibilities.

The *likely* possibilities, on the other hand, were far more limited. This was Nowherested, after all. They didn't have grand tournaments to win or ferocious beasts to slay. Eve had long given up on the idea of becoming a legendary hero saving the land from some apocalyptic threat. As long as she got a better quest than her mother, she'd be happy.

It wasn't that Martha's life goal was *bad* per se. 'Knit the comfiest sweater ever known' was a perfectly acceptable quest, and the *Clothes Mender* class that came with it practically guaranteed her a stable living, especially after advancing it to *Seamstress*. The woman's failed attempts even left Eve with quite the collection of remarkably comfortable garments.

She'd never admit it, but Eve found her mother's quest boring. The same could be said of practically every quest in Nowherested. Sometimes the girl caught herself thinking it wasn't the quests that were unexciting, but the village itself.

More than anything, Evelia Greene yearned to travel. Most of her dreams involved picking up a *Peddler* class and touring the kingdom. How wondrous it would be to see for herself the Cherry Woods, the Great Crossing at Ilvia, or even Pyrindel itself. She wanted none of that monster-fighting nonsense. Others could risk their lives in the wilds; roads were plenty good for her.

Theories on the mechanism behind quest assignment varied. Some scholars claimed the Stones doled out missions randomly, while others professed the monument had some greater plan.

The common thinking among the people argued that the

3

mysterious boulders only formalized a person's true desires, but Eve had a hard time believing *knitting sweaters* was anyone's truest desire. Still, she liked the peasants' theory, if only because it gave her some hope she'd get a worthwhile quest.

A commotion at the head of the line forced Eve from her reverie.

"Stop joking around!" a gruff voice commanded. "What did you *really* get?"

Eve peeked her head to see Wes staring wide-eyed at his stout father.

"I'm not joking! It really says 'Slay the Blightmaw Dragon.'"

"Not in fucking Nowherested it doesn't," the blacksmith spat. "I suppose it gave you some noble warrior class like all the other suicidal fools who go chasing dragons?"

Wes paled. "Um... no, actually." He raised a musclebound arm, turning his palm to the sky. A weak ball of fire appeared in his hand, its flickering glow all but invisible in the late afternoon sun. Though it licked the man's fingers, his skin remained unscathed. "I'm a *Flame Initiate.*"

Eve gaped. Martha stared. All about them villagers looked on in awe.

Mr. Rollund sputtered. "A bloody *magician?* Gods below. Next you'll be telling me little Sally is gonna be a berserker." He jerked his thumb at the eleven-year-old girl next in line for the Questing Stones.

A bead of sweat ran down Wes's brow. "C'mon, Da. Can't we talk about this back at the smithy?"

"Are you kidding?" A portly fellow stepped from the crowd of onlookers, his chef's apron still tied around his waist. "We should be celebrating! Nowherested has its very own hero! Come along, everyone, first round is on me!"

As the gathering broke apart to follow the man, it didn't escape Eve's notice that the very man calling for celebration also happened to own the local tavern. The villagers, largely, didn't care.

While the majority of the spectators moved to start the evening's festivities early, Wes himself didn't follow. Eve gave the new initiate a look of sympathy as his father dragged him back to the smithy to discuss the day's revelations and what they might mean for the future. She pitied them both.

Whether or not Wes survived his quest, Mr. Rollund had already lost his son to the spirit of adventure. Meanwhile the mage now found himself thrust into harm's way, whether he liked it or not. The Questing Stones would not be denied.

For her part, Eve relaxed at the crowd's departure. Fewer onlookers meant less attention as she received her own class and quest. However confident she may have been that her results would be uninteresting, the last thing she wanted was to become the gossip mill's new target. With any luck, Wes would occupy them for the foreseeable future.

The line continued its agonizing crawl forward as each family stopped to congratulate their newly minted *Baker's Assistant* or *Farmhand.* "Why can't they celebrate *after* getting out of everyone's way?"

"Have patience, Evelia," her mother replied. "They're just as excited as you are."

Maybe if you didn't spend an hour coordinating your outfit this morning we would've been done by now. Eve kept the thought to herself; speaking it aloud would only earn her another argument. As it was, their late arrival had left them near the back of the queue, forced to watch as villager after villager learned the true path their lives would walk. Eve bristled.

5

The hours dragged on as the young woman grew inexorably closer to her destiny. By the time Evelia Green stood unimpeded before the upright granite slabs, the summer sun had nearly reached the end of its daily journey. The sky painted itself in a symphony of oranges and pinks, the clouds themselves reveling in the majesty of its color.

Eve ignored the sunset. Pretty as it was, her attention hung elsewhere.

The Questing Stones were six in total, arranged this night in an uneven circle. They didn't glow with arcane sigils or sing a chorus to the heavens. They were rocks. Really big rocks standing vertically in a cluster, but still rocks. Eve's heart pounded as she stepped towards the center.

This was it. Seventeen years growing up in the village of Nowherested, seventeen years of household chores and modeling Martha's sweaters and countless daydreams all led up to this very moment. Eve held her breath.

Unbidden, her status screen popped up along with a second box in the same familiar garish blue.

Life Quest assigned: Head to the next town over and pick up a loaf of bread.

What?

Stomach lurching, Eve panned her eyes over to her status screen.

Evelia Greene
Level 1 Messenger Girl

Seriously, not even 'Messenger Woman?' Just 'Messenger' would've been better! She swore, her mounting frustration at the pointless quest overflowing into the class that came with it. She exhaled. Belittling name aside, the class wasn't all bad. It wasn't *Peddler*, but messengers traveled too, right?

Eve banished the message and status page. She could read the class description later; others still awaited their turn with the Stones. Swallowing down her disappointment, confusion, and excitement, the *Messenger Girl* turned to leave the Questing Stones behind, stepping away from their frigid stillness and into the rest of her life.

* * *

By the time Eve arrived at *The Sower's Mug*, the festivities were in full swing. Proud parents toasted their young *Whittlers* and *Weed-pullers* with full tankards and heaping plates of roast pig and summer vegetables. A teen poured drinks for the rowdy patrons, already practicing his new *Barkeep* class.

Of course, a majority of the recently classed villagers were too young to partake in the alcoholic portion of the revel, but that didn't stop them from feasting on delicious food and far too many sweets.

Eve's mind still raced as she joined her mother at a corner table, anxiously awaiting an opportunity to read further about her new class or try and glean more information about her strange quest. *It couldn't be that simple, could it?*

Martha had other ideas. "Stop worrying," she said, reaching for two glasses of mulled wine. "It'll all work out in the end. At least you don't have something impossible." She gestured across the tavern at Wes and his newly-acquired gaggle of fans. "He's either going to die fighting a dragon or spend his life miserably wishing he'd tried."

From what Eve could tell, the 'miserably' part had already started. Despite the magical class and fawning attention, Wes sat slumped in the corner, nursing his fifth mug of ale. Eve imagined some portion of his foul mood could be attributed to the fact his father hadn't joined him for the festivities.

She shook her head, returning to the topic at hand. "I have the opposite problem. I can get to Fidsworth and back in a *day*. What then?"

Martha shrugged. "You get to be done. Most people don't get that. We try and we try and however close we get to completing our quest, we're never *quite* there." She placed a comforting hand on Eve's shoulder. "Maybe this is a good thing. Pop over to Fidsworth, grab the bread, and move on with your life. Just because they give you a quest doesn't mean the Stones get to define your life."

Eve pointed at the boy pouring drinks. "They defined his life." She swung her hand around at another villager. "And his. And hers. And his. And for some gods-damned reason they decided mine wasn't worth defining."

Martha pulled her daughter into a hug. A second passed as they embraced. And another. All around them toasts and cheers and laughter rang through the air as the two women sat in silence.

When at last she spoke, Martha's voice was naught more than a whisper in Eve's ear. "They didn't define *my* life. I'll never give up on it, but my quest stopped being the most important thing a long time ago. Seventeen years ago to be precise."

A slight grin crossed Eve's face as she pulled out of the hug. "Thanks, Ma. I just... what does this mean?"

"You've always said you wanted to explore; maybe the Questing Stones knew. What's the point of exploring if someone's already told you where to go? Maybe you don't need an epic quest to do something worthwhile."

Eve opened her mouth to speak, but the opening chords of "The Hero Sojourns" drowned her out. Before she knew it, the entire tavern fell into a cacophony of well-rehearsed music and drunken singing along. The village's *Musicians*

—they didn't have a full-fledged *Bard*—had arrived.

Eve allowed the conversation to die down in the face of the crescendoing revelry. She took a sip of her wine, determined to enjoy the evening as well as she could. Martha did the same.

In all it took three glasses of the spiced alcohol for the *Seamstress* to fully commit to contributing her own voice to the collection that filled the noisy tavern.

For her part, Eve spent the evening fighting off the urge to check her status page. Desperate as she may have been to learn as much as she could, she needed this night. She'd waited seventeen years to learn her quest, and shitty or otherwise, she was determined to celebrate it.

It wasn't until a rather intoxicated *Carpenter* keeled over and vomited across her nice leather boots that Eve found a reason to excuse herself from the merrymaking. That was enough. After a pleading look earned a nod from her mother, Eve pushed herself to her feet and made for the exit.

She made it less than halfway home before curiosity won over.

Eve paused her trek, leaning against the back wall of the tanner's house as she reopened her quest log. Whether from the booze, the stench of the mess on her boots, or the information she found within, her stomach churned.

Quest: Head to the next town over and pick up a loaf of bread.

Description: Head to the next town over and pick up a loaf of bread.

Difficulty: Legendary

Unwilling or unable to contain her reaction, Evelia Greene allowed her thoughts to bubble up and manifest themselves into words.

"What the fuck?"

Chapter 2

Why is it Always Wolves?

Eve lay awake late into the night, her eyes flush with the azure light of her status screen. Even as the haze of wine lingered about her mind, she knew she needed sleep. One way or another, she was in for a long day tomorrow.

Still she stared, reading and rereading the information and statistics she'd long memorized.

Evelia Greene
Human
Level 1 Messenger Girl
Health: 99/100
Stamina: 43/150
Mana: 0/0
Constitution: 10
Endurance: 15
Intelligence: 11
Dexterity: 10
Strength: 8
Spirit: 0

Spirit and *Mana* were grayed out as always—magic

remained beyond her purview. In fact, the only change her new class brought to Eve's stats was the increase to *Endurance* and its corresponding *Stamina*.   For the thousandth time that night, she brought up the class info.

Messenger Girl
  Common Tier 1 Class
  Exp: 0/10
  The perfect starting job for a young adult with no training. What could be easier than running messages back and forth?
  +4 Endurance
  +1 Endurance/Level

Passive Ability - Haste
  Your boss needs that message delivered ASAP.   You run slightly faster.

Active Ability - Run Away
  20 Stamina
  The best way to survive a fight is to avoid it.   Double your running speed for 7.5 seconds.

The class was… less than promising. Eve supposed having two abilities for escaping combat could prove useful for avoiding bandits, but monsters were remarkably uncommon in the human lands.

On the flip side, if her quest truly *was* of *Legendary* difficulty, running away didn't seem like a useful option. *Messenger Girl* left her no avenues to actually fight anything and thus no avenues to gain valuable experience. The class was so bad she couldn't even level it up!

She dismissed the thought.   She knew Martha had evolved her class just by making progress on her quest; perhaps Eve could do the same. The *Messenger Girl* tried not to think about what progress on 'fetching a loaf of bread' would even look like. Maybe there was a checkpoint for reaching Fidsworth and another for returning with the bread? What if the quest reward was just the loaf itself?

Eve groaned, rolling over to slam her face into the pillow. *There's nothing I can do about it tonight. I just need to sleep.*

If only it were that easy.

For hours she tossed and turned, slipping in and out of slumber as her mind ran in circles. When sleep finally did take her, she dreamt of desperately fleeing an apocalyptic monster that looked all too much like a giant loaf of sourdough.

* * *

Eve emerged from her mother's shop the next morning sluggish and groggy. No matter how she rubbed them, the sleep—or lack thereof—refused to leave her eyes. The journey would be ever so slightly safer if she could make it home before nightfall. Unfortunately, such a strategy mandated an early departure, so on she walked.

She squinted as the light of the rising sun obscured the road to Fidsworth. It was just her luck that she'd be walking into its blinding radiance both on her morning trip east and her afternoon journey back west. Still, equipped with naught but a few coppers with which to purchase the bread, Evelia Greene took the first steps on her *"Legendary"* quest.

She made it ten minutes before a chorus of cheers rang out behind her. Back at the village's edge, a group of townspeople waved and clapped as one particularly tall *Flame Initiate* took his own first steps.

Wes did not look well. He dragged his feet along the dry dirt road, listing to the side as a hand both rubbed his temples and shielded his eyes from the bright sun. Out of pity more so than a desire for company, Eve waited as he caught up.

"G'morning, Wes."

Startled, he tilted his hand to peek under it. "Oh, hey," he groaned. "Evelyn, isn't it?"

"Evelia," she corrected him, "or just Eve."

"Right. Eve."

"How—um—how much did you drink last night?"

Wes shrugged. "Damned if I know. A bit of advice: Don't get hammered the night before your epic adventure."

"Wise words, oh great hero."

"Ugh, don't remind me. Da's still pissed about the whole thing, meanwhile half the village is bloody worshiping me. Honestly, I'm more excited to get away from them than for all this 'adventure' shit."

He gestured down at the patchwork set of ragged armor he wore. "Not to mention all this. How is it every single citizen of Nowherested has an ancient family heirloom I just *need* to take with me? Mr. Potts even gave me a bloody *sword*. I'm a mage!"

Eve looked him up and down. The man was well over six feet tall and built like an ox. Even given the rusted state of his mismatched armor, he cut a fearsome figure. "You don't look like a mage."

"Take that up with the Stones." He withdrew the worn blade from the loop at his belt. "You want this? It's ugly as sin, but I'm sure it's enchanted to all hells. Apparently Great-Great-Grandma Potts was quite the swordswoman."

Eve reached out to claim the saber, but the moment her hand wrapped around the hilt it plummeted to the dirt.

You are not strong enough to wield this weapon.

She bent over to pick it up, managing to raise the hilt but leaving the tip resting on the ground. "I can barely lift it."

"Ah well." Wes casually grabbed the old sword and returned it to his hip. "Maybe someone in Fidsworth will take it off my hands."

"Good idea. Odds are that thing's enchanted to the high hells. With how rusty it is I wouldn't be surprised if it just explodes in your face. Unstable enchantments are dangerous, you know."

Wes paled, wrapping a tight grip around the weapon's hilt.

Eve changed the subject. "So you're heading east too?"

"I guess? It's as good a direction as any. The Stones didn't tell me where this 'Blightmaw Dragon' actually *is*, so I'm mostly just wandering."

"Don't you want to... I don't know, get some training first? There's a mage's college in Pyrindel."

Wes turned, restarting his sluggish trek. "I doubt I could afford whatever tuition they charge. Maybe if I do a few bounties first."

Eve followed. "Sounds like a plan to me. Better to train up as much as you can before going after your dragon." She shook her head. "I can't imagine what it's like to have a quest like that. What's the difficulty on it, anyway?"

"Epic."

His dragon is easier than my bread! Eve paled.

"Terrifying, right?" Wes misread her expression.

"Yeah," she gulped. "Terrifying."

"So that's my story," Wes changed the subject. "Why are you on the road? Starting your own quest?"

"Something like that. I've got an errand to run in Fidsworth."

"Oh, nice. I could use a few hours company. Just don't go all 'great hero' on me again."

Eve laughed, "I can do that."

The conversation faded as the two groggy—and somewhat hungover—adventurers journeyed on. Truth be told, Eve was grateful for the escort. She didn't know Wes particularly well, but the man seemed nice enough, and having *someone* with a combat class could prove essential should things go as sideways as she feared.

The first two hours passed in relative peace. Wild grass on either side of the road swayed in the breeze. The rising sun burned away the last vestiges of the morning chill as colorful birds flew overhead.

Angry as she was at the Questing Stones and her situation in general, Eve couldn't help but allow some of her frustration to slip away in the face of a beautiful summer day. It was downright pleasant.

Just about halfway to Fidsworth, the growling started.

Eve froze. Wes stopped in his tracks, resting a hand on the hilt of his sword. All of a sudden Eve wished she were strong enough to wield the thing.

The grass shifted.

"There's something out there."

Wes glared at her before whispering back, "I can bloody tell."

Eve strained her ears to listen, but the growls seemed to come from every direction at once.

"Maybe we can scare them off," Wes said. "I don't think they want to eat us. Wolves only growl when they're trying to warn off other predators."

"Since when are you an expert on wolves?"

Wes shrugged. "If I can't chase them away, you should run. I'll have an easier time fighting if I don't have to worry about you."

Eve nodded, already prepared to activate her *Run Away* skill. Gods knew if she could outpace a wolf, but alternatives were scarce.

The first of the gray canines stepped onto the road, its lips pulled back in a snarl and its fur standing on end. Another appeared on its left. And another.

The growling behind them grew louder. Eve swung her head about to see two more of the mangy, skeletally thin wolves making their slow approach.

Wes drew his sword. "Eve? Now might be a good time to run."

Eve ran.

Adrenaline coursed through her with every beat of her pounding heart. She watched as her stamina ticked down, depleting ever faster with the activation of her skill. She breathed. The grasslands flew past. A yelp rang out behind her. She didn't stop.

Eve made it nearly three hundred feet before the timer on her skill ran out. In half a second her legs went from propelling her forward at an incredible speed to being completely unable to keep up with the velocity of the rest of her.

She tumbled.

Eve landed hard. Her hands caught her fall as they could, but such was her momentum that she flipped right over them just as they skidded along the dirt road. Her face took the rest of the blow.

For a second she lay there, wincing in the stinging pain of her scraped-up hands and bloody cheek, until adrenaline forced her to her feet. The cloud of dust she'd kicked up still hung in the air, sending her into a fit of full-body coughs. She pushed through it.

Heart racing, Eve looked back.

Already two wolves lay unmoving in the dirt, but the remaining three circled the muscular *Initiate*. Wes clutched the rusty sword with his left hand, his other engulfed in flame. Frantically he waved the fiery appendage at the hungry predators, but the spell did little more than keep them at bay.

Eve wondered how much Mana he had left.

Shit. She sighed. *I have to do something.*

The flames flickered.

I have to do something now. Against every bit of her better judgment, Eve once again took off into a run—this time towards the beasts. Even if her active ability were off its cooldown, she wouldn't have used it. Unpleasant as falling on her face had been, she imagined it would be far worse to do so at a wolf's feet.

The distance closed.

A wolf pounced, getting a faceful of fire magic for its efforts.

Eve's feet pounded against the dirt road, keeping time with her racing heart.

A second wolf leapt at Wes's sword arm, its teeth sinking deep into his decaying leather vambrace. The hand-me-down saber fell to the ground.

Wes pivoted, swinging his *Burning Hand* at the beast still clinging to his arm. The stench of burning fur filled the air as the wolf yelped, writhed, and eventually went limp, falling to the earth.

Two wolves remained.

At once they lunged, one jerking away as Wes's flames swung at it while the other reached his leg unimpeded. He let out a cry as a pair of jaws wrapped around his calf. The wolf tugged, and Wes collapsed.

He kicked and screamed and swung his fiery hand about haphazardly, but the wolves had him now.

Eve charged on.

She had no weapons, no offensive skills, no plan. Her only advantage came in Wes's prone form granting just the distraction she needed. The adrenaline took over.

Eve reached the closest wolf, putting every ounce of her momentum behind a single kick. A sharp pain echoed up her leg as her foot collided with the beast's side. A sharp crack of breaking ribs joined a pitiful yelp as the creature backed off.

Eve surged forward, stepping past the other wolf which still clung to Wes's leg. She stooped over, wrapping a desperate hand around the fallen sword. Eve pulled.

The *Messenger Girl* dragged more than carried the weapon to the remaining beast. The predator paid her little heed, distracted as it was trying to chew through Wes's decrepit leather. Her muscles ached. Her lungs burned. Her scraped-up palms raged against her as she clutched the hilt with both hands.

Mustering every last drop of her measly 8 Strength, Eve swung.

The old blade struck true, if not deep. Its rusted edge pierced barely an inch into the back of the predator's neck. The beast cried out.

Her blow wasn't lethal, but it was enough.

The wolf released its grip, instinctively leaping back to escape this new attacker. Wes sat upright.

The man lunged, reclaiming the sword from Eve's bleeding hands as he took his swing.

He got it in the throat.

The beast collapsed, taking Wes's sword with it. Eve let out a breath, the sheer euphoria of simple survival already flooding her.

Another growl.

"Shit," Wes swore.

Eve turned, finding the wolf she'd kicked had come limping back. Still it snarled. "Come to die with the rest of your pack?" she taunted the thing.

"Eve?" Wes kneeled in the dirt, his injured leg trailing out behind him. "I'm out of Mana."

"Shit."

"Maybe you should grab the sword."

She halted. "Right. The sword."

Eve reached down, planting a foot on the fallen wolf in her attempt to yank the weapon free. The surviving beast limped closer.

The saber's tip left a line in the dirt as she dragged it back to Wes.

The wolf barked, jumping forward in a ragged pounce. It fell several feet short. Still it approached.

Eve spun around.

The wolf leapt again.

The thing landed hard on the edge of the blade, forcing its point yet deeper into the earth just as its edge pierced the creature's hide.

With nary a whimper, the final wolf fell to the hard ground, dead as its pack mates.

"Holy shit."

Wes collapsed, falling back to lie on the roadside. "Some adventurers we are, huh?   Three hours in and we're already an inch from death."

Eve kneeled at the injured man's side, letting out a laugh as she did.   It was a sharp, full-body thing, echoing through the plains with the kind of distraught mirth shared only by the insane and the remarkably lucky. Wes mirrored her grin.

"Are you okay?" Eve asked.   "Can you walk?"   A number of messages flashed in the corner of her vision, but she dismissed them for now. Wes was more important.

"I'll be fine.   And no, I can't walk."   He held up his wounded arm, pointing to a bronze ring around his little finger. "Ring of Regeneration. Mrs. Lester gave it to me. It's slow, but I should be on my feet in a few hours."

Eve nodded. "Okay—um—good." She swung her legs around, rearranging herself to sit beside the man. "I guess we're waiting here for a bit."

Wes looked up at her. "What about your errand? Didn't you need to do something in Fidsworth?"

Eve shrugged, settling in to get comfortable for the coming wait. She had messages to read. "It's alright," she promised. "It's just a loaf of bread. Fidsworth can wait."

Chapter 3

Practice Makes Perfect

You have defeated Level 4 Gray Wolf: +21 exp!
You have defeated Level 5 Gray Wolf: +27 exp!
You have successfully wielded a weapon beyond your Strength: +1 Strength!

Evelia Greene
  Human
  Level 4 Messenger Girl
  Exp: 12/17
  Health: 92/100
  Stamina: 41/180
  Mana: 0/0
  Constitution: 10
  Endurance: 18
  Intelligence: 11
  Dexterity: 10
  Strength: 9
  Spirit: 0

"Good news?"

Eve slammed her eyes shut to keep them from reflecting

her status for all to see. "No peeking!"

Wes chuckled, "I'm not peeking. You're grinning wider than the north river."

Instinctively she raised a hand to cover her mouth before lowering it with a laugh of her own. "Yes, good news." She twisted her thumb to point at the rusty sword. "Three levels plus a point of Strength for using that piece of garbage."

"Garbage? I'll have you know—wait. Did you say three levels?"

Eve nodded.

"I only got one!"

"Wait, really? But you did all the work. I only got credit for the last two. What's your experience at?"

"Now who's peeking?"

Eve rolled her eyes.

"Alright, alright. Since you asked so nicely, I'm at forty-three out of sixty-three."

"Well, that'll do it. I only needed ten for the first level."

Wes furrowed his brow. "And I needed fifty. And now you're almost halfway to your first evolution. That doesn't seem fair."

"Oh, unfair is it, Mr. *Flame Initiate?*" Eve teased. "Remind me how rare your class is, or what you get for each level in it."

"I—uh—walked into that one, didn't I?" Wes sighed. "I suppose I owe you one. It's an Uncommon class; gives three Intelligence and two Spirit for each level."

"You're shitting me. Five times the exp and five times the stats for a single level of rarity? That's insane."

"Not to mention my level costs go up faster than yours. Just imagine what the *really* rare classes are like. At least the crazy stuff doesn't start showing up until the higher tiers."

Instead of replying, Eve's thoughts turned to her own

class advancement. Would she eventually work her way up to a Legendary class to match her quest? She shook her head. There would be time for daydreaming later.

The *Messenger Girl* pushed to her feet, careful to avoid pressing her scraped-up palms against the dirt.

"Where are you off to?"

"Practice." She pointed at her skinned cheek. "The wolves didn't do this; the ground did. Apparently running away is more dangerous than the skill makes it out to be."

Wes cocked an eyebrow. "You have a skill for—of course you do. Alright, let's see it."

Taking a moment to note the duration of her *Run Away* had increased with her Endurance to nine seconds, Eve stepped off the road and into the wild grass. Better to fall on soft greenery than hard dirt.

Bracing herself for another tumble, Eve took off. The plains raced by as she activated her skill, her chestnut hair blowing wildly in the wind. The seconds ticked by. This time when the ability wore off, she was ready.

Eve jumped.

Instead of her upper body falling ahead of her feet, the girl transferred as much momentum as she could into the leap. She made it six feet into the air before the plummet.

Eve hit the ground running, her knees buckling from the force of the landing. She stumbled forward, barely keeping her balance as her arms flailed wildly.

From his vantage over 350 feet away, Wes applauded. "Do it again!" he called out.

Eve held up her hand in a rude gesture. *Well, that kind of worked,* she thought as her breath caught up with her. *It's not exactly graceful, though. Useful for running away but not charging in?*

She held her position away from Wes for a few minutes as her Stamina recovered and the cooldown refreshed. Already new ideas formed. By the time she once again began to run, Eve had another plan in mind.

As she rapidly approached a still-recovering Wes, the *Messenger Girl* counted down the seconds on her only ability.

Seven.

The wind rushed past, pleasantly chilling the scrape on her cheek.

Six.

The grass swayed beneath her feet, blown to and fro by the speed of her passage.

Five.

Her heart raced with both exertion and joy.

Four.

Eve slowed, actively forcing her pace to diminish beneath a full sprint. The final seconds of her skill ticked away, and again her upper body lurched beyond her legs' ability to keep up. Her arms flailed. Her feet flew wildly forward, each stride falling just short of catching her extended tumble.

Until they didn't.

One solid step followed another, until Eve's desperate stumble transformed into an easy, unenhanced run. She came to a halt just next to Wes, doubling over as she let out bursts of laughter through gasps for air.

"That was fast," the *Initiate* said. "What's the trick?"

Taking a moment to regain her breath, Eve replied, "Just 'cause it *lets* me run twice as fast doesn't mean I have to. Just gotta make sure to slow down before the skill times out."

"Makes sense. Congrats on mastering the art of running away."

Eve smacked his shoulder with the back of her hand.

"Hey, if I'm gonna be stuck sitting here with a hole in my leg, I should at least be allowed a *little* fun."

Eve snorted, turning around for another attempt.

"What're you doing now?"

"Joke all you want," she replied, "but I haven't mastered it yet. Still came in too quick on that one." With a breath and a prayer, she was off.

It took two hours—primarily spent waiting for her Stamina to recover—for Eve to grow comfortable with the skill. She still found herself careening forth whenever she misjudged her speed, but at least she kept her feet every time.

By the time she returned to Wes's side, the stress of the workout and the blistering afternoon sun had left her drenched in sweat.

He didn't even need to open his mouth to get the message across.

"Yeah, yeah," Eve replied to his look, "you don't smell fantastic either. You can buy me a room at the inn when we get to Fidsworth."

Wes raised his eyebrows. "*I* can buy?"

"I saved your ass, didn't I? Besides—" she pulled out her handful of coppers—"I only have enough money to buy my bread. I wasn't supposed to stay the night."

"You're going to Fidsworth for *bread?* Why didn't you just get some from Mrs. Lundt back home?"

"You tell me," Eve said, unwilling to explain further. "How's your leg?" She extended a hand to peek under his shin guard.

He swatted it away. "You don't want to look. Believe me, I wish I hadn't. It's recovering, but it isn't pretty. Give it a few more hours."

"In the meantime—" Eve grabbed the sword, dragging it closer—"let's talk about your gear."

"Honestly, I don't know what half this shit even does. I mean, obviously armor is armor, and Mrs. Lester told me about the Ring of Regeneration, but most of this stuff is so old it'd take a bloody *Historian* to identify it."

"Some of it's gotta be enchanted, right? Let's start with this." She ran a finger over the old weapon, her skin coming back up the color of rust. "Cleaning it would be a good first step."

Before Wes could get a chance to protest, she plucked a handful of grass, wadding it up into a makeshift brush. Pressing the flat of the blade into the dirt, she got to work.

Results were mixed.

While the scrubbing managed to remove *some* of the decay, her improvised tool left its own verdant stain upon the ancient saber. "Shit."

Wes rolled his eyes. "This is why we use *actual* brushes to clean steel."

"You have an actual brush?"

He opened his mouth to speak, said nothing, closed it, exhaled, then finally replied, "Da wasn't about to load me up with smithing supplies when I left this morning."

"That's what I thought."

"Well, I guess you couldn't possibly make it *dirtier.*" Wes reached out to reclaim the sword.

"Hold on," Eve stopped him. "Look at this." She traced a finger along the grass stains. "There are symbols here."

Sure enough, the viridescent marks turned out darker in a few particular areas along the flat of the blade. The shapes spelled out *something*, but for the life of her Eve couldn't determine what. "Any idea?"

Wes leaned over to peer at the runes. "It's not any language I've ever seen."

Eve shrugged, flipping the weapon over to examine the back side. A quick scrub with the grass-brush revealed yet more of the strange figures.

You have learned the basic skill Appraise!

Keen eyes and a quick wit can glean a lot from very little.

Understand basic information about a person or thing.

"Gods below," Eve swore. "I got a new skill."

"Wait, seriously? For rubbing some grass on an old sword?"

"Apparently." Turning her gaze back toward the item, Eve activated her new ability.

Rusted Sword
Rarity: Uncommon

"Don't worry," she said. "It's not exactly useful. Just says it's a rusted sword."

"Gimme that." Wes reached out to reclaim his weapon, turning it over in his hands as he examined the runes for himself. He gave it a few minutes before his shoulders deflated. "Nothing."

"Maybe you have to find something new? I already discovered the runes. Hells, it's not like you're short of crap to look over."

Wes didn't hesitate to drop the blade as he turned his attention first to a leather shoulder pad with frayed seams.

While the man worked, Eve tested her *Appraise* on everything from her dirt-stained pants to individual strands of grass to the road itself. None of the targets provided useful information about themselves or the skill she used, until her attention turned back to her traveling companion.

Level 2 Flame Initiate
Uncommon Tier 1 Class

Interesting, Eve mused. *Does it always tell a person's class, or do I only get Wes's because he already told me?*

She got her answer when, twenty minutes later, he discovered a set of initials stitched into the lining of his vambrace.

"Got it!"

"Nice! Now use it on me. I wanna know what it tells you."

"It tells me that you're a… level question mark *Messenger Girl.*" He sputtered. *"Messenger Girl?* Really? No wonder you have a skill for running away."

"Hey, I'll have you know I also have a skill for rubbing grass on old swords."

Wes fell back in a fit of laughter, his entire torso shaking with mirth as he lay upon the soft grass. Eve mirrored his sentiment, though *she* managed to stay upright. The absolute ox of a man was still giggling when Eve spoke again.

"It gave me your exact level—probably something to do with the fact I out-level you. Though with class rarity having such an impact I imagine that's more important."

Shielding his eyes from the sun as he lay on his back, Wes's tone turned serious. "You know, you're quite a bit better than me at this whole 'adventuring' thing. Maybe you should be the one with the Epic quest."

Eve snorted, if for different reasons than Wes might've assumed. "Not on your life."

"Yep, that's fair. I wouldn't wish this on anyone."

Me neither, Wes, Eve thought. *Me neither.*

* * *

It was well past four by the time Wes was recovered enough to restart their journey. Eve didn't mind the wait. Indeed she rather enjoyed the lazy afternoon, well in need of a rest after the morning's excitement.

The fledgling adventurers wiled the hours away with shared stories and lighthearted banter, each teasing the other for all manner of things in and out of their control. The conversation continued as they reembarked.

Once his wounds had mostly vanished, Wes was kind

enough to lend Eve his Ring of Regeneration for the duration of their trip. Though the dried blood remained, the cuts and scrapes along the girl's palms and cheek knit shut well before the outer structures of Fidsworth came into view.

The blue gloom of twilight colored the air as the travelers finally arrived.

The road through Fidsworth was the same packed-earth as back home, the shops and houses the same hewn wood, and the roofs the same dry thatch. The townsfolk came and went in much the same way as in Nowherested. Even the inn sat just as many lots away from the town's edge as *The Sower's Mug*.

"So, on to the baker, then?" Wes asked.

"Yep," Eve answered as they traversed the town's center. "If I remember correctly, it's right over… shit."

Sure enough, the bakery was precisely where she'd expected to find it. She did not, however, expect to find the building unlit and the door latched shut. "They're closed."

Wes shrugged. "Ah well. You were gonna spend the night here anyway. We'll just get you your bread in the morning."

"Yeah, I just…" Eve trailed off. "It's fine. You're right. I can just get it tomorrow."

Wes turned. "Great. Now *that's* out of the way, I'm in dire need of a hot meal."

Eve nodded, trying not to worry about her quest. *It's late*, she told herself. *Of course the bakery's closed. Everything's fine. It's all normal.* She unclenched her jaw. She'd made it to the next town over; now all she had to do was buy a loaf of bread. If she could wait until evening for Wes to recover, she could wait until morning for the shop to open. Easy.

The Laughing Swine sat mostly empty on this particular night, the denizens of Fidsworth still anxiously awaiting their own day with the Questing Stones. Wes haggled with the innkeeper as Eve surveyed the common room.

What few patrons there were fixed their eyes upon the new arrivals, some with curiosity and others with suspicion. It wasn't common in these parts to see a stranger so heavily armored as Wes, even if his getup looked like it belonged in a trash heap.

One man in particular caught Eve's attention. Though his thick brown hair and unkempt mustache weren't out of place in the farming village, the way he kept his eyes trained on Wes certainly was. His wasn't the cautious gaze of a townsperson watching an outsider, but a deep scowl at some perceived slight.

Just as Eve thought to implement her new appraisal skill, the man leapt to his feet and bolted from the tavern. *Interesting,* she mused. *I wonder what's got him worked up.*

Wes interrupted her train of thought with an iron key pressed firmly into her hand. "One room at the local inn, as requested."

"Right. Thanks. Did—um—did you see that guy just run outside?"

"No? Is something wrong?"

Eve grit her teeth, trying to decide if the man's odd behavior was worth the fuss. Ultimately, it was the layer of sweat which still so uncomfortably glued her blouse to the skin beneath it that forced her hand. "It's fine. I'm going to go wash up." She stepped past the bulky mage and onto the stairs beyond.

A hot bath and a hearty meal later, she'd forgotten all about the strange man in favor of the more familiar worries over her confusing quest and limited class. *At least,* Eve reassured herself as she lay comfortably on the straw pallet, *tomorrow morning I can get that damned bread.*

Chapter 4

The First Milestone

A pounding at her door stole Eve away from the sweet embrace of sleep. "Oy! Open up!"

Eve groaned, rubbing her heavy eyelids as she trudged across the sparse room. She undid the latch. Four men stood outside, each a head taller and a hundred pounds heavier than she. A quick **Appraise** identified them as two *Blacksmiths*, a *Farmer*, and a *Tanner*, all in their mid teens.

"What do you want?"

"Your boyfriend," the *Farmer* said. "Where is he?"

Now, Eve would've liked to snap back with a dry 'excuse me?' or a taunting 'I have a boyfriend? Why didn't he tell me?' but in her grogginess, the best she could manage was a slurred "What?"

"That weasel Randy said he saw you come in with one of those adventurer types. Trouble is, that sword he had don't belong to him."

The man must've taken Eve's exhausted silence as lack of comprehension, because he explained further. "Sword was pilfered from my da ages ago. Hells if I know why your boy painted them green, but I'd know those sigils anywhere."

"He's not my—look, he's not here. And I'm sure if you asked nicely Wes'd be happy to give you your sword back."

The man placed a meaty hand on the wooden door, forcing it to swing farther open.

Eve stepped back to avoid being struck.

The *Farmer* scanned the room, confirming the truth in her words. "We'll see about that. Don't take kindly to thieves 'round here."

Eve opened her mouth to defend her fellow adventurer, to tell the man he couldn't have known the weapon's history, anything in the hope they'd leave Wes be. She never got a chance.

The thugs slammed the door shut.

It took the girl more than a few moments both to finish waking up and calm her racing heart as the encounter sank in. The realization that she, a helpless *Messenger Girl* who couldn't exactly run away in a confined room, had unlocked her door for four strange men in the middle of the night hit hard. "Ma would kill me," she muttered to herself.

At least they were only looking for Wes. Eve's eyes shot open. Wes! "Ayla's tits," she swore in yet another display of behavior that would earn a lecture from her mother. She dashed across the room, rushing to re-don her boots. Magic class or not, Eve didn't favor Wes's odds against four opponents, especially without warning.

Shoes tied, Eve made it halfway back to the room's exit when a hurried tapping rang out behind her. She turned.

"Wes? What the hells are you doing?"

The man, of course, couldn't hear her on the other side of the glass window, but the look on her face was clear enough. He waved her over.

It wasn't until Eve swung the window open to find him desperately clinging to the eave that she remembered they'd slept on the second floor.

"We need to leave," Wes said in the loudest whisper she'd ever heard.

"Why are you here?"

"They tried my room first. Luckily, I was smart enough not to open the door when they started knocking. Just made it out the window before they kicked the door in."

I slept through a break-in? Eve cursed her lack of awareness. "Did you know?"

"That Mr. Potts gave me a stolen sword? Of bloody course not. I didn't even want a non-stolen sword!"

"Right, right. Move over. I'm coming out."

Wes shuffled along the sill, his feet barely reaching the wooden crossbeam that extended an inch from the sheer wall beneath them.

Eve's didn't.

"Shit shit shit," she whispered furiously as she dangled from the open window.

"Okay—um—can you make it over there?" Wes pointed at the vertical beam running down the building's corner, over eight feet away.

"Do I look like I can bloody make it over there?"

"Right. Yes. Um… okay, here's what we're gonna do…" Wes inched away, expertly descending the wooden structure until he reached the dirt below. He held out his arms. "Jump!"

"You're kidding me."

"Eve, we don't have time for this! Those thugs are already searching."

"Alright, alright, just… give me a moment."

She gulped. *Come on, Eve. You can do this. If you can turn back to fight off gods-damned wolves you can face a ten-foot drop. I just need to let—fuck.*

Her hand slipped.

Eve plummeted. Her outstretched toes collided with the

crossbeam they'd so failed to reach, sending waves of pain up her leg as she peeled away from the vertical wall. Her heart raced, somehow convinced this was the moment of her death in spite of all evidence to the contrary.

She fell for but a second before Wes caught her. That is, using the word 'caught' rather loosely. Only one of his extended arms actually intercepted her drop, striking her directly in the upper back. The impact *hurt*.

Fortunately for Eve, the man's failed attempt happened to impact at just the right point to raise her torso above her lower half, spinning her such that her feet hit the ground directly beneath her.

Heart pounding, Eve stood. "Nice catch."

"Nice jump," Wes countered.

"Nice sword."

The companions spun to find the four goons standing on the other end of the alley. Two of them held pitchforks.

The third had a rope.

"Hand over the sword, and maybe I'll let your girl go unharmed. Mostly."

Wes's face curled into a snarl. He raised a hand, setting it alight with strands of flame.

"Is that a no?" The Farmer smirked. "C'mon boys, looks like we're in for some good old-fashioned *justice.*"

Eve looked sideways at Wes. "Run?"

He nodded. "Run."

They ran.

Eve kept back with the initiate, purposefully slowing herself to keep her class's passive ability from outpacing her companion. The thugs gave chase.

Her feet slammed against the hard earth with every hurried step as buildings and alleyways flew by. Her heart raced. Adrenaline pumped. The cool night air blew past. Their pursuers grew closer.

Eve refused to activate her skill, unwilling to leave Wes

in the dust. "We need to lose them!" she panted out through gasps for breath.

"And how," Wes managed, "are we supposed to do that?"

He had a point. The moons above lit the whole village in their silver beams, leaving few shadows in which to take shelter. The late hour meant no passersby to ask for aid, and even were she willing to stop and check, Eve knew well enough each door they passed would be locked.

So on they fled.

The pair made it three more blocks before Eve developed an idea. Without warning, she grabbed Wes's wrist, yanking him down a nearby side street. She led him down to the next crossroad before pointing out a direction. "Double back and sneak your way out. I'll meet you on the road east."

"What're you goi—"

Eve shoved him. "Go!"

He went.

Eve lingered for a moment in the narrow intersection, doing her best to look completely lost. She whipped her head from side to side, miming the action of picking a direction until the sound of footfalls reached the alley behind her. Turning opposite the way she'd pointed Wes, Eve took off.

"That way!"

The thugs followed.

A grin stretched across Eve's face as she led the men along. She dared not look back to gauge their distance, but the echos of their steps and the panting of their breaths confirmed all four had taken the bait.

She regulated her pace, keeping care to always dart down a new path or alleyway just as the men turned the prior corner. They'd only continue if she could maintain the illusion that Wes was just ahead of her, just out of sight instead of across town slinking off into the night.

If all her class could do was run away, Eve was determined to at least be bloody good at it.

She let out a quiet laugh as she rounded yet another corner. She could do this for hours. Barely twenty minutes into her goose chase, her pursuers had already slowed from an outright sprint to a quick jog. On she ran.

It was some time around two in the morning when the four villagers gave up. One by one they bowed out, doubled over as they caught their breath. It would be the only thing they caught that night.

As the last of them—the *Farmer* himself—gave in to his exhaustion, Eve made a point of traveling west. It was better the men thought they'd run home to Nowherested.

Eve grinned as she checked her Stamina to find it still half full. At least all the Endurance her class granted wasn't *totally* useless, even if she'd have preferred pretty much any other stat.

She kept to the outskirts as she turned back toward the eastern road, unwilling to risk running into one of the thugs on his way home. As she followed the moonlit path to her large companion, Eve's thoughts turned again towards her quest.

Was it worth staying in Fidsworth to buy the loaf of bread?

A part of her screamed yes. She'd had an easy enough time escaping the thugs once; surely she could do it again in the morning. That said, the bakery sat in the center of town. A few cries of 'thief!' could turn four pursuers into fifty.

In the end, it was Wes that settled her mind. She'd saved the *Flame Initiate's* ass twice in less than a day, and his own quest would only get harder. Besides, she rather enjoyed his company so far.

"There you are!" Wes's voice pulled her from her

thoughts. "What happened?"

"I led them in circles until they ran out of Stamina. It was easy, really."

"Oh, thank Ayla. I was scared they'd chase you all the way back home."

"Never," she scoffed. "Remember, I've mastered the art of running away. Besides, I couldn't just leave you. You'd die in half a week without my help."

Wes smacked her shoulder.

"Seriously, though, we should keep moving. The further we are from Fidsworth when morning comes, the better."

Wes nodded, accepting her direction. He gestured down the road with an open palm. "Shall we?"

Eve snorted. "Of course, noble sir. We shall."

Twenty paces down the eastern road, a series of messages flashed in Eve's vision. She dismissed them. *It's too bloody late for this,* she thought. *Maybe once we find someplace to sleep and settle in I can—*

"Gods below," Wes swore, his eyes shining blue as they reflected the azure light of his own status screen. "I just leveled up."

"You what?"

"Apparently escaping Fidsworth was an important milestone in my quest. I got a hundred exp."

"You got a—" Her eyes shot open. With a thought, Eve pulled up the message she'd ignored.

Legendary Quest Milestone Reached: Escape Fidsworth!
+1000 exp!

"What—no—that can't be..." Eve fell silent as a dozen more messages popped into view.

Wes perked up. "What's wrong?"

"That," Eve sighed, "is an excellent question."

Chapter 5

The Second Tier

Level Up!
Level Up!
...
Level Up!

"Bandir's Balls!" Eve swore. *Thirteen levels for that? I just ran around in circles!*

Class Upgrade Available: Courier
   Common Tier 2 Class
   Requirements: *Delivery Girl, Errand Girl, Messenger Girl, or Pack Mule base class.*

   From running messages to delivering parcels, you've worked your way up to being a true professional in the field. A proper courier always gets her package to its destination.
   +10 Endurance
   +2 Endurance/Level

There were no other options. Though a bit disappointed to not receive a *Wolf Slayer* or *Thief* class for her escapades so far, Eve wasn't exactly surprised. Her mother had only seen one option for her advancement to *Seamstress* all those years ago; why should Eve be any different?

Maybe tier 3 would provide something more interesting. Hells, she was already past halfway there; she'd have to make sure to do something worth an *Uncommon* class of her own. With a sigh, Eve accepted the promotion.

She noted with glee that the difference in Endurance growth seemed to retroactively apply to all of her levels after unlocking the class change. Considering she'd pushed *seven* past the evolution threshold, the difference meant that many additional points of Endurance. She was pleased to not be penalized for rapid growth, unfair or otherwise.

The new class and levels set her Endurance at a staggering 44. *Forty bloody four. What am I gonna do with all this Endurance?* Thus far her abilities were only good for running away, and while more Stamina was certainly useful, it would never actually increase the power of her skills, just how often she could use them.

Holding out whatever hope she had left, Eve opened up her skill list. There was only one new entry.

Active Ability - Heave
4 Stamina/Sec

It doesn't matter how heavy it is, you've got a package to deliver. Double your maximum carry weight as long as Heave remains active.

The sheer volume and vigor of Eve's sigh attracted Wes's attention.

"Seriously, what is it? Are you alright? Did someth—" His eyes went wide. "Your class changed."

"My class changed."

"So you got a milestone too?"

She nodded.

"But I only got a hundred exp for an Epic milestone. To get level ten you would've needed…"

"More than that." Eve saved him the effort of doing the math. "I got a thousand."

"A thousand?! Eve, what the hells?"

She shrugged. "Good question. Maybe escaping Fidsworth is a bigger part of my quest than of yours?"

"Or," he leveled with her, "there's something you're not telling me."

"Bloody mage Intelligence," she swore, knowing full well that wasn't how Intelligence worked. She sighed. "I got more experience than you because I didn't hit an Epic milestone. I hit a Legendary one."

By some miracle, Wes's eyebrows raised yet more than they already had. "You *what?*"

"It's…" She breathed. "My quest. It's rated as Legendary. For some reason."

"For some reason?"

"I don't fucking know. All it says is 'go to the next town over to fetch a loaf of bread' and that it's apparently super difficult."

"Bullshit."

"My thoughts exactly. It is bullshit. It's complete bullshit. Yet here we are."

"So you just get massive windfalls of exp whenever you make progress? That doesn't seem fair."

"Is it fair that you're a *Flame Initiate* and I'm a bloody *Courier?* For fuck's sake, my abilities are to run away and to carry heavy shit."

Wes opened his mouth, closed it, and deflated somewhat. "No, no, you're right. You get to level up *insanely* faster than I do—at least for now—but I get more stats and two fire spells."

"Exactly! It actually seems pre—wait. Two fire spells?"

The man's eyes lit up. "You aren't the only one who hit

a milestone."

"You got a new spell just for level three?"

Wes gave a sly grin. Without speaking, he raised his right hand. It came alight. Orange flames licked at his fingers, casting their flickering glow across his face. "Burning Hand at level one," he explained, "and more damage at level two."

He closed his hand, pulling it back as if winding up for a punch. Instead he opened his fist as he surged forward, throwing a thin bolt of bright inferno into the night. "Fire Dart at level three."

Eve watched the twinkling projectile fly through the dark sky, its gentle arc leading it towards the ground. "You know what, forget the thing I said about mage Intelligence." She took off.

"What did I—"

She called back over her shoulder, "You're gonna start a brush fire!" With a deep breath, Eve activated **Run Away**. She charged forth, speeding through the dry grass at her inhuman pace. The cool evening air blew through her hair and across her face, eliciting a smile despite the urgency of the situation.

Wes's dart wasn't difficult to find. Although the spell itself had long dissipated, Eve's haste meant only a cluster of the greenery had a chance to catch fire before she stamped it out.

Upon her return, the man greeted her with a sheepish look.

"I'd think with a two-year age gap that *you'd* be the responsible one," she said.

"Sorry." He hung his head. "I saw the new skill and wanted to try it. You know how it is."

Eve sighed, "It's okay. Just... maybe not in the middle of summer. That could've wiped out someone's harvest."

Wes nodded.

"Look," Eve said, "it's late. We're *both* too tired to really be thinking straight, especially after the day we've had. I'm sure we're far enough from Fidsworth that we can call it a night. We can talk about new skills and classes and where we're actually *going* in the morning, alright?"

"I can agree to that," came the reply.

Under Eve's direction, the two companions stepped away from the dirt road to find what comfort they could upon beds of grass. Legendary quests, level gains, and new abilities aside, they'd had more than enough adventuring for one day.

* * *

Eve squinted, groaning as she raised an arm to shield her eyes from the morning sun.

"Good morning!"

She rolled over, doing her darnedest to return to the soft embrace of sleep instead of replying to Wes's greeting. His next words changed her mind.

"Do you want some breakfast?"

Eve sat straight up, throwing her hands in the air to stretch away the night's stiffness. She let out a wide yawn. "What do you have?"

"Meat and cheese, mostly, but Mrs. Yir gave me a few of her scones the morning I left."

Eve's eyes widened. "Scones. Now."

"Yes, ma'am," Wes chuckled, handing her one. "Consider it a thanks for saving my ass."

"Twice," Eve replied through a mouth full of sugary, strawberry-y goodness. "Sounds like you owe me two scones."

Wes wrapped a defensive arm around his pack. "I'd rather take my chances with the wolves."

Eve laughed, shaking her head. "Fair's fair. If I don't see that scone tomorrow morning, there'll be hell to pay."

"What are you gonna do, run away from me?"

"No. I'll run away from you *very quickly.*"

Wes guffawed. "Welp, you got me there. How am I, a measly level three, supposed to compete with your glorious level seventeen?"

"Exactly."

As the pair finished the meal, Eve attributed her high spirits to both the mirthful banter and the pure divinity of the pastry. She'd take Mrs. Yir's scones over some ancient family heirloom any day.

"So," Wes began as they pushed to their feet to continue their journey, "where are you going?"

"Ponsted's the next town over, right? Don't want to risk going back to Fidsworth, and my quest doesn't specify *which* town I need to get the bread from."

"And then?"

Eve shrugged. "Maybe I'll stay with you a bit? If I got a thousand exp for a milestone, imagine how strong I'll be once I finish this damn thing. I always wanted to travel, and based on the last twenty-four hours, you need as much help as you can get."

Wes ignored the dig. "Isn't that too easy? I'd think a Legendary quest would take more than a few days. If Fidsworth fell through, what makes you think Ponsted won't? Or the next town?"

"Then I'll keep going. It's just bread; there's no rush. It's not like my loaf of bread is killing people or destroying livelihoods every day I don't buy it. I could go anywhere, really. Name a town that doesn't have *bread* in it. The real question is where *you're* going."

"East, I guess. I've been thinking over what you said about a mage's college, and I kinda agree. I'm no more ready to fight a dragon than you are. I think Lynthia is the closest city; maybe I can join the adventurer's guild there to earn enough money for tuition."

"Okay, Lynthia it is."

The two walked on in silence, squinting their eyes against the blinding sun ahead of them as it blanketed them in its comforting warmth. Birds chirped as they flew overhead, and the grass on either side quivered with motion as hares and field mice went about their day.

"So—um…" Eve said, "where exactly *is* Lynthia?"

Wes shrugged, humming the 'I don't know' more so than saying it. "East. I'm sure we'll find it if we follow the road long enough."

Eve snorted. "Yep, 'adventure' is definitely the right word."

The travelers *actually* went quiet at that, continuing on through the plains in comfortable companionship. Eve's thoughts drifted as they journeyed, first to the events of the previous night, and then to her future. Already she was only eight levels away from the next class evolution at level twenty-five, and if she wanted something good, she'd need to earn it.

Eight levels—especially in a common class—wasn't long. Not for her.

The hours ticked on as Eve's mind wandered through the different types of skills or spells she might one day unlock. If she was to complete a Legendary quest, why shouldn't she find a Legendary class in the process? Images and daydreams of great powers and incredible feats flicked through her thoughts, each more impressive than the last.

She was just amidst an imaginary encounter with a deadly leviathan when the hissing shattered her reverie.

"Um… Eve? Is that a field hydra?"

The reptilian form stood just over eight feet tall, its musclebound body carried by four thick legs. Its claws scored the dirt beneath its feet. Most intimidating, however, were the eight heads that sprouted from its thick torso, each held several feet into the air by a thin scaly neck.

The thing hissed again in a dissonant chorus of threatening tones.

Wes set his hand alight.

"I wouldn't," Eve warned him. "These things are crazy venomous. One bite and you're dead."

"So what do you recommend?"

"What do I always recommend?"

He smiled. "Right."

They ran.

The field hydra charged, its array of heads gnashing their teeth at the air ahead of it. Were she not otherwise concerned with running for her life, Eve might've laughed at the way the thing's thick legs seemed to waddle after them. That is, she might've until it started catching up.

The creature drew closer. Eve ran faster. Wes didn't.

"It's too fast! We have to fight it!"

"Not if I have anything to say about it!"

Eve slowed, turning around to prepare herself. The hydra gained ground. Wes approached. Eve exhaled.

The moment Wes reached her, Eve wrapped her arms around his waist and activated **Heave.** With a grunt, she lifted.

Pivoting back around, she took off, dumping the twenty Stamina to use her other skill as well. The plains raced by. Her heart pounded. Her Stamina drained. Her breathing quickened.

And Eve smiled.

She smiled for the joy of the wind in her face and the sun on her back. She smiled for the thrill of the chase and the sheer ridiculousness of a five-foot-nothing stick of a girl running off with a two hundred fifty pound mage slung over her shoulder. She laughed, not at some whispered joke or comedic line, but because the world itself was *funny.*

From his backwards-facing vantage, Wes threw **Fire Darts** at the waddling beast. Pained hisses alerted Eve to the man's progress as dart after dart singed the creature's hide. Whenever Wes missed, Eve took care to lead the chase into a circle so she could stamp out any brush fires before they could develop into a second problem.

Minutes passed as they whittled the hydra down, every step and every spell bringing them closer to that coveted victory message. Even when it finally came, Eve didn't stop running. It was only once every budding wildfire in its wake had been summarily extinguished that the companions finally collapsed.

You have defeated Level 15 Field Hydra: +130 exp!

"Ayla's tits," Wes swore. "I got two levels from that!"

"Seriously? I only got one," Eve replied as she watched her Endurance tick up yet again. "Did you get extra experience for doing all the damage?"

He shrugged. "Either that or because I'm so much lower level than it."

"Oh yeah, it's probably that. Perks of being a level three."

"Level five now," he laughed. "And hey, I got an upgrade to both my **Burning Hand** and my passive."

Eve cocked an eyebrow.

"It's just more damage. Nothing exciting, but definitely nice."

"You and your Uncommon class." Eve scoffed. "With your insane stat growth and your new or upgraded abilities every level."

"Hey, keep doing adventurer shit and you'll get one too."

"At the low, low price of almost dying every day."

"To be fair," Wes said, "*I'm* the one who almost died. No

way that thing would've caught you on your own."

Eve smirked. "You know what that means."

"Oh no."

"Sounds to me like I saved your ass *again.*"

Wes shook his head. "Not happening."

"I'm adding this to your scone debt."

"Gods damnit." Wes held his face in his hands.

"Hey, you said it."

"At this rate we'll have to go back to Nowherested just to get more scones."

Eve laughed, lying back on the soft grass. "I'm sure there are other towns that have scones."

Wes lay beside her, the mirth in his voice matching her own. "Just like there are other towns that have bread?"

"Exactly."

The conversation fell silent as the travelers reclined in the grassy plains, their eyes fixed on the azure sky and the few pearly clouds which drifted through it. Another day, another brush with death slipped past. Alone, neither the slim *Courier* nor the bulky *Flame Initiate* could've dreamt of felling a hydra, but together they'd not only won but lived to reap the rewards.

There was more world to see, more adventuring to be done, and Eve loved every minute of it. They had a plan, they had a destination, and, ridiculous as it was, they had a working strategy for the battles ahead.

What more could a pair of young heroes want?

Chapter 6

A Baking Accident

"Do you think these are actually worth something?"

"May as well find out," Wes answered as he stooped over the hydra's corpse with his knife. He slipped a scale into his bag. "Now you've eaten all my food, I've got plenty of space for loot."

"You eat twice as much as I do!"

Wes cocked an eyebrow. "That's cause I'm twice your size. I brought enough to get to Ponsted without resupplying, but *somebody* decided to go off on a Legendary quest without even packing."

"And I would've *finished* my Legendary quest without packing if I hadn't stopped to save you."

Wes shrugged, stuffing another hydra scale into his pack. "It is what it is. We're still a few days from Ponsted, and all I've got left is a few scones."

Eve smirked. "You mean *I* have a few scones."

Wes threw up his hands. "Whatever. The point is we're almost out of food."

"And?"

"And," Wes said as he cut into another scale, "I've always wondered what hydra tastes like."

"No way. They're poisonous; we'll fucking die."

"They're venomous, not poisonous." Wes pointed the tip of his blade just below one of the beast's many jaws. "Venom glands are up here. If we take a cut or two from lower down, we'll be fine."

Eve raised her eyebrows. "You've butchered hydra before?"

"Obviously not if I don't know what it tastes like." He packed away another scale. "But Mr. Braun has, and he told me about it."

"I don't know if I'm more impressed you're willing to eat a hydra or that you actually survived one of Mr. Braun's stories."

"Oh, believe me, I am too. I swear it took him four hours to tell it."

Eve shook her head. "Rookie mistake. Never let him know you have an afternoon off. That man devours free time."

Wes laughed, setting aside the last of the scales as he cut into the creature's flank.

"If you think the scales might be valuable," Eve asked, "what about the teeth?"

He turned to give her a flat look. "You mean the razor edges where all the poison is?"

"Point taken."

"I hope not. Those points are venomous, remember?"

Eve grimaced. "I might charge you a scone just for that pun."

"Right. Yep. I shouldn't have said it." Wes shook his head as he returned to his butchering.

By the time the sunset colored the sky in its usual symphony of colors, the air was filled with smoky goodness as two hydra steaks sizzled over a campfire. Eve had found the flat rock on which Wes cooked, making use of **Heave** for its intended purpose to get it into place.

Though he lacked in the world of spices, the man at least had the wherewithal to bring a pouch of salt on his journey. Unsurprisingly, he used it as another opportunity to tease Eve for her own lack of preparation. She cracked back soon enough.

"So," Wes said through a mouthful of steak, "hydra is *chewy.*"

"I don't think that's the hydra's fault." Eve turned to display the center of the piece she was currently working her way through. It was pure gray. "You cooked it to the eighth hell and back."

"Better safe than sorry," he defended himself. "I'd rather overcook it than get sick off eating raw hydra. If you don't like it, you can cook the next one."

Eve shrugged. "You're the hydra expert. And the fire mage for that matter. It really sounds like your wheelhouse."

"Oh, so you run away and carry shit, and I do everything else."

"You're getting it." Eve laughed as she reclined back, crossing her arms behind her head to stare up at the sunset.

Wes stood. "So, should we keep moving or stop here for the night?"

Eve stayed lying back. "Well, either that hydra had some kind of paralyzing toxin running through its veins, *or* it's been a long day and I'm just really tired."

"No, it's definitely the first one." Wes sat back down a few feet to her left. "You see, I poisoned you so I could have all the scones for myself."

"Ooh, devious of you. I had no idea I was traveling with a criminal mastermind."

"Hey, that's 'Sir Criminal Mastermind' to you. I'm a noble hero, remember?"

"Ah yes," Eve chuckled, "the noble hero who steals a sword and poisons his friend. I remember that story."

"Yeah, well, where's the fun if we're all paladins to Loia? Can't have *every* hero be one of those 'pure of soul' types."

"That would get awfully boring, wouldn't it?"

Wes let out a laugh of his own. "Well, at least we're not bored."

Eve cracked a smile, wide and bright and full of meaning her companion could only begin to guess. "At least we're not bored."

As the sun finally began its nightly rendezvous with the horizon, Eve lay back with a full stomach and a calm mind. Hard earth, dry grass, or comfy inn, she'd take whatever rest she could get.

Come morning, there'd be adventuring to do.

* * *

Eve ran. She did that a lot these days. Luckily, in this particular instance there was nothing lethal giving chase, unless, of course, one were to consider Wes 'lethal' and his casual walk 'giving chase.'

She counted the seconds as the wind swept through her chestnut hair, keeping a careful eye on her ever-depleting Stamina.

119/460

She breathed.

115/460

113/460

Eve slowed her pace, ever so slightly decelerating from a sprint to a quick jog.

115/460

She grinned. Stamina regeneration or not, she obviously couldn't run *forever*. Too little food or too long without sleep and it'd plummet all the same. Still, in battle-time it was effectively infinite. *As long as **Heave** isn't draining it away,* she thought.

Eve stopped to catch her breath, waiting on the roadside as Wes closed the distance between them. He cocked an eyebrow.

"It levels out at one-fifteen," she explained. "I knew the percent regen was higher in the bottom quartile, but I can't believe it only took forty-six Endurance to jog at equilibrium."

"I thought I was supposed to be the smart one."

"No, I'm the smart one. You're the one who sets shit on fire."

"With my blistering intellect."

Eve laughed. "Okay, you win this one. The point is I have enough Endurance to run all day long."

"What about your skills?"

"**Heave** drains faster than I can regenerate, but if I'm below a quarter full I only lose a point or two a second. **Run Away** is a flat cost, but the natural drain from running scales with the velocity. It's not *really* the skill costing more Stamina cause I can still choose not to go at full speed, but it may as well be."

"So how much *does* it cost?"

Eve shrugged. "I'm not about to do that math. More? The skill duration scales with my Endurance, but only half as fast. It was seven point five seconds when I had fifteen Endurance, now it's twenty-three. For now I'm just going to assume the duration will run out before my Stamina does."

Wes gave her a pointed look. "You just don't want to test it."

"No way I'm running that fast without looking where I'm going. I'll hit a tree and die."

Furrowing his brow, Wes over-dramatically scanned their surroundings. "We're in the plains."

"A rock then. One misstep and I'm gone. Who'll look after your helpless ass?"

"Very funny." Wes stepped past her, continuing on down the road. Eve kept silent as she followed.

As the companions rambled on, so too did Evelia's mind. Both her recent discovery and the conversation that followed spurred her on in the direction of Wes.

She liked him. Really, she did. She hadn't known the muscular blacksmith's son particularly well back in Nowherested, but she did now. Somehow, three days of adventuring together seemed to carry more weight than an entire childhood of peace back home.

Sure, he needed saving an awful lot, but that was part of his charm. He joked and teased and took as much shit as he dished out and came up laughing on the other side.

Sometimes Eve wondered how far she'd get without him, if she could just run all day every day, avoiding every enemy and encounter until she got wherever she wanted to be. The trouble was, she didn't know where that might be. She could complete her quest, but then what?

She could run away, but she couldn't fight without Wes's help. She might survive, but she wouldn't *grow*. They were perfect for each other in a strange way. She kept him alive while his vulnerability and firepower provided just enough risk that they could both earn exp.

Then there was the matter of her quest. Wes's need of saving is what made it difficult in the first place, but the Questing Stones had deemed it Legendary before she'd even done that. Had she always been meant to save him? Would she have failed in her quest if she hadn't?

Eve didn't know.

It seemed to her that Wes *must* somehow be wrapped up in her life's quest. Slow and danger prone or otherwise, she'd keep with him. Besides, she liked him, and that was reason enough.

Her musings came to an end when she spotted the smoke.

Wes stopped short. "That wasn't me."

"Unless you can throw that dart way farther than I

thought you could, of course it wasn't." Eve swore. Without waiting for a reply, she took off, racing down the road towards the pillar of black soot on the horizon.

She made it to Ponsted in under five minutes.

An ashen haze hung over the town as Eve walked through the crowded streets. She clung to hope as she stepped past house after house that still stood, untouched by the apparent inferno. The smoke grew thicker. It clawed against her throat and lungs, forcing its way past even the sleeve of her blouse through which she breathed.

By the time she saw the first piece of charred wood, Eve already knew what had happened.

Only one structure had actually fallen to the blaze, its neighbors scorched but otherwise unharmed thanks to the efforts of the local well and the gathered townsfolk who'd come to help. The fire was gone, but its damage remained.

Eve went to investigate. Across the road from the burnt husk, she found a villager sitting in the dirt, leaning against the wall of the inn as he sipped from a flask. His hands were stained with ash and dirt, the wrinkles in his face painted in lines of ebon soot.

Eve approached. "What happened?"

The man's voice scraped through the air, hoarse from exertion and smoke. "Place caught fire earlier this morning. Some kind of baking accident."

Eve collapsed next to him. "I'm sorry."

"Shit like this happens. Nobody's hurt, we kept it contained, and we can rebuild in a few weeks."

"Still," she whispered, "I'm sorry."

The man shrugged. "It's not your fault."

Isn't it? Eve thought. Would the bakery have burned if she hadn't come? Was she cursed to never buy a loaf of bread to fulfill the difficulty requirements of her quest, or was it only Legendary because the Stones somehow knew the string of misfortunes she'd face?

Eve had no answers, and the exhausted villager beside her didn't either. They sat together for a time, two strangers watching smoke waft from the blackened ruins, sharing in the misery of the sight before them.

She couldn't say how much time passed, but the haze had somewhat cleared from the air by the time Wes finally arrived. He extended a hand to help her up.

"I picked up supplies on the way here. There's still a few hours of daylight left. I say we get out of here."

Eve nodded. She took his proffered hand, allowing the man to pull her to her feet. They walked in silence through the streets of Ponsted, weaving their way through villagers going about their daily business.

Eve didn't breathe freely until the last of the buildings fell away and the plains expanded out before her. Though the air here was clear, the smell of smoke still clung to her nostrils. Still they walked.

Wordlessly, Wes reached into his pack, pulling out a scone and handing it to Eve. She took it.

He smiled. "C'mon, we have a city to find."

Chapter 7

Slippery When Wet

You have defeated Level 6 Gnoll: +0 exp!
You have defeated Level 7 Gnoll: +0 exp!
You have defeated Level 6 Gnoll: +0 exp!
You have defeated Level 5 Gnoll: +0 exp!

Eve fell back, cracking a smile as she lowered Wes to the ground. "It's the perfect strategy," she laughed. "They can't hit us if they never get close!"

"You're not the one being slung around like a sack of potatoes," Wes replied, rubbing his sore abdomen. "Your shoulder isn't exactly comfortable."

"Hey, at least you're getting exp for all this."

Wes flashed a smile of his own. "You know the rules, no exp for enemies half your level or lower. That's what you get for rocketing up to eighteen so quick."

"And the world continues to discriminate against those of us cursed with common classes."

Wes snorted. "Tell me again how much you got for your Legendary milestone. Gnolls aside, you've still got more experience than I do."

"Yeah, yeah." Eve waved him off. She knew fair was

fair, even if she gained nothing from defeating the bipedal hyenas. "So how much did ya get?"

"One thirty-six. Got me level six and an upgrade to my **Flame Affinity**."

"Ooh, what's it do?"

"Well," Wes sat down to explain, "originally it was just a percentage boost to fire damage, now it gives resistance too."

"That's it." Eve snapped her fingers. "You're officially the party cook from here on out."

Wes cocked an eyebrow.

"Think about it! You can get the fire going, keep it under control, and even flip the steaks without needing a fork. It's perfect."

"It's only fifteen percent; I'm pretty sure I'll still get burned if I do dumb stuff. And since when are we a party?"

Eve turned up her palms. "We're adventurers and there's more than one of us? Either way, I'm sure we'll pick up more people in Lynthia. As well as it works for now, I don't see the guild approving our 'sack-o-potatoes' battle plan."

"So what'll you do?"

"I'll figure something out," Eve said. "Worst case I can run in and pull people out of danger."

"Fair enough," Wes replied. "You ready to keep going?"

Eve nodded, pushing to her feet as Wes re-shouldered his pack. They left the gnoll corpses behind, unwilling to waste the time or effort skinning the creatures just to collect a few mangy pelts. Hells, they were just as likely to get fleas for their trouble as any money.

The knee-high grass swayed as the companions stepped back onto the road, quivering in a breeze which held a certain dampness and a certain weight to it. Eve watched the sky. Though the afternoon sun still shined unimpeded upon them, gray clouds rolled over the horizon ahead.

"I always liked the summer storms," Eve thought aloud.

"Really?"

"Yeah. There's something magical about rain on a warm day, like the heavens themselves know the sweat on your back and see fit to wash it clean."

Wes snorted. "I'm the opposite. They scared me, growing up. I'd just be out enjoying a bright summer day and suddenly it'd just get so *dark*. Da used to say the thunder was the sound of Bandir's mighty hammer and the lightning was Loia's spear striking the earth."

"Let me guess: if you didn't do your chores, Loia would strike *you*."

He chuckled, "Something like that. I used to think that's how Ma died, pissing off Loia somehow and getting hit by lightning. I'd stay up all night praying She'd leave us alone."

"That's..." Eve raised a hand to her face, covering the grin she bore. "I know it's sad, but it's also really cute. I'm imagining a tiny you cowering under your bedsheets whenever a storm comes."

"I didn't cower!"

"And knowing you, you were never tiny either."

Wes laughed. "Da always said I was a natural born blacksmith."

"Are you? I know the Stones didn't give you much of a choice, but he seemed more put out about it than you did."

"I don't know. I didn't hate working in the smithy, and *everyone* dreams about grand adventures and all that. Maybe it would've been better if I'd stayed home. Like I said, I don't really have an answer."

Eve stepped out ahead of him, turning to look directly in the man's eye. "If the best you can say about working with your da is that you didn't hate it, I think that's your answer."

Wes met her gaze in contemplative stillness, taking a few seconds before quietly lowering his head in a nod. "Maybe you're right." He set off walking again, and Eve fell in line beside him. "What about you?"

"I knew I wanted to travel," Eve said. "Thought I'd get some peddler class and sell things town to town. I like this better."

"Even though it's more dangerous?"

"Dangerous for *you*." She smirked. "I'm a master of running away, remember?"

"Of course, Madam *Courier*, I am at your mercy."

"And don't you forget it."

The pair walked on in mirthful silence, taking joy in each other's company even as the storm loomed. They made it another hour before the rain came.

It began, as such storms often do, all at once. It fell in sheets, soaking both the road and the adventurers on it until not a spot of dry earth or dry skin was left to be found. Eve loved it. While not necessarily warm, the water wasn't cold either, and she much preferred the fresh precipitation over the layer of sweat the summer sun often left her with.

She tugged at her blouse. Whereas most of the girls back home might've been embarrassed—and a few proud —by the way the water made the fabric cling to her skin, Eve didn't particularly care. It wasn't like she had much to keep hidden, and her only company was... well, Wes. He wouldn't gawk even if she wanted him to.

Eve refused to even consider the question of whether or not she did. Now wasn't the time.

Although the downpour was kind enough to wash most of the sweat and dust from her clothes, her shoes received the opposite treatment. It wasn't long before the dirt road turned to mud, leaving the adventurers with the unfortunate choice of walking through the sticky quagmire or upon the slippery wet grass.

Wes opted for the latter up until he went careening forward as his foot slid out from under him. Twice. Eve stuck with the mud.

They didn't spot any lightning so far from the storm's center, but the crash of thunder echoed far across the open plains. Though he hid it well, Eve took careful note of the little winces that spread across Wes's body whenever the cacophony rang out. She knew he didn't want to hear it, but still she mouthed a silent "it's okay" each time it happened. Wes never noticed.

Her eyes fixed on her muscular companion, Eve didn't see the grass quivering on either side of the road. Beneath the drumming of the deluge, she didn't hear sharp-tongued whispering or the skittering patter of nonhuman feet. Hells, had the thunder not chosen to take that particular moment as a break from its rolling, the goblin battle cry might too have been drowned out.

It wasn't.

A ragged 'skreee!' filled the air, matched in chorus six times by the three-foot green creatures that surrounded them. Though their fragile skin was only protected by hide loincloths, Eve cared more about the makeshift spears they each held.

The goblins charged.

Eve charged first. She activated **Heave**, bending low to whisk Wes off his feet. Taking care to scan her surroundings, the *Courier* picked her opening and went for it.

The goblin didn't know what hit him. The poor creature didn't even find a chance to lower its spear before almost four hundred combined pounds of human bowled it over. Eve dismissed the kill message as she trampled it.

One down, five to go.

She dashed through the plains, building up what

distance she could between them and their short-legged pursuers while Wes threw darts over her shoulder. He only cast twice before their strategy fell apart.

"We need to get closer!" he yelled. "The rain's extinguishing my flames before they can hit!"

Eve nodded, slowing her pace as she engaged in her own battle with the wet grass. *I need to focus,* she thought. *One wrong step and we'll—*

Wes's shout interrupted. "Lightning!"

Eve's heart raced. Instinctively, she planted her foot hard to swerve to the side. It landed wrong.

Her leg slid out from under her, sending runner and mage alike tumbling to the soft ground. A bolt of electricity flew past, not from above, but from behind. *Ayla's tits,* Eve swore. *They have a shaman?!*

Wes hurried to his feet. "That's one way to dodge."

Eve ignored the rolling ache in her arm where Wes had landed on her. Her footing escaped her twice as she tried to stand, eventually using the mage as a brace to pull her way up.

The goblins drew near.

Wes threw dart after dart, downing two of the attackers even as the majority of his spells missed or collapsed in a puff of steam under the dense rainfall.

Eve's mind raced as her eyes squinted past the charging monsters. Back on the road, the shaman *danced.* Eve gulped. Whatever magic the creature worked, she needed to stop it. She pointed at the two goblins that still approached. "Can you handle them?"

"I can't dodge its spells in this rain!" Wes drew his sword. "Can you handle the shaman?"

Eve nodded.

With a deep breath, she took off. At first she ran parallel to the road, unwilling to risk dashing straight for the spear-carrying goblins. Turning around would be the first challenge. She charted a wide angle, maintaining as much speed as she dared in the hopes her traction would hold.

It didn't.

She caught herself on her hands as she skidded along the field, happy that her hands came up muddy instead of scraped and bleeding. Eve exhaled. She planted her left knee, placing her right foot directly beneath her as she carefully stood. Her heart pounded. Her instincts screamed she needed to move, needed to go faster, but her mind knew the folly of such ideas.

She'd only fall again.

Eve began slowly once she reached her feet, allowing her speed to build over time. In her periphery, a goblin shrieked. *Get 'em, Wes!* she cheered to herself.

The crackle of lightning ahead wiped the grin from her face. Eve hastened, dropping twenty Stamina to activate **Run Away.** This time, however, she wasn't fleeing.

Again, the *Courier* didn't let herself jump straight to her maximum velocity, forcing herself to limit her pace even as the skill doubled her capacity. She couldn't afford another fall. Eve sped on, setting her course directly towards the dancing caster. Tiny arcs of electricity jumped along the tip of its gnarled branch.

Across her body, Eve's hair stood on end. Her pulse quickened. Her breathing matched it. Rain battered her, oft sending her sputtering as she gasped for air and instead found a mouthful of water.

Still she ran.

Her Stamina ticked down. Thunder rumbled overhead. The distance closed. Twenty feet. Ten.

The goblin leveled its staff, aiming the coming spell directly at her.

It fired.

Eve ducked.

She fell into a skid, sliding along the rain-soaked grass

on her side. The lightning bolt shot through the air above her. Eve's momentum carried her forward. Her extended foot struck the shaman's leg, sending the creature into the mud.

Eve was the first to her feet, already practiced in the art of finding traction on the slick grass. She snatched the fallen staff.

It took three solid hits to the goblin's head before the thing stilled and the kill message appeared.

You have defeated Level 19 Goblin Shaman: +100 exp!
You have successfully wielded a weapon beyond your Intelligence: +1 Intelligence!

Eve let out a breath. She smiled. Her fingers wrapped tight around the wooden staff. It felt more like a large wand in her hand. *Hells,* she thought. *In Wes's it'd probably look—shit. Wes!* She pivoted, scanning the open field to find her friend limping his way back to her.

"Are you alright?"

"I'll be fine!" he answered. "Last one got me in the leg. Hurts like a bitch, but I can still walk. I see you handled the shaman."

Eve laughed. "I made the slickness work for me. Once he hit the ground, I had him. It's good you've got that ring," she changed the subject. "Without it you'd probably have six different infections by now."

"Yeah, yeah, we can't *all* escape unscathed."

She handed him the staff. "Can you use this?"

He took it. "Says it's an uncommon 'Wand of Minor Arcing.' Not sure what that means, but I'm not a lightning mage."

Eve chastised herself for forgetting to **Appraise** the damn thing. "Maybe you can add it to the trash heap you call equipment. I'm sure eventually *someone* will want it."

Wes shrugged, making a point not to acknowledge her comment as he stuck the item through his belt. "So what else did you get?"

With a grin, Eve pulled up her remaining messages.

You have defeated Level 14 Goblin Spear-Bearer: +30 exp!
You have defeated Level 12 Goblin Spear-Bearer: +18 exp!
You have defeated Level 13 Goblin Spear-Bearer: +24 exp!

Eve noted with interest that she got credit for the two goblins Wes had killed while she carried him, but not those he defeated afterwards. "A hundred for the shaman, seventy-two for the others." She smiled as she watched her level and Endurance both tick up.

"Two fifteen for the spear-bearers, none for the shaman. You got him all on your own."

Eve did her best not to beam too visibly at his praise. She was only somewhat successful. "Get anything good?"

It was Wes's turn to grin. "Level seven and a longer range on **Fire Dart**. It doesn't say how long, but I'll take it."

Eve bristled, "I'm still mad you get a skill upgrade every level and I just get more Endurance."

"Hey, don't forget I get Intelligence and Spirit too."

She smacked him.

"Yep, yep, I deserved that. Guess you'll just have to hurry up to twenty-five so you can promote again. Beating a goblin to death with its own staff has gotta be worth *something*, right?"

"Gods, I hope so. Can you imagine if I get stuck with a *third* common class? What would that even look like?"

"*Better Courier*?" Wes joked as he took off down the muddy road. "Maybe *Royal Messenger Girl*."

"Ooh." Eve took a quick step to catch up with him as she joined in the silly conjecture. "Maybe if I'm lucky, I can even make *Page.* Or *Bread-Fetcher.*"

"That'd be perfect for you. Maybe from there you could evolve to the fastest *Baker's Assistant* the world has ever known."

They continued together along the road. Though the rain still fell and the lightning still struck, the rolling thunder fell away into the background, drowned out by the raucous echo of two adventurers in shared laughter.

Chapter 8

Welcome to the Guild

The glass walls of Lynthia glimmered in the distance, its many prisms shattering the afternoon sun into a thousand rainbows. Wes approached. Eve, on the other hand, did the sensible thing and stopped dead to gawk at the work of art before her.

"It's beautiful."

"It is," Wes called back at her, "and you'll have plenty of time to stare at it as we walk."

Eve forced her gaping jaw shut, quickening her pace to catch up to her large companion. "It's gotta get hot in there," she said. "All that glass must…"

"I doubt it. The walls are a quest reward from Ayla herself. She'd be a pretty shit goddess if they made the city miserable."

"Makes sense. Just explain all the hundreds of problems with glass fortifications as divine intervention."

Wes shrugged. "I didn't put them there. Take it up with Ayla."

"Oh, of course. Let me just pop over to the divine plane for a chat with a goddess."

"If you put it like that, it almost sounds as hard as

popping over to the next town for a loaf of bread."

Eve winked. "Almost."

As they walked on towards the sparkling city, Eve slipped a hand into her pocket. Two copper pieces rested there, the same two her mother had given her to pay for her bread. It had only been a few days since she'd left Nowherested, but already the distance seemed an eternity. Multiple brushes with death had that effect.

She absentmindedly rubbed the coins against each other for good luck. In a city like Lynthia, there'd be more than one baker. *One* of them had to have a loaf for her, right? Only so many bakeries could burn down before whatever curse or divine interference that plagued her made itself too apparent. Or so she hoped.

Eve quietly chuckled at the idea of every bakery in Lynthia simultaneously bursting into flame the moment she stepped through the gates. Would the authorities run her out of the city? Could they even hope to discover her connection to a suspicious bread shortage? As per usual, she had no answers. At least the questions were amusing this time.

As it turned out, the only thing that happened when she stepped within the city boundary was a direct assault on all things olfactory.

Lynthia stank.

This wasn't the foul scent of manure in a freshly fertilized field or fumes wafting from the local tannery or the fetid decay of a trash heap in the summer sun, but a demented panoply of all that and more. It clung to Eve's nose, tracing her every step as she walked the rough cobblestone.

How do people live like this? the *Courier* wondered. She swallowed down bile as a breeze blew a fresh wave of the sickening mixture into her face. She hated it. Even as the walls loomed above in all their towering splendor, the stench and the filth and the *thickness* to the air grated against Eve's very being.

Ten minutes later she'd already grown accustomed to it.

By the time they stopped to ask a uniformed guard for directions, the stink had already faded to the back of Eve's mind. By the time they crossed the threshold of the local adventurer's guild, she had more pressing matters to think about.

The place was a menagerie.

Ice Mages and *Axe Throwers* and *Hedge Knights* milled about the common room, laughing and drinking with men and women of every class Eve could've imagined, and a few she'd never have thought to. Interestingly enough, not a one of the guildsmen she **Appraised** had a higher level than she, though Eve was smart enough to know they outclassed her.

Rarity trumped level. An uncommon class five levels lower could easily double her stats, and nothing about these adventurers could be called 'common.'

Their diversity astounded her. The pale, freckled skin and chestnut hair that all citizens of Nowherested shared was practically absent. Guild members displayed every kind and combination of skin tones and hair colors, including a few shades Eve would've thought impossible without magical or alchemical intervention.

Her eyes grew wide when she spotted a *gnome*, but the nonhuman vanished in the crowd before she could point him out to Wes.

Two queues lined the inner wall, one for drinks and one for the clerk. Eve and Wes joined the latter.

"Let me guess," the woman behind the desk greeted them, "the Stones gave you a quest and your backwards town shipped you off to be their great hero?"

Wes reddened. Eve snickered.

"And you," the clerk turned to Eve, "are his naive young

lover who left your quiet life to follow him, not because you're destined for adventure, but because *your* love is special."

Eve's jaw fell open as her brow furrowed in offense. "Excuse yo—"

Wes cut her off. "My *sister* and I want to join the guild. We've seen battle on our way here. I'm sure you'll find we're more than qualified."

Sister? Really? Eve supposed it would at least dismiss any assumption they were lovers, and they *did* look the part. Compared to how different the adventurers all were, she and Wes could practically be twins.

The clerk nodded. "You, I can help. Uncommon classes at tier one are... well they're uncommon. Mages are in decently high demand right now, so you could find a team pretty easily, assuming you aren't a dick, of course."

Wes flashed a grateful smile. "Than—"

The woman cut him off as she addressed Eve. "*You*, on the other hand, don't belong here. Doesn't matter how high your level is or how useful your *brother* is, the guild doesn't take noncombat classes."

"But my quest is—"

"I don't care if your life quest is to join this particular branch of the adventurer's guild on this particular day. The rules are clear. Go home."

"I can't just go back after—"

"Then go deliver some packages for all I care. You're a bloody *Courier*, that's your job, isn't it? Look, I've been through this exact same song and dance with a hundred hopeful idiots just like you. If the Questing Stones didn't want you to be an adventurer, *you aren't*. Go home."

Eve shut her mouth. Rude as she was, yelling at the woman would accomplish nothing. She watched in silence as Wes went through the motions of signing his documents and paying his fee.

For an extra few coppers, he booked a room, a lodging they'd have to share given Eve's inability to do the same. Guild housing was for guild members.

He waited until they made it upstairs before going off. "That *bitch*. Who is she to say you're less of an adventurer than any of those fools downstairs? I bet half of them would've—"

Eve stopped him. "It's okay, Wes. Really. They can't stop me from going on jobs with you, and I honestly couldn't afford the fee anyway. Besides, I'm only six levels away from my next promotion, and that's *sure* to be a combat class."

"Speaking of..." Wes's eyes went blue. "I just hit a milestone."

"Ayla's tits," Eve swore as she noticed her own blinking notification. "So did I."

"Wait, but you didn't... I got a milestone for joining the guild."

Cracking a smile, she checked the message.

Legendary Quest Milestone Reached: Be Rejected from the Adventurer's Guild!
+2000 exp!

Eve doubled over. Heaving, full-body laughs filled the tight room as the milestone sank in. Wes gave her a questioning look.

"I got—" she managed through bursts of laughter, "I got a milestone for *being rejected*."

Wes snorted. "I guess it takes true skill to get turned away with a Legendary quest."

"The worst part is, I can't be mad at that clerk any more. Sure, she's a bitch, but she's a bitch that just gave me five whole levels."

Wes grinned. "Don't worry; I can be angry for the both

of us. Get anything good?"

"It dropped twice as much exp as the last one, but otherwise no, just the ten Endurance. You?"

"Doubled for you too? And here I thought I'd catch up some day. Your quest really is some bullshit, you know that right?" Wes said.

Eve just smirked.

He continued, "Anyway, I got a new passive called **Minor Flame Manipulation**. Not sure exactly what it does, but I imagine it'll at least be useful for not starting any brush fires."

Eve giggled. "Or putting them out once you *do* start them."

"Or that."

"Anyway"—Eve started for the door—"I vote we find some dinner and turn in early. You've got recruiting to do, and I want to stop by the bakery."

Wes cocked an eyebrow as he moved to follow her. "Ooh, gonna start another fire? Which bakery?"

Eve smirked, calling back to him as she descended back down into the common room, "All of them."

* * *

The glimmering city of Lynthia had a lot of bakeries. Fortunately enough, not a one of them went up in smoke over the course of Eve's tour. She did, however, find one that had shut down after defaulting on its debts, one that had mysteriously run out of flour the night before, and one that had been booked out months in advance to prepare cakes for some noble's wedding.

Eve rubbed her copper pieces together as she traveled from shop to shop, greeting each baker who'd taken the day off to visit his mother with a smile on her face. There were three of those.

As the day wore on, she found the string of coincidences more amusing than anything else. Of the nearly two dozen storefronts she visited, Eve's favorites were the couple who'd closed up to go on their honeymoon and the elderly baker who'd gone to celebrate the birth of her grandson.

Well, she figured, *it's good I can do more than burn 'em down.* By her score, Eve counted roughly as many bakers closed for strokes of fortune as misfortune. She took solace in the idea that whatever god had found it funny to saddle her with such a ridiculous quest wasn't outright malevolent.

Eve herself found the situation comedic at times. By the time she reached the baker who'd left his keys at home and thus missed his chance to rise the day's bread on time, she'd already given up on actually completing her quest.

Curiosity more than ambition drove her to continue her search. She knew it wouldn't be this easy, but the act of pushing coincidence to its limits entertained the *Courier* more than she could say.

Her money still rested safely in her pocket when she returned to the guild hall with an exhausted smile on her face.

Even seated, Wes towered over most of the guildsmen as he waved her over to a corner table. He wasn't alone.

A thin man sat across from him. He was every bit Wes's opposite, slim and boyish to the mage's built masculinity. Golden locks draped across his soft face as he smiled at the new arrival. Eve **Appraised** him.

Level 6 Acolyte of Ayla
Uncommon Tier 1 Class

Makes sense given the white robes, she thought, *except for...* "Doesn't Ayla only accept female acolytes?"

The priest reddened. "You can take that up with the Questing Stones. They seem to have a sense of humor lately."

"Believe me, I know." She held out a hand as she took a seat. "I'm Eve."

"Preston." They shook.

Wes explained, "The guild is setting me up in a new team—classic healer, warrior, mage combo. Preston here is our healer."

"And the warrior?"

Preston shrugged. "Some guy called Alex, or that's what the paperwork says. Hells know where he is."

Eve's eyes widened. "An acolyte who swears; color me impressed. Wes, how'd you manage to land the least-holy priestess in the entire church?"

Wes ignored Preston's open mouth. "Same way you landed the most bullshit quest the Stones have ever given. Dumb luck."

"I'm not a priestess, I—"

Eve cut him off. "What use is a priestess if nothing ever hits you?"

"You mean like that goblin never hit me?" Wes retorted. "Besides, a party's gotta have more than just me. You can't carry all of us."

Preston furrowed his brow. "Wait, *she* carries—"

Eve interrupted, "Fair point. Maybe we do need a healer." She turned to Preston, a teasing grin on her face. "Are those women's robes?"

The acolyte hid a smile of his own by lifting a tankard to his mouth. "Is that a corpse's blouse?"

Eve's jaw hung open. Preston sipped his ale. Wes applauded.

"I like this one," he said. "Welcome to the team."

Chapter 9

The Quick and the Dead

Evelia Greene was just about sick of these glass walls. She shielded her eyes from the bright morning sun, but no matter how she turned, the prismatic fortification managed to pierce her measly shade.

"Good morning!" Preston emerged from the gates with a smile on his face. He approached Wes and Eve where the two waited just outside the city. "Excited?"

Wes groaned, rubbing at his temples. "How are you so chipper? You drank more than either of us last night."

"I'm a healer, remember?"

"Right, right, priestess of—wait." Wes froze. "Are you saying you can **Heal** hangovers?"

"Just cause they're self-inflicted doesn't mean they aren't an injury. Ayla's all about forgiveness. She doesn't hold a night of drinking against you."

Wes perked up. "So you'll—"

Preston smirked. "Unfortunately, I'm not Ayla." He pointed at Eve. "I'll heal her because *she* didn't just make fun of me in the same sentence as asking for help."

Wes sighed. "I walked into that one."

"You did."

Eve kept her mouth shut. She stepped forward.

Preston held out a hand. "May I heal you?"

She nodded. "You don't need to ask."

He placed his palm on her forehead. Eve closed her eyes.

The spell *forced* its way in. There was no other word for it. Waves of brilliant energy burst through every corner of Eve's mind, leaving no stone unturned, no memory unseen. It ravaged her very being, leaving each flaw, each indiscretion exposed to the light of day, and only once her every mistake, her every ounce of humanity lay bare, could she be forgiven.

The light left her as abruptly as it came. She wasn't empty. Nor was she fulfilled. As many walls lay broken as new foundations built, and Eve couldn't even begin to assess the injuries to her soul itself. At least the hangover was gone.

"Bandir's balls," she swore. "That was intense. Now I get why you ask permission."

Preston gave her an apologetic smile. "Ayla doesn't exactly respect personal boundaries, so Her acolytes make a point to in Her stead."

"Is it always like that?"

He shrugged. "You get used to it. I'd be a pretty shit teammate if you stop to have a revelation whenever I heal you mid-battle."

"Speaking of which," Wes cut in, "our warrior is late. The guild clerk said just outside the gates at nine o'clock. Where the hells is he?"

"Right here."

All three adventurers spun around at the unfamiliar voice to find a woman towering over them. That is, Eve and Preston found a woman towering over them. Wes found one just below eye level.

"Alex, I presume?"

"Yep."

"You're our warrior?" Wes continued.

The woman scowled, raising a finger to point at the spear on her back. "What's it look like?"

"Right. Anyway, I'm Wes—the mage, Preston's the healer, and Eve's, well… Eve."

Alex cocked an eyebrow. "There was no Eve on the paperwork."

"No, but she's saved my life more times than I can count. Whatever the guild says, she deserves to be here."

Alex tilted her head, never breaking eye contact with Wes. "Long as she doesn't get anyone killed or try and take a cut of my share, she's welcome to tag along. I'm not here to babysit. I'm here to work."

The tall warrior didn't wait for a rebuttal before taking off. Preston followed. Eve and Wes shared a look before scurrying to catch up with the woman's long stride.

"It's just one level," Eve told herself just as much as Wes. "I'll have a combat class soon enough."

"Just one level," he echoed. "Not much time to earn one."

"Hey, I killed two wolves with a sword and the goblin shaman with his own staff. That's *gotta* be enough for a combat class."

"Sure," Wes said, "but you should still use this job as another chance for something good. The last thing you want is to wait another twenty-five levels before you can actually fight."

"Fair point."

They trekked on in silence for a time, both sets of eyes fixed on the new teammates ahead of them. Eve **Appraised** the businesslike warrior.

Level 18 Soldier
  Common Tier 2 Class

She's like me! Eve realized. Then again, just because Alex also had a common class didn't make them the same. *Hers* was meant for combat. No doubt Alex was strong enough to use the spear on her back. She certainly looked the part.

At six feet tall and two hundred pounds of toned muscle, the *Soldier* gave even Wes a run for his money. Hells, with her class she was probably *stronger* than the blacksmith's son. Jet black hair swung out behind her in a tight ponytail, the only hint of femininity Eve could glean without seeing the woman's face. Thick leather armor hid all else.

Eve supposed that was a good thing. She'd rather have a well-protected front line than a pretty one.

At that thought, her eyes shifted to the man walking beside her. Wes too spent the walk gazing forward at the pair of new faces. Eve could only wonder what musings traipsed through his mind. She hoped he wasn't too enraptured with the *Soldier*.

In an effort to prevent him from staring further, Eve raised a question. "They seem to know where we're going. Do you?"

Wes nodded. "It was in the paperwork, which you'd know if you'd actually read it."

"Hey, if they won't let me in the guild, I won't read their bloody documents."

"Anyway," he pushed on, "there's a barrow a few miles south of here, remnant of some forgotten war or something. We've been charged with investigating reports of undead wandering around."

Eve's eyes shot open. "They gave us a necromancer for our first job? Are they insane?"

"None of the reports claim anything over level twenty, so there's no reason to be worried. Besides, our group is pretty ideal for this."

He pointed at the two ahead of them. "Zombies are slow, so Alex won't have any trouble keeping them at spear's length. Corpses this old will be desiccated, so my fire will eat right through them, and healing isn't the only thing Ayla's good for. I'm willing to bet Preston's got a few ways to deal with undead himself."

"And me?"

Wes turned up his palms. "You can outrun them? I don't think the guild really factored you in when they assigned us this job."

"Right, right. Well, I'm sure I'll figure something out. Gotta earn my exp somehow."

"That you do," Wes said as he stared off across the grassland. "That you do."

* * *

Eve wasn't quite certain what she'd expected, but the sight that greeted her when they arrived at the zombie-infested barrow certainly wasn't it. "It's a hill."

"Not just any hill," Wes said. "It's a hill full of dead people."

"Yeah, didn't you know?" Preston smiled. "It's what's on the inside that counts."

Eve laughed. "Or in this case, what's *supposed* to be on the inside but isn't."

"Very funny," Alex commented. "We have work to do." Once again she took the lead, circling the grassy hill until she came upon an opening in its side. The stairs led down, disappearing into the darkness below.

"Well that's not ominous at all." Preston paused at the entryway.

Alex drew her spear. "Good thing you're not going in first. Let's go." She stepped in.

Wes followed, setting his hand alight as he did. His flames threw an uneasy orange glow over the ancient stone, casting flickering shadows into the dark corners of the narrow hallway.

Preston went next, and Eve stepped in after him.

Dry earth lined the walls, supported by stone arches every eight feet. The arches combined with horizontal lines of the same material to segment the walls into rectangular sections, each suspiciously human-sized. Eve wondered just how close she stood to a rotting corpse in its final resting place.

She got her answer soon enough. Not far into the dark barrow, Alex stopped at a piece of wall that seemed to have lost its resident.

"Looks like those reports were right," she said. "Someone's disturbing the dead."

"And the dead are disturbing me," Eve quipped as she stared into the open tomb. Less than a foot of dirt had separated the hallway from the opening within. Less than a foot between them and every other corpse in the place.

"Best to keep moving." Alex ignored the joke. "Keep a count of how many are missing."

Preston nodded furiously, the tension clear on his face. The party continued on.

Eve watched as the healer practically clung to Wes's side, no doubt hoping the large mage would keep him safe should anything get past Alex's spear. Were she not preoccupied with her own mounting nerves, she might've teased the *Acolyte* for it. Instead she walked.

They came across eight more empty graves as the tunnel spiraled into the earth. Each provoked a spike in Eve's unease as the number of creatures they'd have to face slowly incremented. As the party progressed ever downward, a second concern popped up: the tunnel itself.

While the confined space would certainly aid in the process of fighting off several enemies at once, it made Eve's secondary task that much harder. Wes was right; she *needed* a good class, and this was her last opportunity to earn one before her next evolution. If Alex could hold off the entire zombie horde herself, Eve wouldn't get her chance. Even then, her skills weren't much use in a narrow tunnel.

Eve's worries came to a rapid halt as the adventurers did the same.

"Light up ahead," Alex whispered. "We've arrived." She crept forward. The others followed.

Eve breathed a quiet sigh of relief as the tunnel opened out into a wide chamber, only to clench her fists again as their *Soldier* stopped short of entering it.

A hoarse voice echoed through stale air. "Who dares enter my domain?"

"Oh, come off it, Steven," Alex barked. "Did you think I wouldn't know it was you?"

Wes stepped in. "Wait, you know this guy?"

Alex sighed. "He's my ex. We dated for about a month, until I caught him killing cats to practice reanimating them."

"Why didn't you tell us?"

Alex raised her eyebrows. "You think I wanted to admit to dating *that?*"

"Fair point."

"Of course it was me!" the voice called back. "I'm the greatest, most feared necromancer in all of Lynthia!"

Alex ground her teeth. "I *meant* I knew it was you that sent the reports to the guild."

"B-but why would I do that?"

"Because you like to pretend people actually give a shit about you."

Growing impatient, Eve peeked her head around the bulky *Soldier* to glimpse into the room beyond. There were six zombies in all, standing in a semicircle around a man no taller than she. The most feared necromancer in Lynthia's face and clothes were stained with dirt from sleeping on the floor of the catacomb. His hair was ragged and unkempt, and his shirt on backwards.

"Fools! Now you have tread upon my place of strength, nothing can save you! You shall die knowing it was Steven, the world's greatest necromancer, that defeated you!"

Alex lowered her spear. Wes prepared a **Fire Dart**. The zombies shambled forward.

At once the walls on either flank gave way as desiccated hands burst through. Eve yanked her arm away. Preston wasn't so lucky.

The healer lurched to the side as a newly animated corpse snatched his robe. He hit the wall hard. The dirt fell away, and the zombie's head peeked out, its mouth wide open and lined with rotting teeth. A flash of light coursed through the tight space, forcing Eve to shut her eyes.

When she opened them again, the monster had fallen limp.

"Ayla's not fond of undead," Preston bragged.

A cry rang out ahead of them. The healer fell silent as he surged forward to help Wes with his own attacker. Another hand broke through the wall just below Preston's line of sight. It caught his ankle.

The slim blond careened forward, falling directly into Wes. They both went down.

Eve's heart raced. The sound of more falling dirt echoed out behind her, indicating the impending arrival of yet more walking dead. She stared down the hall, watching Alex expertly wield her spear to fend off those encroaching from the front. The *Soldier* took a step forward. Another.

At Eve's feet, Preston struggled to stand, fighting off the grasping hands of two floor-level zombies as Wes shifted beneath him.

We can't fight them all, she realized. The coarse scrape of feet dragging against dirt sounded from the way they'd come. Up ahead, Alex shifted once more, and Eve had her opening.

She charged.

Wes collapsed again to the hard earth as she ran across his back, shooting up to full speed as she activated **Run Away**. A decaying hand reached for her, but she blew right past it. Her heart rate quickened.

She reached the final chamber just as Alex decapitated her second zombie. With a swing of her spear, one more hit the ground. Eve trampled it too.

Steven could only stare as this unarmed, unarmored slip of a girl ran at him. He opened his mouth to bark an order at his undead minions, but he was too late. The slow-moving corpses could do nothing to stop Evelia Greene, and neither could their foolhardy creator.

Eve raised her elbow.

She got him in the throat, her momentum carrying her on until they both collided with the back wall. A terrible crack echoed through the chamber. Fiery pain exploded down Eve's arm as first Steven's back and then her elbow struck the wall. She cried out.

Steven collapsed. Eve followed. The room fell silent. Clutching her aching shoulder, Eve forced herself to survey the room before checking her slew of notifications.

The zombies crumpled, the magic tying them to the mortal plane cut clean.

Alex panted. Wes carefully stood. Preston vomited.

You have defeated Level 28 Necromancer: +480 exp!
You have defeated Level 16 Zombie: +32 exp!
You have defeated Level 15 Zombie: +24 exp!
You have defeated Level 16 Zombie: +32 exp!
...
You have defeated Level 16 Zombie: +32 exp!

Eve swore. *Ayla's tits, it gave me credit for all the zombies?* In a way it was fair; she *had* been the reason they fell. Still, it blew her mind that a single man could be powerful enough to raise that many monsters at only a few levels higher than she. Then again, he *hadn't* been powerful enough to survive an elbow to the neck.

A devious grin overcame Eve's face as she pulled up the final message. It was *long.*

Class Upgrade Avai—

"Gods below!" Wes's curse forced Eve's attention away from the long-awaited promotion.

"What's wrong?"

His eyes shone blue with the invisible light of his own status screen as he reread its contents open-mouthed. "I just unlocked a *Rare* class."

* * *

Wesley Rollund (total xp 1592)
Human
Level 10 Flame Initiate
Exp: 283/484
Health: 43/120
Stamina: 39/110
Mana: 221/300
Constitution: 12
Endurance: 11
Intelligence: 41
Dexterity: 9
Strength: 14
Spirit: 30

Passive Ability - Flame Affinity
You've always had a thing for fire. Fire Spells do 15% bonus

damage. +15% Fire resistance.

Passive Ability - Minor Flame Manipulation
The inferno heeds your whisper. Manipulate small fires with willpower alone.

Active Ability - Burning Hand
10 Mana/Sec
Engulf your hand in flames. Deals fire damage to anything it touches.

Active Ability - Fire Dart
30 Mana
A novice's first projectile. Throw a flaming dart that inflicts fire damage upon whatever it hits.

Chapter 10

Promotion Commotion

"Bullshit," Alex swore. "A *Rare* class at tier two? That's unheard of. You barely even contributed to the fight!"

Preston rubbed the back of his neck. "I—um—I'm sorry about that. One of them grabbed me and I—"

Wes cut him off, "It's alright. These things happen. Instead of worrying about it, go heal Eve."

The *Acolyte* blanched. "Right. Eve. I'm so sorry." He dashed across the room, gently placing a glowing hand on her aching shoulder.

Ayla's light was no less invasive than it'd been before, but Eve was ready this time. She braced herself against the golden onslaught, allowing Her forgiveness to course through the sprained and dislocated joint.

So engulfed was she in the intensity of the healing, she didn't even notice the burst of agony as her shoulder popped back into place. The relief was immediate.

"Now that's dealt with," Alex broke the silence, "how in the hells did you unlock a *Rare* class?"

Wes turned up his palms. "I don't fucking know! The requirement list says some crap about knowing the true nature of fire."

"Well?" Eve stood. "Are you gonna tell us what it is?"

"I haven't technically chosen it yet, but it's the only *Rare* option. *Acolyte of the Devouring Flame.*"

Eve raised her eyebrows. "Say what you will about whether he deserves it; that sounds badass."

Alex grimaced. "Badass and unfair."

"You're right, it is unfair. Just like it's unfair that I got stuck with a noncombat class or Preston's the only guy in an all-female holy order. But it's not his fault. And it's not mine, and it's not Preston's. So maybe you could get off your high horse and stop being an asshole about it."

Alex shut her mouth, grit her teeth, and stormed from the chamber.

Wes turned to Eve. "Where did that come from?"

She exhaled. "Alex isn't the only one feeling a little frustrated. She's been rude since we met her, and I just put off reading my own upgrades so I could hear about yours."

"Then read them."

"Wes—"

"I don't need you to yell at Alex for me, and I don't need you to celebrate my promotion for me. What I need is for you to celebrate *yours*. You saved our asses there, Eve, and you deserve every bit of reward that comes with it."

"Awwww," the healer cooed from across the room.

Eve glared. "Not now, Preston."

The *Acolyte* jumped. "Right. Sorry. I'll just…" He took his leave.

"So." Wes peered down at her. "What'd you get?"

Eve pushed herself to her feet. "Not here. Not… with him." She gestured down at Steven's corpse. "Let's go. I can read while we walk."

Accepting Wes's nod and quiet smile, Eve stepped over the fallen zombies and into the spiral hallway. She forced the necromancer from her mind as she walked; she could deal with those emotions later. For now, at last, she read her messages.

Class Upgrade Available: Envoy
Common Tier 3 Class
Requirements: *Courier or Page base class.*

From humble beginnings, you've fought your way up the ladder into a position with real—if limited—influence. No more do you carry letters or packages, but diplomatic missives of great import.

+15 Endurance
+3 Endurance/Level

Eve dismissed the option outright. *Definitely not taking another Common class,* she thought. *Especially not glorified Messenger Girl.* She opened the next one.

Class Upgrade Available: Starlight Runner
Uncommon Tier 3 Class
Requirements: *Courier, Scout, Thief, or Messenger base class. Use your skills to escape under the cover of the stars. Reach enough Endurance to run through the night.*

The night is your friend, and you're determined to use it. Hide in the shadows, or shine silver starlight to expose that which is hidden.

+25 Endurance
+5 Spirit
+12 Endurance/Level
+2 Dexterity/Level
+1 Spirit/Level

Eve reread the class description. *Well that's vague.* The name certainly sounded interesting, and the stats it granted caught her attention. *Spirit* meant magic. She flagged it as an option, but a few details left her with reservations.

First and foremost, nothing about it read like a combat

class. Useful as stealth may be, she could already escape combat on her own. She needed something that could help the party, and she needed something that would get her into the guild. *Starlight Runner* did neither.

Class Upgrade Available: Medic
Uncommon Tier 3 Class

Requirements: *Put your own life at risk to save another's three times. Rescue someone from certain death by pulling them from combat. Make a personal sacrifice to stay at a patient's side as he recovers.*

Time and time again you've risked life and limb to save another, and should the opportunity arise again, you'll take it. The life of a medic isn't the most glamorous or renowned. You won't be leading armies into battle or defeating ancient beasts, but to those people you save, you mean everything. You are a hero in the truest sense of the word.

+20 Endurance

+7 Spirit

+3 Intelligence

+10 Endurance/Level

+3 Intelligence/Level

+2 Spirit/Level

Eve flagged this one too. Sure, the description seemed to imply the class wasn't a good fit for someone on a *Legendary* quest, but she certainly liked the sound of it. *A hero in the truest sense of the word, huh?* She grinned.

Once again, the presence of *Spirit* meant the class likely had access to magic, but given the low quantities it probably wasn't much. Given the name, they were likely healing spells meant to stabilize a wounded soldier until she could deliver him to safety. The class had two problems.

For one, while technically a combat class to satisfy the

guild requirement, *Medic* was no use for fighting. Gaining exp would be a chore. Beyond that, their little party already had a healer. She liked Preston well enough. He'd even healed her twice in one day, and taking his job didn't feel a great way to repay that.

She moved on.

Class Upgrade Available: Shatterfate Striker
Rare Tier 3 Class

Requirements: Successfully wield a weapon beyond your ability. As a noncombat class, defeat an enemy beyond your level. As a noncombat class, use a defensive ability offensively. Choose not to complete your life's quest when given the opportunity. Accept and overcome the inequality of life.

The gods do not play dice, and neither do you. Unhappy with the life before you, you clenched your fists and stood your ground and whispered defiance at fate itself. You've proven to the divine, to the mundane, and to your very soul that this is the way of things. The path of shattered fate is neither safe nor easy, but know that as long as you choose to walk it, it is yours.

+25 Endurance
+15 Strength
+5 Constitution
+5 Dexterity
+15 Endurance/Level
+6 Strength/Level
+5 Dexterity/Level
+4 Constitution/Level

Eve fell over.

In her distraction, she hadn't seen the dead zombie lying on the floor before her. She tripped over it, her arms windmilling as she careened forward into the opposite wall.

Wes laughed. "This is why we don't read while we walk."

"It's not that…"

Wes gave her a concerned look. "Passing up an opportunity for a witty retort? That's not like you. What's wrong?"

"Sorry, I… I'm just thinking about my options."

He helped her up. "Anything good?"

"How—um—how many stats will you get? Once you take your *Rare* class."

"Twenty a level," he rattled off the answer. "Split between *Intelligence* and *Spirit* with a sliver of *Constitution* in there for survivability. I'd guess it'll be thirty per level once I hit tier three."

Eve nodded. "Yeah that's right."

Wes stopped in his tracks. "Right because you checked my math, or because you *know?*"

The width of her grin told him everything.

He surged forward, wrapping her in a tight hug. A combination of his natural strength and their difference in height left Eve's feet dangling in the air. "Eve, that's incredible! It hasn't even been two weeks!"

"I mean… most of the experience came from my quest, and you know *that's* not exactly fair."

Wes set her down, staring deeply into her eyes as he replied. "Your quest didn't give you a *Rare* class; it gave you a shitty one. You earned it."

"It's not like I—well—" she sighed. "Thank you."

Wes smiled. "Guess it's my turn to play catch-up, huh?"

Eve chuckled, taking a step to continue their walk through the dim tunnel.

Wes only needed a few long strides to catch back up with her. "What are the abilities?"

"I don't know; I haven't taken it yet."

"Wanna hit 'yes' together?"

Eve shook her head. "Not here. I've heard the stories. Grondis the Great slept for thirty days when he jumped to his *Legendary* class. I'm not about to pass out in the middle of a crypt."

"That's a song. Besides, *you* aren't getting a *Legendary* class."

"I'm not getting a *Legendary* class *now.*" she corrected him. "We can wait until we get back to Lynthia."

"Alright, alright." He held up his hands in defeat. "But I'm telling the others."

"What? It's *my* class. They already kno—"

Preston's voice interrupted her from the barrow's exit. "Tell the others what?"

Wes stepped outside. "Eve got a *Rare* too."

The healer's mouth hung open. "Bandir's balls, two rare upgrades in one day? That's amazing!"

Alex stared with wide eyes. "Congratulations. You deserve it." In a single motion, the *Soldier* turned on her heel and strode away.

"Seriously?" Wes watched her go. "How come she yells at me but congratulates you?"

"Because the one time she's seen us fight I saved the day while you fell on your face?"

"Hey! I could've—"

Eve snapped her fingers as the realization struck her. "Speaking of which—" She held out a hand. "Pay up."

"But it's my last one."

"Then get more. If it weren't for me, a zombie would be eating you and it right now."

Wes grumbled as he pulled the pack from his shoulder, digging through it to withdraw the final strawberry scone. He handed it over.

"That looks tasty," Preston commented as Eve took a bite.

"It is," Wes groaned. "And knowing her talent for

getting bakeries shut down, it'll be a while until I can find more. If I can even afford them."

"Come on." Eve licked sugary crumbs from her lips as she spoke. "You still have the hydra scales and that lightning staff/wand thing to sell. Not to mention payment for the job we just did."

"Right, but I imagine a certain *someone* is going to use most of that to pay her guild fees."

Eve smirked. "Oh, sorry, I misspoke. I meant payment for the job *I* just did."

Wes sighed.

Preston guffawed. "She's got you there."

Wes cocked an eyebrow at him. "Strong words for a priestess."

"Hey," Eve stepped in. "*Acolyte,*" she corrected. "He's not a priestess. *Yet.*"

Preston looked up at the tall mage. "Wait a minute, didn't you say your new class is an *Acolyte* too?"

He nodded. "*Acolyte of the Devouring Flame.*"

The healer smiled. "I guess we're peers then, huh? Maybe you can make it to priestess some day too."

Wes scoffed. "Please. We all know I'm going to skip straight to *Lord* or *Master of the Devouring Flame.*"

Preston turned to Eve. "Five silver says he ends up *Fuel for the Devouring Flame.*"

It was Eve's turn to let out a wild giggle. She shook his hand. "I don't have five silver, but you're absolutely on."

The teasing jokes and friendly banter continued on as did the adventurers on their way back to Lynthia and to rest. The mirth of their verbal fencing and the lingering sweetness of the scone on her tongue elevated Eve's mood beyond even the heights of her impending promotion. How she hoped it would all work out.

As the sun fell low on the horizon and walls of glass loomed up ahead, Eve struggled to keep her thoughts from wandering back to the dark barrow.   Necessary or otherwise, she'd killed a man.

She knew she'd had no choice.   Steven was a monster who'd murdered innocent animals to practice necromancy, desecrated dozens of ancient bodies, and threatened to kill her friends. This was no moral dilemma. He'd deserved his fate, and that was that. Still, it stuck with her.

It wasn't so much she felt guilty, or that she questioned the righteousness of her actions. There was just a certain finality to it that left a bad taste in her mouth. Ending a human life was supposed to mean something, and however justified her actions were, it did.

Eve sighed as she and Wes climbed the steps to their shared room. She didn't want to talk about it. Truth be told, she didn't want to think about it. She knew she'd done the right thing; it was just a matter of allowing that truth to sink in so she might move on. She needed a distraction.

Fortunately enough, that very evening the world had deemed fit to grant her the greatest diversion it ever could. A thin smile crossed her face as she sat on the bed.

Class Upgrade Available: Shatterfate Striker
  Rare Tier 3 Class

With a silent prayer to whichever god might listen, Eve lay back, shut her eyes, and hit 'yes.'

Chapter 11

Skills, Skills, Skills

The golden hue of sunrise pierced the thin curtains of the guild dormitory by the time Eve awoke. She didn't even bother to sit up before replacing it with the unsightly blue of her status screen.

Evelia Greene
  Human
  Level 25 Shatterfate Striker
  Exp: 209/1033
  Health: 182/190
  Stamina: 899/900
  Mana: 0/0
  Constitution: 19
  Endurance: 90
  Intelligence: 12
  Dexterity: 20
  Strength: 30
  Spirit: 0

The first thing she noticed was her newly inflated stats. Between the bonus the tier 3 *Rare* class gave and those from her most recent level, the figures left her with quite the grin. They were some *clean* numbers.

She wondered if there was some divine purpose to the perfectly even Endurance, Dexterity, and Strength values, but ultimately concluded that her class itself was evidence enough to the contrary. Sometimes a coincidence was a coincidence. She'd enjoy the pretty numbers while they lasted.

The second aspect of her status which stood out was the exp total. A bit of quick math told her that 1033 was *not* the usual twenty percent higher than her previous level had cost. It was thirty.

Levels are gonna get real expensive real fast, she thought. *So much for that Common class explosive growth.* Of course, the insane stat increase more than made up for slower leveling, and that wasn't even considering the value of actual combat skills. On that note, she had more reading to do.

Ability Upgraded!
  Passive Ability - Haste
  A quicker step is the difference between life and death. You run [END/5]% faster.

The change wasn't massive, but Eve certainly welcomed the less-demeaning description. One fifth of her Endurance for one percent faster movement didn't seem like a great ability, but as she weighed the staggering *fifteen* Endurance she'd gain each level, the ability grew on her. Already she'd be eighteen percent faster with an extra three percent for each level she gained. She'd take that.

Ability Unlocked!
  Passive Ability - Surefooted
  One slip up means death, and you've become familiar with high speeds and difficult terrain. Gain increased traction and

stability.

This one was a bit vague, but Eve had a feeling it had something to do with her battle with the goblins in the slippery wet grass. She'd have to test how well it worked, but if the new skill meant not falling on her face again, it'd be a welcome addition to her arsenal.

Ability Unlocked!
Passive Ability - Battle-hardened
You've seen your fair share of battle, and your body has adapted for it. Gain increased bone density, tendon strength, and resistance to impact injuries.

Eve sighed. *Again with the vague descriptions.* The skill certainly *sounded* useful, especially after she'd dislocated her shoulder elbowing Steven, but she had no idea how exactly it worked, and testing it did not sound fun. Still, it looked promising. She stopped herself from daydreaming about possible upgrades for the ability to open the next message.

Ability Unlocked!
Passive Ability - Enhanced Metabolism
You've grown accustomed to burning through large amounts of Stamina. Gain increased energy efficiency from the food you consume, and increased Stamina regeneration while well fed.

Eve paled. Would she have to start eating twelve meals a night to keep her Stamina up? She could barely afford one dinner as it was. She shivered. The bit about 'energy efficiency' gave her some hope, but the description made her nervous. She didn't want to starve.

At least the good news—if one could call it good—was that she'd now hit the limit on passive abilities. If she managed to unlock a fifth, she could remove anything undesirable. Shaking the uncomfortable thoughts away, Eve moved on to the actives.

Ability Upgraded!
  Active Ability - Charge!
  85 Stamina
Put those feet to work. Whether ducking in or out of combat, a good Striker needs to do it quickly. Triple your maximum running speed for [END/5] seconds.

Now that was more like it. Not only was she free of the insulting **Run Away** skill, but the new version was even *faster*. Eve smiled just thinking about it. Memories of the wind rushing through her hair as she dashed through the plains at high speeds ran through her mind. Triple speed sounded *fun*.

The upgrade wasn't without down sides. The increased Stamina cost she could handle—she had Stamina to spare —but the reduced duration was another matter. Eve supposed the change was inevitable. If the skill still lasted for half her Endurance in seconds, things could get out of hand quickly. In the context of battle, eighteen seconds was still plenty of time.

Ability Upgraded!
  Active Ability - Adrenaline Rush
  8 Stamina/Sec
In the heat of battle, the human body is capable of wondrous feats. You've learned to use it to your advantage. Gain [END/3] Strength for the duration.

Eve's eyes shot open. The new version of **Heave** was the first true *combat* ability she'd picked up. Carry weight didn't help her swing a sword or parry a blow. Strength did.

Sure, she'd have to spend twice as much Stamina if she wanted to whisk Wes or Preston out of danger, but the offensive potential far outweighed an extra four Stamina per second. Compared to her pool of nine hundred, the cost was basically nothing anyway.

Ability Unlocked!
Active Ability - Fate-al Blow
90 Stamina
If you can shatter fate itself, you can shatter a few skulls. Your next melee attack deals [STR/3]% more damage.

"Seriously?" Eve muttered to herself. "Fate-al? Did *Wes* write this?"

The text of the ability itself was pretty simple—standard, even as she understood melee classes. To be entirely honest, she liked having a skill like this, but already Eve couldn't wait to upgrade or replace it, if only to escape the dreadful name.

Ability Unlocked!
Active Ability - Jet
500 Stamina
Momentum is a tool just like any other, and you've learned to wield it. Massively increase or decrease your personal momentum.

"Another one to test," Eve thought aloud. "If it means getting to and from max speed quickly and safely it'll definitely be useful, but... Ayla's tits." She reread the cost. So much for having Stamina to spare; five hundred was more than half her total.

Shit. If she ever wanted to use this in combat, it'd have to be at the very start. Regeneration above fifty percent was *slow*, and unless she took a break mid-battle, she'd never regen above four-fifty. Maybe her metabolism passive could do something about that? Otherwise she'd just have to wait until her Endurance rose even further.

Eve spent a few minutes reading through her ability list twice more as the information sank in. She could work with this. She had a good spread of offense and defense with enough mobility she'd be a nightmare to pin down.

The newly-minted *Striker* was just daydreaming about the way these skills could change and grow with her over time when Wes stepped through the door of their shared room.

"Good morning."

Eve smiled. "So I was right. The class upgrade did knock me out. How long did I sleep?"

"Or," Wes answered, "you had a long day and got a good night's sleep."

"I like my version better."

"Of course you do."

Eve rose from the bed, stretching as she stood. "Are you trying to say I *didn't* sleep later than you because my promotion was bigger?"

"It turns out sleeping in is a lot less pleasant when you're on the floor."

Eve opened her mouth to reply with a scathing witticism before thinking better of it and offering a simple, "Right. I'm sorry."

"It's alright. You've got your combat class now, so you can join the guild and get your own room instead of squatting in mine."

"I'm not squatting! I'll have you know I'm standing perfectly upright, thank you very much."

"Anyway," Wes changed the subject rather than stooping to reply to the pun, "I've got our money. Turns out the hydra scales weren't worth shit, but the enchanter I spoke to paid a few silver for the goblin staff. Said he's gonna use it to teach his apprentice what not to do."

"Welp, silver is silver. What about payment for the necromancer job?"

Wes withdrew another handful of coins. "It was a thirty-silver job, split three ways means my cut's ten. Between meals, renting two rooms, and your guild fees, we won't have much left."

Eve shrugged, scooping up her share as she made her way for the door. "Guess we'll just have to do another job."

"And in the meantime…" Wes turned to follow her.

She called over her shoulder from the hall outside, "In the meantime, I'm getting breakfast."

* * *

Eve approached the counter, filling her voice with every bit of snark she could muster. "Hello, I'd like to join the adventurer's guild."

The clerk's eyes flashed blue as she **Appraised** the *Striker*. "Oh, looks like someone managed to force their way into a combat class. Lucky you."

"Say what you will, at least I *earned* what I've got."

"Too bad what you got won't get you far."

Eve paused. "What?"

The clerk continued, sliding a document over the counter. "Guild fee for a *Common* class is four silver, and no, there's no discount for being stuck at *Common* in tier three."

Eve stared at the woman.

"I assume you'd like to join your brother's team?" She pushed another sheet of parchment across the table. "Sign here, and here."

Dumbfounded by the woman's statements, Eve silently handed over the silver and signed on the dotted line. Another document and another few coins to rent a second room, and the lady dismissed her without so much as a 'welcome to the guild.' Eve didn't mind. Her thoughts were occupied elsewhere.

"**Appraise** me," she ordered as she took her seat at the breakfast table with Wes and Preston. Alex was nowhere to be seen.

"Why?"

"I just had a very interesting conversation with the guild clerk. Apparently I have a *Common* class."

Preston's eyes shot open. "Shit, you're right. It says you're a level twenty-five *Striker*, tier three *Common*."

Wes cut in, "I see the same. It can't be a rarity thing because I'm also *Rare*."

"Let me try," Eve said, using the skill on Wes.

Level 10 Acolyte of the Devouring Flame
Rare Tier 2 Class

She shrugged. "Works fine for me. Maybe it's a tier thing?"

"It can't be," Wes said. "That clerk is tier four."

Eve blinked. "Wait, what? What in the ninth hell is a level fifty doing working a desk?"

Preston explained, "Some adventurers actually live long enough to retire. Besides, it behooves the guild to have a clerk who won't be bullied by every level thirty who thinks she's hot shit."

"Hey, as a level twenty-five who thinks she's hot shit, I was perfectly polite."

The healer cocked an eyebrow. "Were you?"

"She started it!"

Preston laughed. "That's what I thought."

Eve returned to the matter at hand. "But why do I show up as a *Common* class?"

"Your guess is as good as mine. I see you as a *Striker,*

which would imply there's something specifically about the *Shatterfate* part that stays hidden."

"Maybe," Wes chimed in, "it's because that part's not supposed to exist."

"What?"

"Yeah," Eve added, "I agree with Preston. What?"

"You said the class requirements were all doing things you shouldn't have been able to do, like wielding the sword or using **Run Away** to kill something."

"That doesn't explain why other people can't see it."

"No," Wes admitted, "but it's a clue. *Shatterfate* isn't *Rare* because it's strong and not many people have it; it's *Rare* because it isn't like other classes. You *have* to break the system to even get it, so why shouldn't it break the system in other ways too?"

Preston raised his eyebrows. "That's a stretch."

"I'm sure I'm not the first person to change a non-combat class into a combat one," Eve said. "And sure the requirements and the description are a bit unique—the skills all seem based more on the *Striker* part than the *Shatterfate* part. They're good, but they're definitely not unique."

"Well?" Wes grinned. "What are they?"

Eve sighed. "I walked right into that, didn't I?"

Preston chuckled. "You did."

"Alright, fine." Eve settled in, nicking a bite of sausage from Wes's plate. It was cold by now, but the spiced pork played well on her tongue with the little joy of theft. With a smile on her face and a hint of smugness in her voice, Eve launched into her joint explanation and gloating session as she shared the details of her class with her fellow adventurers and new friends.

Chapter 12

*A High Constitution Score Isn't the Only
Way We Protect Ourselves*

Wes spat out his juice. "**Fate-al Blow**? You're joking."

"That's what I said! Hells, if I didn't know better I would've guessed *you* had somehow written my skill descriptions."

"Me? You're the one who went with 'I'm not squatting I'm standing' earlier today."

"Ooooh," Preston taunted. "He's got you there."

"And I stand by that!" Eve said. "Standing-not-squatting is a thousand times cleverer than '**Fate-al Blow**.'"

Wes flashed an incredulous look. "Cleverer?"

"It's a word," Preston backed her up. "It sounds stupid as all hells, but it *is* a word."

"Either way," Wes turned back to Eve, "you're the one with a dumb pun for a skill name."

"Not for long. If you got a new skill or upgrade for every level of *Uncommon*, I'm sure as hells getting one at *Rare*."

"None of mine ever changed names."

Eve turned up her palms. "There's a first time for everything. Maybe I'll just replace it when I unlock a new one. I'm ability-capped anyway, and unless my math is wrong it's only like a twenty percent boost."

Wes rattled off the answer without pause. "It's a twenty percent boost *now*. By the time you promote again it'll be over a hundred."

"You and your Int."

"I'm serious," the mage continued. "There aren't *any* actual damage abilities that scale off Endurance. Considering your **Adrenaline Rush** can convert it to Strength, something like **Fate-al Blow** is going to be your best bet."

Preston added, "Especially if your base damage is already massive from hitting them with insane momentum."

"Exactly."

Eve leveled a glare at Wes. "Since when are you an expert on skill selection?"

He shrugged. "I've been in the guild longer than you, makes me your superior."

She snorted. "Oh, does it, Mr. Tier Two?"

"That's 'Sir Tier Two' to you. This team is a professional outfit."

Preston stepped in, "Professional, huh? Then how come we still know nothing about *your* fancy new class, *Sir Tier Two.*"

Wes held up his hands. "Alright, you win. It's not like I was gonna keep it secret. I'm an *Acolyte of the Devouring Flame. Rare* tier two, mage-type, you know all that. It's fifteen each flat Int and Spirit, then twenty points divided between Int, Spirit, Constitution, and a lone Endurance."

"So... stats of a *Rare* tier two mage."

"Right. The requirements and description talk a bunch about knowing the true nature of fire and wielding its insatiable hunger."

Eve's brow furrowed. "That's not ominous at all."

"Oh, just you wait," Wes continued. "It gets worse. I got two new abilities, both passives. I'm pretty sure the first is really the core of the class, because it lets me gain Mana from nearby natural fires."

"What's a 'natural' fire?" Preston asked.

"Something that's actually burning," the mage explained, "as opposed to the flames around my fist that **Burning Hand** generates."

"So keep a torch or brazier lit and you can cast spells forever?"

He shrugged. "I haven't tested it, and I'd probably have to keep giving it more fuel to burn, but yes. I can turn fuel into Mana. Can't say how fast or efficient it is, but it sounds useful."

Eve looked up from her breakfast. "As long as you don't go burning cities down to fuel your spells."

Wes nodded. "Which gets me to the second passive. I can't make heads or tails of it, so I'm going to show it to you so you know I'm not bullshitting you." His eyes flashed blue as he pulled up his status screen.

Eve and Preston both leaned across the wooden table to stare at the reflection in the man's eyes. Only a single skill description was in focus.

Passive Ability - Whispers of the Devouring Flame
Hear them.

"Ayla's tits," Preston swore. "That's terrifying."

Wes ran a hand through his chestnut hair. "You're telling me."

"Maybe it's a good thing," said Eve. "Maybe our campfire will tell you the future. Or the brazier will give you dating advice."

Wes shifted in his seat. "Or this 'devouring flame' whispers in my ear until I go mad and set you on fire."

Preston placed a hand on his shoulder. "You're not going to go mad. Unless you've done some evil shit without telling us, I don't see how you could've ended up with a detrimental skill. I'm sure it'll turn out to be a good thing."

"He's right," Eve added. "No way that skill turns you insane. I reserve the exclusive right to drive you mad, and any whispering candle is gonna have to wait its turn."

Wes chuckled. "Thanks."

"The real question is, whose skill will drive them mad first: your spooky whispers or the fact I have to live with an ability named fucking **Fate-al Blow**?"

Preston grinned. "I vote Eve. Hers is way worse."

"Yes," Wes admitted, "but what you're forgetting is that I *also* have to live with the knowledge you have that skill."

"Shit," Eve cursed. "I can't argue with that. Better send you to the asylum right now."

"As if you could afford to put me up in an asylum."

Eve snapped her fingers. "Good point. Sounds to me like you, oh dear party leader, should go ask the clerk about getting us another job."

Wes cocked an eyebrow. "So now that you want something, I'm the party leader?"

"Exactly."

Preston laughed. "That's what you get for lording your two days of guild membership over her."

Wes sighed as he pushed himself to his feet. "Alright, fine. At least *I* won't antagonize the level fifty clerk. I suppose next you'll want me to track down Alex and patch things up with her?"

"Actually," Preston said, "I think Eve should do that."

"What? Why me?"

"She empathizes with you," the healer explained. "You proved your worth against Steven, and unlike Wes and me, you didn't luck out with an *Uncommon* class. She'll respect that."

"Oh." Eve paused as the information sank in. "That's actually really insightful. I'm impressed."

Preston grinned. "What can I say? We priestesses are just more in touch with our emotions."

Eve giggled. "Leaning into it now, huh?"

"If the gods-damned Questing Stones are going to have a sense of humor, I will too."

Eve stood, patting the acolyte on the back as she addressed Wes. "So you get us a new job and I'll see about talking to Alex."

"Sounds good to me. Meet back here for dinner?"

She nodded.

"Oh, and Eve?" Wes added. "Don't get stabbed."

"Last I remember, *you're* the one who's been stabbed before. By a *goblin*."

"Actually, never mind," Wes said. "You should aggravate her just like that. I'm sure it'll work out fine."

"You know what?" Eve smiled as she stepped out into the city street. "Maybe it will."

* * *

Eve stopped partway through her journey through the streets of Lynthia when she came across a message depot. She only had a few coins left after paying the assorted guild fees, but what use was money unspent? She'd happily skip a meal somewhere down the line if it meant getting a certain letter sent.

Though the office itself was fairly simple, a strange sense of nostalgia overcame her as she stepped inside. She didn't realize why until she cast the first **Appraise.**

The place was filled with folks of a familiar class. *Messenger Boys* and *Girls* waited patiently for the next job while *Couriers* swapped packages back and forth. Eve smiled. If nothing else, the depot served as a reminder of the life she'd escaped, of the fate she'd shattered. She approached the counter.

Postage to Nowherested was only a silver, but the fee still left Eve with little more than the two coppers she'd started with. She refused to spend those.

Ma,

I'm sure you've figured out by now, but it turns out my quest is a bit harder than it sounds. I'm writing from Lynthia to let you know I've unlocked a Rare *class, I've joined the adventurer's guild, and I'm loving every minute of it. Maybe someday I'll make it home with that loaf of bread.*

Love,
Eve

Eve exhaled as she handed the missive to the clerk behind the counter. She wished the slim parchment had space for more, or that her handwriting wasn't so poor as to fit so little. Most of all she wished her ma could see her now.

She passed right by a bakery as she left the message depot, not even bothering to check if the door was locked. It probably was. Either way, Eve hadn't ventured out into the city to put more bakers out of business. Her first errand complete, she moved on to the second.

She had a *Soldier* to find.

* * *

The *thwack thwack thwack* of dull steel against wood filled the air as Eve crossed the yard. Men and women in varying quantities of armor swung their weapons about in a wide range of skill levels. While some expertly performed complex maneuvers against their wooden opponents, others somehow managed to miss the stationary dummies.

Alex was among the former.

"How did you find me?" she addressed Eve without pausing her routine.

"According to the guard I spoke with, there are only four training grounds in the city. I knew you'd be out practicing after yesterday, so it was just a matter of looking around. It took a bit of running, but that's what I do."

Alex swiped her spear in a series of slashes along the dummy's neck. "Clever, aren't you?"

"I try."

She finished her pattern with a brutal strike that left her spear tip buried in the wooden man's neck. "So why are you here?"

"I wanted to make sure you're okay. We killed your ex and you stormed off and I haven't heard from you since."

Alex turned to face her. "For the record, I'm glad that little shit's dead. He deserved what he got. And I didn't storm off. I'm not obligated to celebrate with you. The job was done and I went home."

"After yelling at Wes."

"Because he was bragging."

"He wasn't bragging!" Eve exhaled. "He was excited to get a new class. You didn't have to bite his head off."

"And I didn't have to cheer him on either. I'm your teammate, not your friend. I showed up on time, I did my job, and I went home."

Eve took a step forward. "That's not how this works. I need to know that I can trust you, that you'll have all of our backs, even if you're pissed at Wes for some gods-damned reason."

Alex matched her, staring Eve down from her superior height. "And I'm telling you I do. Not because I'm your friend, but because I'm a professional."

"That's your argument? We don't have to like you because you're 'a professional'?" Eve scowled. "If you're such a pro, why did you take a mission to go after Steven? Why didn't you tell us, your teammates, that we were hunting your own bloody ex-boyfriend?"

Alex faltered.

Eve pressed on. "If you want us to trust you under the premise that you're a professional, you need to actually act like one. Being a pro doesn't mean being a dick to your teammates, it means not letting personal shit get in the way."

"You're right." Alex spoke through gritted teeth. "I should've told you about Steven. That's on me, and I'm sorry."

"And Wes?"

"What do you want me to say? That I've been fighting my entire life to prove I'm worth more than fucking *Common* and I'm pissed that he gets a *Rare* class for free? Because I fucking am. Happy?"

Eve sighed. "Alex, I'm not here to rub it in your face. I won't speak for Wes because that's his job, but I started as a *Messenger Girl*."

"Did you earn your promotions, or did your fire mage friend carry you to it?"

Eve's laughter elicited a confused look from the tall warrior. "He wouldn't have made it a day without my help. If anything, I carried him. In more ways than one." She exhaled. "I understand your frustrations. I do. But it isn't Wes's fault that he got lucky and we didn't."

"So what do you want, Eve?"

"I want to help. I want you and Wes not to yell at each other. I'd like to be friends if we can."

It was Alex's turn to let out a sigh. "I'm sorry, Eve, but that's not on the table. Not now. I apologize for my lapse in professionalism, and I will strive to perform better in the future."

"Can I know why?"

She turned back to where her spear still rested planted in the dummy's neck. "No. You can't. Now let me practice in peace."

"It won't help, you know," Eve called after her.

Alex pivoted on her heel to stare back at the *Striker*. "Help with what?"

"With your class. Practicing more won't suddenly boost your rarity. It's about taking risks, trying things others wouldn't think to."

"What's your point?"

Eve gestured with open palms. "Look around you. Not a single *Rare* class among them. If you want your life to turn out differently from theirs, you need to do something different."

"Practice isn't about leveling up. It's about surviving. A *Rare* class is only any good if you actually live long enough to use it."

Eve nodded. "I can understand that. It's admirable, even. Hells know I don't have the patience to run drills all day. I just... I know how it is. My advice? Pick something you want, and give your everything to get it." Eve quoted her class description, "Clench your fists and stand your ground and whisper defiance at fate itself. It'll mean taking risks; it'll mean making sacrifices; and it'll mean trusting in the friends you make along the way. I can see the sweat on your brow, and I can see the absolute beating you gave that practice dummy. I know you'll get there. You deserve it."

At last the first chink in Alex's armor appeared in the form of a thin smile. "Thanks. For what it's worth, I think you deserve yours too."

"Of course I do," Eve chuckled. "I fought like hell for it. And you will too. Wes is arranging our next job as we speak."

Alex yanked her spear from its place embedded in the dummy. "Guess I'd better get my practice in while I can, then."

"I guess you should." Eve didn't press any further.

Whatever reason Alex had for keeping her distance from the others, she clearly wasn't ready to share. "I'll see you back at the guild." She turned to go.

"Hey, Eve?" the *Soldier* called after her. "You mentioned not having the patience to run drills. How about something a bit more interesting? I'm sure you're dying to try out your new skills. Why don't you show me what you've got?"

"Are you asking for a bout?"

"You know I am."

Eve spun back around, a smile already stretching across her face. "You're on."

Chapter 13

Everybody Falls on Their Face Sometimes

I hope this traction skill works, Eve thought. The thin layer of loose sand over packed earth gave her some concern as she squared off against the tall warrior. Alex twirled her practice spear—a quarterstaff—from where she stood thirty feet across the sparring ring.

Eve's own hands lay empty. Untrained and unpracticed in the weapons of war, she knew she was just as likely to hurt herself as Alex. She might be unused to her new abilities, but she wasn't stupid.

She ran through each of her skills in a last-ditch effort to formulate some semblance of a strategy for the coming bout. They weren't promising.

The problem was, given Alex's weapon of choice and the abilities at Eve's disposal, her only real option was to use **Charge!** to get in close and **Fate-al Blow** to end the fight quickly. The warrior was smart enough to predict that. After all, how *else* would a melee fighter with no weapon defeat a spear carrier?

At least, Eve reasoned, *she doesn't know my exact skills. Serves her right for skipping breakfast with the team.* There was, of course, one ability that might turn the battle on its head, but everything about it screamed 'terrible idea.'

Jet was right out. Without testing it, Eve had no idea how fast it would make her, and the whopping five hundred Stamina cost implied the answer was 'godsdamned fast.' She shook her head. The last thing she needed was to slam herself into a practice dummy or punch Alex into an early grave. **Charge!** and **Fate-al Blow** it was.

"Ready?" Alex called out.

Eve simply smirked and nodded.

The *Soldier* began her countdown. "Three."

Eve cracked her knuckles.

"Two."

She hopped up onto the balls of her feet.

"One."

She inhaled, clenching her hands into fists.

"Fight!"

Eve dashed in.

Alex raised her spear tip, holding her ground at the ring's edge.

Eve paused just outside of range, ready to dart to the side should Alex lunge. She didn't. The warrior stayed put, tracking Eve's motion with the point of her staff. With her back to the arena's end, Alex protected herself from any attempt at circling her.

Eve darted from side to side, hoping to bait an opening. All she needed was one misstep, a paltry few seconds without a spear between her and her target. She didn't get it.

Okay, new plan. Eve stepped forward, ready to dodge the imminent lunge.

It didn't come.

Shit, Eve swore as her opponent simply continued to track her motion. She stepped in again, further exposing herself to a counterattack. Still Alex refused to strike. *I can't keep doing this*, Eve reasoned. *Soon enough I'll be too close to dodge, and she knows it.*

Her eyes fixed on Alex's spear, Eve stepped in again. And again. Her heart raced with every step as the pivotal moment approached. Either she'd avoid Alex's lunge and push through into attacking range or the weapon would hit home. Another step.

The attack finally came just as Eve's front foot left the ground. The practice spear surged towards her as Alex lunged with incredible force. Eve **Charged!**

Her back foot launched her to the side.

The spear tip flew past.

Eve swung her front foot around to catch her sudden change in momentum. It slammed into the packed earth, sending a jolt of shock up her leg but failing to regain control of the motion. Her upper body continued lurching to the side at inhuman speed.

Her right shoulder hit the ground first. Her face followed. The sand scraped against her exposed skin as her momentum carried her several feet along the surface of the practice ring. Stinging pain flowed through her cheek and shoulder, that of the fall matched by the embarrassment of how it came to be.

It was her own damned fault.

Eve pressed a palm into the earth to push herself up, but a hard shape pressing into the back of her neck kept her in place.

"I win."

Eve groaned, nonverbally accepting defeat. Alex withdrew her spear, replacing it with an open hand.

Eve took it.

"Well fought," the *Soldier* complimented as she helped Eve to her feet.

"Well fought? I fell on my face."

Alex grinned. "Exactly. I'd say you learned more from

that bout than any day of practice could've taught you."

Eve raised a lone eyebrow in as skeptical a look as she could manage.

The warrior explained. "You know what your problem is? You're too clever for your own good. Given your level, I'd guess you've been adventuring for a few months at least, and I'm willing to bet every insane plan you've come up with and every risk you've taken has worked out."

Eve didn't bother to correct her. "What's your point?"

"My point is, we all fall on our face sometimes. Welcome to the real world. Cleverness will only get you so far; the rest is work."

Eve sighed, rubbing the back of her neck. "You're right. I should've tested and practiced more before getting into a fight. I've never even *tried* to **Run Away** sideways before, let alone **Charge!**"

"Wait," Alex snorted. "You have a skill called **Run Away**?"

"Had," Eve corrected. "I was a *Courier*, remember? Don't bother making fun, Wes has already exhausted pretty much every joke there is about it."

Alex shook her head. "It's a good thing I'm not Wes. I would never make fun of a person's class, especially not after they've proven they're better than it."

"Thank you, Alex. For the bout and for... the advice, I guess."

The tall warrior clapped a hand on Eve's shoulder. "We're teammates, remember? It's my job to keep you alive. This is just as much a part of that as anything I do in the field. Now go find Preston and get those scrapes patched up. If we're going on another job later, I want your ego to be the only part of you that's taken a hit."

Eve laughed, raising a hand to her forehead in mock salute. "Yes, ma'am."

Alex chuckled. "Good work, soldier. I'll see you in the

field. You're dismissed."

* * *

Eve braced against the invasive mercy of Ayla's light as Preston healed her injuries.

"At least you didn't dislocate your shoulder again. Maybe this new class is worth something after all."

She grimaced. "Are all the gods like this or just Ayla? I don't need a bloody divine revelation every time you patch up a few scrapes."

Preston shrugged. "Hells if I know. I'd bet if I worked for Loia you'd end up in a battle frenzy instead of feeling absolution."

"Feels a lot more like scrutiny than absolution. Does She *really* need to root through my entire past to stop me bleeding?"

"Like I said, Ayla's not big on boundaries."

Wes paced across the small bedroom. "I'm just impressed you actually got into the ring with her. You fell on your face the first time you used **Run Away**; why should **Charge!** be any different?"

"And immediately after falling on my face I saved your ass, remember?"

Wes snorted.

"Look," Eve explained, "Alex is angry you got a class you didn't deserve, and she thinks I'm cocky and too clever for my own good. I needed to humble myself, and failing in the ring was the perfect opportunity."

"How long did it take you to come up with *that* excuse?"

Eve grinned. "Twenty minutes. I thought it was a pretty good one, actually."

Wes laughed. "For Preston, maybe, but I know you well enough to know you'd never take a dive like that."

"You know what Alex said when I told her about **Run Away**? That she wouldn't even consider making fun of someone for their class. Maybe I should go stay with her

118

instead of putting up with your bullshit."

"Please." Wes leaned against the wall with his arms crossed. "You love my bullshit."

Preston chuckled, "He's got you there."

"No," Eve said, "I love your *scones*. Speaking of…"

Wes held up a hand. "I'm trying, I'm trying. I found a baker who makes them, but they're not cheap. I can pick some up once we get paid for the job tomorrow."

"Oh." Preston perked up. "That reminds me. What exactly *is* this job?"

"There's a troll, apparently, in the hills east of Lynthia. It's labeled as standard difficulty, so the pay's not great but it shouldn't be *too* dangerous."

Eve looked up. "Honestly, I'm okay with that. We don't have to *almost* die on every single mission. An easy one will be a nice change of pace."

"I agree," said Preston. "I'm super close to level ten—I don't need to risk my life to get there."

Wes cocked an eyebrow. "You sure? Getting a *Rare* requires a bit of risk."

"I don't *need* a *Rare* class. I'm a healer, remember? I'll be useful either way, and *Uncommon* is perfectly reasonable at tier two."

"Yeah," Wes teased, "but if you don't unlock something different, you'll be stuck in your holy sisterhood. You know you can't get exp once you've unlocked a promotion."

Preston snapped his fingers. "Good point. Maybe I should murder a few people to get into Loia's good graces."

Eve giggled. "If it means no more of Ayla's bloody mercy, I'm onboard. Who should we kill?"

Preston rolled his eyes. "Maybe I should just stop healing you every time you fuck up."

"Or," Wes added, "you could stop falling on your face."

Eve let out a sharp laugh. "I think we all know neither of those things are about to happen. Falling on my face is as much a part of my class as healing is of yours." She stood, crossing the rented quarters in but a few strides. "The real question is, how many times will I fall on my face before one of you saves *my* ass for a change."

Wes smiled. "Well, I get another chance tomorrow. You aren't the only one who got a new class."

"True enough." Eve smirked as she swung open the door to head down for dinner. "This troll doesn't know what's coming for it."

* * *

The next morning, as with their first job, the four adventurers met up outside the city gates. Just as before, Alex didn't say much of anything before leading the way east. At least this time they weren't hungover.

Eve spent most of the journey at speed, running various tests on **Charge!** for the sake of avoiding another slip up. She found that similar to its predecessor, the skill sent her tumbling if she let it wear off while running too fast or tried to get moving too quickly.

She supposed that's what **Jet** was for, but the massive Stamina cost still put her off testing the ability. The last thing she needed was to enter battle with the troll with her most valuable resource depleted.

The improved traction and stability from **Surefooted** seemed to help, but Eve couldn't pin down exactly how much. She *felt* like she was accelerating, decelerating, and turning faster than before, but she had no way of measuring the difference. Perhaps the passive would scale with Endurance too. She certainly hoped so.

Eve put an end to her running as the party reached the first of the hills, deciding it better they stick together as they approached the troll's den. Wes greeted her on her return.

"Hey, I've been thinking. Stronger bones or whatever your passive gives you, I'm not sure punching things at high speed is a great idea."

"Sure," she replied. "A spear or some daggers would probably fit better with my class, but we don't *have* those, and I definitely can't afford to buy some."

"We might not have the optimal weapons, but we do have *a* weapon." Wes smiled as he withdrew the rusty sword from his belt. He handed it to her.

"You don't mean—"

"You need it more than I do, and now you've got a class that gives Strength you can actually use the damn thing."

She admired the old weapon, its runes still colored green from the grass she'd tried to clean it with. "Now we just need to figure out what its enchantments actually do."

Wes chuckled. "Explode when you break them, most likely. Assuming it *is* enchanted. For all I know those sigils are someone's name."

"Yeah, the guy you stole it from."

"Hey, the guy *Mr. Potts* stole it from."

Eve snorted. "Tell that to the thugs back in Fidswo—"

Alex cut her off with a furiously whispered, "Quiet!"

Eve froze, her grip tightening on the weapon's hilt as she scurried up the hillside to join Alex. The four adventurers stopped just short of the summit, peeking over the hilltop into the valley below.

Eve swallowed down bile. It wasn't the hideous, shaggy-furred brown monster nor the collection of old bones scattered about the space which so churned her stomach, but the blood that stained its misshapen chin and the corpse over which it leaned.

Preston retched.

Wes paled. He whispered, "Is that a…"

Alex answered with steel in her voice, "A human, yes. And it'll be the last one this *thing* ever kills."

Eve clenched her fists. "So what's the play?"

"The play is I'm gonna burn the ever-loving shit out of it."

"Wes, shouldn't we—"

The first **Fire Dart** was already in the air before Eve could finish her warning. Instead, she cursed. "Shit."

The troll cried out as the attack struck it, singeing some fur but failing to set it alight. Its bloody fangs glimmered in the noonday sun as its roar filled the small valley.

Alex charged. Eve followed.

She waited until she crested the hill to activate her skill, allowing the downward slope to aid in her acceleration. Her class-induced velocity pulled her away from the *Soldier* at her side as she neared the nine-foot monster, leaving Eve with a terrible sense of facing the threat alone.

Wes's next spell helped assuage the feeling as it set the thing's hair aflame, forcing the troll to pause as it batted out the flames.

Eve leveled her weapon to skewer the beast.

A guttural bellow assaulted her ears as she drew near.

Her vision narrowed.

The creature raised a meaty arm, ready to swipe at this small but quick attacker.

Eve readied herself to dodge.

It swung.

She stopped short, allowing the thick appendage to pass right in front of her before closing in for the lethal blow.

Or at least that was the plan.

Her foot caught on a stripped bone hidden in the grass, pushing her sure-footedness beyond her skill's ability to help. The femur rolled beneath her boot as she careened forward.

The troll's swing struck true.

Pain exploded in Eve's side as the attack sent her flying. She landed hard on the grassy hillside, luckily avoiding any of the decaying ribs or other pointed bones that may have impaled her. She didn't feel lucky.

Panic rose as she gulped for air but her lungs refused to cooperate. She planted a palm in the dirt to push herself up, but her arm collapsed beneath her. It bloody *hurt*. She gasped once more, the panic subsiding as her aching chest allowed a modicum more oxygen than before.

The troll roared.

The earth beneath her trembled as the creature stomped its way over. Eve watched with wide eyes and a pale face as it came. Once more she tried to stand and once more she failed.

The monster approached.

Alex beat it there. With a cry of "healer!" she stood her ground in front of Eve's prone form, her spear leveled at the encroaching troll.

It swiped. She lunged.

The thing cried out as a red slit appeared on its arm. It recoiled.

Wes launched another **Fire Dart**, and again the beast stopped to extinguish burning fur. Alex lunged again.

Eve lost track of the battle as Preston finally reached her and Ayla's piercing light claimed her full attention. The wounds ran deep, and so too did Her forgiveness. It just wasn't *pleasant*.

By the time the blinding radiance of Her judgment and Her mercy faded from Eve's eyes, another light took its place: the azure glow of a notification.

You have defeated Level 13 Hill Troll: +30 exp!

Such a low level? Shit, Eve swore to herself. *At least the others probably earned a lot.*

The string of curses coming from Preston somewhat confirmed her theory. "Ayla fucking damnit!"

Alex gave him a curious look. "What's going on?"

Wes's mouth hung open in awe. "I'll tell you what's going on: he just got his class upgrade."

"And?"

"Take a look."

Alex froze. "Oh. I'm so sorry."

Unwilling to wait any longer for an explanation, Eve pushed herself up to turn towards the youthful healer. With first a gasp and then a hand clamped over her mouth to keep herself from laughing aloud, she **Appraised** him.

Level 10 Priestess of Ayla
Uncommon Tier 2 Class

Preston met their looks with a beet-red face. "If any of you says a gods-damned word, I swear on Ayla's bloody tits that I will murder you in your sleep."

The valley fell quiet. Three adventurers stared at their healer in perfect stillness, the gentle rustling of the grass in the breeze the only sound to reach their ears. Seconds passed.

Preston was the first to break, the corners of his mouth slowly creeping up until his scowl could hold no longer. Alex followed suit.

For the minutes that followed, were any citizen to peek into that particular valley a few hours east of Lynthia, they would find four guild members standing over the corpse of a hill troll laughing like the lunatics they were. Better yet, said onlooker wouldn't even be surprised at such a scene.

Indeed, for all of history there has never once been an adventuring group worth its salt that didn't have some amount of lunacy to go around, and neither the gods nor the Stones nor the adventurers themselves would have it any other way.

Chapter 14

Practice Makes Perfecter

"And go!"

Eve **Charged!**

Unkempt chestnut strands blew wildly in the wind as she flew across the training yard. She squinted against the assault of the dry summer air, unwilling to falter or slow even as her eyes accumulated a misty sheen. They could water all they wanted; she had a lap to run.

She forced herself to slow as she approached the line in the sand, dropping to only a touch above double her unmodified running speed. She'd done this turn enough in the past two weeks to know **Surefooted**'s limits, and by Ayla, she was going to push them.

The ball of her foot just barely skidded into the lap marker as she reversed her direction, her velocity hitting zero for a fraction of a second before she shot off back the way she'd come. Eve smiled.

It took a few seconds for the air to blow her hair back out of her face, a fact of the maneuver she'd grown all too frustrated with. She'd have to take a page out of Alex's book and tie it back. *That or cut it off*, Eve mused. *I'm not just a village girl any more; I don't need to worry about finding a good husband.* Adventurers wore their hair however they damn well pleased.

The idea left a quiet grin on her face as she burst past the starting line, calling "time!" as she decelerated in the space behind it.

Wes grinned as he rattled off the answer, "Five point three six seconds."

She stared at him. "Honestly, why do you waste time casting spells? Clearly the true purpose of all that Int is so you can be a human sundial."

"Please, I'm way better than a sundial."

Eve rolled her eyes. "Anyway, that's pretty close to a third of my last time."

"Which means **Charge!** also triples the speed from your **Haste** passive."

She beamed at him. "This is going to get pretty insane pretty quickly." Eve attempted a bit of quick math in her head before deciding she didn't need to know the exact ratio. The important discovery was that her **Charge!** didn't just set her running speed to a flat figure but would continue to scale as her Endurance grew.

Wes tilted his head. "Quickly is relative. You won't be getting any faster any time soon unless you actually start leveling up again."

*Or if I start using **Jet**,* Eve thought. She knew from its cost alone the ability must've been powerful, but still she hesitated to actually *test* it. A low max Stamina would only be an excuse for so long.

She shook her head, returning herself to the conversation at hand. "I know, I know. I just need to find another quest milestone and I'll start rocketing up again."

"Or," Wes pushed, "we could start taking harder jobs."

"No way."

"Yes way," he argued. "Eve, these standard jobs are earning enough to pay for rooms and meals and strawberry scones but not much else. The whole point of coming here was to save up to afford tuition at the mage's college."

Eve sighed. "Look, I want more money just as much as you do. For hell's sake, look at me. This blouse used to be white." She picked at the sickly brown-yellow fabric and its mottled stains of dirt, sweat, and blood. "I need clothes, I need armor, I need weapons that aren't a rusty old sword, and I know as well as you do that standard difficulty jobs are never gonna pay for that."

"So you agree? A more dangerous job means more pay, more exp, and a better chance at hitting a milestone."

"It also means more chance one of us dies. We aren't in a hurry, and sure, I'm not getting much exp from our current jobs, but you and Preston *are*. There's nothing wrong with racking up a few more levels before trying the risky shit."

Wes met her stare with a level gaze. "Is this about the troll?"

Eve glared back. "Does it matter? I'm getting as much practice in as I can because I don't want my fuck up to be the reason one of you gets hurt. There's no rush. We can always take a bigger job later."

He nodded. "You're right. There's no rush, but we can't wait forever either. I'm sure I'm not the only one getting a little impatient. Alex has a class promotion coming soon, and I guarantee you she'll want to do something between now and then."

"I know, Wes. I know. It just doesn't have to be *now*. We can wait a few more weeks to make sure we're ready before we go charging into some monster-infested ruin."

Wes shut his eyes as he let out a breath. "Okay."

"Thank you," Eve said, wiping the sweat from her brow. "For waiting and for helping me practice."

He grinned. "You're very welcome. Now come on, let's

get back to the guild hall. Drinks are on you."

* * *

"Ayla's tits, I needed this," Preston said through a deep exhale as he set down his half-empty tankard. He sat with Eve and Wes at their regular corner table in the adventurer's guild common room, enjoying a cold ale at the end of a warm day. Alex, as per usual, was absent.

Eve asked the question on everyone's mind. "Where have you been all this time, anyway? I've seen *Alex* more than you in the last few days."

Preston flung his head back in a somewhat overdramatic show of aggravation. "Ugh, you have no idea. Apparently becoming an ordained *Priestess of Ayla* is an entire bloody job of its own. The ceremonies and the rituals and the gods-damned *praying* just never stops."

Wes gave the man a gentle look. "Are... um... are you sure you're cut out to be a priest? I know you take whatever class the Stones give you, but it sounds like you *really* don't fit in with Ayla's lot."

"Don't even get me started. Yesterday I had to go through a *ritual cleansing*. Imagine me, naked as the day I was born, being washed and anointed by a dozen leering old ladies."

Wes choked on his drink, his face taking on a brilliant shade of cherry red.

Eve laughed. "And here I thought Her *healing* was invasive. They really didn't design their rituals with male acolytes in mind, did they?"

"No." Preston vigorously shook his head as he lifted his flagon again. "No they did not."

"Well, hey," Wes coughed as he changed the subject, "at least you got a milestone for all that, right?"

"A milestone? Why would their pointless rituals be worth a milestone?"

The bulky mage raised an eyebrow. "For getting

ordained? Doesn't your quest have to do with the order? I figured that was a requirement. Why else do you put up with them?"

Preston snorted. "I put up with them because they give me food to eat and a place to stay. The ceremonies are awful, but I can walk into any cathedral in any city and find a hot meal and warm bed without spending a copper. I can survive a few creepy old women if it means I don't have to worry about starving for the rest of my life. If nothing else, I've saved enough silver to afford to drink away the bad memories."

Eve let out a bright guffaw as she raised her glass. "I'll toast to that."

They drank.

Wes shifted in his seat. "So, if your quest isn't about climbing the order's ladder, what is it?"

Preston swallowed. "That's—uh—that's a bit of a personal question, don't you think?"

The man shrugged. "You're the one who just told us to imagine a bunch of old ladies wiping you with oils."

"Fair point."

Wes leaned in, resting his elbows on the wooden tabletop. It bent under his weight. "So what do you say? I'll show you mine if you show me yours."

"Actually"—the healer pulled away, resting his back against the wall—"I think I already know what yours is."

"Really?"

"Yep." Preston smirked. "Because it's the same as every other farm boy with an *Uncommon* tier one that walks in here. Kill some big bad you've never heard of, save the day, and all that."

Wes's face fell. "How in the hells—"

"You see, the thing about the creepy old ladies is that they *talk*. They've all had their own adventures and by Ayla do they have stories to tell about it. Most of them are boring as sin, but a few are actually useful."

"Ooh," Eve laughed. "The *Priestess* knows his shit."

"So I'm right?"

"On all fronts," Wes admitted. "It's an *Epic* quest to slay the 'Blightmaw Dragon.'"

Preston grinned, downing the rest of his ale. "Anyway, you're not the one I'm interested in." He turned to Eve.

"Me?"

"*You* aren't the stereotypical farm boy. I want to know what got a *Courier* to 'whisper defiance at fate itself.'"

Eve raised her eyebrows. "Same deal?"

"Same deal."

"Alright." Eve pulled closer to keep her voice down in the crowded tavern. "My quest is to head to the next town over and pick up a loaf of bread."

"Bullshit," Preston swore. "That's not a life quest; that's barely even an afternoon's work."

Eve turned up her palms.

Preston pushed. "What's your *real* quest?"

"That is my real quest. Remember when you said the Stones had grown a sense of humor? I told you I knew what you meant, and this is why. I've got the most bullshit quest there's ever been."

"So?" the healer asked. "Have you finished it, then?"

"That's the thing. I can't. Every time I try, something goes *just* wrong enough that I can never get my hands on a loaf of bread. Bakeries burn down, bakers take a day off, Wes gets mauled by wolves and we don't make it to town until everything's closed for the night. Turns out *Legendary* quests are pretty hard."

Preston rubbed his chin. "That's an interesting set of coinci—wait. Did you say *Legendary?*"

"I did."

Preston froze. Instead of fawning over her for her greatness or further investigating the enigma that was her life quest, his face grew pale as he muttered to himself. "Ayla's tits. You're *her*."

Eve furrowed her brow. "I'm who?"

The healer leapt to his feet. "I have to go."

Concern flooded Wes's face. "Is everything okay?"

Preston stepped away from the table. "Yeah—I just—I need to think."

Eve called after him as he made his way to the door. "What about our deal?"

Her only answer came in the form of the guild hall door swinging shut as Preston vanished into dark streets beyond. "What's his problem?"

Wes exhaled. "Whatever it is, it's *his*."

Eve stood. "I'm going after him."

The mage grabbed her arm, pulling her back to the table. "No you're not. He said he needed to think, and you're gonna give him time to do that. He's drunk, you're drunk, I'm drunk. Now's not the time for serious conversations. Find him in the morning."

She sat back down, crossing her arms in frustration. "Ugh. He's hiding something. He'd better not go back on his deal."

"You can worry about that if he does."

"Alright. Fine." Eve drained her tankard before slamming the empty iron cup back onto the table. "But you're buying the next round."

"Okay, but if you pass out I'm not carrying you upstairs."

"Oh, come on," Eve laughed. "I've carried *you* enough times, maybe you should return the favor."

Wes shook his head with a quiet chuckle but didn't protest as he pushed to his feet to buy a round of whiskeys. By the time the two companions finished the sharp drinks, they'd forgotten all about Preston and his untold secret.

Eve returned to her room that night in high spirits, both

because there was a smile on her face and because the quantity of spirits in her belly was rather high. She had, if only for now, replaced the chaos and instability of travel with the relative safety of life in the city.

She knew eventually her team would out-level the easy jobs and move on to riskier fare, but that was a problem for another day. Indeed, as she drifted to sleep in her small but cozy room above the guild hall, all of her problems were problems for another day.

* * *

The rising sun had just begun to cast its brilliant rainbows through the glass walls of Lynthia when Eve stepped out into the empty streets. She rubbed the sleep from her eyes as she shut the door behind her. Taking a deep breath of the sharp morning air and the stench of city life that came with it, Eve set off for Ayla's Cathedral.

The *Striker* was loath to wake so early after a late night drinking in the common room, but she had a healer to speak with. She knew Preston slept at the cathedral, but gods knew how she'd find him if he awoke and left before she could get there. So she ran.

Eve made it less than a block before she activated **Charge!** Everything was more fun at high speed, and the early hour left the city absent the normal hustle and bustle that might've prevented such an endeavor. She picked up speed.

Houses and shops and the odd pedestrian flew past as Eve ran, turning down alleys and thoroughfares as she made her way. She may not have ever *seen* Ayla's Cathedral, but that was no deterrence to an adventurer of her caliber. She'd given herself plenty of time to find it.

She entered into a wealthier quarter of the city, where the homes stood three or four stories tall, each surrounded with a lush garden and a high wall for privacy's sake. The avenue was wide and devoid of obstacles, allowing Eve more room to *breathe.* She ran faster.

With every stride she seemed to float in the air for the magical seconds between her back foot leaving the hard stone and her front foot hitting it once more. There was a rhythm to it.

Until, without warning, her foot failed to find the ground.

She stopped short, hanging motionless in the air as her feet dangled beneath her. Eve's eyes shot open. Her heart raced. She fought to swing her head around, desperate to analyze her surroundings, but an invisible chain held it fixed in place. She gulped.

A male voice rang out behind her. "Well, well, well, what do we have here?"

A woman answered. "Another adventurer who thinks they're above the law."

Eve tried to snap back with a witty retort, but her mouth refused to open. All she managed was an angry hum.

The two figures casually strolled down the street and into Eve's field of view, revealing their embroidered tabards. Eve cursed to herself, *Shit.* She recognized the eagle-head crest of Lynthia where she saw it.

The man turned to stare at her, his eyes flashing the familiar blue. His thick handlebar mustache seemed to dance from side to side with every word. "Let's see... Evelia Greene, level twenty-five *Striker.*" He shut the status screen. "Do you know how fast you were going?"

Once again, Eve tried and failed to speak.

The guard smiled. "I thought so."

Behind him, the woman scribbled information down in a large notebook. He gestured to her. "My colleague here is writing you an infraction for breaking the city speed limit. If you want to go above double-speed, you can do it outside of Lynthia."

Eve managed yet more angry hums but little more in the

way of protest.

Rolling his eyes, the guard pressed an enchantment on his vambrace and the restraints around Eve's head went slack.

"I didn't know! I swear I just got here. Nobody said I couldn't run full speed."

The woman snapped, "Ignorance is no excuse. I don't care what your level is or who you work for; the law still applies to you. You're not hot shit, you're not some legendary hero, you're a *Common*-er just like the rest of us, and you'll follow the same rules as the rest of us." She ripped off a sheet of parchment and handed it to her partner.

Eve's hands would've quivered in fear had they been able to move at all. "Wh-what's gonna happen?"

The man rolled his eyes again. "You're not gonna cry your way out of this. You'll pay a fine and if we catch you breaking the law again you'll be exiled."

"How much?"

"A hundred silver."

Eve had to stop herself from cursing aloud. "I don't have that kind of money."

The woman scoffed. "You adventurers are a resourceful bunch. I'm sure you'll figure something out."

"And if I can't?"

"That's not my problem."

Eve's eyes widened. "Excuse me?"

The man glared. "You heard me. You have two weeks. If you don't pay a hundred silver to the office of the magistrate by then, you'll be hearing from us again."

"And you do *not* want that to happen," his partner finished.

"This is bullshit."

The man smiled, his mustache somehow staying perfectly horizontal as the corners of his mouth turned up *above* it.   Eve was too distracted by her situation to contemplate the absurdity of the sight.

"Bullshit or not," he said, "it's happening."

The guard gingerly placed the slip of parchment on the ground in front of her before giving Eve a smile. Together, the pair strode back the way they came, disappearing beyond Eve's ability to crane her head and watch them go. By the time the enchantment wore off and she returned to the support of her own two feet, the guards were long gone.

Heart still pounding as her mind raced through the news, Eve bent down to snatch up the ticket, finding the woman had drawn a crude outline of a middle finger along the back.   Eve wondered if they did that for all their citations or just this one. Either way, she crumpled it in her hand as she turned to storm her way back to the guild and to Wes.

Preston could wait. She knew exactly how she'd earn the silver for this *stupid* fine, even if it was an option she'd been actively avoiding all week. She could avoid it no longer.

It was time to take a *real* job.

Chapter 15

A Real Job

Eve placed a hand on the wooden desk, leaning over as she met the clerk's gaze. "I need a threatening-tier job."

The high-level desk-worker didn't even bat an eye. "Why?"

Eve faltered. "Excuse me?"

"Why?"

She swallowed. "Because I'm level twenty-five and these standard jobs are only dropping crumbs."

The woman rolled her eyes. "Last I remember, your *teammates* aren't level twenty-five, and you're a gods-damned *Common*-er."

"They'll back me on this. Wes needs money, Alex needs to do something impressive before her upcoming promotion, and Preston will take any excuse he can to get away from the cathedral."

The clerk leaned back in her chair. "Are those supposed to be reasons I should give you a riskier job?"

Eve shrugged. "Do you care if we live or die?"

"That's not a reason why I *should*."

"Alright, fine." Eve exhaled. "I know these jobs are in low demand. Everyone willing to risk their life on a guild mission has already out-leveled this kind of shit. I don't need to clear out the dead city of Elchnia, I just need something with a bit more risk to it and the pay to match."

"Okay." The lady leaned in. "You're right. I've got about a dozen high-paying jobs your team technically qualifies for that *nobody* wants. All rated as threatening. All too dangerous for the likes of you."

Gods damnit, Eve cursed to herself. *I'm not a bloody* Common-*er!* She knew she couldn't actually say it. The clerk would only accuse her of lying, and the last thing she needed was to further antagonize the woman. Instead, she dropped any sharpness from her face, softening her gaze to wordlessly communicate her sense of desperation. "Please. I need this."

The clerk sighed, reaching into a drawer to withdraw a sheet of parchment. "The enchanter's guild is offering five hundred silver to anyone who can clear out the Burendian ruins to the northeast. You're welcome to any loot you find —they just want it safe enough they can study the enchantments on the place."

Eve scanned the paperwork, confirming the location and details of the commission. It was perfect. "Why this one?"

"It's the only one you have a chance of actually surviving. The difficulty's based on an estimate instead of an actual **Appraise** of whichever big bad the buyer wants dead."

Eve gulped. "Great." She snatched up the parchment. "I'll take this to my team, thank you."

The clerk called out after her as she began to turn away. "Oh, by the way, I see you have a fine on record. I'll go ahead and redirect a portion of your cut to pay it."

"You can do that?"

The woman laughed. "Of course I can. Did you think you were the first adventurer to get slapped with a speeding ticket? We practically fund the city guards ourselves."

Eve paused. "Wait. If you knew why I needed the silver, why did you keep asking questions?"

A thin smirk stretched across the clerk's face. "Would you have thought I gave you the best job for your team if I didn't make you work for it?"

Eve rolled her eyes. "You're a real pain, you know that, right?"

"Just doing my job."

The *Striker* shook her head, muttering to herself as she walked away. "And being a real pain about it." The parchment felt good in her hand, like a silver-backed bank note just waiting to be exchanged.

She smiled once more as she set off to find Wes. They had a ruin to explore.

* * *

The late-summer sun was already high in the sky by the time the four adventurers met up outside the city gates. Shimmering rainbows danced along the dry grass as sunlight refracted through the magnificent walls of transparent glass. Eve paid them no heed. Her mind was elsewhere.

Preston didn't say a word as the party began their northbound trek. Though Eve took note of the bags under his eyes and the shadows upon them, she also knew that clenched jaw and directed stare for what it was. Determination.

She elected not to inquire after his strange behavior quite yet. He'd tell her about his quest when he was ready, and there would be plenty of time for that to happen. They had a long day's journey ahead of them.

Absent their talkative healer and given Alex's usual disinterest in socialization, Eve and Wes spent the first hours of their trip chatting amongst themselves about this and that before running out of nothing to discuss and falling silent as well. The afternoon dragged on.

It wasn't until the four companions settled in for their first night on the road that Eve dared approach with an attempt at conversation.

"Hey," she hesitantly greeted, plopping down beside the quiet priest. "I bet you're glad to get away from those priestesses."

Preston sat directly on the soft grass, hugging his knees to his chest as he watched Wes set up the campfire. "Yeah. I am."

"Look," Eve cut to the chase. "If you don't want to tell me your quest, that's fine. Wes and I were worried about you when you ran off like that. You don't have to tell me everything, but I need to know if we're okay. If *you're* okay."

He didn't meet her gaze as he quietly nodded. "I'm alright. I just—you're not the only one who got a cryptic quest description, and I think learning about yours may have given me a clue about mine."

"Do you want to talk about it?"

He shook his head. "Not yet. Not until I know for sure."

"As long as your quest isn't to shut down every bakery in Leshk, I think we'll be fine."

Her joke managed to elicit a soft chuckle from the man. "No, it's... not quite *that* strange."

Eve smiled. "Good. Then it doesn't matter what it is, or if you don't want to tell us; we'll help you with it anyway."

Preston raised an eyebrow at her.

"That's what friends do, Preston. I can't speak for Alex because she's... well, Alex, but Wes and I are your friends, and we're here for you."

In the twilight gloom, Eve couldn't see the shift in the healer's expression as he turned back to stare forward, but she took the wistfulness in his voice as a win. "Friends?"

he asked.

"Friends," she answered. Pushing herself to her feet, Eve patted Preston on the shoulder as she moved to approach the campfire. "Now come on, let's eat our share of the dry rations while we can. You'll be wishing for them when we run out in a few days and have to survive Wes's cooking."

"I heard that!" the fire mage called over his shoulder.

"You were meant to!" she answered.

"So you're insulting your scone-dispenser now?"

"So you're insulting your not-dying dispenser now?"

"Hey." Wes pointed. "Technically, you're my tertiary not-dying dispenser. I've got a healer and a warrior now."

"And so far," Preston stepped in, "we've saved Eve more than anyone else."

Eve stamped her foot. "That was once! See if I trip and fall on a random bone again."

"Knowing you," Wes teased, "it'll happen twice more *today*."

"He's right, you know," the healer added. "Falling on your face is a hallmark of yours."

Eve exhaled. "So this is what I get for trying to make peace with you."

"What? Did you think I *wasn't* going to help Wes make fun of you?" Preston smirked as he used her own words against her. "That's what friends do, Eve."

She held up her hands in defeat. "Alright, alright, you win this round. But only because I've run out of *Priestess* jokes."

"Don't worry." Wes clapped her on the back. "You've got a whole fifteen levels to come up with more before he evolves again."

Preston blanched.

"Good," Eve said. "There's no way I let this slip by without at least a few more solid jabs."

"Of course not." Wes laughed before echoing the phrase for himself, "Because that's what friends do."

The three continued their amicable jokes and japes and conversation for some time as the blue twilight faded into the silver starlight of a summer night. They cared little for the darkness of the sky or the ghost of approaching autumn sending its chill along their skin. They had warmth aplenty as they sat around their campfire, told their stories, and ate their meals, once again companions in the truest sense of the word.

* * *

Wes faltered when the tree line first came into view. "You didn't tell me we were going into the northern woods."

Eve looked askance at him. "Where did you think these ruins were? You know there's nothing *truly* dangerous in the plains."

"Right..." Wes breathed. "I just... You've heard the stories about that place."

"The stories I've heard are that only adventurers go there because it's dangerous. We're adventurers, Wes."

"She's right," Alex broke her usual silence to step in.

"I am?"

"Yep. There's hostile monsters in there, but nothing we can't handle. You'd have to get through the forest into the mountains to find the really scary stuff. Besides, according to our info, this ruin isn't even that far north."

Eve grinned. "There you go—we'll be fine."

"Yeah, yeah, I know," Wes said. "It's more... this is it, you know? Until now we've just been running around the plains doing the odd bit of hunting. All the great hero stories start in the woods."

Eve rolled her eyes. "So do all the great lumberjack stories."

"Come on." Alex forged on. "The sooner we find these ruins the sooner we can get started."

Wes and Eve shared a quiet nod before continuing on after the *Soldier*. The forest loomed. Despite her brave words, Eve couldn't help but hold her breath as the sun first disappeared behind a canopy of verdant needles. The air turned cool.

Eve grew more and more vigilant as the pines grew denser around them. She'd never admit it, but she too had heard tales of creatures lurking in the woods, and she wasn't about to be caught off guard. With every shift in the wind, shadows danced in her periphery. No matter how she told herself there was no beast waiting to pounce, her heart rate refused to calm.

The sense of silent unease remained firmly in place as the minutes dragged on. Eve hoped they'd find the entrance to the ruins soon. She wouldn't get a wink of sleep if they had to camp beneath the oppressive gloom of the canopy, even if their destination would prove far more dangerous than a simple forest. At least ruins had walls.

Alex was the first to enter the clearing.

There wasn't a plentitude of open space, but the ten-foot diameter ring of empty air was as welcome a sight as Eve had ever seen. Mostly she was glad to see the sun again, delivering its afternoon warmth just as it banished the shifting shadows. The others, however, were less interested in the clearing itself than in what it contained.

"Is this it?" Preston asked.

Wes stared at the hillside opposite them, and the mossy stone arch which held open the way into it. "It certainly looks like it."

"It is," Alex said. "Look." She unceremoniously pointed to a simple wooden signpost beside the ruin entrance. Its message was simple.

Claimed by the Enchanter's Guild—Lynthia Branch

Eve smiled. "Welp, that's as much confirmation as we could've asked for. Shall we?" She stepped forward.

Alex held out a halting hand. "You know the drill." She drew her spear. "Me first. Wes? Can we get some light?"

The mage nodded, holding up his own hand as it burst into flame.

"Alright," the *Soldier* said, taking the first careful step through the crumbling archway. "Let's go."

Eve grit her teeth as she took her place at the back of the formation. She only made it half a stride into the dark entrance before a notification pulled at her attention. She opened it.

You have entered the dungeon: Burendian Outpost! Fight well.

Chapter 16

Dungeon 101

The party forcibly halted as their vanguard froze in her tracks. "We need to leave. Right now."

"Alex?" Eve asked, trying to look around the massive fire mage that stood between them. "What's wrong?"

The *Soldier* cursed to herself. "Those bastards didn't tell us this place had naturalized into a dungeon." She backpedaled, colliding into Wes before turning to face the others.

He kept his **Burning Hand** held high to keep from singeing her. "What difference does it make? Now we get a bonus for clearing the—"

She cut him off. "No, you don't understand." Her voice quaked as did her hands, matching the frantic look in her fire-lit eyes. "It was a dungeon that k—" She stopped herself. "We need to go."

Eve pressed against the side wall to slip past the slim healer. Standing on her toes, she could just peek over Wes's shoulder to look Alex in the eye. In as gentle a voice as she could manage, she asked, "It was a dungeon that *what*?"

The warrior swallowed, clutching her spear in a white-knuckle grip. "If those assholes at the enchanter's guild didn't tell us this place had naturalized, what *else* did they leave out? Dungeons are dangerous."

"Alex." Eve kept her voice even as she attempted to calm the woman down, "we knew this was going to be dangerous going in. We're practiced, we're prepared, and we're high level enough for a challenge like this. Tell me this isn't the perfect opportunity for you to get a *Rare* tier three."

Slowly, the tall *Soldier* bobbed her head up and down in a hesitant nod.

"Good." Eve gave her a confident smile. "Now let's show this dungeon what we're made of."

Gritting her teeth, Alex turned forward, leveling her spear as she continued down the dark corridor. The others followed.

"I don't like this," Preston whispered to the *Striker* behind him as they walked. "Miss Professional is the last person who should be getting rattled like that."

"Wes is right," Eve replied. "All this means is we get an extra reward at the end. Alex *is* a pro, and I'm sure whatever's bothering her won't get in the way of her fighting just as hard."

The healer nodded. "Alright, you're the boss."

Eve's eyebrows shot up. "I am?"

"I mean… um…" Preston backpedaled. "We should be focusing. This place *is* dangerous."

She gave him an incredulous "…right," before shutting her mouth and returning her attention to their surroundings. There wasn't much to see.

Mossy stone lined the walls, the individual blocks of carved limestone bound together by no mortar Eve could determine. The tunnel floor was pieced together with the most even cobblestone she'd ever seen. Had she not looked, Eve might've thought she walked on a single flat slate.

The orange glow of Wes's fire flickered across the tight space. Eve whispered silent thanks that his skill released no smoke, or else she'd fear for the quality of their limited air. At least the downward slope of the corridor would've sent any fumes rising back the way they'd come.

They made it fifteen minutes into their descent before Alex called a halt. "There's a room up ahead. Too dark to see inside."

Raising his other hand, Wes lobbed a **Flame Dart** over the warrior's shoulder. Eve watched it fly. The burning projectile arced through the air, bathing the chamber in a flash of light.

For an underground outpost, the chamber was massive. Easily eighty feet wide and fifty across, the space elicited a quiet sigh of relief from the *Striker*. *Finally*, she thought, *I've had enough of these cramped tunnels.* Her class didn't do well in tight spaces.

Opposite them, the cavern housed what could only be described as an oversized door. It towered over the adventurers, as imposing as it appeared impregnable. The structure itself appeared to be two massive, homogeneous pieces of stone split directly down the middle. A seal sat upon its center, carved to appear as a sunburst with a spiderweb of twisting lines emanating from it across the entire door.

And then the **Flame Dart** collided with the opposite wall, and the intricate structure vanished as the cavern returned to darkness.

Alex stepped forward, leveling her spear. "Eve, to the front. Nothing's coming up behind us, and I don't want you stuck in that tunnel."

Preston and Wes stepped aside as Eve made her way up. "What's going on?" she whispered.

"While you were gawking at the architecture, I was

doing my job. There's a nest of something in the left corner."

Eve gulped. "Right. Hold on." She reached back to withdraw the rusty sword from Wes's side. "When we get back to Lynthia, remind me to buy a belt."

Alex ignored her comment. "I'm going to hold the tunnel entrance. Wes, your primary job is to make sure we can see. Pick off any enemies if you get a chance. Don't hit Eve." She pointed with her spear. "When you're ready, I want you to throw a dart in that corner."

"Got it." Wes prepared the spell.

Eve held her breath. This was just another fight. She'd survived all sorts of encounters before; whatever forest creature had made its home in the dungeon entrance would be no different. If the door was any judge, they weren't even *inside* the ruins proper yet. She gripped her sword.

Wes threw the dart.

This time she kept her eyes fixed on the room's left corner, ready to **Appraise** whatever appeared before Wes's flames ran out. Her mind almost blanked when she saw them.

A half-dozen furry brown creatures huddled together. Eve estimated each to be roughly waist-high, with floppy ears pointing up another foot or two. *Bunnies? Our first encounter in the dangerous ruin is a nest of* bunnies? *They'll probably even leave us alone. They're so fluff—*

Level 28 Managorged Hare

"What the shit?"

The dart landed directly on the hares' nest, setting the pile of twigs and fur aflame.

Six angry growls filled the chamber.

Eve stepped onto the balls of her feet, ready to run.

"Well at least we have another light source."

Preston hesitated. "Are you sure we want to..."

"That's not just twigs in that nest," Alex said. "Look."

Eve squinted, the growing blaze blinding to look directly at in the dark cavern. She cursed when she saw them. Along with the wood and leaves and tufts of loose fur, alabaster bones littered the den. These hares had killed before, and Wes had just destroyed their home.

The oversized lagomorphs charged.

Eve **Charged!**

She darted out to the side to begin, unwilling to race directly into the mass of fluff and teeth. She kept her eyes fixed on the approaching hares, counting the seconds as they disappeared into the chasm of darkness between Wes's light and the burning nest.

Another **Flame Dart** launched across the room, casting its dim illumination on the creatures. Eve picked her target.

One hare, slightly larger than the rest, lagged behind the drove. Eve shot after it.

She angled her blade to meet directly with the creature's neck without the need for a swing, with her arm lined up behind it to reinforce its position. Just like she'd practiced. The last thing she needed was to get her weapon stuck in a heavy corpse.

Her heart raced. Her feet slammed into the smooth stone. She activated **Fate-al Blow**.

Shock ran up her arm as the sword connected. She held fast. The force of the strike twisted her upper body back as her momentum carried her onward, but she kept to her feet. Two weeks spent at the training grounds proved their worth.

The blade passed clean through.

Eve dashed on, rebuilding her distance from the rest of the drove as her target's head fell to the cavern floor. *One down, five to go.*

Wes's barrage managed to down a second beast as its fur caught alight, filling the cavern with hideous squeals and the stench of burning hare. Eve cringed before forcing herself to refocus.

She watched just out of reach as the four remaining bunnies made it to Alex's position. The *Soldier* kept her spear back, waving it slowly to ward off the creatures.

One pounced.

The warrior swung at it, but the thing was too fast. The spear's edge missed as the beast instead collided with the shaft. The blow knocked it off course, but it landed unbleeding on its feet.

Another leapt at the spearwoman, taking advantage of the opening left by its companion. Alex threw up an elbow to protect her face, unable to bring her weapon to bear in time. Unnatural, inch-long claws scored her vambrace. Blood dripped to the cavern floor.

Wes swiped his **Burning Hand** at the creature, forcing it to jump away.

Ayla's golden light joined the mage's orange as Preston healed the surface wound.

The remaining duration of Eve's **Charge!** ticked away. If she wanted to do something before the ability went on cooldown, she'd have to do it now. Raising her sword once more, she dashed in.

Another fiery projectile forced the rearmost hare to reel back, distancing itself just enough from its drove-mates for Eve to single it out. She took aim, activating **Adrenaline Rush** to put an extra burst of Strength behind the attack.

Just as she neared the four-foot bloodthirsty hare, it jerked forward to rejoin its peers.

The rusty sword struck. Again Eve's upper body twisted as she continued on, but no rabbit head fell to the stone floor absent its body. Instead, her blade dug deep into the creature's center. It cried out in agony as it collapsed, the sword still embedded in its ribcage. As its final act, the managorged hare robbed Eve of her only weapon.

She spent the final seconds of her **Charge!** distancing herself from the three remaining monsters. She turned back around just in time to watch Wes set another aflame. She tuned out its cries.

The final two creatures leapt at once, overwhelming Alex's defense as they came from several directions. She stopped one. The thing impaled itself on the warrior's spear thrashing around for an agonizing second before falling limp. Its companion caught the woman on the shoulder.

The force of the collision sent Alex tumbling. She landed hard on the cold stone, the beast atop her.

Wes was ready.

He swung his **Burning Hand**, still alight for its purpose of illumination. The hare shrieked. It clawed at the downed *Soldier* as the flames caught hold and began their spread. Alex echoed its cries. "Get it off me!"

"I don't want to burn you!"

Eve called out from her vantage across the cavern. "Then bloody kick it!"

Wes's eyes widened as he remembered magic wasn't his only tool. Stepping back, he wound up for the same maneuver Eve had used to get the wolf off his leg on their very first day together.

He kicked it in the ribs.

The hare rolled off its victim, landing gently atop the corpse of its companion. It cried out a final time as the flames continued to spread, their eternal hunger inexorable as they claimed the last of the den.

By the time the blaze reached the last of its fuel and itself died out, Preston had already patched up the worst of

Alex's wounds.

"Everyone alright?" he asked as he helped the *Soldier* return to her feet.

The chorus of yeses was all Eve needed to turn her attention to the flashing notifications in her peripheral vision.

You have defeated Level 28 Managorged Hare: +93 exp!
You have defeated Level 26 Managorged Hare: +81 exp!
You have defeated Level 26 Managorged Hare: +81 exp!
You have defeated Level 25 Managorged Hare: +75 exp!
You have defeated Level 25 Managorged Hare: +75 exp!
You have defeated Level 25 Managorged Hare: +75 exp!
Level Up!

Ability Upgraded!
Fate-al Blow cost reduced!

Eve dismissed the notifications, somewhat disappointed her ability upgrade had only been a thirty Stamina drop in the cost of her least favorite skill. She supposed the first *interesting* ability change would come at level thirty, but that deduction was pure guesswork. Still, she grinned. A level was a level, and watching her stats tick up would never fail to satisfy.

"Anyone get anything good?"

Wes smirked as he boasted, "Level fourteen and a new active ability. Lets me make nearby fires burn hotter for a time."

"Thirteen for me," Preston piped in. "As well as a lower cooldown on my **Healing Touch**."

"I got nothing," Alex said as she planted her foot on one of the corpses to withdraw her spear from it. "But I'm just on the verge of twenty-four."

"Good." Eve grinned at her. "More time to fulfill

evolution requirements. We've got a lot of dungeon ahead of us."

Wes snorted. "Assuming we can even get the door open."

"Before we do that," Preston interrupted, "shouldn't we talk about these hares? I don't know about you, but I'm pretty sure they aren't supposed to get this big. Or this high level."

Nodding along, Eve approached the beast she'd killed to reclaim her stolen sword, copying Alex's planted-foot technique to yank it out. "I'm not sure what 'managorged' means, but I imagine it has something to do with living in a dungeon."

"No." Alex shook her head. "Dungeons won't do this." She pointed at the bloody tip of her spear. "Or that."

Eve squinted across the dark room before realizing she had a bloodstained weapon of her own. She inspected the blade.

Sure enough, ethereal wisps of undiluted white drifted off the viscous liquid. All over the weapon, the translucent strands wafted into the air like tiny lines of wafting smoke. It was captivating. Eve stared as she swung the weapon to and fro, watching the pretty tendrils trail behind it. "Is that... Mana?"

"It looks nothing like mine," Wes said, "but mine isn't pure. It's fire Mana."

"So this is what, raw Mana?"

He shrugged. "It would make sense, but I really can't say. The hares were labeled as 'managorged' so I guess their blood is full of raw Mana?"

Preston stepped in, "the body isn't meant to hold Mana. The soul is. Whatever these hares came into contact with, or whatever they ate, put that magic in a place it shouldn't have been."

"So what now?"

The healer turned up his palms. Alex answered instead. "Now we know we're in for enemies that use unaligned Mana, which I guess we should've known already. The enchanter's guild wouldn't have been interested in a place without enchantments."

Shaking her head to refocus away from the pretty lights, Eve stooped over to wipe her blood on the fur of a dead hare. "Speaking of enchantments," she said as she returned the blade to Wes, "how are we gonna open that door?"

The fire mage scratched his head. "Now *that* is a very good question."

Chapter 17

Enchantments Are Fun

Eve stared up at the massive double door, its inscriptions only lit by Wes's flickering flames. "It's an enchantment, right?"

"That would make sense," Alex replied. "We are here for the enchanter's guild."

"So how are we supposed to get past?"

Wes shrugged, stepping up to the entryway. "Maybe we should just..." He raised his hand in a closed fist before knocking three times against the carved slab. Nothing happened. "Okay, first, *ow.*" He cradled his knuckles against his chest. "And second, I'm an idiot. Who knocks on a stone door?"

Eve held her head in her hands. "A hundred Int and he still pulls shit like this."

"You've got a better idea?"

"I'd start with not hurting myself. Look, it's clearly enchanted, but it's probably been centuries since anyone's maintained the thing. What if it's out of Mana?"

Preston raised an eyebrow. "How can a door run out of Mana?"

Eve turned up her palms. "You're the caster, you tell

me."

"I'm not an enchanter, though. My Mana comes from my connection to Ayla, and operating oversized doors isn't exactly a part of Her domain."

All eyes turned to the party's other spell-caster.

"Don't look at me," Wes protested. "I can make it hotter if you want, but that's about the extent of my abilities. Fire Mana and all that. And before you ask, no, I'm not strong enough to melt stone. Not yet, anyway."

The group fell silent for a moment as its members thought through the problem separately.

Eve was the first to speak. "Wait. If you can't recharge the door because you have specialized magic, don't we just need a source of raw Mana?"

"And where are we going to... oh."

She continued, "These hares grew giant *somehow*. Maybe all that Mana in their blood came from the door."

Preston jumped up. "Eve, you're a genius!"

"I know." She smirked. "Now let's see about putting the Mana back where it came from."

"And how are we supposed to do that?"

"Hells if I know," Eve said, already making her way back to the nearest dead hare—one of Wes's. "But Mana's literally *spilling* out of these things. I vote we just put some hare's blood on the enchantment and see what happens."

"Is that a good idea?" Alex asked. "For all we know the enchantment is for repelling intruders."

Eve answered over her shoulder as she dragged the furry creature towards the others. "It didn't repel the hares. Seems more likely it's for opening the damn thing." She stopped at the door's base. "Can I borrow a knife?"

Wes offered his.

In a rough, jagged motion, Eve sliced open the burnt corpse, allowing its blood to spill directly onto the inscribed stone. The adventurers held their breath.

As they watched in silent trepidation, a dim alabaster glow began to creep up the web of jagged lines that coated the door. It didn't hum, it didn't pulse, it simply *spread*.

Seconds passed as the ethereal light made its way to the round seal at the slab's center, setting the engraved sunburst aglow. It didn't appear as a sun to Eve's curious gaze; more a moon given the softness of the illumination and the silver of its hue.

Up and up the Mana stretched itself, falling ever dimmer the higher it climbed. It never reached the top. The pearly glimmer flickered twice before it began to fade.

Eve's heart sank as the Mana disappeared, returning the room to the same fire-lit gloom in which it had begun. Nothing had changed.

"It wasn't enough."

Wes shrugged. "We've got five more hares, let's use them."

"Not quite," Alex said. "The ones Eve killed will have bled out too much already. Unless you have a way to get a pool of blood off the floor, we're down to just two."

"If one wasn't enough, will two be?" Preston asked. "It looks like the Mana we put in just leaked right back out."

Eve quietly stared at the Manaless enchantment, her mind elsewhere.

Wes turned back to the remaining hares. "No reason we can't try. Eve's already made a mess of my knife; may as well get even more blood on it."

"Alright," Preston agreed, gesturing down to the hare Eve had cut open. "Let's get this drained one out of the way first."

It wasn't until Wes had cleared away the singed critter that Eve finally spoke her thoughts. "Maybe that's not a good idea."

Wes looked up at her. "What are you talking about?"

Instead of answering him, Eve turned to Alex. "Earlier

you said the enchantment could be for repelling intruders. It could be, but not in the way you meant. What if it isn't for opening the door, but for keeping it shut?"

"So a giant magical lock?"

"Exactly. And if it's out of Mana, maybe it's unlocked."

Wes leveled with her. "So what, we just push it open?"

Eve's reply came in the form of a quiet smile and a confident step up to the structure. Bracing herself against the stone, she leaned in and *pushed*. It didn't budge. Her arms strained against the weight of the thing. Her feet held firm thanks in part to the extra traction from **Surefooted**. With a breath, she heaved.

The door shifted. It moved no more than half an inch before halting again, but that tiny motion was all she needed.

Wes joined in, adding his not insignificant weight to the attempt. Alex followed. Even Preston with his slight form and unenhanced Strength applied what little force he could. Eve activated her **Adrenaline Rush**, heaping yet more power behind the group effort.

All at once the stone barrier overcame whatever years of decay had held it fast, swinging wide in a single motion. Eve stumbled forward, barely managing to keep her feet as the door opened.

Wes fell on his face.

"Ayla's tits," Preston swore. "You'd think opening a centuries-old ruin swimming in enchantment would be a bit more complicated than just bloody *pushing*."

Eve chuckled. "That's why I'm the boss. Always try the simple way first."

"The hare's blood was your idea."

"Alright, fine," Eve admitted. "Always try the simple way eventually."

"That's more like it," Wes laughed.

Alex snapped, "Focus up. We're still in a dungeon.

Back in formation. Eve, stay near the front."

The three quietly nodded as they obeyed, accepting the truth in Alex's words. Together, they stepped through the newly-opened door into the room beyond.

The immediate thing Eve noticed was the floor. It was made of the same unnaturally smooth cobble as the chamber outside, but white light emanated from the gaps between. The glow *pulsed* every few seconds, bright spots racing along the grid-like cracks as if they had someplace to be. Perhaps they did.

The space itself was long and narrow—some sort of entry hall by Eve's estimation. Its twenty-foot width would give her plenty of space to run should she need it, even if she hoped she wouldn't. Something told her such hopes were futile.

Opposite them, the cavern branched in two directions, each only lit by the dim fluorescent glow from the enchanted floor. Before she could even begin to wonder which path was the correct one, Eve's attention turned to the construct that sat between them.

"If that's not a guard, I don't know what is."

Ten individual marble slabs rested against the wall betwixt the two exits, arranged in such a way to match the general shape of a man. Or a Burendian, assuming the long dead species looked remotely similar. It didn't move as the party approached.

As they walked, Wes extinguished his **Burning Hand** to conserve Mana, leaving the group illuminated only by the ghostly glow from beneath.

The strange angle cast unnatural shadows across the adventurers' faces, granting Eve the eerie impression that she traveled amongst a group of revenants long due their inevitable grave. She shook the thought from her head. No doubt she appeared the same.

They made it more than half way through the spacious

entry hall before the golem came alive.

White light coursed over the marble blocks like so many jagged bolts of lightning as first the head, then the arms, then the torso began to levitate. The flows of Mana met in the space between the slabs, coming together in bright nodes as if taking the place of a normal joint. They formed the knees, the hips, the shoulders, and elbows of the thing as it pushed itself away from the back wall to take its first step.

The room quaked.

Dust rained down from the ancient ceiling, planting another concern in the back of Eve's mind. She didn't have time for that now. She gripped her sword.

The golem leapt.

Alex shouted, "Run!"

The party charged forward as the construct flew overhead, landing hard on the ground behind them. The chamber shook once more as loose pebbles fell from the stone above.

Alex pointed at the branching paths ahead of them. "Get to the tunnels! Preston, Wes, I want you behind me!"

Cut off by the marble golem by the way they'd come, the casters dashed down the leftward path to take shelter. Alex and Eve pivoted to face the thing.

Eve muttered, "If I weren't terrified, I'd say that thing looks ridiculous." In a way it did. The crisp corners and faces to its smooth rectangular torso and limbs made the golem's blocky appearance feel somewhat clumsy. Its movements were anything but.

Gracefully rising from its kneeling landing, the thing turned to them. It approached.

As per usual, Wes landed the first blow. Dart after dart struck the twelve-foot construct, leaving black singe marks on its pristine marble but otherwise accomplishing nothing. His flames washed harmlessly against the enchanted stone, unable to melt or burn the sturdy material. Still the golem came.

Eve **Charged**, leaving her sword to strike at one of the glimmering joints. The construct swung first.

She dashed to the side, her feet sticking fast to the smooth stone as she turned on a razor's edge to dodge the blow. Her momentum lost, Eve backed away to prepare for another run.

The enchanted sentry made it to the tunnel's mouth before she could.

Alex didn't even try to strike at the thing. It swung a thick arm overhand at the leather-clad warrior, forcing her to leap to the side. No spear could block such a swing.

Their vanguard separated from them, Preston and Wes sprinted farther down the left hand path to distance themselves from the goliath.

The golem's head twisted, turning as if to gaze with an eyeless face at Eve and Alex off to its right. A second passed. Eve's breath quickened. *If that thing goes after the boys, they'll be dead in a heartbeat.*

She gripped the hilt of her sword, grit her teeth, activated her **Adrenaline Rush,** and ran in.

Eve was ready for the swipe when it came. Unwilling to compromise her momentum, she poured every ounce of Strength into a mighty leap. The marble slab passed harmlessly beneath her.

Inertia carried her forward.

As she flew, Eve grasped her weapon with both hands, dumping the last of her dwindling Stamina into **Fate-al Blow**. She'd only get one shot.

A hideous crack rang through the cavern as the rusty blade collided with the construct's marble head.

The stone won.

Pain shot up Eve's arms as her sword snapped. Panic entwined with despair flowed through her for that fraction of a second as she still hung in the air with a broken blade in her grasp. They'd never get a chance to see her fall.

This was no ordinary sword.

In a single moment, whatever untold ancient enchantments that had lain dormant on the old weapon broke open. No longer bound by its decaying runes, the blade's Mana burst free in a brilliant explosion of pure white.

The force of the blast threw Eve back. Once more she flew through the air, this time landing hard against the cavern wall. Skin tore and bones cracked as she rolled down the chamber's side, hitting the floor just outside the rightmost pathway. Alex raced to her side.

Eve's heart raced as her health reached the single digits.

A horrific rumbling shook the ground beneath her as the explosion rocked the ruin's very foundations. This time it wasn't only dust which fell.

Alex wrapped two desperate hands around Eve's ankles, dragging the wounded *Striker* into the mouth of the nearest exit with as much haste as she could muster.

The last thing Eve saw was a cascade of falling rock and a little blue light indicating there were messages to be read.

And the world went black.

Chapter 18

Revelations in the Ruined Ruins

Wes staggered to a halt as a terrible crash rang out behind him. He turned around just in time to watch the tunnel entrance disappear in a cloud of dust and falling rock. His stomach dropped.

"Ayla's tits," Preston swore. "They did it."

"Did it? They collapsed the bloody cavern!"

"Check your notifications."

Wes obeyed.

You have defeated Level 35 Burendian Sentry Golem: +840 exp!
Level Up!

The news did little for his sinking mood. "Shit." He took off back the way he'd come, charging towards the entry hall they'd so narrowly escaped. A wall of rubble blocked his way. "Gods-damnit, Eve."

Preston caught up to him, placing a gentle hand on his arm. "What is it?"

"If that cave-in was enough to kill the golem..."

Preston finished the thought, "Then it was enough to kill

the others."

Wes nodded.

The *Priestess* stepped forward. "You don't know that. They could've escaped down the other tunnel or back out towards the entrance. Hells, they're probably going back to find help as we speak."

Wes pulled away from the man's comforting touch. "Or they're buried in that rubble and we're going to die in here."

Preston paused, his eyes flashing blue for a moment before he opened his mouth to reply. "It's okay, Wes. Eve is alright."

Wes echoed the healer's words back at him. "You don't know that."

"She's okay."

"How can you say that?"

Preston insisted, "Because I know!"

"Don't give me any of that 'have faith' crap. You know the gods don't work like that."

"It isn't crap."

Wes tensed. "Then what is it?"

"Look, I can't speak for Alex, but Eve is alive. I know it."

The mage didn't remove his gaze from the fallen rock. His brow lowered into a scowl. "Don't bullshit me, Preston."

Preston grew louder. "It's not bullshit!"

"Then how do you know?!"

"Because I haven't failed my quest!" Preston slapped a hand over his mouth as if to recapture the escaped words, but it was too late. His shout echoed down the empty hallway as if to taunt him for his loose tongue.

Wes waited until the last of the reverberations faded before turning to look him in the eye. "What are you talking about?"

Preston replied through the hand atop his mouth. "I shouldn't have said that."

"Does this have to do with why you ran off the other night?"

"I don't even know if she's the one it's talking about. It's just… she showed up out of nowhere with a *Legendary* quest and it just made so much sense."

"Preston, what in hells are you talking about?"

He finally lowered his hand as the words spilled out. "Eve isn't the only one who got a super vague and confusing quest."

"What?"

Preston sighed. "I was fifteen when I got my turn with the Questing Stones. My class isn't the only joke they played on me. It's an *Epic* quest, and it's got three hells of a failure condition."

Wes raised an eyebrow. "And that would be…?"

The healer sighed, his eyes glowing blue as he stepped in close to the towering fire mage. "See for yourself."

Wes nodded as he stared down into the shorter man's eyes to read the text reflected therein.

Quest: Don't Let Her Die.
Description: Don't let her die.
Difficulty: Epic

"Gods below."

Preston blinked away the screen and stepped back. "That's what I said."

"And you think Eve is 'her'?"

"I don't know, Wes." Preston shook his head. "I don't know. She's the most likely of everyone I've met so far."

"And if you haven't failed your quest, that means she's still alive."

"Exactly."

"Then what are we waiting for?" Wes turned away from the wall of rubble to start down the unexplored path. "If they're stuck too, we need to find a way out."

Preston scurried to catch up to him. "Is that a good idea? I can't deal damage, and the last monster we fought wasn't exactly flammable."

"Don't care." Wes kept walking. "Even if I don't have a quest for it, there's no way in hells I'm letting her die."

* * *

Eve awoke to an aching everything and an obnoxious azure light filling her vision.

You have defeated Level 35 Burendian Sentry Golem: +660 exp!

Seriously? I didn't even get a level from that? That thing was insane! Eve grumbled internally as another message popped up.

You have survived extreme damage against all odds: +1 Constitution!

Now it's just taunting me, she mused. Eve couldn't say what exactly 'it' was, but hells was she annoyed with it. *One measly Constitution for that?* Her groan came out audibly this time.

"Eve!" Alex materialized by her side. "Are you alright?"

"Good question," she managed, pushing herself to sit against the tunnel wall. An Eve-shaped imprint remained on the floor in the dust and pebbles that had fallen over her while she'd slept. She winced. "I've got... twenty-nine health."

"Excellent. It's working."

Eve raised one eyebrow. "What's working?"

Alex reached behind her to pick a glass vial off the enchanted floor. It was empty. "The health tincture. It's slow and shitty but you should be on your feet in an hour or so."

"You gave me a—" Eve stopped herself before bringing up how expensive such a cure could be. Alex already knew that. Instead, she asked a different question. "I used to be worse, didn't I?"

The *Soldier* nodded. "And you weren't getting any better."

Eve gulped. "Thanks." She flexed her left hand, glad at least one of them still worked. Hopefully Alex's tincture would repair the havoc the explosion had wreaked on her right. "How long was I out?"

"Twenty minutes? Can't really tell down here."

"And the others?"

Alex shook her head. "I don't know." She gestured at the heap of fallen earth and marble that walled off the way they'd come. "Can only pray they aren't trapped too."

Eve swore. "What if they are?"

"Then once you're recovered, we hope these tunnels meet up again farther in. Or that at least one of them leads to another way out."

"Shit."

"Shit is right," Alex snapped. "I *told* you dungeons are dangerous."

"How was I supposed to know—"

Alex cut her off. "That hitting a block of marble with a rusty sword wasn't going to go like you planned? Some gods-damned forethought."

Eve glared. "Last I checked, we're only alive *because* I broke that sword."

"We're only here because *you* couldn't afford your speeding ticket."

"And everyone signed off!" Eve's voice echoed across

the barren hall. "Wes and Preston both needed the exp, and last I checked you were desperate to unlock a *Rare* class."

"Well I fucking didn't."

Eve froze. The tunnel fell silent as the words sank in. "Alex, I'm so sorry. Did you get an *Uncommon*, at least?"

"Two of 'em. I can be a *Defender* or a bloody *Spear Maiden*."

"Those—um—those sound useful." Eve knew the words rang hollow the moment she said them, but she had to say *something*. "Have you picked which, yet?"

"I haven't. And truth be told I don't want to. They're the same gods-damned thing." Alex sighed. "I just—I figured after everything that's happened, I deserved to be more than a generic 'woman with a spear.'"

"Of course you do," Eve continued her attempts at comfort. "And there's always another promotion. I know level fifty is a while away, but..." She paused as the thought struck her. "Wait. What 'everything' *has* happened? When we first stepped foot in this place you freaked out for a minute."

Alex neither replied nor met Eve's gaze.

The *Striker* pressed. "You've been in a dungeon before, haven't you?"

The warrior kept silent, her eyes glued to the floor before her.

Eve forced her voice to soften. "You might as well tell me. You've saved my life twice now. It's not like I'm gonna go share your secrets with people." She exhaled. "I'm only up to thirty-five health; we're going to be here for a while. You don't have to talk if you're not comfortable, but we still have half a dungeon to clear, and I don't want whatever happened to you to get in the way of that."

Eve tried to run a hand through her hair, but the

chestnut strands were so tangled she barely made it past her ear. "I don't need your life story, but I do need you to trust me."

Silent seconds passed between the two adventurers as Alex stared through the stone beneath them. The ghostly pulses of white light lit up her face from below, granting the woman an air of quiet melancholy. Or perhaps that was just her expression. Either way, her gaze stayed empty as she whispered her reply. "They died."

Eve swallowed as she gave a gentle nod. "Who were they?"

"Jason and Priya and Liam. My old team."

"You didn't get to level eighteen on your own, then."

"Nobody does." Alex kept her voice low, barely muttering the words loud enough to reach Eve's ears. Reach they did. "They were all just like Wes. Born into starting at *Uncommon* like they were slated for great things from day one. Took them a while to get used to working with a *Common*-er like me, but by the time we all hit the second tier we were close as could be."

The *Soldier* sat petrified, her only motion that of her lips as she told her tale. "The dungeon was my idea. I wanted to prove myself. It wasn't hard to get them onboard—they wanted me to succeed just as much as they did. That's just the kind of people they were." She paused.

Eve kept her own mouth shut, allowing Alex whatever time she needed to gather herself.

She continued, "We took the job for three hundred silver. For three hundred gods-damned silver. The cheap bastards wouldn't even pay up when I was the only one who made it back. 'We didn't pay you to fail,' they said, as if it wasn't their own bloody fault for rating the job so low." Alex shook, her hands clenched in quaking fists. "I made it three weeks before I ran out of money."

"So you joined us."

Alex nodded. "So I joined you."

"Ayla's tits, Alex. That's terrible. And now I've dragged you into the same situation all over again. I'm so sorry."

"Like you said, I signed up for this."

Eve let out a breath. "Is this why you refuse to spend time with us?"

She didn't reply.

"Alex?"

The teardrop glimmered in the ethereal lighting as it struck the floor. "I can't go through that again."

"Alex, I... I can't begin to imagine what you're feeling right now, but you can't just shut us out. We're a team."

"Going out drinking together isn't a guild requirement."

"It isn't," the *Striker* said. "But not behaving like you expect us to die at any minute is an Eve requirement. We aren't your old team. Alex, I won't pretend we're all expert adventurers, but we're not clueless either. I need you to have faith in us."

Alex sniffled. "I thought faith was supposed to be Preston's thing."

"No, Preston's thing is disdain for his patron goddess."

The *Soldier* let out a half-hearted laugh as a smile peeked through her teary face. "If we get out of this, I'll buy the drinks myself."

Eve gave a gentle grin. "That's all I can ask."

"Can—uh—can you do me the favor of not sharing this with the others? I don't want—"

"Of course not. You trusted me with your story—I'd never break that trust."

For the first time, Alex looked up to meet Eve's gaze. "Thanks, Eve. I—um—I'm glad we talked."

"Me too. That's what teammates are fo—"

"Holy shit." Alex cut her off with the uttered expletive. The woman's eyes flashed blue before Eve could even ask what was wrong. "I unlocked a new class."

"Now?"

"I just got the notification. Ayla's tits, it's a *Rare*."

"Alex, that's fantastic! What is it?"

"*Unbowed Survivor*. The—um—the requirements list is a bit strange."

"Can I see?"

A moment passed before the woman silently nodded. Pushing herself to her feet, Alex crossed the narrow tunnel to allow the *Striker* a good look at the reflection in her wet eyes.

The description was long. Eve mentally flicked through prerequisite after prerequisite, ignoring all sorts of bits about facing certain death or overcoming high-level foes. They'd all done that, and they'd all done that before the cave-in. The more she read the more she wondered why this class change had only appeared now, until she reached the final item.

Make the first step towards recovery.

"Congratulations, Alex. You deserve it."

"I wouldn't have got it without you." She took a step back, wiping her face on her sleeve. "Thank you, Eve. For listening."

She grinned. "Listening's the easy part. You did the real work." Eve paused to check her slowly refilling health bar. It was back above a hundred. "Now go ahead and accept it. I can keep watch while you sleep. We've still got a dungeon to clear."

* * *

Alexandra Reeve
Human
Level 25 Unbowed Survivor
Exp: 36/835
Health: 481/590
Stamina: 59/250
Mana: 0/0

Constitution: 59
Endurance: 25
Intelligence: 9
Dexterity: 17
Strength: 61
Spirit: 0

Chapter 19

The Alchemy Lab

Eve clutched the hilt of Alex's belt knife with white knuckles as they began their exploration. The short blade was a tool, not a weapon, but it was better than nothing. She silently mourned the loss of her sword, no doubt trapped beneath the fallen rubble and shattered into a hundred pieces. Hopefully after her fine she'd have enough money left over to buy a new one.

Alex led the way forward, her spear poised to ward off any surprise attackers. However prepared they might've been, a single thought loomed between the two adventurers. Neither dared speak it aloud.

They wouldn't survive another sentry golem.

It was a miracle they'd all lived through the first one—assuming Wes and Preston even *had*. When she wasn't desperately hoping she wouldn't come across another beast as threatening as the prior one, Eve quietly wondered how the men fared. They were even *less* capable of surviving another Burendian construct.

The thoughts fled from Eve's mind the moment she saw the first door. It had been a sturdy thing once, built of thick oaken planks and bound in iron. No more.

Alex simply had to prod at the rotting wood with the butt of her spear to set the entire thing free of its hinges. It slammed flat into the room beyond with a resounding thud.

Eve cringed at the noise, jerking her head to peer farther down the hall. If there *were* more monsters to be fought, they either didn't hear or didn't care about the door's collapse. Satisfied nothing was coming to kill them, Eve followed Alex out of the tunnel and into the side room.

It was a bedchamber. Or at least, it had been a bedchamber in some forgotten age. The wooden bed frame sagged with rot, any shred of linen or straw long eaten by some combination of pests and the ravages of time.

A decrepit chest of drawers was the only other piece of furniture. Eve thought to search it for loot, but the idea of touching the decaying wood sent her stomach churning. The top of the thing had collapsed into the first drawer, and Eve got the distinct impression she'd have to break it apart to access any of the lower ones anyway.

Sharing a shrug with the tall warrior over the striking amount of nothing they'd found, Eve returned to the long hallway.

The adventurers came across a number of identical sets of quarters as they explored, taking care to fully investigate each and every one. Alex came up with a way to get the doors open quietly by kicking them at the base so they fell outward into her waiting grasp. Eve didn't envy the dirt and shards of rotted wood she had to wipe off her hands each time, but Alex never complained.

As they cleared room after room, a lingering idea began to grow at the back of Eve's mind. It took eight sets of bedchambers in total before she voiced it. "Why aren't there any bugs?"

"Why should I know? Chalk it up to ancient pest-removal enchantments."

Eve shook her head. "That's not my point. *Something's* eaten all the bedding and a good chunk of this wood, but I haven't seen a single insect."

"They ran out of linens to eat and died a hundred years ago?"

"Then there would be dead bugs."

Alex froze. "You think something's eaten the bugs."

Eve nodded.

"Shit. Alright. So there's *possibly* some other monster out there. Maybe a managorged something or other."

"That's good, though," Eve said. "I'd rather a giant managorged snake or whatever than another construct. At least I can stab a snake."

"Well, there's not much else we can do but keep an eye out."

"Which we're already doing."

"Which we're already doing," Alex repeated. "So, shall we?"

Following the *Survivor's* lead, Eve continued on down the long hallway. The pair investigated two more empty quarters before they came across an oaken door unlike any other. Though the same thick planks and iron bands held it together, these stood untouched by decay's inexorable approach. It was pristine.

"If this thing isn't enchanted, I don't know what is."

Alex ignored the comment, reaching out to tap the door with the butt of her spear. It held fast. With a gesture, she ushered Eve to step back as she swung her weapon's base at the rustless iron handle.

The door swung open without so much as a squeak.

Eve didn't question the wisdom of exploring a room that almost certainly didn't hold the way out. They were hired to clear the place, and by the gods she was going to do it. Even if the obviously enchanted side room proved dangerous, it could also prove full of loot. The adventurer's dilemma urged her on, and Eve was determined not to leave empty handed.

Fortunately enough, the room did not hold any immediate threats. There were no golems or giant hares or lethal enchantments, just a stone countertop lining the walls. Whatever magic pulsed across the floor outside stretched up to encapsulate the walls and ceiling of the space, shining plenty of light upon the counters. Their contents immediately claimed Eve's attention.

Hundreds of pieces of immaculately crafted glassware cluttered the space. Flasks and vials and all sorts of strange alchemical contraptions Eve couldn't even begin to identify sat as if undisturbed for millennia. Perhaps they had been.

A layer of dust coated each item, leaving an ashen mark on Eve's finger as she reached out to touch a tall beaker. She tried to wipe it on her trousers, but it somehow came back even dirtier. She *really* needed new clothes. "Do you think this stuff is worth anything?"

Alex turned up her palms. "To an *Alchemist* probably, but I don't have a way to safely transport a bunch of glass."

Eve nodded, continuing to scan the countertop for anything worthwhile. Nearly all the glassware sat empty, though a number of pieces had dark stains along their sides, their contents long spilled or evaporated. A few even held the crumbled remains of a cork that had long failed at preventing exactly that.

"It's curious," the warrior said. "I didn't know the Burendians did much alchemy. Thought they were all focused on Mana and leylines and enchantments."

Eve shrugged, not looking away from her task. "That's already more than I ever knew about them. Maybe whoever owned this lab was an exception."

"Maybe... if only he'd left his notes behind..."

Eve chuckled, "If only."

The two continued their rummaging for a few silent minutes before Alex's voice echoed through the ruined laboratory, "Found something!"

Eve turned to find the warrior held five identical spheres in her upturned hand. Each was no more than an inch and a half in diameter, made of sheer stone with a piece of circular crystal on either side. The dark glass appeared as if meant to be a window into the stone's interior, but as Eve stared into it she saw nothing. Her **Appraise** delivered better results.

Minor Burendian Mana Core

Rarity: Rare

Alex grinned. "Now *these* are worth something." She slipped them into her pack. "Any enchanter or craftsman worth their salt has a use for 'em."

"Finally," Eve said, "some actual loot." With a smile of her own she returned to scanning the countertop, passing over all manner of impressive craftsmanship until one particular piece caught her eye.

Instead of a long-decayed cork, a glass stopper rested atop the round-bottom flask, keeping its contents liquid despite the ravages of time. The serum within was roughly Mana-potion blue, but a number of ethereal silver strands streaked through it. They glimmered as she picked the container up.

"I've got something too," she called Alex over. "A potion of some sort."

Eve swirled the liquid around, watching as it lit up with tiny lightning bolts with each spin around the flask.

Alex stared. "It's beautiful."

Eve nodded. Whatever this was, it was clearly magical in nature. She **Appraised** it to limited success.

Volatile Compound
Rarity: Legendary

"Shit," she swore. "It's bloody rare." A thought struck her as she swung the bottle yet faster to analyze the brilliant lights. "You wouldn't happen to know what 'volatile' means, woul—"

The flask exploded.

Shards of shattered glass fell to the floor as the strange liquid sprayed out in all directions. Alex threw up a hand, her exposed palm taking the brunt of the spill. Eve wasn't so lucky.

Most of the deep blue serum struck her directly in the chest. It seemed to pass directly through her dirt-stained blouse, leaving the garment dry as it hit the skin below.

Eve burned.

Her heart, her lungs, her very soul erupted in an icy inferno. The agony was unrelenting. She opened her mouth to scream, but no sound escaped.

Alex cried out enough for the both of them.

Eve fell to her knees, clutching her hands to her chest. She tried to breathe but the air refused to come. Panic mounted. The blaze spread, coursing through her veins with ice and fire and lightning and *pain.* Such pain.

She hit the ground hard, barely noticing the impact against the cold stone. She had other worries.

Dark spots appeared in her eyes, slowly spreading across her vision as the maelstrom did through her body. A second passed. Another.

Before Eve could even think to regret her decision to ever come to this gods-forsaken ruin, the world went black.

* * *

Preston hung close to Wes's side as the two crept down the ancient hallway. Though the ghostly pulses of white light across the cracks in the floor rendered his **Burning Hand** unnecessary, the fire mage still kept a spell at the ready.

The gesture was more of a comfort than a strategy. He knew he could throw a dart just as quickly from his side, but the thought of having a hand poised to strike gave him some confidence. Not much, but some. He could only hope whatever monster they found wasn't immune to his flames.

Wes shuddered. The golem encounter ran through his mind over and over again, reviving the sense of helplessness he'd felt as his spells washed harmlessly against the enchanted marble. *That's the trouble with fire magic,* he reasoned. *It can be unstoppably powerful or completely useless.* Some things just didn't burn.

The two adventurers stopped at each decrepit bedroom they passed, diligently checking each for monsters or loot. They found neither.

By the fourth bedchamber they searched, Wes decided he'd had enough of getting *nothing* from the deserted quarters. He set his hand alight. "I'm going to burn the bed frame."

Preston's eyes shot open. "What? Why?"

"My passive," the mage explained. "I can use a natural fire to regain Mana." He kicked the rotted wood. "It's not like this stuff's good for anything else."

"And the smoke? I don't see any chimneys."

Wes shrugged. "It'll mostly stay in this room. By the time it's a problem we'll be long gone anyway." He bent over to pick up the fallen door. "Here, we can even close the door."

"Alright," the healer said, stepping back into the empty hall, "but I'm waiting outside."

Wes nodded, leaning the decaying door against its former frame. With a quiet breath, he placed his **Burning Hand** onto the ancient bed.

The dead wood came alight in seconds, the blaze quickly spreading to consume it entirely. Wes smiled. A familiar warmth coursed through him as the fire burned. His Mana pool ticked up as he bathed in the beauty and comfort of the inferno. It felt good. It was *his*.

We hunger.

"Gods damnit," Wes cursed to himself. "These bloody infernal whispers."

Feed us so we may be strong.

Wes tried to shut the voice out, resolving for the hundredth time to replace the passive ability that generated them as soon as he could. He stepped away from the burning wood, dimming but not silencing it.

Burn.

Wes's gaze turned to the chest of drawers, the only other piece of furniture in the room. He shook his head. "I don't take orders from a fucking bonfire," he muttered. "Great. Now I'm muttering to myself like a madman." He supposed madmen heard voices too.

He stayed alone in that room until the blaze finally burned itself out, keeping low to avoid the smoke that coalesced along the roof. He uttered a quiet thanks that the whispers were gone for now as he rejoined Preston in the ancient hallway to continue their delve.

At least now he had a full Mana pool.

* * *

Eve blinked the darkness from her eyes as she came to beneath Alex's watchful gaze. Her chest still ached with a shadow of the frigid hellfire that had ravaged it, but the pain was manageable. She breathed.

"Gods damnit," Eve swore as she rubbed her neck. "I've gotta stop blacking out. That's twice in one day."

"Both times for exploding something you shouldn't have exploded." Alex clutched her right hand to her chest, her left covering it from Eve's view.

Eve ignored the comment. "Are you alright? Hells, am *I* alright?"

"We're alive," the warrior replied. "You were only out for a few minutes. Whatever that stuff was, it seems to have passed pretty quickly."

"Mostly passed. I still feel it."

"Me too," Alex said. "But nothing like before."

"Right." Eve pushed herself to her feet. "How's your hand?"

"See for yourself."

Alex withdrew her uninjured hand to reveal the damaged one beneath. Jagged lines of ivory lightning raced across her skin, glowing with the same ghostly light that filled the room. They stretched all the way down her wrist before disappearing beneath her vambrace. "Your neck looks the same."

Eve's eyebrows shot up as she spent a second futilely attempting to get a glimpse of her own neck. Realizing her stupidity, she turned around to peek down her blouse. "Shit," she swore. Sure enough, the same jagged web covered her skin, far denser than that on Alex. The lines seemed to pulse with her heart, as if every beat pumped Mana through her just as it did blood.

"Shit is right. My hand still works, but the lines aren't getting any dimmer and the burning feeling is still there."

Eve nodded. "Same here. What happens if they never go away?"

"That's what worries me," Alex said. "I'm sure there's a researcher in Lynthia that can help us, but we have to live that long first. The quest doesn't make me feel any better."

Eve froze, just noticing the flashing notification in the corner of her vision. "The what?"

"Just read it."

She didn't have to tell Eve twice.

The *Striker's* vision went blue as she scanned the new

message. She let out a curse as its contents sank in. "Gods below. Is this a good or a bad thing?"

"I don't know, Eve," Alex said. "I don't know."

Her eyes wide and her heart racing, Eve looked through the message once more.

Secondary Quest assigned: Legacy of the Precursors
Stage One: Discover the serum's effects.

Chapter 20
The Leyline

Evelia Greene
Human
Level 26 Shatterfate Striker
Exp: 914/1086
Health: 211/240
Stamina: 525/1050
Mana: 483/0
Constitution: 24
Endurance: 105
Intelligence: 12
Dexterity: 25
Strength: 36
Spirit: 0

"Ayla's tits."

Alex perked up. "What's wrong?"

Eve met her gaze with azure-lit eyes. "Check your Mana pool."

"Ayla's tits," Alex echoed. "I've got a hundred Mana."

"Shit. I've got almost five times that."

"It makes sense," the warrior said. "You got hit with

more of that serum."

Eve swallowed. "So… what does this mean?"

Alex shrugged. "I'm no caster, but even *I* know bad things happen when you overload on Mana."

"So what do we do?"

Alex stood, gripping her spear in defiance. "We finish this gods-damned dungeon as fast as we can and hope there's a way out on the other side. We can find help in Lynthia, but we have to live that long first."

Eve nodded, stooping over to reclaim Alex's knife from where she'd dropped it. She took a moment to thank the gods she hadn't fallen on it when she'd passed out.

The two women left the alchemy lab together. As they walked, Eve watched the web of jagged lines on Alex's hand. They looked alien. Wrong. Eve cringed as her thoughts turned to her own set of lightning bolts running up her neck and torso. She could almost imagine the foreign magic tearing her apart as it coursed through her veins. Her stomach churned.

The adventurers fell into a pattern of efficiently checking each room for monsters and loot before moving on to the next one. An hour in, the single bedrooms began to give way first to bunk rooms crowded with the collapsed remains of triple-layered servants' cots and then to all manner of rooms absent any furniture altogether.

Eve wondered if these empty chambers had somehow been cleared out, or if the Burendians had died out before they'd ever seen use. The thought sent a chill down her spine.

Why stack up cots three-high just to have a bunch of empty rooms? Had whatever wiped out the ancient race given warning? Perhaps the insects had managed to devour these pieces of furniture before whatever monster lurked ahead had devoured them in turn. Eve sighed. It was no use speculating.

Her mind had returned to worrying about the pulsing sensation of heat at her chest by the time they found the kitchen.

Stone countertops lined the massive chamber, split into individual workspaces. Each came equipped with its own hooded chimney directly above what appeared to Eve as just more counter. "Did they set fires right on the stone?"

Alex shook her head. "It's enchanted. Like everything else here. Probably set the pan right onto the stone and dumped Mana into it."

Eve sighed. "Please tell me this isn't what the guild is interested in. I swear if they're paying five hundred silver for bloody cooking enchantments…"

The *Survivor* laughed. "Could be. Or they could be after how to make a golem. Or the thousand other wild things down here."

"Fair point."

"Come on." Alex swung open the door back into the hallway. "Better keep moving."

Eve lingered in the ancient kitchen for a second, lost in thoughts of the ancient race doing something as mundane as *cooking*. The heat in her chest grew warmer. With a quiet gulp, she scurried after the towering warrior. They had no time to waste on idle imaginings.

The pair continued on to investigate dining rooms and meeting spaces and even a gods-damned *garden*. At least, Eve assumed the square patches of barren soil had been a garden before whatever remaining denizens of the ruin had devoured all the plants. Not a one of the dozen various chambers produced anything of interest.

By the end of their second hour of exploring, Eve stopped to ask a question. "How's your hand?"

"It's fine?" Alex answered hesitantly. "It feels warm, but it's not burning or anything."

"I think my chest is getting hotter."

Alex's face fell. "That's not a good sign."

"None of this is a good sign."

"Like I said, we'll just have to—" Alex froze, her voice suddenly dropping to barely a whisper. "Do you hear that?"

Eve strained her ears.

A gentle scraping echoed down the cavern ahead. If Eve squinted, she could barely make out a long thin shadow jerking back and forth in the distance, but the ethereal light of the enchantments blurred the visage.

Tightening her grip on Alex's knife, Eve gave the warrior a nod. They crept down the passage together.

Eve's heart raced with every careful step. The scratching sound grew louder, more frantic. Could whatever it was sense them? She held out her knife, ready to **Charge!** should the thing come barreling down the hall at them. It never did. By the time she grew close enough to **Appraise** it, she knew why.

Level ?? Leygorged Widow

"Holy shit," Eve swore as they stopped just short of the twitching spider leg. "It's stuck in there."

The massive beast pressed against the tunnel opening, desperately swiping a barbed leg at the two adventurers. With every miss it scraped against the floor, leaving a deep scratch in the enchanted stone.

"Gods below," Alex mouthed. "I knew Mana could make things bigger after the hares, but Ayla's tits. That's gotta be at least twenty feet tall."

"Poor thing grew too big to fit into the tunnels."

Alex snorted. "That 'poor thing' probably ate every other living creature in this place." She raised her spear. "So, what's the plan?"

Eve shook her head. "Where's Wes when we need him?

185

This would be perfect for him to just sit back and throw darts at."

Alex cocked an eyebrow. "Are you saying we should wait?"

"We might as well. Whatever that chamber is, it's *large*. I'd bet the other tunnel meets up with it eventually."

"Alright," Alex agreed. "We'll give them a bit of time to catch up in case they explored slower than we did. But if your chest or my hand starts to get worse, I say we go for it. I'd rather die fighting a giant spider than because I was too scared to try."

"Okay." A pulse of warmth echoed across Eve's torso. "Let's hope they didn't get into as much trouble as we did."

* * *

Wes had just about had it with rotting bedrooms. Eighteen and counting was more than enough decayed bed frames and collapsed dressers to carefully search through.

Preston agreed. "I bet the others have found all sorts of valuable loot while we're stuck on bedroom duty."

"Knowing Eve, she's stumbled her way into clearing half the dungeon already."

The healer laughed. "And/or she's fallen on her face."

"I'd wager both." Wes smiled. At least he was stuck with someone worth talking to instead of that dreadfully boring warrior. *I swear to Bandir, if I have to hear one more comment about bloody 'professionalism' I'm gonna snap.*

"Well, well, well. What do we have here?" The conversation fell silent as Wes swung open another rotted door to find a staircase in lieu of the umpteenth bedroom. In addition to along the floor, the lines of illumination stretched across the outer wall of the spiral steps as they descended into the earth below.

The pulsing white aura gave the stairway a sense of magnificence, as if it led directly to the heavens themselves. Wes stepped in.

"Is this a good idea?" Preston asked. "I'm pretty sure the way out isn't down there."

"We're here to clear the dungeon," Wes answered over his shoulder. "And this is part of it. I mean look at this thing. It's gotta be important."

The blond priest nodded, gathering his wits before following Wes down the brilliantly lit steps.

On and on they descended, delving ever deeper into the unknown. By the time he lost count of the number of steps, Wes began to lend credence to his theory they'd find one of the heavens at their base.

Instead they found a door.

Unlike the decaying wood of those above, this was made of solid stone. A sharp web of ghostly white pulsed across it. Preston reached for the handle.

"Ow!" He jerked his hand away, his fingers already blistering. "It's bloody hot!" The room flashed gold as he healed himself.

"Let me," Wes said. The iron loop felt warm in his grasp, but left his skin uncharred. "Fire mage, remember?" With a cocky smirk, he swung the door open.

The world went white.

"Ayla's tits!" Preston swore. "That's fucking bright!"

Wes shielded his eyes with a hand as he stepped into the room.

The chamber itself was rather barren. Aside from the number of iron tools which hung from hooks on the far wall, its only feature was a steel hatch embedded in the floor at its very center. Wes couldn't look directly at it.

Blinding colorless light blasted the room from a thin crack along the trapdoor's center. Wes approached.

"We should leave," Preston called after him. "Whatever that is, the worst thing to do would be to get close to it."

"It's Mana," Wes said. "Unless I miss my guess, getting

close is *exactly* what we need to do. How do you think this place naturalized?"

"Ayla's tits. You think there's a bloody dungeon core in there?"

Wes bent over, shutting his eyes as he blindly groped around for the hatch's handle. "Only one way to find out."

Not even his magically induced fire resistance could protect him from *this* heat. Wes wondered how the steel wasn't glowing red as it singed his palm. At least he had a healer behind him. He grit his teeth and *pulled*.

The hatch flew open, sending the fire mage stumbling backwards.

Holding his robes over his eyes to help shield them from the worst of the oppressive light, Preston stepped forward. "You're right. There's something in there."

Wes followed suit.

The trapdoor revealed a torrent of light, the same hue as the enchantments all about them but a millionfold as bright. "Gods below. Is that a—"

"A leyline. There's a reason the Burendians built their settlements underground."

Wes pulled away, grabbing a pair of long-handled tongs off the wall. He squinted as he peeked through the tiny holes in his shirt at the raging current of Mana and at the dark shape resting near its top.

"Let me." Preston held out a hand. "I have more Spirit; I can handle more Mana than you."

Wes shook his head. "Neither of us could handle a drop of this. I'll need you to heal me."

"No," Preston insisted. "If you collapse I can't out-heal the damage you'll take. You know I'm not strong enough to pull you to safety."

"But I am."

Preston nodded.

With a sigh, Wes stepped behind the slim *Priestess,*

handing him the steel tongs. "Tell me when you've got it."

"Alright." Preston tensed.

Wes wrapped an arm around the man's waist, ready to rip him away from the opening at a moment's notice. "Ready?"

The healer nodded. With a breath and a prayer, he plunged the tongs into the deluge below.

The earth shook. The enchantments around them flickered. The torrent raged. Preston screamed.

Ghostly wisps twirled up the ancient tongs, dancing along the steel as they reached for Preston's exposed hands. He reached in deeper.

Wes dug in his heels, fighting to maintain his balance as the ground quaked beneath them. He prayed. Preston's body shook before him. An eternity passed in seconds.

"I got it!"

Elation flooded through the fire mage as he leapt backwards, yanking Preston with him. The two landed hard on the stone steps. Preston fell limp. The healer's skin burned against Wes's, but he held him all the same. "Preston? Are you—"

The room went black.

Every jagged line, every bright light, every enchantment in the place winked out. The darkness pressed in against them, every bit as suffocating as the light before it. Until it wasn't.

Preston's eyes shot open, his irises shining in brilliant gold. It was a warm glow, a gentle glow. One Wes had felt —and resented—many times before. Ayla's light spread through the priest's slack form, coating the whole room in Her resplendent illumination.

Wes watched in awe as Preston channeled every ounce of foreign Mana into healing the very wounds it had wrought.

And then it was gone.

The earthquake stilled, and the enchantments flickered back to life, and Preston's chest heaved with a powerful breath. He smiled.

Wes exhaled as relief flooded through him. "You did it. Holy shit, Preston, that was amazing!"

The healer sat up. "Being a *Priestess* has its perks."

"That it does," Wes chuckled. "I guess I can't tease you about it anymore, huh?"

"Not if you ever want your share for finding this." Preston held up a fist-sized obsidian sphere, handing it to Wes. It was cool to the touch, despite the maelstrom in which they'd found it.

Minor Dungeon Core
Rarity: Mythic

Wes grinned. "Sounds like a deal." He slipped the core into his pack before extending a hand to help Preston up.

The priest took it.

"Now come on," Wes said as he led the way back up the stairs and towards their next challenge. "Let's get the hells out of here."

Chapter 21

So About that Giant Spider...

Eve paced impatiently back and forth across the hallway, an eye fixed on the foot-thick spider leg at all times.

The appendage and its owner sat deathly still, as if under the impression it would escape their notice should it avoid all motion. The tactic might've worked were it still the size of a copper instead of the twenty-foot monstrosity it'd become. Eve wouldn't forget the thing *without* its looming presence.

Though its eyes rested too high on its face to peer into their tunnel, the women got a clear view of its deadly mandibles. They glistened with the sheen of venom, something Eve determined to be the least of her worries. The thing's fangs were thicker than her leg. It wouldn't need any toxins to bite her in half.

"Where the hells are they?" Eve cursed as heat blossomed in her chest, pushing past the realm of discomfort to that of pain. It came in waves, each burning hotter than before.

"They'll get here when they get here," Alex answered from where she sat leaning against the wall. "Maybe they've been more thorough in their searching?"

"We don't even know for sure that their tunnel leads here."

The warrior shrugged. "Maybe you're right. Between you passing out after the golem and you passing out in the lab, they should've had a pretty big head start on us."

"Shit. What if something happened to them?"

"We'll worry about that if it happens." Alex looked up at Eve. "For all we know, their tunnel is just longer than ours. Maybe they found a treasure room and are trying to haul a ton of loot with them. The plan is a good one. Wait as long as we can before taking on the widow."

"You're right, you're right." Eve tried to calm herself down. "I'm sure they're fine. I just don't like—ah fuck!" She doubled over, clutching a hand to her chest. It burned.

"Eve!" Alex shot to her feet, racing to the *Striker's* side just in time for the feeling to fade.

"I—I'm okay." Eve braced herself against the wall as she stood upright. Fiery pain lingered across her torso, but the wave had passed. "We might have to act sooner rather than later."

"That bad?"

She nodded.

"Alright." Alex turned to stare down the monstrous spider. "So what's the plan here?"

"Well, it's blocking the way into the main cavern, so we'll have to fight it from here. I keep the leg busy while you stab it with your spear?"

Alex sighed, "It's not ideal, but we may not have a choice. Maybe if we can get it to back off a bit you can slip into the larger area to have space to run?"

Eve gripped her knife. "On the count of three?"

Alex nodded. "One."

"Two."

"Thre—"

The tunnel went black. The earth around them quaked

as the ancient enchantments winked out. Eve looked up at Alex, the only light in the room that from the glowing lines across her skin. "What in the—"

The enchantments flickered back to life, somehow brighter than before. Eve spun to watch the mouth of the passage.

The spider was gone. *Now's our chance!*

"Three!"

She **Charged!**

The cavern was massive.   Towering stone arches stretched fifty feet into the air, each lined with the familiar shimmering enchantments. To the far side, Eve spotted a spiral staircase leading upwards.   A glimmer of hope welled up in the back of her mind. The second sight that greeted her compounded it.

The leygorged widow lay on its stomach with its face pressed against the side wall, six of its legs stretched out behind it while the other two reached ahead.   *Another tunnel!*

A grin managed to fight through Eve's burning chest and racing heart.

She weaved through the twitching hind legs, reversing her grip on the dagger for an overhand strike.   With a mighty leap, Eve threw **Fate-al Blow** and **Adrenaline Rush** into the blow, hammering the belt-knife into the obsidian carapace.

It struck just above the beast's rear end.

The monster twitched as the steel blade sank two inches into its abdomen. It didn't hiss. It didn't screech. It simply stood.

Eve clutched the hilt of her knife as the spider rose to its feet, yanking her up with it. Her legs dangled below her as she questioned the wisdom of her choice of attack. Her chest pulsed with fire.

In a single motion, the creature jerked its massive body,

wrenching Eve's hand from the dagger's hilt.

She flew backward.

The *Striker* landed hard on the enchanted floor, the scores and holes the monster had carved over the years scraping up her back.

The spider turned, skittering across the ancient stone to exact revenge on this morsel that poked it. Alex got there first.

Her spear raised, the warrior dashed in, sidestepping a sweeping leg to plant her weapon directly in the beast's maw.

It recoiled.

Eve took the opportunity to clamber to her feet. "I can barely scratch it!"

"Then try harder!" Alex yelled back. "Aim for the eyes!"

Easy for you to say, she thought to herself. *You can actually reach them.* Agony surged across Eve's chest as Alex engaged the spider once more. She fought to keep her footing as the pain sent her reeling.

She cursed, gritting her teeth as she forced her focus outward. Now wasn't the time. *Step one: get my knife back.* Eve dashed to the right, keeping her distance as she circled the beast.

Alex kept it busy with a series of sidesteps and warding strikes, but they both knew she was one misstep from death.

Eve hastened.

Reaching the spider's rear, she leapt for the weapon still embedded in its abdomen. Her fist found only air as the beast surged forward once more. She scampered back to gain some distance before her next attempt.

A crash rang out. Brilliant raw light flashed through the room. Alex screamed.

The creature fell to its stomach, its legs still twitching. It wasn't dead yet.

Eve raced around the massive beast to check on Alex.

The *Survivor* lay against the back wall, thrown there by whatever had caused the crash. Shattered bits of spear-handle pierced her bleeding right hand as she desperately clutched it. It glowed no more.

The Mana!

Eve skidded as she reversed direction, her **Surefooted** keeping her stable.

The spider twitched, its legs shifting beneath it as it recovered from Alex's blow.

Eve ran faster, pushing the final seconds of **Charge!** as hard as she could. Her chest ached. Her heart pounded. She jumped.

Her hand collided with the knife's hilt just as the monster lurched to its feet, taking Eve up with it.

She held fast.

The inferno within her mounted as she pulled herself up. The spider shifted beneath her. She prayed.

The agony built, coursing fire through her veins.

Now!

Eve *pushed*.

Her body burst with energy, searing her eyes with its blinding brilliance. Sight was the least of her problems.

The knife shattered, its metal unable to handle the sheer power she forced through it. Shards of steel pierced her skin. Even more pierced the ebon carapace.

The blast sent her flying, colliding into the back wall with a sickening crunch. Pain piled upon pain as her blood fell to the stone, casting the white enchantments in a crimson hue. She forced her eyes open, unwilling to lose consciousness. Not again.

Eve stared down the fallen spider as black spots danced across her vision.

Notifications flashed in her periphery.

She grinned.

The fire in her chest had faded, its pain replaced by the singed flesh and broken bones it had left behind. She'd bloody done it.

Her relief faltered as darkness continued to spread over her damaged eyes.

Until it didn't.

Golden light flooded through her, scrutinizing every aspect of her very being as wounds knit shut. She shuddered beneath Ayla's judgmental gaze but accepted every aspect of Her forgiveness as the price for Her healing.

The pain was but a distant memory by the time her vision returned.

"Thank bloody Ayla you made it!" she called to Preston where he stood at the tunnel's mouth. "Since when can you heal at range?"

Wes answered for him, "Being a *Priestess* has its perks."

Eve laughed as she pushed herself to her feet, crossing the chamber to wrap the man in a tight hug. "Your timing is impeccable."

"Yeah, well, we got caught up *doing our job*." He reached into his pack to withdraw an orb of pure jet.

Alex gaped. "Is that—"

Preston shook his head, pointing at the spiral stairway. "Let's worry about getting out of here first, then we can swap stories."

The party agreed, and Alex took the lead up the stone steps. It took a group effort to overcome the layers of earth and grass which had grown atop the trapdoor, but the adventurers' combined strength proved enough to clear the way to open sky.

Eve never thought she'd be so happy to see a cloudy night.

Their battles survived and their adventures done for the day, the four companions crowded together around Wes's campfire to tell their tales and read their rewards.

You have defeated Level 52 Leygorged Widow: +1560 exp!
You have cleared dungeon: Burendian Outpost: +5000
exp!
Level Up!
Level Up!
Level Up!
Level Up!

Ability Upgraded!
Passive Ability - Battle-hardened
Gained 20% explosion resistance!

Ability Upgraded!
Passive Ability - Surefooted
Increased stability on moving surfaces!

Ability Upgraded!
Active Ability - Adrenaline Rush
Cost reduced!

Ability Upgraded!
Active Ability - Fate-al Blow
Now applies to magical attacks!

Eve pondered the meaning of her skill upgrades, especially
given they seemed to match with the events of the past few
days. *Gods-damnit*, she swore. *Even my bloody class thinks
I've exploded too many things*.

The level thirty upgrade was the most compelling.
Unless she could somehow replicate the burst of Mana that
had killed the spider, she *had* no magical attacks to boost.
Eve cursed again. She'd really hoped to get a significant
change for the milestone level, and *this* wasn't it.

Perhaps the upgrade implied she'd get a magic attack someday? The existence of her secondary quest seemed to lead in that direction.

Wes and Preston received no credit for downing the leygorged widow, but the two were plenty happy with the whopping chunk of exp from the dungeon itself. It was hard not to be. Preston leveled four times off it alone.

Their levels claimed and their abilities upgraded, Alex and Preston disappeared back into the depths of the ruin to carve up some spider meat for their supper. While they did, Wes turned to Eve.

"Are you alright?"

"I think so?" She turned up her palms. "My chest doesn't hurt any more, and the weird Mana-lines are gone. Status still says I have twelve out of zero Mana, but that's a hell of a lot better than four hundred. And hey, maybe this secondary quest will have some interesting rewards."

Wes carefully nodded. "We should still get you and Alex to a magical researcher as soon as we get back. Twelve Mana isn't nothing, and if you still have the quest it means Preston's healing didn't fix whatever the problem is."

"Right. Like I said, we'll look into it."

"Good." Wes sat back. "I just don't want you to get hurt."

A hint of red tinged Eve's face at the thought of Wes worrying after her. She banished it with great prejudice.

"Alright," Preston's voice rang out from the trapdoor behind them. "Who wants to learn what spider tastes like?"

Eve shuddered. "Not me. If that meat's got as much Mana in it as I think it does, it's not worth the risk."

Alex's face fell. "Shit."

The fire mage shrugged. "Fine by me. I actually *have* a Mana pool."

Without waiting for the others, he got to cooking.

The smell of roasting meat taunted the women as Preston and Wes feasted on seared spider. Reaching into her pack, Alex handed Eve a chunk of stale cheese. "Well hey," she muttered, "at least we don't have to eat Wes's cooking."

"I heard that!"

"She meant you to!" Eve answered, graciously accepting the food.

It wasn't an easy dinner to chew, nor a particularly tasty one, but Eve enjoyed it all the same. Any meal felt wondrous after such a brush with death. Her spirits grew as she thought of the silver that awaited them in Lynthia, as well as whatever deals they could make with Alex's five enchanted spheres and the dungeon core.

Things were looking up, and Eve reveled in it.

Until Preston's voice rang out with wavering trepidation, "Um... Eve? You're glowing."

Her eyes shot open. Heart suddenly racing, Eve peered down her shirt to confirm the healer's words.

Once more her skin pulsed white. "Shit." She checked her Mana.

182/0

"I've gained Mana."

Wes cursed. "You've what? How?"

Eve gulped as yet another notification appeared in the corner of her vision. "Hold on. I think I might know."

Ability Upgraded!
Passive Ability - Ethereal Metabolism
Mana is just another source of energy, one your body has learned to produce. Convert a portion of the food you eat directly into Mana.

Eve's shoulders slumped as she exhaled through gritted

teeth. "We're going to need to hurry back to Lynthia, after all."

Chapter 22

A Voice in the Mist

The late summer sun was already high in the sky by the time the adventurers embarked on their journey south the next morning, not that they could see it above the leafy canopy. The forest felt lesser, somehow.

Dancing shadows of shifting branches no longer caught Eve's eye in quite the same way. Little twitches in the brush were lurking beasts no more. As fears went, the dark held little sway before the absolute nightmare she'd felled last night.

No, the fearsome northern woods failed to quicken her pulse or quiver her hands. Her own skin did that plenty.

From time to time as the party walked Eve would raise an arm in front of her, watching as the skin of her neck glowed ethereal light upon it. Her chest pulsed with warmth as the Mana coursed through her. She could only wonder what damage it wrought.

The hours dragged on as Wes set a blistering pace, one Eve was happy to match. The sooner they got home, the better.

The trouble was, after delving below ground in one place and surfacing in another, the party had little idea where exactly they *were*. The trees provided little in the way of landmarks. Alex navigated generally south by the angle of what sunbeams pierced the canopy, but that would only get them out of the woods. Finding Lynthia again was another matter.

As things were, Eve had an awful lot on her mind when she stepped away from the others to relieve herself in the privacy of a nearby tree. Indeed, so distracted was she by the fire in her chest and the uncertainty of their whereabouts and the mystery of both her quests that she failed to notice the first tendrils of fog that crept in.

It came like a tide, sweeping through the underbrush as it climbed inexorably higher. By the time Eve stood and re-clasped her pants, the mists had reached her waist. Her chest. Her throat.

She **Charged!** through the brush, her heart racing as the unnatural fog poured in.

"Wes!" she called. "Alex, Preston! What's going on?"

No reply came.

Eve's stomach sank. She hadn't been that far; where had they gone? The mists climbed higher.

She tilted her head up, holding her face above the rising tide as long as she could before it enveloped her. She held her breath.

The world went white as the fog eclipsed her vision, casting the nearest trees and shrubs as no more than dark silhouettes. It was cool against her skin, almost refreshing in contrast to the blazing Mana within her. The glowing cracks upon her exposed neck reflected against the suspended droplets, casting visible beams of light in their jagged pattern.

She took a step forward. Her lungs burned as she wandered through the fog, unwilling to breathe whatever magic had so filled the air. The mists gave her little choice.

She inhaled with a gasp, the moist air coating her throat

enough to elicit a fit of coughs. After a moment's recovery, she called out once more. "Guys? Where are you?"

The voice that answered was none she knew.

"They can't hear you."

A figure appeared before her, at first just a shape in the fog. It wasn't until he stepped closer that she knew him for a man.

There was little by which to identify him. His trousers were plain if a lustrous shade of black, while his shirt and vest were simple cotton. Eve never saw his face as the mists danced and twirled about it.

She **Appraised** him.

Level ?? The Man of the Mists
 Unique Tier ?? Class

"Who are you?" she asked with more confidence than she felt.

The shape tilted its obscured head. "A rather strange question to ask of a man in a mask."

Eve held her ground, swallowing the growing urge to panic as it welled in the back of her throat. "You're the one hiding from a level thirty."

The laughter came from everywhere at once, somehow echoing through the fog when no other sound would. "You have courage. Perhaps they were right about you. Or perhaps you lack the subtlety to realize what a single voice can do."

Eve certainly didn't feel courageous. Her hands twitched and her heart raced and the cool mist sent chills down her spine. At least her thoughts were distracted from the warmth in her chest. She fought to keep her gaze level with the strange man. "What do you want?"

"Straight to the point," the man sighed. "Efficient, if a little boring. Don't you have something else you'd like to ask about? Or rather, someone else?"

She froze. "What did you do to them?"

Hidden though it was, Eve could practically *hear* the grin on the man's face. "That's more like it. Your friends are unharmed, if perhaps a bit lost. It's remarkably easy to lose one's way in the fog. I imagine they're more worried about *you.*"

Eve's shoulders relaxed as a portion of her tension drained away. Whoever this was, he'd come to talk. She considered stepping onto the balls of her feet to **Charge!** away, but in this fog she'd just as soon run into a tree as actually escape.   Besides, if he wanted her dead, there wasn't much she could do about it. Instead, she replied with another question. "Should they be?"

"Not yet. Not for some time, I'd imagine, and certainly not from me." The figure stepped closer, the mist around his head swirling ever-denser to keep his face concealed. "You have a ways to travel yet."

"What do you want?" Eve repeated herself.

"My associates are always on the hunt for promising new talent. *Legendary* quests don't come about often, especially ones with as much… flexibility as yours."

Eve's eyes widened. "How did you…"

"Know?" A smugness filled the man's voice. "It's my business to know, my dear girl. In fact, I'm sure they all know about you and your quest by now. That is, all those who matter."

The use of the words 'dear girl' sent a shiver down Eve's back. "Those who matter? What are you talking about?"

A chuckle rang out, this time only from the man before her.   "What indeed.   I'm sure you're clever enough to realize when there's a larger game ahand. Your human kingdom is a pawn of a pawn. My associates and I are players."

Despite the implication of the words and the strength of

the man who spoke them, one particular aspect of the speech stood out to Eve. The question left her mouth before she had a chance to stop herself. "Isn't it afoot?"

"Pardon?"

"The phrase," she explained. "There's a larger game afoot."

"You play chess with your feet?"

Eve paused, realizing the foolishness inherent to correcting the grammar of a man who could murder her with an absent thought. She held her breath.

"You're a curious one, Evelia Greene. Well suited to the quest you've been given."

"What do you know about that?" she pressed. "You said it was flexible, but I've really just been wandering aimlessly and trying to survive."

"That's the beauty of it. Your path is unset, and not even I can see where it leads. Such freedom is a gift few ever know. The only price is also the only guarantee: whatever you do, the dangers shall be great and the impact worthy of legend."

Eve cocked an eyebrow. "That sounds like a really fancy way of saying it's *Legendary* but you don't know why."

The cackling returned, again from all directions as if the fog itself found humor in the words. "You'd be surprised how often the way you say something holds more sway than the something itself. Eloquence has every right to a place beside wit and strength."

"Spoken like a man with neither."

More laughter. "Courage it is, then. You'll do well in the greater game. When the time comes."

"Is that why you're here?" Eve asked. "To recruit me onto your team?"

"Not quite. My faction is but one of many, and more than mine have their eyes on you. The Stones have marked you of interest, and the world has taken heed."

"I'm not leaving my friends." Eve held her ground, her heart racing as she outright defied the power before her.

"Even if you were ready, I'm not asking you to. We value loyalty, and I would rather have yours intact. No. There will come a time when your growth outpaces theirs, when one by one the danger of your company turns them away or ends them altogether. Perhaps a few will embrace the risk and find their way to the world at large. Perhaps not. Either way, I'll be waiting."

"So you've ambushed me in the middle of the woods to tell me you're waiting for my friends to die off?"

"Nothing of the sort," the man said. "Others will come with offers and threats and promises and lies, anything to put another piece of their own onto the board. When the time comes, I want you to remember that I was the first to approach you. To reach out and speak with you as an equal. That has to count for something."

"And if I turn them away? What if my quest is to join one of them, or to leave you all to your squabbles and keep my own friends?"

"That's your choice." The voice darkened. "You're free to live as a pawn if you like, but no matter what you'll remain on the board. At least with me you'll know for which color you play."

"So I can either go work for someone directly or be manipulated into this fight of yours anyway?"

"They said you were clever."

The man stepped forward, his right hand outstretched. Mist rushed in, condensing in his upturned palm. He closed it, reaching out to place a cold and rigid object in Eve's own hand. He curled her fingers shut over it. "Think of me," he said, "when you're ready to stop being a pawn."

Eve nodded.

The figure turned, striding away with casual confidence.

Just as the fog swept about his dark form, swallowing him up in its pale beauty, he paused. "I wouldn't tell your companions about our meeting. Especially not her. I know the jealous type when I see it." Another step and he was gone.

Eve stood alone, breathing in the cool mist as she played through the encounter in her mind. Unless he'd tricked her **Appraise** somehow, she'd just had a conversation with a living legend. She wondered how high level he truly was, or how he'd managed to unlock a *Unique* class.

She didn't know what was wilder: that a being so powerful had sought her out, or that apparently he wanted her *help*. Or at least her allegiance. She shivered.

Her heart still pounding, Eve carefully opened her hand to see the token he'd left her.

It was a chess knight, white as pearl and cold as steel. Though almost two inches tall, it sat near weightless in her hand. Tendrils of mist flowed off the beautiful piece, another reminder of from whence it'd come.

Eve slipped the knight into her pocket, clinking it against the two copper pieces her mother had given her for the loaf of bread. She wondered if she'd ever get the chance to spend them.

Dismissing the thought with a shake of her head, Eve turned her musings elsewhere. A notification blinked, and she had a bad feeling about what it might mean. The last thing she needed was *another* secondary quest.

Legendary Quest Milestone Reached: Meet the Man of the Mists!
+4000 exp!

Level Up!

Eve almost let out a sigh of relief when she read the

message, a glimmer of joy even blossoming at the level up. Her comfort came crashing down as she realized the implication of the milestone. If the encounter was a milestone, it must mean the man himself was a part of her quest. The knight suddenly felt heavy in her pocket.

"Eve!"

She slammed the status screen shut as Wes's voice echoed through the fog.

"Eve, there you are!" Three figures materialized before her, a **Burning Hand** guiding them like a beacon. "Are you alright?"

The *Striker* nodded. "I'm okay." She gave Wes her best 'we'll talk later' look before repeating herself. "I'm fine."

"Good," the mage said. "This fog is insane."

As if at his command, the moisture in the air seemed to burn away. Eve smiled as the forest around them revealed itself. "Whatever it was, it's gone. C'mon guys." She stepped past them, taking the lead. "Let's go home."

Chapter 23

The Lynthia Institute for Magical Afflictions

"So let me get this straight," Wes said from where he sat on the side of his bed in the tight guild quarters, "we spent a half hour wandering around in supernatural fog so some *guy* could have a private conversation with you?"

Eve rubbed her neck, leaning against the back wall to maintain *some* amount of personal space. "When you put it like that, it makes it sound so..."

"Overdramatic?"

"I was going to say inconsiderate, but that too."

Wes shrugged. "You'd think someone that powerful could just... I don't know, walk up and ask to have a word?"

"He wanted me to keep the meeting secret. Specifically from Alex—said she was the jealous type."

"Oh shit. Yeah I can see why. You saw how she got when I got my *Rare* class."

"No—it's not like—" Eve struggled to explain. "She's been through some shit, and I don't think she's really recovered." She shook her head. "That's not the point. This man of the mists guy didn't want you all to know about him."

Wes cocked an eyebrow. "Did he think we just wouldn't ask where you went in that fog?"

"What are you saying?"

"You basically vanished," the mage said, "for a long time. And then when you reappeared, you acted like nothing happened. It's like he *wanted* you to look like you were hiding something."

Eve swallowed. "He said I'd have to leave you all behind sooner or later. Maybe he was trying to speed things up."

Wes's voice filled with vigor. "That's not going to happen. You and I are in this together, and if you think Preston is letting you out of his sight, you're sorely mistaken."

Eve straightened. "Preston?"

"You aren't the only one who learned a new secret while we were separated. He asked me not to tell you, but rest assured Preston is here for the long haul."

"Um… alright." Eve paused, wondering what exactly Wes meant.

He didn't give her much time to think. "So what all did your high-level mystery man say?"

"All sorts of vague shit about how Leshk is a pawn of a pawn and there's a bigger game ahand."

Wes furrowed his brow. "Don't you mean a bigger game afoot?"

"That's what I said! He insisted people don't play chess with their feet. Actually, he was *really* fond of his chess analogies." She reached into her pocket, withdrawing the ivory knight. "He gave me this."

Wes stared at the tendrils of mist as they wafted off the chess piece. "What does it do?"

"Hells if I know. **Appraise** just says it's a 'token of the mists.'"

Wes snorted. "So he gave you a souvenir."

Eve chuckled, "Maybe the next guy I meet will give me a bishop. I can put together the most confusing chess set ever seen."

"So does the token mean he wants you to be his knight or he's somebody *else's* knight?"

Eve rubbed her temples. "It's open for interpretation? Maybe he just likes horses."

He rolled his eyes. "It sounds like all we really know is some guy with a *Unique* class and a flair for the dramatic wants you to work for him once you've leveled up a bit more."

"That—uh—that about sums it up."

"So what are you going to do?"

"For now? Nothing." Eve pushed away from the wall to stand fully upright, drawing uncomfortably close to Wes in the process. "Alex and I still need to find someone to help us with the Mana thing, not to mention selling the loot from the dungeon. I can worry about mysterious job offers from creepy mist-men when I have new clothes and my chest isn't on fire."

"Fair point." Wes pushed to his feet as Eve opened the door out into the hall. "Preston and I can see about selling the dungeon and Mana cores while you find your researcher."

"Great. I'll meet you back here in a few hours." Eve paused as she stepped from the small bedroom. "Oh, and Wes? Hold on to a few of those Mana cores. I think I might have a use for them."

An amused grin crossed the man's face as he jokingly saluted. "Yes, ma'am."

"Good." Eve smirked. "You're dismissed."

* * *

A bead of sweat dripped down Eve's brow as she glanced around the waiting room at the Lynthia Institute for Magical Afflictions. To her left a man curled his face into an agonized snarl as his hair burned with purple fire. Across from him sat a woman with one eye turned obsidian black. Behind *her* was a pair of teenage girls carefully cradling what appeared to be a horned toad. An **Appraise** told Eve otherwise.

"This place is depressing," Alex muttered as she stared at a man with feet at the ends of his arms.

"You can say that again," Eve replied. "I had no idea there were so many curses running around."

"It comes with the territory," the warrior said. "Break into enough ancient crypts and you're bound to wind up hexed sooner or later."

Eve shuddered as she watched a bald, sunburnt man vomit into a bucket for the third time. "Remind me never to go wherever *he* went."

"Alexandra Reeve?" a nasal voice called from across the room.

The two adventurers shared a look before quietly standing and weaving their way through the busy waiting room to the open door on the other end. A gnome of all things ushered them in.

The examination room clearly displayed the poorly funded state of the place as Eve and Alex sat upon the rough table. The only other furniture was a broken chair and a wooden stepping stool, upon which the *Cursebreaker* promptly stood.

Without looking up from his clipboard, the hairless bespectacled gnome asked with a tired, monotonous tone, "Where and by what were you cursed?"

"A Burendian ruin," Eve explained. "And it's not exactly a curse. We found a volatile compound in an alchemy lab and it spilled on us."

He lowered his notes. "An alchemy lab? In a Burendian ruin? How unusual. I've never known them to practice alchemy."

"That's what I said," Alex stepped in.

Raising his eyebrows, the gnome returned to scribbling away on his clipboard. "So what are the symptoms?"

Eve started from the beginning, describing the compound itself before going over the maelstrom of agony it had inflicted before fading to a gentle warmth in her chest. She told of finding the massive influx of Mana, as well as the growing fire beneath her skin leading up to the explosion that had killed the leygorged widow. She ended with mention of the secondary quest and the evolution of her metabolism skill.

"For what it's worth," Alex added, "my quest has a different name. It's probably because only my hand got hit, but mine's called 'Hand of the Precursors.' And it's my **Survivor's Recovery** that upgraded to give me Mana regeneration even though I don't have a Mana pool."

Eve cocked an eyebrow, wondering why Alex hadn't shared that information with her. Come to think of it, she didn't know *any* of the warrior's skills.

The gnome's voice ended her train of thought. "Curious. Mana overload is a known phenomenon, but I've only read about it in cases of mages trying to cheat their way to more power. Allow me to just..." he trailed off as he dug through his pockets to retrieve a shard of yellow glass. "Your hand, if you please."

Alex obliged, holding out the afflicted appendage. The gnome peered at it through his colored glass, analyzing the jagged lines of glowing white Mana.

"Oh dear," he said. "Oh dear oh dear oh dear." He released Alex's hand as he turned to gaze at Eve's torso.

She tugged her shirt down as far as she could without exposing herself to the clinician. "What do you see?"

"As you may know, the Spirit stat represents one's ability to open a space in their soul to contain Mana. When a mage casts a spell, they're channeling it directly from that space into the world itself."

The gnome shook his head, lowering the enchanted glass to look the adventurers in the eye. *"Normally* overload occurs when an idiot purposefully tears a hole in their soul to force more Mana in. The treatment is slow, but most patients recover. Your case isn't normal."

Eve furrowed her brow. "What do you mean?"

"The Mana isn't in your soul at all. It's in your body."

Alex cursed.

"Moving past your friend's foul language," the gnome addressed Eve, "her sentiment is correct. The human body isn't made to store Mana. Build up too much, and you'll explode or burst into flame or experience any number of particularly unpleasant ways to die."

"So we just need to be sure to drain any excess?" Eve asked, remembering how they'd killed the spider.

"That's a start. It'll keep you alive for the time being, but human flesh isn't meant to *channel* Mana either. Regular healing might help, but you *will* eventually burn yourself out."

Eve chewed her lower lip as she thought through the gnome's words. Alex spoke up. "So what are we supposed to do?"

"My professional recommendation would be to replace the skill that's generating Mana as soon as possible. Failing that—as I suspect you might—reach the fourth tier and unlock a magic class. I can't say for certain, but we can hope that developing a natural pool might redirect the Mana into your soul."

Alex scowled. "So your solution is to level up and hope the problem goes away?"

The gnome shrugged. "I'm sorry, but I can't help you. You're not cursed, and as far as your classes are concerned, this may even be a good thing."

Eve exhaled. "Alright. Thank you. We'll—um—we'll

figure something out."

The vertically challenged clinician nodded, turning to open up the door back into the waiting room. "I wish you the best of luck. If you *do* find out where your secondary quests lead, please come back and let me know. It'll be useful information should someone else turn up with your condition."

"We will," Eve said, ushering a still-smoldering Alex from the examination room. "Good—um—good luck with your other patients."

He gave her a half-hearted smile. "Never a dull moment." With a quiet shrug, he unceremoniously turned to call in the next unlucky patient.

Eve and Alex waited until they'd stepped back into the busy street before discussing the meeting. "Well that was useless," the warrior started.

"I wouldn't say that," said Eve. "We learned the serum forced Mana into our bodies instead of our souls, and that we can fix it by leveling up."

"We can *maybe* fix it by leveling up. For all we know we'll keep getting abilities that generate Mana until we explode."

"If that compound was a death sentence, it wouldn't have come with its own quest," Eve insisted. "We just have to figure out..." She trailed off as a notification flashed in her periphery.

"I got it too," Alex said, her eyes turning blue with the screen's reflection. Eve's followed suit.

Secondary Quest Stage Complete: Discover the Serum's Effects
+1000 exp!
Stage Two: Adapt to the changes.

"Well there you go," Eve said. "The quest agrees. We just

need to wait and level up a bit and make sure to vent any excess Mana when we build up too much."

"I don't like it. Just waiting and leveling up doesn't sound like much of an adaptation to me—we were already doing that."

"In that case, you can start worrying about how to get rid of built-up Mana without a huge explosion." Eve didn't wait for a reply as she turned to stride down the cobblestone road away from the institute.

"And where do you think you're going?" Alex called after her.

"I need a new weapon, and I still have some silver left over after that fine," she answered over her shoulder. "I'm going shopping."

Chapter 24

Shopping!

Eve found Wes waiting for her at the mouth of Emerald Street, so named for the viridian hues that glimmered across the cobble. The other colors of the rainbow as cast by the towering glass walls were still present, but this particular avenue's position within the city lent itself to the greener tones. Eve couldn't begin to understand why.

The "how was the clinic?" was only half-formed in Wes's mouth by the time Eve stepped right past him to attack the pack on his back.

"What are you..." the bulky mage managed as Eve rooted through his belongings.

"Ah-hah!" she cheered as her hand found one of a half-dozen parchment-wrapped parcels. She gave him a victorious smirk as she unwrapped the strawberry scone. She took a bite.

The perfect blend of juicy strawberries and soft pastry and oh so much sugar washed over her tongue. Her head lolled back and her shoulders un-tensed and she let out an exaggerated moan.

Wes rolled his eyes. "Who's overdramatic now?"

"I think I'm the *perfect* amount of dramatic." Eve blew

through his incredulous look. "Did you really think you could hide them from me?"

"How silly of me." Wes shook his head. "How could I forget your **Scone Detection** passive?"

Eve swallowed her second bite of scone, reaching up to pat Wes on the back. "That's why I'm the hero and you're the trusty companion."

"Last I checked, you're the one who can't even step foot in a bakery."

"Which is exactly why I need my trusty companion to run errands for me. To hells with the blightmaw dragon, your real quest is to keep me supplied with scones."

"Something tells me killing the dragon would be the easier of the two." Wes laughed.

"Maybe for the low cost of a lifetime supply of strawberry scones, I, the legendary hero, will help with your little dragon problem."

Wes snorted. "Why don't you worry about that once you've fixed your little exploding problem?"

"What do you think we're doing here?" Eve stopped outside a simple shop with a picture of an anvil carved into the door. "This the place?"

Wes nodded, swinging open the wooden door to usher Eve inside. "Yep. I stopped by four different smithies while you were at the clinic. She's the best."

Eve surveyed the array of weapons and armor lining the walls as she stepped up to the unmanned counter. "Did you judge them based on some secret blacksmith's son knowledge or by just **Appraising** them and picking the highest level?"

"A little of both. Half the smiths in this city are too high level for me to **Appraise**." He unceremoniously picked a bronze bell off the countertop and rang it.

The woman who appeared was perhaps the most stereotypical blacksmith Eve had ever seen. Her black hair was cut short to keep errant sparks from igniting it, her skin coated in a thick layer of black soot, and her frame stout enough Eve might've thought her part dwarf if such a thing were possible. Her **Appraise** was promising.

Level ?? Arcane Smith
 Rare Tier 4 Class

How does a blacksmith even get to level fifty? Eve wondered.

The woman's gruff voice pulled her from her thoughts. "What do you want?"

Wes fished the three remaining Burendian Mana cores from his pack while Eve explained, "I need new weapons. A sword for me and a spear for my friend. They need to be able to store and discharge raw Mana, hence the cores."

"No."

Eve furrowed her brow. "What?"

"I said no," the woman barked. "I'll do the spear, but there's no way in hells I'm letting you leave with a sword in your hand."

"Then I'll go somewhere else."

She shrugged. "Any smith worth their salt will tell you the same thing. I'm sure some idiot will take your money, but the smart ones don't let buyers make that kind of mistake. Dead adventurers don't make good return customers."

"What are you talking about?"

The *Arcane Smith* leaned in, looking at Eve dead on. "You're a *Striker*. Means your entire class is built around dashing in, getting a few quick hits, and getting out. At that kind of speed, a sword'll get stuck in the first thing you hit."

Eve's eyes widened as she remembered the fight with the managorged hares, when *exactly* that had happened. "Um—okay—no sword. What do you recommend?"

The woman looked her up and down. "You don't need reach because you have mobility, and you don't need a long blade because you won't be parrying any time soon. Since you got three cores there, I'd say a spear for your friend and a pair of daggers for you. I'd also recommend a mace or flail to go with them, but that'll be more expensive, and you wouldn't want it enchanted like that."

"Why not?"

She slammed a closed fist into her open palm. "Blunt weapon explodes with Mana, you'll lose half your force to just knocking it away from whatever it hit." Her two hands flew away from each other at equal speed.

With a nod, she replaced the fist with a pointed finger, sticking it between those of her open hand. "Stick a blade in 'em, and more of the blast will deal real damage." She pantomimed a blast forcing her fingers apart.

Eve shook her head, understanding the logic and feeling the meager supply of silver in her pocket. "Alright, no mace for now. And wouldn't a dagger get just as stuck as a sword?"

The *Smith* snorted. "Not in anything *you'll* be fighting. Least not for another tier."

Eve raised an eyebrow, thinking of Alex's knife getting stuck in the carapace of the leygorged widow. Then again, she *shouldn't* have attempted to fight that monstrosity. "Okay, daggers it is. How much would it be to make two knives and a spear with the Mana cores?"

"To make? A hundred silver. More if you want anything fancy. A third of that to modify some pieces my apprentice made for practice with those cores of yours."

Wes stepped in. "I'd like to see those pieces."

She gestured to a table near the back piled high with simple blades. "O' course. They're good work; just every adventurer in this gods-damned city thinks they need their iron dagger made by a master smith."

Wes rummaged through the pile, looking over each piece for little details Eve never could've gleaned. He returned to the counter with two ten-inch daggers and a basic spearhead.

"You've an eye for quality," the smith admitted as she glanced over the items. "That'll be thirty-five silver—twenty-two for the daggers, thirteen for the speartip. Forty-five if you want a steel shaft on that spear."

Eve balked at the steep price tag but nonetheless reached into her pocket to dig out all but three of her remaining silver. "Can you cover the spear and shaft?" she asked of Wes. "Alex will pay you back."

He grumbled as he counted out the requisite coin but deposited them on the counter all the same.

"Good," the woman huffed. "Come back tomorrow and I'll have your weapons."

Eve thanked the *Arcane Smith* for her quick work and sound advice before leading the way back out onto the green-tinted cobblestones. She instinctively wrinkled her nose at the city's oppressive stench for the few seconds before she grew re-accustomed to it.

Wes squinted as the crystalline walls refracted sunlight directly into his eyes. "So where to next?"

"I need clothes," she replied, "but between the speeding ticket and those daggers my cut from the dungeon job is down to three silver. Maybe I could find someone with some hand-me-downs or old rags they'd be willing to sell. *Anything* would be better than what I've got." She tugged at the torn and stained blouse she'd worn since leaving Nowherested.

"Yeah," Wes said, extending a hand to gesture at a ragged boy picking pockets in the street. "I think that street urchin is better-dressed than you."

"Well, we can't all leave home decked out in ancient heirlooms from half the town."

Wes pointed where his left shoulder pad was coming apart at the seam. "To be fair, most of this shit is barely fit for a vagabond."

"At least you can afford to replace it. Hells, for a hundred silver you could get some enchanted armor. I can't even buy *clothes*."

"Well… technically you can." Wes stopped short below a sign reading *Thander's Threads*. He reached into his pocket. "The bakery isn't the only stop I made this morning. It turns out one minor dungeon core and two Burendian Mana cores sell for a grand total of sixty-five silver. I spent one on strawberry scones, so your cut comes out to—"

"Sixteen silver," Eve finished for him, her face already splitting into a wide grin. She leapt at him, wrapping the oversized mage in a tight hug. "Thank you, Wes."

He stiffened under the embrace. "It's—um—really, I didn't do anything. Hells, we wouldn't have *any* money if you hadn't talked us into going to the ruins." He pulled away, handing over her share of the silver. "Now go buy whatever you need."

Eve placed a hand on the doorknob to the clothier's before turning back. "Why didn't you lead with this?"

"I was going to," he said, "but you skipped straight to the scones. Besides, I wasn't going to miss an opportunity to make fun of you for looking like a street urchin."

She laughed, "Just like I wasn't going to miss a chance to say you look like you're wearing the guild's trash heap."

Wes smiled. "On that note, I've got some shopping of my own to do. I'll see you back at the guild hall. We just cleared our first dungeon, after all—first round's on me."

Eve watched him turn and stride down the emerald street, waiting for him to disappear around a bend before stepping into the shop herself.

The look of disgust the man behind the counter gave her

was all the salesmanship he needed.

Eve's nineteen silver bought her four simple but well-made blouses, several sets of undergarments, a new belt, and two pairs of sturdy 'adventuring pants' as the flamboyant tailor had called them. Thander, as she assumed he was named, even insisted she purchase an above-the-knee cotton skirt for nights on the town, citing that there was more to life than gritty dungeons and deadly combat.

Or, rather, his exact words were more along the line of, "Girl, those hips need all the help they can get. What you have is legs—use them! You gotta have some *fun* before you're an old fart like me."

In her state of combined embarrassment and shock at the tailor's outrageous comments, Eve neglected to mention that with his dyed hair and pierced ears, he didn't look a day over thirty.

Unfortunately, her limited funds didn't stretch quite far enough to cover a replacement for her rapidly degrading boots, but they at least would last for another job or two. Thander, of course, made a point of recommending "the greatest cobbler of all time" and assuring she would visit as soon as she returned from whatever deadly mission came next.

In the end, she left *Thander's Threads* in a fresh blouse and her new skirt, the clothier stepping away to burn her old clothes the moment she left the changing room. Arms laden with her purchases and pockets once again weighed down with only two copper pieces and an ivory knight, Eve weaved through the crowded Emerald Street.

She made it less than two blocks before a familiar voice drove her to halt.

"Fifty silver for a fucking spear? What kind of scam are you running?"

Eve paused, cursing to herself as she realized her

mistake. Of *course* Alex would go shopping on her own. With a sigh, she stepped into *Armelia's Weapon Emporium*. Sure enough, she found the *Survivor* yelling at the clerk.

"Alex…"

"Hold on, Eve," the warrior snapped. "I'm negotiating."

She cocked an eyebrow. "Negotiating? It looks like you're waving a spear at the poor man."

Alex's eyes turned upward at the for-sale weapon she held over the counter. She lowered the tip away from the salesman.

"Okay," Eve exhaled. "Why don't you put the spear down? You don't need it."

"Well of course I don't need *this* overpriced piece of crap, but I do need *a* spear. But that's not the point—"

"No, that *is* the point. Or more importantly"—Eve gestured at the spear's tip—"you won't be buying *that* point."

Alex glared at her.

"Gods below." Eve paled. "I'm turning into Wes." She shook her head. "Look, I meant it to be a surprise, but we commissioned a new spear for you. Got a blacksmith to turn some of those Mana cores into weapons that can store Mana."

"What?" Alex froze. "Eve, that's…"

"Don't thank me yet. I couldn't afford it, so I told Wes you'd pay him back." She jerked her thumb at the salesman behind the counter. "Still less than half what this guy's charging, though."

"Well what are we waiting for?" Alex dropped the too-expensive armament, its steel shaft clanging against the wooden floor. "Let's go."

Eve followed her out of the cluttered store, scurrying to catch up with the warrior's long strides. "No, it's—uh—it'll be ready tomorrow."

"Oh." Alex stopped. "Damn. I was hoping to get some

practice in with the new weapon."

"I mean…" Eve stepped in front of her. "You don't *have* to practice today. We're all getting together for drinks at the guild hall tonight…"

"You know I don't do that, Eve."

"You can't keep distancing yourself. Look, I know you're still recovering from what happened with your old team, but we aren't them."

"Eve, I…"

The *Striker* sighed. "We just survived a gods-damned dungeon, Alex. We got a huge payout in silver and exp, and you even got your *Rare* class. If that's not worth celebrating, I don't know what is."

Alex didn't reply.

"Okay," Eve said. "You don't have to spend time with us if you don't want to. I hope you'll change your mind." She shrugged. "If you do, you know where we'll be."

With a quiet breath, Eve turned to stride away from the quiet *Survivor*. Her skirt swayed in the breeze as she navigated the busy streets towards the guild hall. Eccentric or otherwise, Thander had been right about one thing.

With or without her warrior friend, tonight Eve was going to have some gods-damned *fun*.

Chapter 25

Jet!

Eve awoke to a world of pain. Her head throbbed with the gallop of a thousand stallions, each kicking up a cloud of sand from the desert that was her throat. She reached for the cup of water she kept by the side of her bed, but found it already knocked to the floor, its contents long dried.

She groaned.

In a battle that should've rewarded exp for all its difficulty, she fought her way to her feet, keeping care to maintain both her unsteady footing and her unstable stomach. At least her chest didn't hurt.

She braced herself against the wall as she swung the door open, stumbling more than stepping into the hall. Through the hazy gaze of her squinted eyes, Eve barely spotted the familiar set of white robes.

"Healing," she wheezed.

Preston stopped at the top of the stairs, turning back to spot her. "Eve! I—um—right. Let me just..." He raised a hand and the hall flashed gold.

Eve didn't even wince as Ayla's light coursed through her, patching up her various wounds all the while judging her for the actions which had inflicted them. She simply stood as the goddess of mercy rifled her every rash decision and impure thought, forgiving them all with the same vigor as always.

By the time Her divinity vacated the premises, Preston was gone.

Eve pressed on down the wooden steps, too distracted by thoughts of breakfast to wonder why a priest who normally slept at Ayla's cathedral had been in the guild hall at such an early hour. She found Wes in the common room with a plate of eggs and meat.

"G'mornin'," he greeted through a mouthful of sausage.

"Ugh," Eve replied, snatching his water-skin as she sat. She drained half of it before speaking. "What happened last night?"

"Whiskey happened last night. Among other things. The main one *you* need to know about is over there." He pointed over his shoulder at the wreckage of a wooden table stacked upon the log pile to be burned with the rest of the firewood.

"Shit."

Wes smiled. "Let's just say you aren't the first adventurer to get drunk and destroy guild furniture, but you're almost *certainly* the first to do it by exploding."

Eve checked her Mana to find it resting at a neat 10/0. It ticked up as she took a bite of sausage. "Well that explains why my chest didn't hurt when I woke up this morning. They're not kicking me out, are they?"

"Nope," Wes chuckled. "Like I said, you're not the first. If they kicked out everyone who broke one of their tables, they'd run out of adventurers pretty quick. They just make you pay for it." He snapped his fingers. "Speaking of which, you owe me five silver."

"Only five?" Eve raised an eyebrow.

He shrugged. "They buy it cheap. No point splurging on nice tables if drunken idiots are just gonna destroy them."

"Well this particular drunken idiot will pay you back once we finish the next job."

"Broke again?"

"Yep," Eve sighed. "Turns out speeding tickets and custom daggers and new clothes are *expensive*." She didn't mention the two copper pieces that still rested in her pocket. Those had one purpose and one purpose only.

"In that case, you know where the desk is."

As she turned to see who sat behind said desk, Eve threw her head back, groaning for the third time that morning. "How is that clerk *always* there? Don't they take shifts or something?"

"Hells if I know. High-levels work in mysterious ways."

"If by 'in mysterious ways' you mean 'at the front desk,' then yeah." Eve chuckled at Wes's annoyed look. "Alright, alright, fine." She pushed herself to her feet. "I'll go negotiate our way into another job."

"Fair luck, brave hero!" Wes called after her. "Keep your wits as you venture into the dragon's maw!"

Bereft of witty replies, Eve gave him a rude gesture over her shoulder as she approached the desk.

"Let me guess," the receptionist greeted her, "you can't afford to pay for the table you destroyed?"

"You know, most people consider eavesdropping rude."

"Who said anything about eavesdropping? Half this guild couldn't afford to buy a new table."

Eve gave the woman the most incredulous look she could muster. "Do you have a job for me or not?"

"Ooh, the *Common*-er thinks she's hot shit because she survived a dungeon. Did you fail to satisfy your death wish?"

Eve bristled. "You know as well as I do we only took that job because I got slapped with a bullshit speeding ticket."

"And you're only taking this one because you broke a table."

Eve sighed, forcing herself to relax her shoulders and unclench her fists. "Whatever I did to piss you off, I'm sorry. I know I'm not from here and I'm new to the guild but for fuck's sake I'm trying. You don't have to be such an *asshole* about it."

The woman tilted her head. "Alright. Apology accepted." She spun around to rifle through a file cabinet behind her, withdrawing a single sheet of paper. "Here you go. It's a solo job, but I'm *sure* you can handle it. Pay's ten silver."

Eve narrowed her gaze at the rude clerk's sudden about-face but declined to comment. Further antagonizing the tier 4 with control over her jobs didn't feel like a wise choice. Instead, she snatched the parchment off the woman's desk, muttered a quiet "thanks," and made her way for the exit.

"Where are you off to?" Wes called after her.

"Solo job!" she answered from where she stood with her hand on the door. "Just gotta run some errands first."

"Try not to die!"

"No promises," she laughed. "Enjoy your day off."

Wes raised a forkful of sausage as if in toast as Eve stepped out into the busy street.

The *Striker* lingered just outside the guild hall, considering which of her two destinations she should visit first. In the end, it was the chance the blacksmith hadn't quite finished with her daggers yet that made her decision. A goal in mind and a task at hand, Eve turned to weave her way through the passersby to find the practice field.

She had an ability to test.

* * *

The loose sand crunched beneath Eve's boots as she stood alone at the back corner of the training yard. Clangs and grunts and shouts echoed all about her as guards and soldiers and adventurers alike sparred against training dummies and each other. Eve paid them little mind.

Her eyes flashed blue as she reread the skill description.

Active Ability - Jet
500 Stamina
Momentum is a tool just like any other, and you've learned to wield it. Massively increase or decrease your personal momentum.

Sure would be nice if I could spend Mana on this, she mused, trying to ignore the spread of the white lines across her skin.

Truth be told, she'd been remiss in her duties as a teammate and adventurer to ignore the ability for so long. At eighteen hundred, she had more than enough Stamina to pay its hefty price, and her list of excuses not to maximize her toolkit had run dry.

Shaking her head as she dismissed the azure screen, Eve mentally prepared herself for a long morning of falling on her face.

She grit her teeth. She bent her knees. She leaned forward. *Here goes.*

Eve **Jetted** forward.

She shot across the training yard like from a cannon. Her heart raced. Her torso pitched forward. She jerked her foot forward, just barely catching the ground in time to make her first stride.

There would be no second.

Even with her **Haste**-empowered run speed, Eve's legs failed to keep up with her body's momentum. She tumbled.

The coarse sand and packed earth scraped against her bare palms as she caught herself, skidding a dozen feet down the training ground. At least her face remained unscathed. For now.

"Okay," she muttered to herself as she stood, shaking her skinned hands to either side. "Gotta **Charge!** *before* using **Jet**."

She brushed a tangled lock of hair behind her ear as she reset for another attempt. She readied herself. She breathed. She activated **Charge!**, keeping still as the first few seconds of the ability ticked away.

And off she went.

Eve hit her maximum speed in less than a second, **Jet** accelerating her forward beyond what even her **Surefooted**-enhanced traction could ever manage. Wind rocketed past her, sending her hair billowing as her feet shot forward to catch each stride. She made it three steps this time before her legs lost pace with the rest of her.

In all it took four attempts before Eve got a handle on the fundamentals of **Jet,** including a twenty-minute break halfway through to recoup her Stamina. The trick, as she found, was to hit the first step at a backwards angle so her knees could absorb some of the superfluous momentum. Perhaps she could maintain the full speed once her **Haste** scaled a bit more, but for now she needed to slow herself.

Her palms stung and her wrists ached from the series of falls, but she took pride in the fact not once had she caught herself with her face.

Gods-damned **Ethereal Metabolism**, she cursed to herself during one of her recharge breaks. *I can't eat to restore Stamina because I'll end up overloaded on Mana too.* A quick check told Eve that her meager breakfast had already imparted over fifty points of the pulsing light.

Her stomach growled even as she reminded herself of the cost of Mana burn. She'd exploded enough times for one day.

Pushing herself to her feet as her Stamina closed in on

half full—high as it would get without food or sleep—Eve continued on to the next maneuver: **Jetting** to a standstill.

She managed this one without a single tumble, though her first attempt did send her stumbling backward as her legs instinctively moved to keep running even as the rest of her stopped short. The sensation itself was strange. It wasn't as if she collided with a wall or skidded to a halt. To Eve's eyes it seemed the world itself had simply decided to stop moving around her.

The key problem she came across with the technique wasn't one of balance or traction, but of convenience. With every **Jet**, her *body* leapt into or out of motion, but her clothes lagged behind. In her form-fitting pants and well-fastened blouse, the effect was little different than a bit of air resistance. She quietly praised her earlier judgment to wear the outfit, imagining how troublesome a skirt would be in such a situation.

The real trouble was her hair. Sure, the wind blew it back and away from her face as she **Charged!** forward, but each time she **Jetted** to a halt it flew into her eyes—an annoyance for now, a possible death sentence in a fight. She'd have to buy some pins and ties for it once she had money to spend.

Her final step—so she began after yet another Stamina break—was to put the skill through its paces. She started with the most obvious use case: dodging an attack.

Her tests proved... less than stellar. However she contorted her body or placed her feet, time and time again Eve found herself skidding on her hands or shoulder after a failed sideward **Jet**. The ability simply didn't leave enough time to rotate her body before sending her into the dirt.

She was, after hours of trying and failing and waiting to recover, able to develop a sort of compromise: jumping. Eve found that if she leapt and turned her body midair, she could activate **Jet** to shoot off in the new direction, hitting the ground running with the same minor slowing method as before.

The maneuver required some setup, precious seconds she might not have in the middle of a fight, but even with limited control, the ability to turn on a copper could be lifesaving. Eve ended the session on that win.

That afternoon, as she caught her ragged breath and allowed the late summer sun to dry the sweat off her brow, Eve's mind wandered through the less conventional uses for the costly ability. She daydreamed of **Jetting** upward for a mighty leap or backward to evade an attack.

Of course she didn't attempt such foolishness. She may have been inexperienced, but she wasn't stupid enough to try complex acrobatics without a healer present. Another time, perhaps.

Eve walked away from the training yard battered, bruised, scraped up, and bleeding, but she smiled nonetheless. She knew every skinned elbow and twisted ankle here was one avoided in the heat of battle, and she'd take that trade any day she could.

Besides, as Eve stepped along the uneven cobblestones of the glass city, she had another reason for grinning from ear to ear.

The time had come to retrieve her new daggers.

Chapter 26

A Little Off the Top

"Gods fucking—" Eve cursed as she slit the tail off yet another sewer rat. "I swear by Loia's bloody middle finger if I ever see that receptionist's smirk again, I'll wring her fucking throat, tier four be damned."

Sewage sloshed against her chest as she tied the severed tail to her belt, making nine by her count. *Solo job my ass,* she swore internally this time. *A level two could do this.* As it was, Eve avoided using *any* of her abilities as she waded through the filth. **Charge!** had splashed enough of it onto her face for her to learn *that* lesson.

Given the stench of the streets above, Eve had been surprised Lynthia even had a sewer. She wasn't any more. Having seen the crumbling stone walls, the complete lack of any sort of maintenance walkway, and of course the unmoving chest-high river of shit, Eve instead wondered how the city didn't smell *worse*.

The ground—for lack of a better term—beneath her feet was the worst. Eve tried not to think about the sticky substance that clung to the soles of her boots with every step. *Just one more rat to go,* she told herself.

Eve spun the dagger in her hand, admiring its sleek

form and the mastery with which the Burendian Mana core had slotted into the crossguard. She **Appraised** it for the ninth time that day.

Manacharge Dagger
  Rarity: Rare
  Mana: 18/500

Its twin at her waist sat uncharged, ready to store the magical results of her next meal—another thing she tried not to think about. The smell of sewage didn't mix well with daydreams of dinner.

Her hair clung to the back of her neck, tied back with the first rat tail she'd claimed. She'd already managed to splash too much of the vile sludge onto her chestnut locks; the concern at this point was keeping it out of her face. The makeshift tie did little good.

An echo tugged at the edge of Eve's attention. She froze, straining her ears to track the sound: light scratches across stone. She smiled.

The *Striker* pushed on through the horrid waste, dagger at the ready as she crept towards the skittering rat. She spotted it in her periphery, crawling along a crack in the stone wall. She held her breath.

Eve lunged, swinging her weapon in a sideward strike. The creature squealed and stilled as a notification appeared in her vision.

You have defeated Level 3 Sewer Rat: +0 exp!

Eve sputtered as the motion sent her hair flying into her face, leaving a trail of filth across her cheek. "You know what? Fuck this." She grabbed the end of her ponytail, pulling it above her head with her left hand. Her right raised the dagger to it.

A single, quick motion sent the razor-sharp blade through the chestnut strands, severing them. Eve reclaimed the rat tail holding them together before letting her once shoulder-length hair fall to the sludge.

She left it there, floating atop the river of sewage as she cut her final trophy and waded away to claim her reward.

* * *

Eve slammed the door to the adventurer's guild behind her, storming through the common room with her fistful of rat tails. *Shadowblades* and *Paladins* and *Occultists* alike turned away and pinched their noses as she passed, rightfully averse to her stench. Eve cared little, practically allowing herself to drip filth onto the floor. Let them all see what she'd been through.

Curiously enough, the other guildsmen were happy to step out of her way as she approached the counter. Being covered in sewage had its perks.

Eve slapped her severed vermin-bits on the wooden desk. "Ten tails, as requested."

The clerk looked up at her with raised eyebrows. She didn't smirk. She didn't laugh. She didn't roll her eyes. "Well done," she simply said, sliding ten silver coins across the table. "Your pay."

Eve scowled but didn't comment.

"You know," the clerk added, "some adventurers have never trudged through a sewer to kill a few rats, and it really shows." The *Striker* opened her mouth to retort, but the receptionist beat her to it with an uncharacteristically warm look. "Welcome to the guild."

Eve only managed a furrowed brow and a surprised "thank you" before the clerk called up the next person in line. Taking her dismissal for what it was, she turned towards the narrow stairs, replaying the brief conversation in her mind as she embarked on the monumental task of washing up.

Two baths, a silver coin spent on *laundry*, and an entire bar of soap later, Eve sat at a newly purchased table in the guild common room as a certain *Priestess* fussed over her hair with a pair of scissors.

"It's such a shame," Preston rambled as he tidied up the rough cut her dagger had made. "You have such a lovely chestnut. I'd hate to see it turned into a mess."

"Chestnut," Eve scoffed. "It's fucking brown."

"Speak for yourself." Wes ran a hand through his own hair, now longer than Eve's where it rested just over his ears. "Yours may be brown, but *mine* is roasted chestnut."

She rolled her eyes. "Our hair's the same color."

"Yep." Preston smiled as he leaned down to confirm his trim on each side of Eve's head was level. "And that color is chestnut."

Eve shut her eyes as the healer moved on to evening out her bangs. "How did you even learn to do this?"

"My da's a *Barber*. Level nineteen. He taught me the basics, even let me practice on my brothers." Preston chuckled. "You should've seen some of the messes I've made."

Eve's eyebrows shot up, eliciting a sharp "hold still!" from the healer. "I hope you're not making a mess of me."

"If you keep moving, I might," he replied. "Don't worry. I've had *lots* of practice. You're going to end up with a bit of a boyish style 'cause that's all I know, but that's what you get for cutting it so short."

Per his instructions, Eve stopped herself from shrugging. "Honestly, as long as it stays out of my face and I don't look like a *complete* mess, I don't really care."

"Well it's good you have me," Preston said as he carefully snipped along. "Lesson number one is never cut your own hair."

"Hold on," Wes stepped in. "I'm still caught up on the earlier bit. You have brothers?"

"Three of 'em," the *Priestess* replied. "All older. Believe me, I'm lucky Da was there to stop them beating me up whenever I cut their hair. I deserved it."

"Where are they now?"

"Oh, here and there." Preston flourished with his scissors. "Danny's in the city guard, Reid's in a banking office somewhere, and Charlie's working as an apprentice to a local alchemist. Don't tell him I said this, but I swear he's got a crush on his boss. Anyway, we all get together for drinks every now and again, but I don't really see them that much these days."

"That's a shame," said Wes. "I'd love to meet them sometime. Do they—uh—know about your quest?"

Eve narrowed her eyes at the question, remembering how cagey the healer had been about his life quest.

"They do," he answered curtly before falling silent. The conversation stalled as Preston seemed to devote his focus to the task at hand before suddenly stepping back with a grand flourish. "And done!"

Eve ran a hand over the back of her head, feeling the sharpness of freshly cut hair. It stopped above her ears, just long enough to lie flat on the top of her head. Her bangs swept to the side, leaving her forehead completely exposed. Nothing about the new look excited Eve, but the newfound shortness would definitely make life easier.

"Thanks, Preston," she said. "I'm just going to assume it looks nice." Absent a mirror, she couldn't say more, but she had every faith in the healer's abilities.

"You're very welcome," he called over his shoulder as he crossed the common room to fetch a broom.

Eve took it from his outstretched hand, volunteering herself for the job of sweeping up the hair trimmings. "So —um—you were talking about that quest of yours?"

Wes and Preston shared a quiet look before the *Priestess* scowled and turned back to Eve. "It's not a big deal. I'm more interested in yours, actually. Why haven't you completed it yet?"

She shrugged. "Because the universe is conspiring to stop me? Besides, what would I even do if I finished it?"

"The same things you're doing now? You don't need a relevant quest to be an adventurer. And hey, once you've fetched your bread or whatever, you can always visit the Stones again to pick up another *Secondary* quest."

"I don't know, Preston."

The healer smiled. "You should at least keep trying. Look at it this way: if the universe is conspiring to stop you, you might as well make it *work* for it."

Eve planted her foot. "You know what? You're right."

Wes stood. "Eve, I'm not sure that's a good idea. I don't think the Stones are going to let you finish your quest until you actually do something *Legendary*. You shouldn't push it. Remember what happened in Ponsted?"

She shook the image of the burning bakery from her mind. "No, no, I should go. Hells, maybe with my *Shatterfate* class I can actually do it." Eve tossed the broom handle to Wes, who fumbled it twice before catching it. "I'll be back in a bit!"

The *Striker* turned, striding across the common room. As she swung open the door, she made a point of ignoring Wes's words of warning, choosing instead to heed Preston's call of "good luck!"

From where she stood on the cobblestones of Lynthia, the fallen sun cast twilit gloom across the streets and alleys. The final glimmers of sunlight still graced the very tops of the glass walls, sending brilliant beams of orange and yellow and pink across the city's rooftops. Eve picked a direction and started walking.

Late as the hour may have been on the bakery-adjusted scale, the *Striker* knew for certain of an establishment that sold ales as well as breads. With any luck they'd still have a loaf in stock.

She kept her spirits high as she wandered the streets, looking on as butchers and leatherworkers and carpenters disappeared into their homes and the scavengers and streetwalkers and drunkards took their place.

Gone was the symphony of banging hammers and haggling shoppers and shouting merchants. Now was the time for the opening chords of the songs of night. Songs crafted of professional *Bards*, of raucous laughter, and of lustful wails. The city at night was a panoply of vice and crime and joy and love, and Eve reveled in it.

The bakery came all too soon.

Golden lamplight spilled through the windows of *Breads and Brews*, all the sign Eve needed of their ongoing business. A smile crossed her face as she stepped ever closer. Her heart began to pound as she imagined what kind of quest reward she might receive. It was a *Legendary* quest, after all.

It's too easy, she thought. With every stride she imagined the building going up in smoke, or selling their final loaf, or shutting down for the night. Eve shook her head as she imagined something moving in the shadows of the alley behind the bakery. *Just a cat,* she told herself as she stepped past the alley's mouth.

It was no cat.

An arm shot from the darkness, snagging her wrist with brutal speed. Eve only managed half a gasp of shock before a meaty hand slammed over her mouth. Her heart raced. Adrenaline and panic joined forces as they coursed through her. She reached her free hand for a dagger, but a second figure emerged from the alley. Two thick arms wrapped around her from behind, holding her in place as she squirmed.

Eve panicked.

Her mind raced through her every option, cursing

herself for storing all her Mana in the weapons. Unable to reach them, she was without it. She thought to **Charge!** away but the hands which bound her proved as iron.

A masculine grunt rang out behind her as she activated **Jet**, but her captor held.

"Fuck!" he swore. "She's squirmy."

"Hold on, hold on," his companion rambled.

Eve twisted and kicked in desperation as she heard the sound of a stopper coming uncorked. Her efforts proved in vain.

Her final thoughts as the stranger held the vial to her nose were many. The first, and most pressing, was that these were no simple thugs. To overcome **Jet** implied a level of strength she'd not yet faced. The second were the words the man said as a fog began to overcome her.

"Sleep now, girly. Boss wants to have a word with ya."

Just before the spreading fog could overcome her consciousness, an image appeared in the corner of her vision, flashing a familiar blue.

Legendary Quest Milestone Reached: Be Kidnapped!
+8000 exp!

And the world went black.

Chapter 27

Not That Kind of Job Offer

The first thing Eve saw as the fog began to drift clear of her mind was a flashing blue notification. *Gods damnit,* she cursed to herself. *That's three times in less than a week. I really gotta stop passing out.* Whether or not being drugged by a pair of burly men dragging her into an alley counted as a valid excuse for blacking out was an entirely separate matter.

Some combination of unwilling and unable to push past the lingering lethargy that still clung to her body, Eve forwent rising from the soft surface on which she lay. For now, she kept her eyes closed and opened the message.

Level Up!
Level Up!

Ability Upgraded!
   Passive Ability - Battle-hardened
   Gain poison resistance!

Well that would've been fucking nice, Eve mused. Just like with the explosion resistance, her skill had decided to upgrade the second *after* she needed it.

Ability Upgraded!
  Active Ability - Jet
  Jet in any direction!

Eve furrowed her brow as she reread the ability. *Now that is interesting.* As far she knew, she already could **Jet** in any direction, at least so much as she'd tested. *Does this mean I can Jet up to launch myself into the air? Or use it to catch myself mid-fall?* Scenes of leaping off high cliffs only to **Jet** to a halt just before hitting the ground flashed through Eve's mind. It sounded like fun.

A sultry voice pulled Eve from her reverie. "Good morning, my sweet. Did you have a nice nap?"

The *Striker* snapped her status screen shut, pushing herself upright to find she sat on a bed of pillows. A cursory scan of the room displayed an abundance of luxury and an awful lot of red. Crimson curtains of flowing silk draped across the corners, segmenting little nooks of plush cushions like Eve's own. Embroidered velvet—also red—caressed her exposed palms as she leaned against them.

The source of the voice—or so Eve assumed—was the chamber's only other occupant. Despite the silver sheen of her hair, the woman's skin was free of wrinkles. She sat upon an ornate mahogany desk, strewn about it as if posing to show off her curves. It might've made for an alluring sight if not for her choice of attire.

Her dress was, for lack of a better term, frumpy. The baby blue monstrosity sagged in all the wrong places, covering the woman's flawless skin in a way that even a Bishop of Ayla might find overly modest. Wrinkled sleeves stretched all the way to her wrists, ending in a poof of white lace that Eve found tacky if not outright hideous.

"Where am I?" she eventually managed.

"My office," the stranger replied. "I have a few questions for you."

"And you are?"

"Call me Agatha." She smiled, her gorgeously made-up face parting to reveal a practically glimmering set of pearly teeth.

Before replying, Eve decided now was as good a time as any to **Appraise** her captor.

Level ?? Lady of Whispers
Unique Tier ?? Class

Great, it's the man of the fucking mists all over again, Eve cursed to herself for what felt like the hundredth time that day. "Alright, Agatha. You're free to ask, but I have questions of my own."

"Ooh, trading questions. I do love this game. A bit overdone, but that's true of all the classics, I suppose." The woman's smile shifted from alluring to predatory in a moment. "Why don't you begin?"

Eve refrained from pointing out Agatha just *had* begun on the basis that technicalities were no fun. "Where are we? For real this time."

"The upper floor of the Gilded Hyacinth, one of my establishments. Fourth building down on Vermillion Way in the grand city of Lynthia."

Eve opened her mouth to speak, but the stranger held up a shushing finger. The muted cries of pleasure that penetrated the floor beneath them in the momentary silence told Eve all she needed to know about what kind of 'establishment' Agatha meant.

"Now," a venomous sweetness filled the woman's voice, "my informants tell me you took an off-the-books solo job for the guild's receptionist. What was it?"

"Huh?" Eve faltered. *"That's* what I'm here for?" She snorted.

"Do you have to ask?"

Eve turned up her palms. "Alright, sure. That clerk's a bitch and she made me wade through the sewer to kill rats."

Agatha's irises flashed gold for a quarter of a second. She tilted her head. "Curious."

Eve furrowed her brow as she asked her next question. "Why do you care about the receptionist?"

"She's up to something. I don't know what or why, but I tell you, my dear, I'm going to find out. She's not tied to any of the players I know. Who does she work for?"

"Um... the guild?" *She's gods-damned paranoid,* Eve mused. The man of the mists *had* told her others would reach out, but she hadn't exactly expected it to happen so soon, nor for it to be a strange old lady spouting conspiracy theories about the guild clerk. Having two goons snatch her in a dark alley didn't seem like an effective recruiting technique, either.

Eve shook her head. "Maybe it has something to do with my speeding ticket. The clerk *was* rather unfazed when I told her about it. She could be colluding with the city guard."

Agatha waved her off. "No, no, that was perfectly legitimate. Speeding is dangerous, you know."

Eve sighed but didn't comment.

The brothel owner continued on to her turn. "Why might she send you my way?"

"What?"

Agatha sighed. "Must I explain it for you, my dear? She knows I keep an eye on this city and that I wouldn't miss an off-the-books job like this. If the job itself wasn't important, she must've intended to arrange our meeting."

"I—um—I really don't know. I don't think she was

thinking that far ahead. She's always been rude to me, and she knew I needed money to pay back my friend after I destroyed a piece of guild property. She was just trying to haze me. You think there's more to it?"

"Was she?" Agatha pressed.

Eve shrugged. "As far as she's concerned, I'm just some *Courier* who worked her way to a *Common* tier three." She smiled. "Do you have need of *Strikers?*"

The strange woman sat upright, her posture immaculate as she stared down at Eve from her seat atop the extravagant desk. "But you aren't, are you? You're far more interesting than that."

"Maybe," Eve said, "but she doesn't know that." She crossed her arms. "I think it's my turn."

"I believe so," Agatha replied. "I'll admit I got a bit lost in that last exchange."

Eve exhaled. "Why kidnap me? You could've just sent me a letter or asked me directly. Hells, I'd be remarkably pissed at you right now if—" She stopped herself before admitting she'd received a milestone for the experience.

"If it weren't for my level?" she assumed. Eve didn't correct her misjudgment. "A number of reasons. Horrible as it may be, the world doesn't bat an eye at a girl being snatched into a dark alley. Mysterious letters from high-levels draw attention. Think of it as a lesson. The next thing you find lurking in the alleyways might not be so hospitable."

"Is that right?" Eve snorted. "How do you live your life if high-levels can't show their faces in public?"

Agatha held up a finger, swinging it side to side as if chastising a child. "No, no, dear thing. It's my turn. What are the details of your quest?"

Interesting, Eve wondered, thinking back to her conversation with the man of the mists. "You don't already know?"

"Why should I?"

Eve raised her eyebrows. "It's a *Legendary* quest to buy a loaf of bread."

Once again the woman's irises flashed gold. Her eyes shot wide open. "So that's why…"

The office fell quiet for some time as Agatha muttered to herself. Eve took the opportunity to ask her next question. "If you knew the receptionist sent me on a job and how to find me in the alley, how could you not know where I went?"

The madam grinned. "I have eyes in the guild hall, not in the sewers. I've found they don't make for interesting rumors. The real question is, what to do with you?"

"You could let me leave?"

"Where's the fun in that?"

Eve sighed. "Alright then, another question. You mentioned 'players.' Who are they and what are they playing?"

Agatha smiled. "You're catching on. It's a game of power and a game of survival. The rules are simple: amass as much wealth and influence as you can without waging open war or otherwise jeopardizing the survival of civilization."

"It sounds like a bunch of bored high-levels squabbling against each other."

Agatha's smile widened as she let out a sharp, salacious laugh. "That's more accurate than you know." She leaned back to reach into an open drawer on the other side of the desk, withdrawing a folded parchment. "To that end, I have a job offer for you."

Eve raised an eyebrow as a particularly loud moan of ecstasy rang out from the floors below. "Not here you don't."

"Oh, no. I'm afraid you wouldn't last a day in this line of work. I have a much more *interesting* path lined up for you."

Eve told her the same thing she told the man of the mists, "I'm not leaving my friends."

"I should hope not. You'll need them. What do you think of this?" She handed over the parchment.

"This is guild paperwork," Eve noted as she scanned the details. "Why not just go through them?"

"So that impolite friend of yours can't interfere. You'll find she's a diligent one."

Eve nodded, failing to remember a time when the rude clerk *wasn't* at her desk. She didn't mention that spending all day behind a desk left little time for whatever schemes the madam seemed to expect. "I'll bring it to my companions, but I can't make any promises. Eight hundred silver is a lot of money, but most of them are still flush from the last job."

Agatha smiled. "Of course. What more could I ask?"

"Is that all?"

"That's all I have for now. You may go, if you wish."

Eve refolded the parchment and slipped it into her pocket, turning away from the desk towards a leather-cushioned door. She paused with her hand on the doorknob, craning her neck back to the strange madam. "Actually, I have one more question, if you don't mind. Why are you dressed like that? You're *clearly* gorgeous, but that dress just…"

Agatha blinked. "My, my. Brave of you to ask a question like that." She gestured down to the hideous dress. "I'll have you know this used to be the height of fashion. I'd say when, but you know a true lady never reveals her age." She scowled. "Then again, a true lady doesn't ask questions out of turn."

Eve opened her mouth to apologize, but the madam beat her to it. "Consider it a favor. I'll ask that question you owe me when next we meet. Whenever that may be." She raised a hand. "Now, please, return to your friends. We wouldn't want them worrying after you."

"I—of course not." Eve turned the handle, swinging open the door to admit yet more overdramatic cries of passion from downstairs.

As the *Striker* moved to exit the ornate office, Agatha called after her. "Oh, and Eve? This could be a wonderful opportunity to prove you're worth that token in your pocket."

Eve froze, stopping herself from asking how she knew about that. She'd already asked one question out of turn. Instead she swallowed and grit her teeth and stepped out into the staircase, shutting the office door behind her.

She wondered, as she passed all manner of sweet boys and working women, whether Agatha had spoken with the man of the mists or simply rifled through her pockets while she was unconscious. As she stepped through a dark common room filled with scantily clad barmen and waitresses, Eve averted her eyes from the tempting display. She'd not be spending a coin here.

The former *Messenger Girl* shook her head, dismissing all speculation as she stepped back out into the night. She had no interest in this high-level bullshit. In fact, after her experience trying to purchase that loaf of bread, Eve decided she'd just about had enough of trying to decipher cryptic messages and strange quests.

For now she could just be an adventurer of the guild, and that was okay. No grand plots, no mysterious games, and no bloody heroism. Agatha could go fuck herself.

Still, Eve reached into her pocket to feel the folded parchment beside her copper coins and ivory knight. Even split four ways, eight hundred silver was a lot of money.

Come to think of it, she could really use a nice set of armor.

Chapter 28

The Comfiest Sweater Ever Known

"So you're saying a *Unique* high-level had you grabbed, drugged, and kidnapped so she could send us on a *bounty?*"

Incredulous—and a bit rude—as she was, Alex made for a welcome sight pacing around the common room of the adventurer's guild. Sure, an official team meeting wasn't the same as actually socializing with the rest of them, but Eve would take what she could get.

"Pretty much," she replied through a mouthful of stew. A collage of spices danced across her tongue as pieces of meat and potato melted in her mouth. She swallowed. "It's a lot of money."

Preston sat up. "You can't seriously want to *take* it?"

"I don't know," Wes said. "We *do* need money. Eve is basically broke, and I'm still trying to save up for tuition to attend the mage's college."

Alex froze. Preston gaped.

"What?"

"God's below." Alex rubbed a hand across her forehead. "I forgot you two grew up in the middle of nowhere."

Eve furrowed her brow. "What are you talking about?"

Preston's face softened as he placed a hand on Wes's shoulder. "The mage's college isn't a school. It's not that kind of college. It's more... um... a loose association of high-level mage types."

"And/or a powerful cabal that runs the government," Alex added. "There's about a dozen companies like that that run the higher-risk jobs. Tier fours and fives pretty much; the adventurer's guild feeds right into them."

Eve jerked a finger towards the clerk where she sat at her desk across the room. "Is that how we got stuck with her, then? Hit tier four and decided not to join one of these companies?"

The warrior shrugged. "Probably." She turned back to Wes. "Either way, you don't need tuition money. Tier two *Rare* like you? They'll be chomping at the bit to recruit you once you hit fifty."

Wes put a thoughtful hand over his mouth and chin. "What about the rest of you?"

"I don't know, Wes. Preston and I will be fine; tier three *Rare* is good enough, and healers are always in demand. Eve though? Unless her level fifty promotion actually **Appraises** correctly, she might have a hard time."

The *Striker* shook her head. "We're getting sidetracked. We can worry about what comes after the guild..." She gestured wildly as she struggled to find the right words before settling on, "after the guild."

"Alright, fine," Alex said. "I still vote we don't take this job."

"But you don't even know what it is!" Eve protested.

"Whatever it is, it's shady. If this Agatha lady were legitimate, she would've gone through the guild like everybody else."

"But she doesn't want to because she thinks the clerk is up to something." Eve paused, setting down her spoon. "Look, there's a drake somewhere east of here that's disrupting trade.   This is exactly the kind of thing adventurers should be doing, and Agatha is paying more than double what a bounty like this normally goes for."

"Maybe there's a reason for that."

Eve shrugged.   "Maybe.   I don't know.   Maybe that reason is that she's a bajillion years old and is going senile."

"Could be," Preston said.   "My grandpa used to think the seamstress next door was plotting to murder him.   Old age can mess you up."

Alex counted on her fingers.   "So either she's senile and paranoid, or the clerk really *is* up to something, or she's lying about the whole thing for some ineffable reason."

Wes stepped in, "Maybe she's just so rich she doesn't know what jobs like this normally pay."

"Yeah, the *Lady of Whispers* doesn't know basic commission pricing."

Eve let them argue as she lifted the bowl to her mouth to wolf down the rest of her stew, more intent on eating while it was hot than asserting her point one way or the other. There would always be another job.   As she returned the wooden dish to its place on the table, the *Striker* noticed a familiar pale glow shining upon it.

Gods-damnit, already? she cursed, reaching a hand for the hilt of a dagger.   *That was fast.*   She winced as the frigid inferno scorched her veins on its way out, the jagged lines disappearing from her skin as her Mana pool hit zero once more.

Eve returned her attention to the conversation at hand just in time for Wes to slam the parchment onto the table.

"I say we do it.   The paperwork looks official enough, and if the old lady wants to pay a premium to avoid dealing with the witch behind the counter, I'm not going to get in her way."

"He's not wrong," Preston added, tracing a finger over

the guild seal. "Besides, it's only a drake. It's not like she's having us break any laws or anything."

Eve nodded. "We can at least travel out there and see what there is to see. Worst case I take a look around and **Charge!** out if it looks too dangerous. Hells, it's a guild-approved job so we don't even have to find Agatha to get paid."

"I don't know," Alex said. "It's a risk, no matter how you slice it."

"Adventuring is a risk." Eve smiled. "And don't tell me you aren't dying to try out that fancy new spear of yours."

"It *has* got over a hundred Mana stored in it," the warrior admitted.

"It's settled then." Eve pushed herself to her feet. "Meet up tomorrow morning at the usual place?"

A chorus of nods gave her her answer, including a reluctant one from Alex. "I'll see you then."

Meeting adjourned, Eve turned to vacate the common room, eliciting a question from a curious Preston. "Where are you off to?"

"I've got four silvers to my name," she answered, "and I'm gonna spend them. I've gotta have *something* to hold all my loot. It's high time Wes wasn't the only one with an actual pack."

The mage's eyes shot open. "If you're willing to start carrying your own supplies, I'll buy you a pack myself."

"Don't worry about it," she called from the doorway. "After this job, three silver will be nothing."

"Try not to get mugged on your way back!"

"C'mon, what're the odds I get jumped twice in two days?" Eve left the common room with a smile on her face, practically skipping as she weaved through the late-afternoon foot traffic.

Visions of herself decked out in form-fitting leather armor inscribed with all manner of powerful enchantments danced through her mind. She could afford it with two hundred silver. Hells, with that kind of money she could even pick up a blunt weapon to complement her daggers.

As she approached the general goods store, Eve's daydreams shifted towards calculating just how many strawberry scones she could buy with the reward for Agatha's drake. She settled on 'a lot.' Of course, she'd have a hard time buying them if she couldn't step foot in a bakery.

Maybe if I don't try to buy bread, fate will let me into a bakery, she thought. *Or I just have to find one that's already sold out of bread but still has scones.* In the end she decided to have Wes handle her scone-buying for the foreseeable future.

To her chagrin, the first shop Eve visited only sold handmade artisanal leather bags for triple the price any reasonable customer would ever pay. After a few minutes wasted on a failed attempt at haggling, she moved on to a second, slightly seedier establishment.

She walked away with a pre-used shoulder-pack of rough canvas. Its seams frayed in a few places, and the iron clasp took a bit of force to latch into place, but it would serve its purpose. Though a rusty brown bloodstain spattered across the bag's back spoke to the ill end of its previous owner, Eve knew well enough she'd soon coat the item in stains of her own. Given the fate of her old clothes, dirt was an inevitability.

On her way back to the guild for the night, Eve stopped at the message depot she'd visited all those days ago. It took nearly thirty minutes of waiting in line and another twenty of tapping her foot while the *Courier* behind the counter searched for any letters with the name 'Evelia Greene' on them, but the paper-wrapped package he handed over was well worth it.

She stopped just outside the depot, leaning against the

stone wall as she ripped open the attached note.

My dearest Evelia,

I can't overstate the relief I felt upon receiving your letter. It's a mother's lot to worry, especially after her daughter doesn't come home from a simple errand. I'm excited to hear things are going well in Lynthia; I'm sure with your Rare class you've become quite popular. I'm so happy you're getting your chance to travel.

I wish you the greatest of luck, and I want you to know you're always in my heart. Stay safe out there.

Love,

Ma

P.S. As it turns out, you departing on your quest has somewhat rekindled my enthusiasm for my own. You'll find my latest attempt enclosed. I hope you like it.

Warmth—of a purely nonmagical variety—flooded Eve's chest as she read and reread the letter. Sure enough, tearing through the remaining paper revealed a red woolen sweater, expertly knit as were all Martha's creations. Eve held the garment to her face, reveling in the soft caress of the fabric.

It smelled like home.

Wafting scents of Mrs. Yir's pastries and Mr. Ilan's famous roast pig and Mr. Potts' well-tended rose garden sent Eve on a journey in her mind. She clutched the sweater tight in her bare hands, holding on to each and every memory it provoked. Happy as she was to spend her days adventuring with the wonderful friends she'd made, Nowherested would always keep a special place in her heart. How could it not?

That feeling of love and the smile that came with it stuck with the *Striker* as she made her way through the stretching shadows of twilight to find her bed.

She was two blocks away when she saw him.

A boy, no more than eleven, sat alone in a dark alley. His face was scared and dirt-stained, his skin only protected by a shirt and pants he'd long outgrown. Only the wretched nature of his malnourished frame allowed the clothes to fit at all.

Eve froze as she watched him shiver in the evening chill, the warmth of summer already fading to the ghost of coming autumn. She swallowed.

She had no food to give, no alms to bestow. The *Striker* rubbed a hand across the soft wool of the sweater, heart already aching at the situation before her. She knew what she had to do before she even stepped into the alley.

"Here," she said, kneeling down before the urchin, "you need this more than I do."

The boy hugged his knees to his chest, looking up at the stranger with fearful eyes.

"I—um—I'm sorry I don't have anything else to give," Eve managed.

He didn't move.

Taking one final moment to reminisce in the softness of her mother's work, Eve placed the sweater on the stone between them. "I'll just... leave this here."

She stood, clenching her jaw in resolution as she moved to vacate the alleyway. Eve paused before stepping back into the street as the sound of rustling fabric rang out behind her. She smiled.

Eve knew it wasn't much, that it wouldn't keep him fed or protect him from the dangers of the streets, but at least this lonesome child in a cold world might once again feel the shadow of a mother's embrace.

As Evelia Greene returned to her warm bed at the adventurer's guild with a bittersweet joy tugging at her chest, another Greene woman tucked herself beneath three layers of quilts miles away.

Martha sipped at her nightly hot cocoa, soothing herself the way she always had when worrying after her adventurous daughter. She managed to spill some all over her nightgown when the notification popped up.

Life Quest Complete: Knit the comfiest sweater ever known.

She didn't even bother to read the experience bonus or level up notifications or her quest reward. None of that mattered. All Martha cared about, and indeed all she needed to know, was the message itself and the truth it implied.

More than her skill as a *Seamstress* or expertise with a knitting needle, it celebrated one simple, incredible, wonderful fact.

Eve was okay.

Martha slept better than she ever had that night, the comfort of her bed or the warmth of her cocoa no match for that of the love in her heart.

Chapter 29

There's a Drake in my Boot

A warrior, a mage, a healer, and a rather strange rogue walked together through a set of familiar hills. Not too long ago, this same quartet had made the journey here to do battle with a troll, an experience at least one of them would've preferred to forget. She had no such luck.

"I wonder if there's still an Eve-shaped imprint in the grass somewhere around here."

"Give me a moment and there'll be a Wes-shaped one," she snapped back.

"Woah there." He held up his hands. "Violent today, aren't we?"

"Well, we *are* on our way to kill something," Preston chimed in.

Eve rubbed the back of her neck. "Sorry, I—um—didn't sleep well last night."

Wes's voice turned gentle. "Would this have something to do with you showing up at the guild practically in tears?"

"Wait, what?" Preston gaped. He smacked Wes on the shoulder. "Why didn't you tell me?" He turned to Eve, his expression immediately softening. "What's wrong?"

"Nothing's *wrong*," she insisted.   "It's just... I sent a letter to my ma a while back, and yesterday she replied with one of her sweaters. I gave it to this little orphan boy because he wouldn't stop shivering and he was just so *thin* and..." she sighed. "Is it wrong that I kind of wish I'd kept it?"

"Are you kidding? If I had something my ma made for me like that, I wouldn't give it up for the world.   That orphan could freeze to death for all I care."

Eve stopped short to gawk at the healer. "You really are the worst *Priestess* ever."

Preston shrugged. "I've been saying that for years; take it up with the Stones."   He exhaled.   "What I'm trying to say is: you did something good, something a hell of a lot of people wouldn't have had the willpower to do.   You should be proud."

"Thanks, Preston."   She hugged the healer from the side as they continued their trek.

"That's what I'm here for."   He returned the gesture. "Spiritual support."

Wes spoke up, "I thought you were here to heal us."

"Right, right."   He grinned.   "Spiritual support and keeping you all from getting yourselves killed."   With a laugh, he pulled away from Eve.   "Alright, that's enough cuddling. We gotta be in the right mindset for murdering an innocent animal."

Eve snorted.   "Innocent my ass.   According to the paperwork, this drake has killed three people."

Wes snapped his fingers. "Three people *that we know of.*"

Alex, in her customary, boring way, interrupted. "And it'll kill four more if you all don't shut up."

"Oh, come off it, Alex," Wes insisted. "We've got at least a couple of hours before we even enter its territory."

"That's assuming the paperwork is accurate," she said. "Can we at the very least refrain from announcing our presence to the high hells?"

Eve held up her hands defensively. "Alright, alright, we'll be quieter." She gave Wes a shrugging roll of her eyes the moment Alex turned her attention back to the road ahead.

The conversation fell silent for a few moments as they each thought their own thoughts. Eve spent the time pondering what exactly this drake had done to anger the *Lady of Whispers*. She could understand the old woman being paranoid enough to think the clerk would sabotage the job listing, but kidnapping Eve and paying such a high fee raised some questions.

In all likelihood Agatha had some stake in whatever trade route the beast was disrupting. Whether it was secrets or goods or illicit substances, Eve didn't particularly care. If this drake was killing people, and someone wanted to pay her to stop it, she was onboard. Still, the mystery of Agatha's and possibly even the guild clerk's involvement tugged at her mind. Enough so that she spoke up, albeit quietly to satisfy Alex.

"What if we just left?"

Wes raised an eyebrow. "Hmm?"

"I mean, there are jobs everywhere, right? Why should we stay in Lynthia?"

"Because it's my home," Preston asserted.

Eve tilted her head. "But it's also the place with all the creepy old ladies who watch you bathe."

"Hey, I'll have you know that was part of a holy ritual and also that you're absolutely right; we should leave immediately."

Eve laughed. "I'm just tired of getting speeding tickets and being kidnapped and dealing with that asshole receptionist. Besides, we're kind of getting to the point where we have to walk a long way to get to any jobs worth doing. Why not save time and travel out to a frontier town?"

"I don't know," said Wes. "We haven't been in Lynthia that long—shouldn't we take a bit more time before moving on?"

"We'll have to go back anyway to turn in this drake quest. We don't have to decide anything until then."

"Alright." Wes nodded. "I do like the idea of just heading north and power-leveling until we all hit tier four and can start talking to those mercenary companies."

Preston snorted. "Still set on joining the mage's college?"

Eve chuckled. "Maybe he's just tired of smelling like a sewer every time he steps onto the street."

"I'll give you that," the healer admitted. "Lynthia *does* stink."

"So north it is? More jobs, more monsters, and more dungeons, fewer creepy old ladies and rude clerks."

Wes faltered. "I'm not so sure about the 'more dungeons' bit. Remember last time we—"

He stopped short as a cry rang out, echoing across the hills from the road ahead. Though no words survived the bloodcurdling screech, Eve had no trouble identifying it as distinctly human.

"Shit," Preston cursed.

Alex leveled her spear, taking off into a calculated run forward. "Let's go!"

The boys followed. Eve **Charged!**

She didn't bother keeping to the road, instead making a beeline directly for the summit of the nearest hill. The wind swept around her as she ran, her heart racing faster with every step. Eve threw back her arm, allowing her pack to slide off it and fall to the ground. She could worry about loot and supplies later.

By the time she reached the closest peak, the cries had already silenced. She was too late.

A green-scaled monstrosity, easily thirty feet long from tail to tip, chewed on a limp and bleeding corpse—a wandering *Bard* if the worn lute on the ground next to him was any indicator. Eve's heart sank as she watched it chomp down once more on the poor man before dragging the carcass away from the road. She drew her daggers.

"Wait!" Alex called from her vantage on the path below.

Eve grit her teeth, her blood burning as she forced herself not to run in. "It killed him," she growled.

The warrior scurried up the hill. "Which means we don't need to rush in to save him. We wait, we follow it, we let your **Charge!** come off cooldown, and we attack while it's feeding."

Eve swallowed, slowly nodding as she watched the duration of her most important skill slowly tick away. With a sigh, she shoved her daggers back into her belt. "Alright."

The women watched from the hilltop as Wes and Preston caught up and returned her bag, waiting for the drake to carry its prey towards whatever den it kept. Eve took the lead after it.

The creature's bright scales glimmered in the sun, running up and down its entire body to meet in brutal spines across its back. Vicious claws sank into the soft earth as it walked, tugging up clumps of grass with every step. Its most intimidating feature was that which most infuriated Eve: its deadly maw.

The thing's snout was wide enough to completely envelop the dead man's torso, his limbs swinging limply in the air as his blood dripped down the drake's chin. The beast trekked on.

The four companions kept their distance from the predator, tracking its movements as they prepared for their time to strike. It came twenty minutes into the hunt.

In a small valley curiously absent of any sort of nest or

remains of other kills, the monster curled up to pick apart its prey. Eve drew her knives, checking the Mana on the one she'd been charging for the past days.

Manacharge Dagger
Rarity: Rare
Mana: 298/500

It'd have to be enough. Her **Appraise** of the creature itself proved less informative.

Level ?? Lesser Drake

"At least it's lesser," she muttered, "whatever that's worth."

"Ready?" Alex asked.

Three heads nodded yes in answer.

"Let's do this." The warrior leveled her spear, advancing into the valley. Eve followed, keeping at her side for the time being. The drake, too distracted with its meal, failed to notice their approach.

Alex landed the first blow.

The air flashed white as her spear dug into the creature's side, sending a deafening boom echoing through the valley. A horrific roar followed. The burst of Mana sent Alex reeling backwards as the drake recoiled.

Eve **Charged!** slamming her uncharged dagger into the beast's flank. Her momentum drove the blade deep, but it slid free as the monster stood. Inertia carried her forward, sending her careening beneath the creature's massive frame. Her heart raced as a combination of practice and **Surefooted**-ness kept her in control enough to dodge the thick leg that came crashing down before her.

The *Striker* took the opportunity to plunge a dagger into the muscular limb, again choosing to use the uncharged weapon. She'd only get one shot at her own Mana explosion, and Eve had loftier plans than taking out a leg.

Her knife sliced through the creature's hamstring, sending it collapsing back to the earth as Eve dashed away. It turned to snap at her, but a **Fire Dart** to the eye pulled its attention away.

Alex stepped between Wes and the monstrosity, posturing her spear to keep its maw at bay. It lunged anyway.

The *Survivor's* spear caught it in the mouth, piercing its cheek just enough to send the attack wide. A wicked fang passed just barely by Alex's head, driving instead through the warrior's shoulder. Her armor didn't even slow it.

She screamed, clutching desperately to the drake's lower lip as it raised its head, taking her with it. Gold and orange filled the valley as Preston and Wes alike channeled their spells.

No amount of healing could free the writhing warrior. She remained conscious by some miracle of her class and Constitution, continuing to strike at the beast with everything she had even as it swung her around like a child's plaything.

Eve dashed in. Her **Charge!** still ticked as she raced around the raging draconid, but its seconds were running low. **Adrenaline Rush**ed through her. She activated **Fate-al Blow.**

Alex cried out.

Wes distracted the beast with another **Fire Dart.**

Eve leapt.

The dagger missed its mark, striking inches away from the drake's exposed throat. Inches were close enough.

Three hundred points of raw Mana exploded into soft flesh, unhindered by the viridian scales which the blade had done its job to bypass.

Eve **Jetted** to the side, tearing Alex from the creature's maw as her skill launched her away from the burst of energy and blood. Pain shot up her arm as the two landed hard on a nearby hillside.

A piteous wail rang through the valley as the drake failed to find the necessary breath to properly roar. It crashed to the ground, tail and snout alike thrashing about in agonized rage. The party stood clear.

The *Striker* winced as golden light forced its way into her, patching up her various wounds even as it condescended her for getting them. She and Alex both made a complete recovery under Preston's holy glow, each making it to their feet in time to watch the creature finally still.

A wide grin stretched across Eve's face as the notification appeared.

You have defeated Level 41 Lesser Drake: +3920 exp!

Ayla's tits, she cursed to herself. *That's a lot of exp for a level forty-one.* In the post-battle high of fading adrenaline, Eve didn't even care it wasn't enough to level up. *With their lower levels, Wes and Preston probably got a shitload.*

She opened her mouth to inquire what kinds of rewards her tier two companions had received, but the echo of a muffled squealing from behind the next hill stopped her short. "Did you hear that?"

"It sounds like…" Wes trailed off, scurrying up the slope to peer into the valley beyond. "Holy shit."

"What is it?" Preston called up after him.

"There's a nest," the mage answered. "And, uh… apparently drakes have hoards too."

Chapter 30

Drakes Have Hoards Too

Eve stood atop the shallow hill, carefully surveying the valley below with narrowed eyes. "This has got to be the shittiest dragon hoard I've ever seen."

Wes cocked an eyebrow. "And how many dragon hoards have you seen, exactly?"

"None," she chirped. "But this one's still the worst."

She had a point. The layer of stolen shoulder packs, bedrolls, and broken tents demonstrated just exactly *how* the draconid had come across its ill-gotten gains. Most notably, an inordinate number of pots and pans littered the trash heap. Eve wondered if the drake had intercepted a shipment of cookware or simply attacked a particularly well-equipped chef.

"Aww, cut her some slack," Preston said. "It's not like she had an entire mountain of goblins desperately mining to bring her tribute. She did what she could."

Alex grimaced. "You mean she killed innocent people to steal their supplies."

"Wait," Wes stepped in. "She?"

"Male drakes don't lay eggs." The healer pointed across the hoard towards a grass nest where a glimmering eggshell lay shattered. A muffled squeak rang out from somewhere amidst the clutter.

"Shit," Eve cursed. "There's a baby somewhere in this mess, isn't there?"

Preston perked up. "We have to help it!"

"We have to what?" Alex asked.

"We just killed its mama. The poor thing needs us."

"We killed its mama that, need I remind you, ate an innocent person while we fucking watched!"

"To be fair," Wes chuckled, "I wouldn't exactly consider *Bards* 'innocent.' Or 'people' for that matter."

"Hold on," Eve interrupted. "If we killed its mama, does that mean there's a papa around here somewhere?"

Preston shrugged. "Paperwork only mentioned one. Either papa's already dead or he's wandered off somewhere. I don't know enough about drake behavior to say for sure, but if he were here we'd probably know."

The *Striker* tilted her head. "That's good enough for me. Come on, let's see if she hoarded anything worth salvaging." She took off down the hill eager to sort through the massive collection of odds and ends. She might not have gotten a level for killing the drake, but she sure as hells was going to get some loot.

Wes waded in after her.

"Be careful!" Preston called as he too carefully descended into the clutter. "You don't want to accidentally step on the little guy."

Eve rolled her eyes at the warning but nevertheless minded her step as she maneuvered around a broken wagon. Baby monsters aside, there were enough sharp points and broken edges in the vicinity that tripping and falling would be ill advised. Still she continued, picking through the frayed ropes and spent torches for anything worthwhile.

Even Alex joined the effort, shifting the chaff aside with

the butt of her spear to see what hid below.

Unfortunately, only the women seemed to put any real effort into the search for valuables. Preston spent the time peeking around and under various pieces and making soft cooing noises, while Wes understandably flicked between picking through the hoard and reading his status messages.

Eve was just in the middle of shoving a coiled rope into her pack when a muttered expletive drew her attention.

"Bandir's balls," Wes cursed. "Look at this!" In his hand he held a battered iron pan into the air as if it were a torch.

For a moment, the other three adventures simply stared in silent confusion at the gesture, before, like a torch, the dented metal came alight with orange flames. The crackling blaze licked at the dark iron, consuming it with the same insatiable hunger as it did all things.

In her awe at the impressive display, Eve failed to notice the shadow that fell across Wes's face or the flash of fear that flickered with it. He recovered well.

"Wes, that's awesome!" Preston said.

"Isn't it? No more fireproof golems for me." He looked up at the flaming cookware, still structurally sound even as the inferno claimed it. "Looks like it'll take a while to make its way through, though."

"That's a good thing," Eve said. "If you could burn through walls, you could burn through buildings. You don't want one stray **Fire Dart** to burn down a dungeon with us inside."

"True enough," he replied, "but I can always extinguish anything I start with **Flame Manipulation**." A wide grin overtook the mage's face. "Oh and by the way, it's not **Fire Dart** anymore."

The *Striker* laughed. "Let me guess, **Dart of the Devouring Flame?**"

Wes snorted. "No, I've only got three abilities 'of the devouring flame.' It's **Fire Bolt** now."

"Look at you." Preston lifted his head from where he'd been searching. "You're a full-fledged fire mage now."

"You kidding?" Eve smirked. "He's not a full-fledged fire mage until he knows **Fireball**."

"Hey, I'm better than that. *Fire Mage* is a tier two *Uncommon*."

"Hold up," Alex's voice broke apart the lighthearted banter. "I think I've found something." She reached into the debris to withdraw a wooden club topped with a fist-sized chunk of steel lined with brutal ridges. It looked like something that would leave a dent. "It's not enchanted, but we could definitely sell it for a few dozen silver."

Eve and Wes shared a look as they recalled what the blacksmith had told her. "Actually," Eve announced, "I think I could use it. It'll be hard to keep hold of, but something blunt would be great for an opening blow with a **Charge!**'s worth of momentum behind it."

The *Survivor* paused, opening her mouth for a few seconds before actually speaking. "Right. Looking at you, I keep forgetting you have a lot of physical force behind your mobility."

Eve furrowed her brow, looking down at her admittedly stick-like frame. "I'm not *that* frail."

Alex pointed the morningstar at Wes. "Standing next to him you are."

She rolled her eyes at the overly muscular fire mage. "*Everybody* looks frail next to Wes. Just give me the mace."

Wes opened his mouth to either protest or brag, but Alex didn't let him.

"Right, right," she said, wading through the sorry hoard to hand over the weapon. "Here you go."

Eve grasped the leather-bound handle, swinging the powerful club. The weapon felt eerily light in her grip, bringing up memories of dragging the rusty sword through the dirt with both hands. She marveled at the difference an extra seventy Strength made.

"Okay, next question," Eve wondered aloud as she held the weapon to her waist. "How exactly does one belt a morningstar?"

"I think it's a special strap," Alex offered. "I'm sure any leatherworker could make you one."

More things to buy, Eve thought to herself as she shoved the mace into her pack. *There's always more things to buy.* She turned to Wes and Preston. "Come to think of it, Alex and I both bought new weapons with our dungeon money, but you two are still in the same gear. What gives?"

Wes chuckled. "I can't believe it took you so long to ask. I commissioned a staff from a local enchanter. It wasn't ready in time for this job, but I oughta be able to pick it up once we get back."

Preston didn't look up from his search as he called out his own answer. "I'm saving it. Sent some to my da, but I'm holding on to the rest in case something happens. You don't *have* to spend all your money the moment you get it."

"Yeah, well, that's easier when you don't have a speeding ticket that needs paying and worn-out clothes that need replacing and a deadly Mana generating *thing* that needs dealing with."

Wes grinned. "Not to mention Mr. *Priestess* over there gets free housing at the cathedral."

The healer turned up his palms. "We can't *all* be Ayla's chosen."

"Thank the gods for that," Eve muttered as she returned to her search.

Minutes turned to hours as the four adventurers filtered through the hoard, turning over broken carts and damaged gear to find those few pieces still intact. In addition to the rope and morningstar, Eve soon found her pack stuffed with a set of cutlery, a pair of dark leather boots that looked *vaguely* her size, and a brown, hooded cloak with only a few bite-holes in it.

The party's pile of things to sell, on the other hand, grew substantially. The collection was mostly made up of basic steel weapons, given their resistance to biting, clawing, and other drake-borne damages. A few of the swords, axes, and spears were stained with blood, evidence that their former owners had at least put up a fight before falling to the draconid's maw. Most shone clean.

The vast majority of any defensive gear they came across wasn't even worth considering. It made sense that armor of any kind wouldn't survive its wearer's death by drake. To be entirely honest, Eve was rather impressed the beast had managed to remove so many cuirasses, vambraces, and chausses from its meals with as little damage as it had.

Of course, 'little' was relative. Most pieces were significantly chewed up if not outright torn in half, but they remained recognizable. Mostly.

Alex practically cheered with uncharacteristic enthusiasm as she strapped a metal kite shield to her back. Sure, it was a bit dented, and whatever sigil that had once colored its front had been long scratched away, but it fit the *Survivor* well. After all, what good was a tank without a shield?

Eve was just evaluating the ruined state of yet another bedroll—apparently the creature had thought them chew toys—when a yelp rang out behind her. She turned just in time to find Preston frantically hopping on one foot as he tugged at his boot.

"I found it!"

Wes was the first to reach him, helping stabilize the healer as he removed his right boot. Eve and Alex made their own way over as the men hunched over Preston's discovery.

The *Striker* arrived to find a foot-long lizard wrapped around the *Priestess's* arm, its claws harmlessly retracted into its tiny little feet. "Look at him," he gushed. "He likes me."

"Good for it," Alex replied, reaching for her belt knife. "Now let's put it down before it bites you."

Preston spun to put himself between Alex and his new charge, otherwise completely ignoring her comment. He looked up at Wes. "Do you think he's hungry? He looks hungry."

"Only one way to find out," the mage said, digging through his pack for a piece of jerky. Tearing off a bite-sized chunk, he held it out towards the hatchling. Sure enough, it wolfed down the morsel with a vengeance, expertly avoiding Wes's fingers in the process.

"Awww, he knows his mommy." Preston stroked the creature's head with the tip of his index finger as it ate.

"Wait, how come *I'm* its mommy?" Wes protested. "You're the *Priestess*."

"You two can't be serious," Alex spoke up as they boxed her out. "That's a dangerous animal."

"I'm gonna name him Reginald." Preston continued to ignore her. "Does he look like a Reginald to you?"

"That *thing* is going to grow to be the size of a gods-damned house!"

"Eh, let them have their fun," Eve said. "They can always release it once they realize how stupid an idea this is." She shook her head. "Come on, let's get moving." She nodded towards the stack of weapons they'd collected for sale. "We've got packing to do."

The warrior grumbled and rolled her eyes and gripped her knife but did eventually turn to follow Eve to the hillside where they'd left their spoils. They had to leave a few of the more worse-for-wear pieces behind for lack of bag space, but by the time Eve's, Alex's, and Wes's packs were stuffed full, the party had more than enough wares to sell upon their return.

After a quick stop to carve off a few scales from the fallen drake to prove they'd killed it, their job in the hills was well and truly done.

So it was that laden with food, supplies, trophies, and enough weapons to arm a small village, that Eve, Alex, Wes, Preston, and Reginald turned around to make their way back home.

Chapter 31

Money to Burn

Eve sat upon the soft grass, leaning against her pack as the exhaustion of the day's adventuring washed over her. The collection of swords and axes and knives they'd claimed from the drake's hoard kept her backrest upright at the cost of significant lumpiness. She shifted as the handle of a dagger on the other side of the canvas dug into her back.

The four companions sat together under the starry sky, having elected to make camp for the night rather than try and find their way back to Lynthia in the dark. The array of camping supplies they'd just looted may or may not have had an impact on that decision.

A crackling campfire held off the creeping chill of coming autumn, casting its orange glow across their tired faces. For all his protests that it was perfectly safe, Eve hadn't let Wes light the fire. The last thing they needed was to set the bloody dirt ablaze.

Still, the fire mage stared at the burning twigs with a furrowed brow and a slight, but noticeable, grimace. In his hand he absentmindedly flipped a copper penny, serenading the gathered adventurers with the rhythmic *ting* and *slap* of a coin flicked and caught.

For her part, Eve couldn't believe he was still mad about the campfire thing.

Preston spent his attention fawning over Reginald, hand feeding the oversized lizard with little bits of charred meat left over from their dinner. It wrapped itself around his arm, somehow managing to cling to the warm healer without digging in its claws.

Eve **Appraised** the creature, more out of boredom than any expectation of useful information.

Level 1 Hatchling Drake

Yep, she thought, *useless as usual.* She wondered if there was some way to upgrade the skill or otherwise glean more information from it.

Alex, meanwhile, spent the time running a whetstone along the tip of her spear, glancing up regularly at the baby monster with a combination of disdain and suspicion. While Eve didn't necessarily *expect* the hatchling to murder them in their sleep, she could understand the warrior's feelings. They *had* watched its mother kill a man.

It took Preston running out of scraps to feed Reginald to finally break the silence. "Hey, Wes, heads or tails?"

The mage flipped and caught the coin once more before replying, "Call it in the air."

Another *ting* rang out as he flicked the copper piece, firelight reflecting off its spinning surface with a warm glimmer.

"Heads!"

Wes caught it in his palm, slamming it into the underside of his forearm. "And the answer is..." He withdrew his hand, revealing a small green flame consuming the coin. "Fire! I guess you lose."

Eve snorted.

Preston grumbled, "If I didn't have a drake occupying

my arm, I would so smack you right now."

Wes chuckled, flipping the coin again. A trail of emerald fire followed it as it spun through the air. "You have to admit it looks pretty."

"You sure about that, Wes?" Alex's voice pulled at their attention. "Until we get paid back in Lynthia, I don't think you really have money to burn."

The party froze.

In dead silence, three pairs of eyes turned to gape at the ever businesslike *Survivor*.

"What?"

"Did you..." Preston managed. "Did you just tell a joke?"

"Bandir's balls," Wes swore. "She has a sense of humor after all."

Alex huffed, "Just because I choose not to joke around with *you* doesn't mean I'm incapable of it."

Eve met the warrior's gaze, a genuine grin stretching across her face. She gave a gentle nod. It was, of course, not her place to tell the others Alex's reasons for keeping her distance, but that didn't stop her from appreciating progress where she saw it.

Alex shook her head, breaking eye contact. "You know what? It's late; we're clearly all tired; I'm going to bed. You jokesters can figure out first watch amongst yourselves. Wake me when it's my turn."

"I'll handle it," Wes volunteered. "You all get some sleep."

Eve nodded, flashing a grateful smile before rolling onto her side. The warmth of the fire washed against her back as she drifted off, leaving Wes alone to gaze into its crackling glow.

* * *

"Where did you get this?" The guild clerk looked up from the folded parchment and pile of drake scales to cock an eyebrow at the four gathered adventurers. "I didn't assign this job."

All eyes turned to Eve, who held up her hands in an exaggerated shrug. "The buyer came to us directly. I guess she heard about our exploits and decided we were best for the job."

The receptionist managed a truly striking amount of incredulity in the look she gave them.

"What?" Eve asked. "It's not *so* farfetched, is it?"

The woman sighed. "You know, you're better than I gave you credit for." She unlocked a drawer in her desk, counting out the contracted payment. "Eight hundred silver, as promised. Good work."

Eve blinked.

"You did well," the clerk elaborated. "Come back tomorrow and I might have another job for you."

The *Striker* opened her mouth to reply, but a quick call of "next!" prompted Wes to gather up the coin and usher her away. She hated the swelling sense of pride she felt at the receptionist's kind words, detested that she should care about the opinion of such a vile woman. But she did.

Eve forced her thoughts away from the receptionist as Wes doled out the silver. There simply was nothing for reversing a foul mood quite like receiving a heavy purse. The ten-silver pieces reduced the sum to a manageable quantity, but Eve still reveled in the heft of the pouch. Perhaps more exciting, even, than the beauty of a payday was another fact driven home by the weight of her pack: they weren't finished yet.

Alex took the lead out of the guild hall, directing the party towards a steel smith she knew would give them a fair price.

Eve squinted as the famous glass walls refracted the midmorning sun directly into her eyes, doing her best to follow the warrior's blurry form as she deftly maneuvered through the crowded streets. Though she managed to keep to her course without bumping into *too many* passersby, she did fail to notice when Preston peeled away. When they finally did arrive at their destination, it took Wes's explanation for her to even realize his absence.

"He's off to the cathedral," the mage said. "Wants to research how to care for a baby drake, and apparently Ayla's got quite the library."

Eve shrugged. "Ah, well. It's not like he was carrying any of the loot. The freeloader."

Wes laughed. "Right. How many bones did you break on that job?"

"Hells if I know."

"Exactly."

Alex's voice cut into their conversation from where she held the door to the smithy. "Enough gossiping, ladies. We've got weapons to sell."

"Hey, I'm not a lady," Wes protested. "And Eve sure as all *hells* isn't one."

Eve gave him a rude gesture.

"See, look at that unladylike behavior. She's making my point for me."

She snorted. "Maybe Preston was right to call you Reginald's mommy. You certainly sound a lot like *my* ma."

"Any more backtalk out of you and you're grounded."

Eve guffawed, breaking out into a massive grin as she stepped past him into the smithy. Wes followed in a fit of laughter of his own, eliciting a disappointed head-shake from Alex.

Much as the tall *Survivor* insisted they maintain a steady, professional front while negotiating the sale of their loot, they agreed upon a price all too easily. Apparently there had been a huge uptick in newly classed adventurers. Eve didn't stop to think about what that might've meant.

In all, the hardest part about the deal was the simple act

of actually unloading the gear onto the wooden countertop. As it turned out, just throwing a bunch of weapons into a shoulder pack resulted in a rather hazardous game of pickup-sticks. By the second time she accidentally slit open her hand on an exposed blade, Eve began to resent Preston's absence.

Fortunately enough, the smith was perfectly happy to lend her a few bandages, especially after Wes refused to share his ring of regeneration. The mage had cuts of his own.

Alex somehow escaped the process unscathed, either through surprising dexterity or a defensive ability she hadn't shared with the others. Come to think of it, Alex hadn't shared *any* of her abilities with the others. Eve made a note to ask her about it when she had a chance.

Thirty minutes later saw the *Striker* practically skipping from the smithy, her pack comfortably lighter and her purse wonderfully heavier. With a quick word to Wes to confirm their celebration at the guild hall and a few inquiries about armorers to Alex, Eve split from the others to go about her shopping.

She resolved, of course, not to spend the entirety of her newfound two hundred fifty silver—she'd learned her lesson after breaking the table and ending up killing rats in the sewer—but by the gods she was going to spend some of it.

Her first stop was to find a replacement for her canvas pack. It had been a sound enough purchase when she'd first obtained it, but the *other* trouble with stuffing a bunch of weapons into a bag is the damage they do to said bag. Why couldn't the drake have hoarded sheaths too?

A few silver spent and Eve was once again confident her pack wouldn't spill its contents at a moment's notice.

Moving on, she at last visited the cobbler Thander had recommended days ago, replacing her peasant's boots with a much sturdier pair, complete with treaded soles to complement her **Surefooted** skill.

Eve's final—and most expensive—stop in her shopping extravaganza was at the leatherworker Alex had recommended. Between modifying her belt to include a loop for her morning star and commissioning an entire set of leather armor, this particular errand put her down over a hundred silver. She didn't regret it.

Still, even in the knowledge she'd gotten a good deal on essential protection, leaving the armorer's shop empty-handed stung. At least he'd promised to work quickly, pointing out a completed set that was *almost* Eve's size. She'd have to return tomorrow to pick up the adjusted outfit. At least he'd done her belt there and then, so she didn't have to worry about the morning star dealing any more damage to her new pack.

She returned to the adventurer's guild that night with a spring in her step, eager to drink and laugh and celebrate their victory as well as to learn what exciting toys the others had spent their prize on. That staff Wes had mentioned commissioning interested her the most. A simple boost to fire damage wouldn't take *this* long, right? No doubt the mage would be more than happy to brag about it once he had the weapon in hand.

After a quick visit to her room to deposit her gear and change into fresh clothes, Eve descended into the common room. She was the first to arrive.

Unperturbed by the tardiness of her companions—Wes had to track Preston down to deliver his share of the loot-money before doing his own shopping—Eve claimed a table and ordered the first round. She thought to herself, as she nursed her first intoxicant of many that evening, of how remarkable it was to have come so far so quickly.

Not long ago she'd been a *Seamstress's* daughter in Nowherested, and now here she was drinking ale in the adventurer's guild with enchanted daggers and a gods-damned *morning star* at her side. She thought back to her dreams of being a *Peddler* and traveling the world. How quaint they'd been. How unambitious.

Eve realized, though, as she took a gulp from her tankard, that she hadn't actually done all that much traveling. Sure, she'd come to Lynthia and seen the great glass walls, but that was about it. Maybe it *was* about time to move on.

The *Striker's* musings came to a screeching halt as the guild door swung open to admit the absolute last person she'd expected.

Alex strode into the room.

"You came," Eve pointed out the obvious as the warrior claimed a seat at the table.

"What? Can't an adventurer share a drink with her teammates?"

Eve smiled, holding up her near-empty mug. "She most certainly can."

Alex lifted her glass to the air, spilling a bit of ale as she and Eve clinked their tankards together. "To a job well done and money to burn."

The *Striker* laughed, giving Alex a meaningful look as she echoed the toast. "To a job well done and money to burn."

Chapter 32

Eight Hundred Silver Can Buy A Lot of Alcohol

Eve collapsed to the loose sand and packed earth of the training yard, cackling madly as she sucked the cool night air into her lungs. Wes, less accustomed to such falls, rubbed the back of his head as he groaned through a crazed smile of his own.

"Seventh hell, guys!" Preston cursed through the fit of shared laughter. "You seriously fought a hydra like that?"

Eve's abdomen ached from laughing as she sat up. "Bloody ridiculous, right?"

Alex snorted. "Gods-damned brilliant is what it is. Who needs a tank when you have a *Courier?*"

"At least until you fight something with a ranged attack," Wes commented, wincing as Preston sent Ayla's light through his sore back. "Or until the grass is wet and Eve pulls her famous 'falling on her face' maneuver."

Eve smirked, pushing herself to her feet. "He's only saying that 'cause he didn't see me take out that goblin shaman. It was the slide tackle to end all slide tackles."

Alex stepped up, handing Eve back the tankard she'd been holding. The *Striker* took a gulp.

Wes reclaimed his own beer from Preston. "Alright, alright. I'll concede you do get points for beating it to death with its own staff."

"One point," Eve corrected. "Of Int, remember?"

"Right, right," Wes chuckled, "because you weren't smart enough to use the staff. The staff a *goblin* was wielding."

Eve took another swig of her ale. "If only Int worked like that, maybe you wouldn't have needed a *Courier* to look after you."

"Girls, girls," Preston interrupted, "stop fighting. You're both pretty."

"Please." Wes ran a hand through his hair in an over-exaggerated flourish. "I'm not pretty. I'm *gorgeous.*"

Preston winked. Alex rolled her eyes. Eve snorted.

For his part, Reginald nestled himself comfortably in the healer's golden hair.

"Wait, shit." The seriousness of Alex's tone put a sharp end to the banter. "We have a problem."

Three pairs of eyes turned to look askance at the tall warrior only for her to turn her tankard upside down. "I've run out of ale!"

"A terrible fate, indeed!" Preston remarked with the most snobbishly noble accent Eve had ever heard.

Wes raised his own mug to his mouth, downing its contents in a few massive gulps. He lowered it with a belch. "I appear to have the same problem."

Eve paused to finish her own beverage before adding a "me too!"

"Alas, alack, how horrible!" Preston cried out. "This hellish affliction of alelessness is spreading!" He took a sip of his beer, leaving a line of foam across his upper lip. "My dear adventurers, I hereby charge you with the noble quest of curing this foul disease before it spreads further."

Wes kneeled before him. "My lord, I swear on my life

that we shall complete this quest, so you may be spared the horrific pain we now endure." He leapt to his feet, calling out as he strode away. "Onwards to glory!"

Alex and Eve shared an exasperated look, chuckling to themselves for a moment before the *Striker* dashed after the errant mage. She grabbed his arm once she caught up.

"Unhand me, wench! I am a master wizard on a noble quest!"

Eve laughed. "Of course, wise spellweaver. It's just..." She pointed back the way he'd come. "The guild hall is that way."

Wes lifted his left foot into the air, spinning on the other in a dramatic about-face. The maneuver sent him stumbling, careening forward for several feet before he caught himself.

Eve doubled over laughing at the display, tears welling in her eyes as her entire body shook with mirth. After a quick recovery and a bit of power-walking to rejoin the others, the *Striker* and friends took to the streets of Lynthia.

The city was alive. Not even the late hour could deter the denizens of the glass city from their goings-on. Instead of shops and smithies and market stalls, they flowed to and from the taverns and brothels and gambling houses, spreading such life and cheer that even the chill of a cloudless night couldn't pierce their warmth.

Eve reveled in it. She winked at the streetwalkers and laughed at the drunkards and swayed to the music pouring through the many open windows. Such music it was. Tunes of joy and adventure and love and melancholy stretched like so many tendrils into the starlit street, each tugging at the heartstrings of passersby with the singular message that *this* was the tavern for them.

Where Eve walked along the thoroughfare, the melodies twisted together into a dissonant symphony of emotion: conflicting, ugly, and eminently human. She treasured every second of it.

The party continued on. Preston looked up with gentle eyes and a wide smile as he listened to Wes spout his drunken nonsense. Alex paused outside one particular barroom, swaying her head to the lilting soldier's lament that played within until Eve tugged her along. Together they skirted around a drunkard pissing against the wall of a flower shop.

It was in rather triumphant manner that they arrived at the guild hall. Wes was the first inside, bursting through the door before striking a clumsy pose and thunderously declaring he'd come on a noble quest to defeat the evil beast of sobriety. By Eve's reckoning, said beast had died hours ago.

True to his mission, Wes bought the next round, spilling more than a little of his hard-earned prize on the already sticky common room floor. Nobody particularly minded.

Eve, having by then consumed more calories of ale than of food, ordered a meat pie for the table. She had silver to spend, after all, and this *was* a celebration. The others were more than happy to dig in. Even Reginald claimed a few scraps for himself before disappearing into Preston's sleeve.

"I thought," Alex voiced through a mouthful of pie, "that familiars were only for witches."

"Maybe I am a witch," he laughed. "An evil witch who's tricked you all into thinking I'm an innocent *Priestess*."

"That would certainly explain all the swearing," Eve said.

"If you *are* a witch in disguise," Wes slurred, "you're doing a shit job of hiding it."

"Fair point," Preston admitted. "No self-respecting witch would disguise themself as a male *Priestess*."

"So not only are you a witch—Alex pointed at him

—"you're a witch with no self respect."

Wes guffawed. "I like drunk Alex. We should hang out with her more often."

The warrior held up a finger as if making an elaborate point. "Drunk Alex is an elusive creature who only makes appearances on rare occasions. And on Fridays."

"I'll toast to that." Preston raised a tankard. "To Fridays!"

"To Fridays!" Wes echoed.

Eve furrowed her brow as they clinked glasses. "But it's Tuesday."

Preston awkwardly held a finger to her lips. "Shhhhh. Don't tell Alex that. She'll disappear."

"Oh shi—" She clapped a hand over her mouth.

The conversation once more devolved into a chorus of raucous laughter, only fading as a level 19 *Bard* whipped out his lute and strummed the opening chords of *Emma's Eve*. The entire common room sang along to the bawdy lyrics, dragging the party into the aura of mirth.

At some point during the fourth verse—Eve wasn't exactly sure when—Wes excused himself. Preston soon followed, citing a need to visit the privy. By the time the music died down, neither had returned.

Eve took the opportunity to speak freely with her remaining companion. "I'm glad you decided to join us. Really, I am."

"It's nothing." Alex swirled her half-empty tankard. "Just a few drinks with some friends."

"It's not nothing. I know you wanted to keep your distance. Hells, if I'd been through what you have, I'd be the same. I don't know what I'd do if I lost Wes, or any of you, really."

The *Survivor* sipped her drink. "I'm sure you'd live through it. You've got your *Legendary* quest to complete, after all."

Eve exhaled. "Assuming it even *can* be completed. I've given up trying, to be honest. Whatever my quest wants from me, it certainly isn't a loaf of bread."

"Maybe you've just gotta find the most badass loaf of bread ever made."

The *Striker* laughed. "Of course! Flour ground from Renth's gilded wheat, water from the spring of eternal youth, kneaded by a horde of stampeding centaurs and baked in dragon fire."

Alex snapped her fingers. "Now you're thinking like an adventurer."

Eve sighed, resting a hand on the side of her empty mug. "So you know pretty much all of my story. What about yours? How'd you end up at the guild?"

"It was that or join the guard. There was no way Da was gonna let me join the army, not after..." She shook her head. "Anyway, the Stones made me a *Cadet*, so combat was really my only option. I even got the same generic *Personal* quest half the army has."

Eve cocked an eyebrow.

"Prove Your Valor," Alex explained. "It's the kind of quest that infantrymen get before walking off to die in some nobleman's border dispute. I wasn't about to give my life for some rich fuck I've never met, so I joined the guild instead. Got paired up with a team, did some jobs, you know the rest."

Eve nodded, remembering their conversation in the Burendian ruins. "I'm sorry you had to go through that."

"Yeah, well, shit happens sometimes," the warrior slurred. She blinked. "Speaking of shit happening, you're glowing awfully bright right about now."

Eve shook her head, glancing down at her chest to see the white lines along her skin shining bright enough to appear through her shirt. It took her a few seconds to realize the burning sensation she felt was from the Mana and not the booze. "Oh hells." She flicked open her status screen, shutting one eye to stop the numbers from moving around.

Evelia Greene
  Human
  Level 33 Shatterfate Striker
  Exp: 5292/6817
  Health: 312/520
  Stamina: 1320/2100
  Mana: 581/0
  Constitution: 52
  Endurance: 210
  Intelligence: 12
  Dexterity: 60
  Strength: 78
  Spirit: 0

She cursed as her health pool lost another three points as she watched. The burning grew hotter. "Gods below, that's a lot of Mana." Eve hands shot to the daggers at her waist, the energy scorching her veins as it ran through her. By the time her pool hit zero, her left dagger was already full. She lost another fifty health in the process.

"You alright?"

She nodded. "For now. I'm worried it's getting worse. I hit five-eighty just now; that's higher than even the serum put me."

"I figured that was part of the quest," Alex said. "We're supposed to adapt to the changes, right? Maybe that's what this is."

"Sure," Eve replied, "as long as the changes don't kill me."

"I've been tracking it. Having consistent regeneration rather than your weird food-eating system makes it easier.

It's definitely getting worse. I'm lucky my health regen ability makes up for the damage the Mana deals."

"Yeah," Eve echoed, "lucky."

"Hey, think of it this way, you got hit with more of the serum, and you got a harder secondary quest, so you'll get a bigger reward at the end."

Eve laughed. "Knowing my luck, I'll end up replacing it with a quest to buy a magical tea cake."

"Great, after discovering the only Burendian alchemy lab *I've* ever heard of, we need to find a Burendian bakery too?"

"Maybe that'll be the quest. Build the first ever Burendian bakery. Instead of dumping excess Mana into our weapons, we can bake it into the pastries."

"Now that's the kind of venture I could get behind," Alex chuckled. "Once we're done with all this adventuring business we'll use the money to start a—" She cut off with a curse. "Gods damnit. Preston forgot his pet."

Sure enough, Reginald scampered across the wooden table for the remains of the meat pie, happily chomping away at a piece of burnt crust.

Eve sighed, reaching out to scoop up the scaly hatchling. It wrapped its tail around her thumb. "I should probably get to bed anyway. I'll bring Preston's new familiar up to Wes's room; *he* can deal with it until morning."

The two adventurers pushed to their feet at once, each stepping away from their shared table. Alex was the first to bid goodnight.

"You too," Eve replied. "I am glad you came. We should do this again sometime."

The warrior nodded, her eyes unfocused as her mind wandered elsewhere. She shook her head as she returned to the present moment. "Right. Another time." With a thin smile, the *Survivor* unceremoniously turned and half walked half stumbled her way out of the common room.

Eve exhaled, watching Alex leave before making her own path around the few remaining revelers and passed-out guildsmen towards the stairs. It had been a truly marvelous night, one she'd sorely needed after the stresses of adventuring.

So it was that with a tense grip on the handrail to overcome her unsteady footing that Evelia Greene set out first to return a certain baby drake to its reluctant 'mommy' and then to find the welcoming comfort of her bed.

Chapter 33

The Kneads of the Many

The stairway swayed as Eve climbed it, taking care to plant both feet on any given step before moving on to the next one. It was slow going, but Eve's spinning mind needed all the stability it could get. When she finally reached the top, she steadied herself against the wall for a brief moment of breath and celebration of her triumph before the drakeling wrapped around her arm reminded her of her task.

She slammed on Wes's door. There was no response. Eve contemplated shouting through the thin wooden barrier, but the late hour combined with the row of other doors along the hallway eliminated *that* idea. The last thing she needed was a bunch of angry adventurers.

He's probably passed out in there, she thought, reaching for the doorknob. It wasn't locked. *I could just leave Reginald insi—*

Her mind ground to a halt as the door swung open, revealing a very much not-passed-out Wes standing in the room's center. It wasn't shock at finding her friend still awake that so stunned the intruding *Striker.* It wasn't his apparent toplessness or the exposure of his bare skin and rippling muscles that reddened Eve's cheeks.

It was the white-robed *Priestess* he held in his arms.

"Eve..." Preston started. "What are yo—"

"You forgot your lizard," she blurted. Reginald leapt from her grasp, darting across the floor to hide under Wes's discarded shirt.

Wes blushed, stepping away from the lithe healer. "Eve, maybe you shou—"

"I'm going to bed." She cut him off, clumsily turning to stumble back into the hallway. Preston followed her out.

"Wait—Eve." He caught up to her, placing a comforting —and stabilizing—hand on her shoulder. "Look, I'm sorry that we—"

"What do you have to be sorry for? You're both adults; you can do whatever you want."

Preston shrank back at the sharpness of her tone. "You're not going to tell Alex, are you?"

"I'm not gonna—what? What does Alex have to do with this?"

"She—uh—she has a thing for Wes."

Eve's eyes widened. "No she doesn't."

"Believe me, she does. It's subtle, but it's definitely there."

"Yeah, if her *thing* is that she resents him for getting a *Rare* class so easily."

Preston sighed. "Eve, as your spiritual advisor—"

Eve snorted.

"Okay, as your *friend*, I'm asking you: don't tell Alex about us. It really should come from Wes, and he's resisting but I'm working on that."

"Alright. Fine. Whatever." Eve blinked. "I'm going to bed. You two have your fun."

"Oh, wait, one last thing." Preston held up a hand, sending a cascade of golden light through the intoxicated *Striker*. Though the fog of alcohol lingered in her mind, the churning of her stomach and the looming headache faded away. "In case I'm not here when you wake up. Drink some water."

"Hold on..." Eve's sluggish brain worked through the man's words. "The other morning, when you healed my hangover, I never figured out what you were doing still at the guild..."

Preston winked. "Sleep well, Eve." He turned, stepping away before disappearing back into Wes's quarters.

Eve lingered in the hallway, wondering how she'd missed the signs. The way Preston clung to the bulky mage for safety in combat, the fact Wes had never once looked at *her* in anything but a gentlemanly manner. Hells, she should've realized it the morning she saw Preston in the guild hall when his lodgings were at the cathedral.

As far as Alex went, Eve suspected Preston might be full of shit. She sure as hells hadn't seen any evidence of such. Either the *Priestess* wasn't as good at reading people as he thought, or Eve herself was completely blind. Possibly both, given the evening's *other* discovery.

She shook her head, stumbling her way back to her own bedroom. Revelations aside, the day had been long and the hour was late. She could process the information and chastise herself for her obliviousness once she'd had a good night's rest.

Eve's final thoughts as sleep took her were of the many jokes and japes and teasing comments that the discovery so conveniently laid out before her.

* * *

Eve awoke to a grumbling stomach and a blinding beam of sunlight through the shutters she'd forgotten to close. She rubbed her eyes, pushing herself out of bed to begin the process of cleaning off the dirt and sweat and spilled beer from the prior night in order to make herself *somewhat* presentable. At least her head didn't hurt.

She strapped her daggers to her waist before heading downstairs, well aware that the act of breakfast would necessitate access to the weapons. She smiled at the ridiculousness of the thought as she reached the common room.

"Good morning," she chimed at Wes as she plopped down to join him. "Sleep well?"

He looked up from his cup of tea, the dark shadows under his eyes clashing with the smile on his face. "Fantastically, actually. Just not very *long*."

Eve flagged down the barman, flashing a silver piece to order a plate of eggs and sausage. "That's okay, length is less important than girth anyway."

"How does sleep have gir—" Wes's jaw fell open. "Eve, what the fuck?"

She smirked across the table. "Where is her holiness, anyway?"

"Gone," he said. "Has errands to run and all that."

"Don't we all," Eve replied. She sat back with a massive grin as the server deposited a heaping plate of protein on the table in front of her. "My armor oughta be ready today."

"Oh, that reminds me. I need to stop by that enchanter I commissioned. He should have my staff by now."

"Oooh, that's exciting. I bet Preston and Alex have all sorts of new toys too."

Wes chuckled. "Well, if you consider Reginald a new toy..."

"Or you," Eve laughed.

Wes blushed.

As if on cue, the guild's door swung open to admit a frazzled Preston, still wearing the same wrinkled robe as the previous night. He made a beeline to his two companions. "We have a problem."

"Let me guess, you got a bullshit speeding ticket?"

Preston rolled his eyes.

Wes leaned in. "What's wrong?"

"I was chatting with sister Selma—who's an absolute dear, by the way, you all should meet her—when Reginald climbed out of my sleeve. Once she got past the whole 'seven hecks you have a monster on you!' Selma was kind enough to let me know that apparently you need a *license* to keep wild animals in the city."

Eve shrugged. "So get a license."

"That's the thing," the healer explained. "They're bloody expensive. You have to register as a monster tamer and take an exam and pay an exorbitant amount of money."

"Makes sense." Wes nodded. "They don't want people keeping dangerous pets."

Preston smacked him. "Reginald isn't a pet! He needs me. He needs *us*."

"Okay," Eve thought aloud, "So it's illegal to keep him, and you won't just release him into the wild—"

"Because he's too small to fend for himself," the *Priestess* added.

"Right. Of course," she said.

"So you want to hide him?" Wes asked.

"Not quite." Preston flashed a sheepish grin. "I want *you* to hide him."

The mage's eyes widened. "You can't be serious."

"I am! There's no way I can keep him at the cathedral. I share a room with the three nosiest *Priestesses* to ever live. They'd find him in an hour."

"But I have my own room here at the guild," Wes finished for him.

"Exactly."

The two stared each other down, Preston looking up at the bulky fire mage with begging eyes and an innocent smile. He pulled the hatchling from his sleeve, making a show of stroking the back of his head. Reginald purred.

"Alright, fine," Wes gave in. "I'll keep him here until we can come up with a longer term solution. We can only hide him so long. Soon enough he won't fit in your sleeve anymore."

"Thank you thank you thank you!" Preston beamed, passing the oversized lizard across the table.

"Yeah, yeah," Wes said, petting the baby monster. "You're just so cute I can't resist."

"Keep it in your pants," Eve quipped.

For the umpteenth time in the last twelve hours, Wes reddened. "I was speaking to Reginald!"

"Don't keep Reginald in your pants," Preston said. "He likes sleeves much better."

Wes groaned, rubbing his temples with his left hand while the hatchling reveled in the warmth of his right. "You two are impossible."

Eve laughed, shoveling a forkful of fried egg into her mouth. "Please, you love our antics."

"I'm so glad I don't have a hangover right now," Wes said. "I can't imagine dealing with you two with a headache."

Preston smiled.

"Hells," Wes continued, "hungover me wouldn't even be able to *look* at you."

Eve furrowed her brow. "Look at me? What are you— gods damnit." She cursed as she turned her vision downward, confirming that already the radiant web of raw Mana had returned to the skin of her neck and chest. "But I've barely eaten anything!"

Wes shrugged. "I guess a few sausages is enough? Maybe protein makes for better Mana generation."

"No, no, I was talking to Alex about this last night," Eve muttered. "It's getting worse." She reached for the dagger on her right hip before remembering she'd filled that one up already.   At least the one on her left still had some space.

"I'm going to need a better way to dump all this Mana," she said through gritted teeth as she emptied her overloaded pool into the weapon.   "That or fight something after every meal."

Preston placed a hand on her back, sending a burst of Ayla's light to heal her Mana-dealt wounds.   "Time for another job, then?   Drain all that Mana into some big bad and earn enough coin for a better sink while you're at it?"

"Actually, I have a better idea."

Wes cocked an eyebrow. "What's up?"

"Why don't we just leave?   We've been talking about moving on anyway, and away from Lynthia I can explode to my heart's content.   As long as Preston's there to heal me, that is."

The *Priestess* snapped his fingers.   "That's perfect!   We won't have to worry about keeping an illicit drake within city limits if we *aren't* within city limits!"

"Are you sure?" Wes asked.   "We have a good thing going on here."

"Do we?   So far I've run afoul of the guards, the guild receptionist is awful, I've been kidnapped in the streets, and now you've agreed to keep an illegal monster in your bedroom."

The mage's eyes flicked down to the hatchling in his hands and back up to the no-longer-glowing *Striker* across from him.   "Alright.   If you can convince Alex, we can head north.   Powerlevel for a bit like we talked about."

Eve grinned, leaving her half-eaten breakfast behind as she pushed herself to her feet.   "I can do that.   Just need to pick up my new armor and a few supplies and we can head out tomorrow morning."

Wes nodded.   "You shouldn't need much.   That drake had a pretty good stock."

Preston pointed at her leftover sausage. "You planning on eating that?"

She shook her head. "I would if I could. Daggers are almost full—I don't want to risk it."

"Excellent." He pulled the plate over. "I left the cathedral before I had a chance to get breakfast."

Eve rolled her eyes but refrained from commenting. "I'm off, then. See you tonight."

Wes waved goodbye as she turned to make for the exit.

Already brimming with excitement for her new armor and the prospect of journeying on to see new horizons, Eve stepped out into the busy street. The sight that met her left her reeling.

A mass of men and women crowded the thoroughfare, each adorned with a white apron or picket sign. To cries of 'no grain means pain!' and 'we knead cheap wheat!' they marched.

Once she'd had her fill of gaping at the display, Eve hailed another spectator to inquire about the gathering.

"The city council just approved a new tax on wheat," the stranger explained. "It's high enough to put half the bakers in the city out of business. They're going on strike to protest, but the council works at the speed of government." He shrugged. "Until then, there won't be a single loaf of bread in all of Lynthia."

Eve snorted, her mouth widening into an open smile. She fell back, collapsing against the guild's outer wall as the laughter took her. She laughed and she laughed and she laughed. The man gave her a curious look, but she was too distracted by the ludicrous nature of the city's bakers going on bloody *strike*. It was gods-damned funny.

As the procession passed and Eve recovered her senses, she weaved through the streets of the glass city with a grin plastered across her face. What better sign could she have asked for? Whatever hijinks, shenanigans, or escapades the future had in store for her, one fact stared Eve right in the face.

The time had come to leave Lynthia behind.

Chapter 34

Show and Tell

For the seventh time in the twenty minutes she'd been waiting outside the northern gate, Eve swung her arm in a full circle, reveling in the freedom her armor provided. "Plates" of hardened leather protected the rigid areas of her body while a softer, more flexible material allowed her joints their almost complete range of motion.

It was at her abdomen that the system failed. The thick chest piece remained solid all the way below her belly button, forcing her to bend at the waist or the knee should she, say, drop one of her daggers on the floor of the guild common room. Eve supposed it wasn't a huge loss. Unless she needed to double over in pain—something the armor should hopefully prevent *anyway*—she couldn't see a reason to complain.

The noonday sun shined warmth upon her bare neck, reminding her yet again that she *probably* should've bought a helmet. If only the leatherworker had one that didn't swivel around her head and block her eyes whenever she made a high-speed turn. Maybe she'd find a better one in her travels.

The other piece she missed were the gauntlets so

commonplace among agility fighters. Though she was no rogue in need of nimble fingers for illicit deeds, Eve *did* have a valid reason for leaving her hands exposed: the daggers at her hips. Channeling Mana through a barrier of leather was beyond her ability; she required skin contact both to charge and activate the enchanted weapons.

The morningstar that hung on her left side needed no such accommodation. Its brutal, bone-crushing ridges more than anything sold the message that she meant business. Eve smiled at her reflection in the great glass wall, marveling at her transformation from a simple village girl to the spitting image of a veteran adventurer.

A certain fire mage shattered her reverie. "Well damn, Eve, if you weren't so short I'd say you looked like an actual threat."

"I'm not short!" All five feet of her turned to glare up at the newly arrived caster. "You're just freakishly tall."

"Right, right." Alex appeared from behind Wes's bulky figure, her own significant height further proving his words. "You're perfectly normal; it's everybody *else* who's too tall."

Preston rounded the corner into the field outside the city just in time to jump to Eve's aid. "Ooh, nice armor! You look like a real adventurer."

She grinned. "See, *Preston* doesn't think I'm short."

Wes snorted. "That's 'cause Preston's short too."

The *Priestess* gaped. "Sounds like someone never learned adventuring lesson number one."

"Don't die?" Wes guessed.

"Close," Preston said. "Don't piss off your healer."

Eve laughed. "Sounds like the same thing to me."

"Oh, I'd never let you die," he said. "But see if I heal your next hangover, why don't you?"

Wes grimaced.

"On that note," Alex stepped in, "it looks like we're all

here." She gestured down the northbound road. "Shall we?"

The party nodded their assent, and together they embarked on the first steps of their journey away from the glass city. Eve twisted her head back to gaze upon the prismatic walls and the rainbows they cast several times as the minutes dragged on, until at last Lynthia faded into the horizon.

"So," Eve broke the lingering silence, "are you going to tell me about your new toy?"

"What, this old thing?" Wes pulled the six-foot staff from its binding on his back. "If you *insist.*"

Preston chuckled, turning to whisper to Eve, "He's been waiting for a chance to show it off all morning."

She had to admit it looked impressive. Faint runes decorated its dark iron shaft, meeting along the tip where it split into four sharp prongs which clutched a fist-sized crimson gem. Eve might've guessed it ruby were it not for Wes's explanation.

"The core came from a greater salamander, strong enough to hold half my pool in fire Mana. The whole thing's enchanted to naturally pull in energy from nearby fires, which has the added benefit of keeping me from accidentally setting it alight. Not to mention it does this." Wes grinned, raising both the staff and his free arm to the sky. As his left hand came alight and launched a **Fire Bolt** to the heavens, so too did the brilliant gem, matching his spell with a bolt of its own.

Eve watched as both projectiles flickered out before returning to the earth. "Did your staff just cast a spell?"

Wes beamed. "Yep. As long as it's got enough charge, it'll echo whatever I cast. It even lets me choose a different target, though I—um—need to work a bit on my aim."

Alex shook her head. "It's not worth it. Trying to aim at two different things at the same time is a fool's task. I've seen poorly-trained *Rangers* try and fire two arrows at once enough times to know it just means you miss twice as fast."

The fire mage smirked. "Those *Rangers* didn't have a hundred and thirty Intelligence."

Alex shrugged. "You're free to try. Who knows, maybe you'll figure it out."

"Just don't burn down the woods while you're at it," Eve added.

"Please, I wouldn't set fire to an entire forest. Not on purpose, at least."

Eve rolled her eyes, turning to look at the brand-new canvas messenger-bag that hung from a long strap at Preston's side. "So what've you got in there? Finally decided to carry your own supplies?"

"Well I couldn't exactly leave my stuff at the cathedral this time," the healer said. "With any luck I won't have to step foot in that horrid place again." He patted the bag with a gentle hand. "Got some general supplies, food for Reginald, and some potions."

Eve thought back to seeing such items for sale in Lynthia and balking at their high price. "Why do you need potions when you can just heal yourself?"

"Not without Mana," he replied, "so most of them are for that. I did get a *few* health tonics, just in case something happens to me. I can't heal myself if I'm passed out. Plus a couple general antidotes. I have spells for curses and diseases, but nothing that helps with poison."

"That's... remarkably well thought out," Eve commented.

The healer smiled. "We don't *all* need fancy enchanted gear. My job is to keep everyone alive, and this is the best way to do it."

Eve peered over her shoulder, casually lifting the canvas flap to peer into his bag. Her eyes widened in surprise as she found a dozen clearly labeled, miniature leather pouches like so many tiny wineskins. "Aren't potions supposed to come in vials or bottles or... something?"

"Maybe if your alchemist doesn't know what he's doing," Preston explained. "What kind of adventurer wanders around with a bunch of glassware? Sounds like a recipe for broken shards and spilled potions."

Eve turned to cock an eyebrow at Alex, remembering the health tincture the warrior had given her in the Burendian ruins. It had come in a glass vial.

Alex reddened but didn't comment.

"Anyway," Preston continued, "that's basically it. Just potions and supplies." His golden hair shuffled and shifted as a viridian drakeling peeked his head through the healer's bangs. "And Reginald, of course."

Out of simultaneous curiosity, boredom, and a nagging feeling that the creature looked slightly bigger than before, Eve **Appraised** him once more.

Level 3 Hatchling Drake

"How's he leveled up?" she asked. "Has he been hunting mice?"

Preston shook his head, carefully so as to not risk Reginald's perch. "He's a hatchling, Eve. He levels just from eating until he's grown."

Wes laughed, "I wish I could level from eating."

Eve's stomach grumbled. "Gods, me too. All *I* get for eating is draining health and random explosions."

"You can borrow my spear for tonight," Alex offered. "The health regen on my **Survivor's Recovery** more than makes up for a bit of Mana burn."

"Thanks, Alex. I'm going to see about dumping some once we stop for the day. I'm just worried I'll get to the point where a single meal is too much for my daggers."

The warrior nodded, flashing a comforting smile before returning her attention to the road ahead.

"So what about you?" Wes asked. "We've got my staff, Eve's armor, and Preston's potions; what'd you get, Alex?"

The *Survivor* spun, pulling her kite shield from her back. "Redid the straps and commissioned a few enchantments. Watch this." Securing the thing to her left arm, Alex slammed its pointed base into the packed road. With a quiet glow, the dirt itself shifted around it, forming an earthen reinforcement to hold the shield in place. "Won't work if we end up in another stone ruin, but anywhere else I'll be a lot harder to dislodge."

Eve gestured at the web of white light along Alex's right hand. "Can you charge it with your—"

She shook her head. "It needs earth Mana, so no. Fortunately the enchantment's relatively cheap. I just need to leave it partially buried every night and it'll keep charged."

"Look at us," Wes said with a wide grin, "all geared up and ready for adventure. Those legendary monsters of the north better watch out."

Eve snorted. "More like Foot's Garrison had better watch out. You're just as likely to burn the place down as help keep it safe from monsters."

Preston giggled to himself. "I know it's called that because it's at the foot of those mountains, but Foot's Garrison will never stop sounding ridiculous."

Wes joined in, "What's next? Toe's Keep?"

Eve rolled her eyes, tuning the pair out as they brainstormed sillier and sillier names for the frontier town.

As the hours dragged on and the conversation died down, the *Striker's* thoughts turned away from her new gear and rumbling stomach towards ideas of what lay ahead. Daydreams of exploring ancient dungeons and felling deadly foes played out in her head, paired, of course, with wistful imaginings of exp earned and levels gained.

Far away as her next promotion was, both Wes and Preston grew closer to their own. Eve wondered what the devouring flame had in store for Wes, or if Preston would eventually escape the clutches of his rather impolite goddess. Truth be told, she'd run out of *Priestess* jokes.

By the time the party stopped just short of the looming tree line beneath the blue glow of twilight, Eve's mounting hunger could be ignored no more. Her normally massive pool of Stamina fell to double digits as her body failed to find the energy to refill it. She didn't wait for Wes to start the campfire before digging into her supply of rations.

Alex looked on with concern. "Didn't you want to vent some Mana before eating again?"

"I'd rather keep my daggers full in case we encounter something," Eve explained through a mouthful of jerky. She swallowed. "I'll dump my pool once I'm done eating."

"Are you sure you're alright?" Preston asked. "You're already glowing."

White light raced along her body, stretching in jagged tendrils up her neck. She took another bite. "Food first, Mana later."

Despite her dismissive words and pressing hunger, Eve did a quick check on her Mana pool. Already it sat at just over a hundred, not enough to hurt but plenty to stop her health from regenerating above half. Still she ate.

Eve made her way through two chunks of aged cheese, three strips of salted meat, a handful of berries, and more hardtack than she'd ever thought she could stomach before Wes placed a hand on her shoulder.

"You need to stop." A gentle worry colored his voice. "Eve, you've had two meals' worth of food. Mana aside, we'll run out of rations before getting to Foot's Garrison."

She froze, taking note of the brilliant glow of her skin

and the inferno coursing through her veins. Still her stomach rumbled. "Shit." She pulled up her status.

Evelia Greene
Human
Level 33 Shatterfate Striker
Exp: 5292/6817
Health: 112/520
Stamina: 231/2100
Mana: 821/0

Her jaw hung open. "My Stamina's barely recovered. It's all gone to Mana." Her health ticked down before her eyes. "Preston, I need—"

Her voice cut off as Ayla's invasive light poured into her, fighting off the frigid storm of burning Mana with its combined healing and unwelcome scrutiny. "Go," the healer said, "dump it."

Eve nodded, jumping to her feet to dash away from the group. She would've **Charged!** had she the Stamina to spare. Ayla's light followed her as Preston channeled the spell at range, keeping her health topped off even as the Mana ate away at it.

She made it two dozen yards before collapsing to the grass, planting both palms in the cool greenery. At her bidding, the Mana came forth.

The explosion sent her flying.

Eve tumbled through the air, spinning wildly as she flailed for some semblance of control. She found none. She landed on her right hip, thankfully avoiding the side with the morningstar. She didn't feel thankful.

Preston raced to her side, switching to his more powerful **Healing Touch** as she recovered from her fall. Seconds passed in quiet discomfort before the pain and Ayla's mercy alike faded away, replaced only by the continued ache of an empty stomach.

Wes helped her to her feet. "Are you alright? What happened there?"

Eve gulped. "My Mana generation isn't just getting worse; it's taking away from my normal metabolism."

Alex furrowed her brow. "What does that mean?"

Eve chewed on her lip as she reread the description on her secondary quest. "It means," she eventually said, "I need to 'adapt to the changes.'"

Chapter 35

Those Damned Scones

A horrific growl echoed across the canopy as the four adventurers cut through the thick foliage that had made its way onto the road. "Careful, guys," Wes warned. "It sounds like there's a wild beast on our trail." He chuckled. "No, wait, that's just Eve."

A combination of too sluggish, too hungry, and too exasperated to come up with a witty reply, Eve settled on the classic, "Fuck you too."

"When the quest said to 'adapt to the changes,'" Alex said, "avoiding food altogether wasn't exactly what I had in mind."

"What else can I do? I can't just keep exploding all the time; Preston's gotta run out of Mana eventually."

"And you've gotta eat eventually," the healer snapped.

"I know, I know," the *Striker* admitted. "I'm just hoping if I go a while without, I can remind my body it needs energy too, not just Mana." Not experiencing the terrible burning pain that came with having too much Mana running through her veins was an added benefit she neglected to mention.

"It still sounds a lot more like 'avoiding' the changes

than 'adapting' to them," Wes said.

Eve shrugged. "You have a better idea?"

"Eat something! Explode if you need to, or have Preston heal through whatever damage the Mana does to you, but you need food."

The *Priestess* nodded along to Wes's comments. "I don't know how fast it drains you, but I can keep up a few dozen health points a minute for *hours* before I run out. Hells, if you could channel that Mana of yours without exploding, I could even *use it* to heal you."

"Let's not go down that road," the fire mage argued. "Remember the dungeon core? Last time you got a dose of raw Mana, you had to use all of it keeping *yourself* alive. Can't heal Eve if you're too preoccupied with not dying."

"Whatever we do," Preston said, "it'll have to happen soon. Look at her; she can barely walk."

"I'm right here."

"Right," Wes added, completely ignoring Eve's words. "She can't wait for a class promotion."

"Could you two stop talking over me? Gods, you're like my ma and da all over again."

Preston turned. "Don't you talk to your parents like that, young lady! Your father and I are trying to help you."

Alex laughed aloud from where she stood chopping through a low branch blocking the way.

Eve sighed.

"Oh that reminds me." Wes swung his pack around his shoulder, flipping it open to dig through it. His hand returned wrapped around a strawberry scone. "I've still got one left over from before the drake job. Didn't have a chance to get more before we left what with the strike and all, but this one oughta still be good. It's only a *few* days old."

Her stomach grumbled once more as she eyed the treat. Even dried out and stale as it was, it tempted her. Oh how it tempted her. Her mouth watered. *No. It's not worth it.* Divinely delicious or otherwise, no week-old pastry was worth the pain it promised. Eve shook her head.

Wes's eyes practically leapt from his skull as Eve turned to keep walking, leaving him behind still holding an uneaten scone. He turned to look at Preston.

The healer shrugged. "She'll give in eventually. She's gotta eat *sometime*. My bet's on a hot meal once we get to Foot's Garrison."

Wes grinned, stowing the treat back in his pack. "You're underestimating the power of the scone."

"Bet you five silver I'm not. Your stale hunk of pastry can't come *close* to a homemade dinner fresh from the stove."

The bulky mage held out a hand. "You're on."

They shook.

Alex and Eve alike rolled their eyes at the wager, pressing on down the overgrown path towards their destination.

At the back of her drained mind, the *Striker* wondered how the frontier town had let their road fall into such disrepair. Surely Foot's Garrison was just as much in need of trade and supplies and travel as any other settlement. She hoped they had gone the right way. Then again, she'd rather be lost than discover Foot's Garrison had fallen a decade ago without telling anybody.

The adventurers hacked and shoved and burned the encroaching foliage, more so to clear the way for future travelers than for their own passage. They were perfectly capable of climbing over a few shrubs, thank you very much. Hells, with any luck, the village would pay them for the service.

The party journeyed onward, ever watchful of the shifting shadows and rustling leaves of the northern woods. That is, *Alex* was watchful. Preston spent most of the time huddled up next to Wes for safety whenever the wind shifted *too* much, while the mage himself devoted his focus to igniting brush on the road without allowing his flames to spread elsewhere.

For her part, vigilance wasn't even in Eve's vocabulary. Not today. Sure, she vigilantly heeded her grumbling stomach and dwindling Stamina pool, but watching for potential threats was beyond her ability.

The hours ticked by in relative peace as the group progressed, only stopping for the night once the sun had well and truly shed its final ray. As Wes passed around rations of dried meat and cheese and hardtack, Eve arranged her pack as a pillow and lay down to rest. She'd have sleep for dinner that night.

* * *

The following day began much the same as the prior one had ended: with everyone else eating while Eve's belly ached. It was a quiet throb, coming in gentle waves that fell somewhere between nausea and actual pain.

Wes looked on with concern as she forced herself to her feet, gathering her gear to set off once more. Eve didn't protest when he reached out to take her pack away, shouldering it beside his own. She simply gave a smile of thanks.

The days blurred together as churning turned to aching turned to recurring pangs of sharp pain. Drinking from her water-skin seemed to help, but hydration was a poor substitute for nourishment.

By the time the walls of their destination came into view, not even a night's sleep could raise her poor Stamina above single digits. Eve wondered how long ago she'd have collapsed were it not for her rather insane amount of Endurance. Two hundred and ten of a single stat was a lot, no matter how one looked at it.

The wooden fortifications of Foot's Garrison were as

overgrown as the road there. Vines and moss and even the odd flower littered the barrier of vertical logs, lending an air of decay and new life to what certainly looked like an abandoned outpost.

The adventurers stopped below the tightly-shut gate, sharing looks of confusion and worry amongst themselves.

"I swear, this place is supposed to be occupied," Wes insisted. "The guildsman I spoke with said it's *the* hub for intermediate adventurers looking to break into the big leagues."

"And—uh—how old was this guildsman?" Preston asked. "Looks like nobody's lived here for decades."

Alex shrugged. "Only one way to find out." She held an open hand perpendicular to her mouth as she called out, "Anyone there?"

"Yeah, yeah, I'm coming, I'm coming," a muffled voice answered.

The four companions shared a surprised look as the gate drifted open to reveal a bored-looking woman adorned with the gray and red of the Leshkian military.

"Oh, thank Ayla," Preston said. "We were afraid this place was abandoned."

The guard furrowed her brow. "Why would you—" Her eyes flicked up to gaze at the thick vines coating the outer walls. "Gods damnit, Barry." She turned back to the new arrivals. "That'd be the work of everyone's least favorite *Druid*, Barry. Whenever he gets drunk he thinks it's funny to turn the place into a bloody garden. Wishes he was born an elf, that one."

Eve blinked at the mention of the mythical race, to say nothing of the eccentric *Druid*.

Alex managed to maintain *some* semblance of professionalism. "The road here was pretty overgrown too. We cleared it out."

"Good," the soldier barked. "Saves me the trouble. And

don't be expecting payment. If we had the money to hire out adventurers whenever Barry makes a mess of things, it wouldn't be *my* job." She ushered them in. "Anyway, welcome to Foot's Garrison. Inn's that way, job board's that way, graveyard's that way."

Wes cocked an eyebrow. "Graveyard?"

"You'll need it sooner or later. You're adventurers, aren't you? Two things adventurers are good at: drinking and dying."

Alex's mouth hung open for a second before she collected herself. "Alright then. I guess we'll just... head to the inn. Thanks for the directions."

The guard nodded, giving them a smile as they stepped inside. She closed the gate after them.

Eve, for the most part, paid little attention to the exchange. She didn't have much to spare. The *Striker* simply trudged on after her companions as they made their way through the town. She could take a tour of Foot's Garrison later; all her mind could manage at the moment were thoughts of a comfortable chair and a stacked plate.

She feverishly tried to fight off that second image, but it was a persistent one. Roast pork and rabbit stew and game pies danced about her vision as she followed Alex's lead. Eve was already salivating by the time she stepped inside *The Foot's Rest.* Not even the remarkably unappetizing name of the establishment could deter her.

"Welcome, dearies," a grandmotherly voice greeted them from across the common room. "You're just in time for tea." The plump woman spun around from the table over which she'd been leaning, revealing a porcelain tray clutched between two mitted hands. "I've made strawbe —"

If she'd had the Stamina to spare, Eve would've **Charged!** the innkeeper then and there. As it was, her mad dash was more of an unbalanced tumble through the assorted chairs and tables that littered the space between them.

"Oh dear, hungry, aren't we?"

Eve shoved two of the scones into her mouth at once. Their crisp, sugar-coated exterior exploded across her tongue just as the soft, still-steaming inside melted in her mouth. The tartness of fresh strawberries balanced beautifully with the sweetness of the pastry, coming together in a symphony of flavor, texture, and *joy*.

"I told you so," Wes muttered where he still stood at the inn's doorway. "Nothing beats the power of scones."

"Not so fast," the healer protested. "I said it'd be a hot meal fresh from the oven. Those look plenty hot to me."

The mage patted Preston on the back. "We'll call it a draw."

Fire already blossomed in Eve's chest by the time she reached for thirds. She didn't care. It didn't matter if the food turned to Mana instead of nourishment or if the experience would leave her writhing in agony. She needed this.

She managed to down five of the sugary treats before collapsing to the hardwood floor.

"My heavens." The innkeeper pulled away the tray of scones. "Is she alright?"

Wes and Preston raced to her side as Alex pulled the elderly *Hostess* away to explain the situation.

Eve saw none of it.

An icy inferno raged within her as her **Ethereal Metabolism** converted every calorie of the delicious snacks into pure Mana. Her pool skyrocketed.

Mana: 381/0

She grit her teeth.

Mana: 812/0

Her knuckles whitened as she clenched her fists.

Mana: 1391/0

A whimper escaped her parched throat.

A soft hand touched her forehead, sending waves of golden light through her very being. Two sets of thick fingers wrapped around her wrists, pinning them to the ground to keep her from thrashing as Preston went about his work.

The maelstrom roiled.

Black spots danced across Eve's vision as agony consumed her. White Mana scorched her very being, burning and freezing and melting and *raging*. Her health plummeted, only held stable by the constant stream of healing magic.

The two forces battled within her, laying waste to veins and arteries and organs alike as Ayla's mercy faced off against the remarkable destructive power of the raw Mana.

"Don't explode," Alex practically shouted into her ear. "Not here, not inside. You'll just be back where you started. You need to *adapt.*"

It hurt. By the gods, how it hurt. Eve couldn't bring herself to acknowledge the warrior's words, but she held on nonetheless. People could die if she unleashed this much Mana in the town's center. She slipped in and out of consciousness as the fire within her grew too hot to bear only to recede in the wake of the *Priestess's* spell. Still she held on.

Twice as she lay there on the common room floor did Preston send Alex digging through his pack for a Mana potion only to down the thing in one gulp. The healer never ceased his channeling.

After seconds or minutes or hours of unyielding pain—Eve could scarce tell the difference—the Mana seemed to settle.

"Did you do it?" Nerves shook Wes's voice. "Is she—"

Secondary Quest Stage Complete: Adapt to the Changes

+2000 exp!
Stage Three: Discover their Legacy.

Level Up!

"Look at her eyes!" Alex gestured to the familiar blue reflection of a status screen. "I think she's done it!"

"Thank Ayla." Preston exhaled.

"C'mon," Wes said, "let's get her upstairs."

Eve's consciousness had already begun to fade as two pairs of capable hands gently lifted her, maneuvering her limp form towards the cramped stairway and a soft bed. Before sleep could finally take her, however, Eve managed to read but one more notification from the list that blinked in her periphery.

Race Change Unlocked: Manaheart!

Chapter 36

Manaheart

Eve blinked the sleep from her eyes as the faint glimmers of early dawn pierced her window. The room was spacious, far larger than the one she'd enjoyed at the guild hall, even if the bed itself was a tad lumpy.

All things considered, she felt downright wonderful. Sure, her lower back ached from sleeping on it weirdly, and her *ego* was certainly a touch bruised from collapsing in the middle of the common room only to wake up alone the next morning, but her *body* was fine. No more did she burn with the fires of unspent Mana.

What she *did* burn with, however, was the realization that she wore just her underclothes beneath the thin sheets. Eve hoped that… she gulped. She didn't know what she hoped. Knowing him, Preston had probably insisted on privacy as he'd stripped off her armor. The neat way her clothes sat folded on the foot of her bed seemed to support the theory.

At least as a healer, he was probably professional about it, not to mention that Preston of all people was familiar with being exposed to unwelcome glares from the opposite sex.

Eve shook the thought from her head. There were more important things to worry about, most pressingly the flashing notifications at the corner of her vision. She opened the first.

Race Changed: Manaheart!

The conjunction of your previous skills, inability to manipulate Mana, and accidental participation in the science experiment of a dead race has created something unique. Something new. For the first time in millennia, a step has been taken towards the Burendian dream of true balance between life and Mana. Good luck.

Through the combined efforts of magic and alchemy, you have overcome the inner workings of life. No longer are you bound by the limits of chemical energy. You are a being of Mana.

Eve reread the message. *Well that's... vague,* she thought. She wasn't even entirely sure what 'chemical energy' *was.* The Manaheart looked down at herself.

"I still *look* human," she thought aloud. In fact, other than the familiar white glow coming off the jagged lines along her chest and neck, Eve appeared no different than the day she'd left Nowherested. She'd need a mirror to confirm the assessment.

The idea of being transformed into 'something unique' was at once exciting and terrifying. What if healing spells didn't work on Manahearts? What if her body needed some obscure resource she'd never heard of just to get by? Eve froze. What would her mother think?

Eve dismissed the thread of anxiety with a look towards her notifications. There was no use worrying when she hadn't even gathered all the facts available to her.

Ability Upgraded
Ethereal Metabolism

319

Overcome the inefficiencies of flesh. Mana is the purest form of energy, and your body has learned to use it. Metabolize food directly into Mana. All bodily functions require Mana instead of Stamina.

That last sentence was enough to widen Eve's eyes, giving her sufficient pause to set aside the array of messages in favor of checking her status.

Evelia Greene
Manaheart
Level 34 Shatterfate Striker
Exp: 475/8862
Health: 560/560
Stamina: 0/0
Mana: 194/2250
Constitution: 56
Mana Density: 225
Intelligence: 12
Dexterity: 65
Strength: 84
Spirit: 0

Unsurprised as she was, Eve still gulped at the word 'Manaheart' where it had once said 'human.' No doubt it would take some getting used to. The next line of the unsightly blue screen reminded her she'd leveled up amidst yesterday's chaos. She wondered if the upgrade to **Ethereal Metabolism** counted as her level-up reward or if another ability change awaited her in the notification list.

And then she saw it.

Stamina: 0/0

"Gods below," she swore. A bit of quick math confirmed the sum matched up with what had once been her Endurance. Her mind raced. Even without the need for

Stamina, she clearly would still need to eat. Her **Ethereal Metabolism** made that clear enough. But what about water? If her body had replaced its chemical functions with the use of Mana, did she still require hydration? Her dry throat argued that it did.

The question of sleep arose in her mind. If she metabolized nourishment directly into Mana, was a full night's sleep still necessary? The description of the skill upgrade had mentioned overcoming inefficiencies. Eve wondered what exactly it meant. Once more she cursed the vague nature of the messages.

The curious absence of Endurance from her stat sheet only added to the mystery. Eve shook her head. There had to be more in her remaining notifications. Sure enough, a series of messages explained.

Statistic Gained: Mana Density
With the ability to store Mana in one's very flesh comes the need to quantify how much can be stored. Mana Density measures how much Mana you can store in the limited space of your earthly form without leaking or taking damage.

Statistic Lost: Endurance
Race [Manaheart] does not have access to the Endurance statistic. All points and future gains have been redirected to its closest analog.

Eve furrowed her brow as she considered the new information. She hadn't expected to gain an entirely new *statistic*, especially when one already existed to measure Mana capacity. She recalled that Spirit measured one's ability to make room within their soul for magical energy. Apparently Mana Density was for space within one's body. Then again, the description seemed to imply the amount of space within her body was set, and the new stat just allowed her to pack more Mana into said space.

Eve shrugged.

She was no scholar, and the complexities behind statistic names and effects were well beyond her expertise. As long as her abilities still worked and she wasn't losing power, she wouldn't worry about it too much. The basic mechanics of how this change would affect her life concerned her more. She moved on.

Ability Altered!
Active Ability - Jet
500 Mana
Momentum is a tool just like any other, and you've learned to wield it. Massively increase or decrease your personal momentum in any direction.

"Oh, thank Ayla," Eve muttered. She hadn't even considered what would've happened if all her skills still cost Stamina. Seeing no other changes to **Jet,** she continued through the notifications. **Fate-al Blow** and **Charge!** underwent similar shifts towards Mana use, maintaining the same price as before, if of a different resource. **Adrenaline Rush** was another story.

Ability Upgraded!
Active Ability - Mana Rush
X Mana/Sec
The strength of a Manaheart is determined by the energy that runs through their veins. You've learned to manipulate it to your advantage. Gain [X*MND/20] Strength for the duration.

So she *had* received a skill upgrade for reaching level thirty four, and gods was it a doozy. Assuming 'MND' was the abbreviation for Mana Density, Eve had just unlocked a *massive* well of Strength. Sure it scaled at one twentieth instead of one third, but a bit of quick math confirmed that the original price of X equals four would give her about half as much Strength as the old version.

Eve's mind raced with ideas. At twenty Mana a second, she could add her entire Mana Density to her Strength. Gods, if she wanted to dump her entire Mana pool into the skill, she could break ten *thousand* for a few seconds. Combined with the Strength scaling on **Fate-al Blow**, she'd have nine hells of a first strike. She'd have to be careful, of course, to cancel it quickly. If her body required Mana to live, she didn't want to find out what might happen if she ran out.

She would, of course, have to test the skill. For all she knew, there was a cap on how much she could spend or a minimum duration she'd have to pay for. She could hardly reach ten thousand Strength if the ability wouldn't let her spend more than ten Mana a second. These descriptions were way too vague.

The *Striker* took a breath as she dismissed the last of the notifications. Her thoughts continued to run through the various changes as she finally rose from the lumpy bed and moved to dress herself, pocketing a few silver from her pack. She left her armor where it lay. It seemed unlikely she'd be attacked at the breakfast table.

With a meal in mind, Eve swung open the unlatched door to step into the empty upstairs hallway. She stopped short halfway through to stare into a mirror that hung upon the wall.

Sure enough, the familiar jagged lines still crawled up her neck, but the skin of her face itself remained untouched. The same couldn't be said for her eyes. The same white web traced along her irises, making the green circles appear shattered into a dozen pieces. Cool as they looked, it was her pupils that drew her attention.

They had turned white.

"Definitely not human," she mused. Raising a hand to her face confirmed her recolored eyes glowed just as bright as the lines along her chest. Eve took a moment to thank the gods she didn't have a stealth class. No way she'd escape notice with these beacons on her face.

Eve shook the thought from her mind as her stomach grumbled from days of malnourishment, and if her sub-two-hundred Mana pool was anything to go by, it was justified in its complaint. She continued on to the common room.

Only one of the many tables of *The Foot's Rest* sat occupied, as a lone warrior with an enchanted spear nursed a cup of hot tea.

"Eve!" Alex shot to her feet. "Are you alright? Preston wouldn't let us check on you."

Eve smiled. Saving her life *and* guarding her decency, she'd have to reward the healer somehow. She wondered if he took payments in scones. "I'm okay, I think. Where are the others?"

Alex raised an eyebrow. "Have you ever known those two to wake up at dawn?"

"Right. Well, I'm glad to know at least *one* of my teammates was worried about me enough to not *sleep in*," Eve said with over-exaggerated disdain.

The *Survivor* sat back. "Nah, I always wake up this early." She chuckled to herself. "Seriously, Eve, how are you?"

Eve took a seat across from her companion. "Hungry, mostly. I had—um—a *lot* of notifications to read this morning."

Alex raised a hand to beckon the young man behind the bar. "You can tell me all about it while Peter here gets you some breakfast."

Eve gave the warrior a curious look at her casual use of the man's first name but declined to comment. The heaping plate of ham and sausage and eggs and—thank Ayla—leftover scones that soon appeared before her more than distracted her from the thought. It took Alex's prompting gesture to remind Eve she had a story to tell.

"Well," Alex said as Eve wrapped up her tale and shoved another forkful of egg into her mouth, "that definitely counts as 'adapting.'"

Eve swallowed. "Well it *did* say I completed that stage of the secondary quest. Now I've just got some vague mission to 'discover their legacy.'"

Alex shrugged. "Probably just means you need to level up more and explore more Burendian ruins. Maybe we can find an expedition into one of the more dangerous ones." She paused, resting a hand on her chin as she mused. "A race change kind of makes sense if I think about it. That gnome at the institute in Lynthia said the *human* body isn't meant to store Mana. He didn't say anything about… whatever you are."

"Speaking of leveling up," Eve said, "have you checked the job board? There's gotta be a few dungeons around here, right?"

"Too many," Alex corrected. "There's too many dungeons around here." She conjured a sheet of paper from some unseen pocket, unfolding it and sliding it across the table. "This is the only one we're even close to qualified for."

Eve scanned the rough map and scribbled description. "Demons, huh?"

"Demonoids." Alex nodded. "Mostly lesser ones if the listing is accurate. Wes might have a hard time dealing with them if they're from one of the fiery hells, but Preston will be especially useful."

"Pay's shit," Eve gestured to the hundred-silver reward for completing the dungeon.

The *Survivor* turned up her palms. "That's what you get

for tackling dungeons so far from the cities. Sure there's more of them, but fewer people care enough to pay up. Higher level you get, the more your money comes from loot rather than commissions."

"What kind of loot do demons have?"

"Hells if I know."

Eve opened her mouth in a wide smile of silent laughter at Alex's choice of words.

Alex groaned. "Gods, you're no better than Wes."

"*I* didn't just make a demon/hells pun."

"It's a common expression!" Alex insisted.

"Whatever you say," Eve laughed.

Alex held her head in her hands.

The *Striker* pushed herself to her feet. "Anyway, while we wait for the two lov—" She caught herself. "The two layabouts to wake up, I'm going to get some practice in."

Alex nodded in approval. "Practice is good. See you in a bit."

Eve checked her status as she crossed the empty common room, taking note of her rapidly rising Mana pool. The messages she'd read had implied it could overflow, and she sure as hells didn't want it to do so indoors. She could experiment with that once she had Preston around her to heal any damage it dealt.

At least now she had a good way of dumping extra Mana, one she was all too excited to try out. Eve smiled. She may have finished that leg of the quest, but by no means was she finished adapting to the changes. For the time being, that meant one thing and one thing only.

She had an ability to test.

Chapter 37

A Hell of a Time

"So besides the—um—the glowing thing," Wes said as his eyes traveled over Eve's inhuman form, "what actually changed?"

Eve instinctively moved to brush her hair behind her ear, forgetting she'd cut it too short to even reach said ear. "I just told you; it's—"

"No, no, I get the whole 'Mana instead of Stamina' thing," Wes interrupted, "but what does that actually *mean*?"

The *Striker* turned up her palms. "Other than not exploding and being able to eat again? I don't know. My Mana regens the same way Stamina used to—up to half without food—and since I still don't have any Spirit, I'm pretty sure the change hasn't turned me into a spellcaster."

"You mentioned efficiency, though," Alex chimed in with detail from Eve's prior telling of this same story. "And running on Mana has gotta change how your body functions *somehow*."

"Well I still need to eat and sleep and drink. Maybe more efficient means I don't need as much? My Mana did fill up pretty quick as I ate breakfast."

"Wait." Wes stopped in his tracks, forcing the entire party to pause their trek through the thick pines of the northern woods. "So instead of breaking down food to get nutrients from it, you're turning it directly to Mana?"

Eve furrowed her brow, uncertain where the mage was going with this line of questioning. "Um... yes?"

Wes's voice fell to whisper. "So—um—do you still poop?"

Preston smacked him. "Wes! You can't just *ask* that."

"What? We were all thinking it."

The healer held his head in his hand. "Well, *now* we are."

Eve exhaled. "I'll add that to the list of 'things we'll find out later.' It's only been a few hours; all I've tested so far is the new ability."

That piqued the party's interest. "New ability?" Preston asked. "What is it? What'd you learn?"

"It's an upgrade, really. **Adrenaline Rush** is **Mana Rush** now—I guess because I don't have adrenaline anymore?" Eve shrugged. "The main thing is it's got a scaling Mana cost, and gods does it scale."

She briefly explained the numbers and math behind them before continuing on to talk about her experiments with the skill. "The bad part is it's got a minimum duration. I actually *can't* cancel the ability within ten seconds of using it."

Wes blew through the calculations in under a second. "You can still hit two *thousand* Strength if you're willing to dump most of your pool. More once you've leveled up and have a bit more Mana Density."

Preston whistled. "He's right, Eve. That's gods-damned ridiculous. Most Tier *fours* don't have that kind of firepower."

Eve smirked. "Most Tier fours are human. Don't get me wrong; I'm not complaining. It's just... weird. The skill description says nothing about a minimum duration, and ten seconds feels super arbitrary."

"All abilities have their limits," Alex said. "And yeah, the descriptions are shit sometimes. That's why we test things. My guess is your body can't handle two massive stat changes one after the other like that, so it makes you wait a bit before losing all that Strength."

"Maybe." Eve exhaled. "I don't know. I'll have to keep an eye on my Mana and do the math ahead of time. If I accidentally activate **Mana Rush** for too much and get locked out of canceling it for ten seconds, I could run dry. Natural regen can only do so much, and I don't want to wind up without any Mana left over to keep my body running."

"Maybe you'll just pass out like most people do when they run out of Stamina," Preston suggested.

"Or maybe I'll take damage or maybe my heart will just stop," Eve continued. "It's not something I want to test."

"Right," the healer admitted. "Fair point."

"So—um," Wes changed the subject, "remind me what kind of demons we're supposed to be hunting?"

"Demonic ones," Eve answered.

Alex sighed. "The listing didn't say. All we know is a cave in the Teeth naturalized into a dungeon a few years ago, and apparently there's demons there. The details are too limited for my liking, but it's the only job within our level range so... here we are."

"Are you sure we should be heading into the mountains?" Preston asked. "I thought it was supposed to get *more* dangerous the farther north you go."

"Well, if you'd rather stay in the woods and fight level ninety manticores, be my guest."

The healer gulped. "Demons it is."

Eve scratched her neck. "Preston, you're a *Priestess.* Shouldn't you be jumping at the chance to kill demons?"

"Ayla isn't exactly the demon-slaying type. That's really Loia's or Steilinar's area of expertise. Sure, if one of those demons curses you, I'm your man, but actually fighting them?" He grimaced.

"Alright," Alex thought aloud, "so Preston stays on the backline. Got it. We'll have to wait until we know more about these demonoids to plan anymore than—"

A horrific growl from ahead cut her off.

"Is—um," Preston stammered, "is that them?"

A blast of frigid air swept through the trees, sending a chill down Eve's spine. She placed a hand on her morningstar.

A figure appeared in the shadows of a nearby pine. Another followed in its tracks. And another.

They were eight in all, canine in shape, but that was where the familiarities ended. Where might've been fur and flesh was instead a sharp and skeletal form of deep blue ice. To a beast they stood near as tall as Eve herself, prowling across the forest floor and leaving a trail of frozen foliage in their wake.

Most off-putting, however, were the eyes. Eve might not have realized their demonic nature were it not for the soulless orbs of blackest obsidian which met her gaze. She shuddered.

"Speak of the demons..." Wes let out a nervous laugh to accompany his bad joke.

Alex strapped on her shield. "Gonna need to finish this quick. I can't keep eight hostiles away from the casters for very long. Not on this terrain."

Eve grinned as she grasped her mace. "On it."

She **Charged!**

The hellhounds dashed in, ignoring the running *Striker* in favor of assaulting the juicier targets before them.

Alex lowered her spear.

Eve skirted around the pack, singling out the demon at

the back. *Perfect.*

Energy coursed through her veins as she dumped a hundred points into **Mana Rush**. It'd drain half her pool by the time she could cancel it, but a *thousand* extra Strength was no joke. Especially if it meant an extra three hundred percent damage from **Fate-al Blow.**

The morningstar passed clean through her target.

It shattered.

Shards of unnatural ice flew out in all directions as the hellhound dissolved under the force of the blow. Eve smirked. Damn that sound was satisfying. She let out a laugh as her momentum carried her away from the rest of the pack. She didn't need the kill notification to confirm the beast hadn't survived becoming a pile of broken ice.

She checked her Mana. *1291/2250*

Two demons lunged at Alex at once, overworking her defense enough for a third to reach her spear arm. Frozen teeth dug into her forearm, eliciting no more than a startled grunt from the seasoned warrior. Her defensive skills and Preston's light kept her standing as the creature tugged and twisted.

Alex held resolute, keeping her spear and shield leveled at the rest of the pack.

Eve ran in.

Another swing, another shattered hellhound.

Again, the *Striker's* momentum pulled her away from the fray.

827/2250

We really do need to end this fast, she thought. *Maybe a hundred per second was too much.*

Eve froze as she turned back for another pass.

The demons burned.

Orange flames licked at their icy flesh, tearing through the pack with insatiable vigor. Of the six still-living demons, two already writhed on the forest floor. The motion did little good, as the blaze simply spread to consume the dry needles and branches and even the dirt itself. The other four whined and growled and yelped but kept their feet as the fire devoured them.

As if on cue, the fire mage raised an open hand to the sky. It glowed red as he clenched it into a fist.

The inferno raged. At once it flared up, the flames themselves flashing a blinding white at their center.

Six kill notifications appeared in Eve's vision.

A warrior, a healer, and a whatever Eve was stared in silence at their muscular companion.

Preston was the first to break it. "Ayla's tits, Wes! What the hells was that?"

Wes smirked, lowering his staff. "An old ability, actually. I've had it since the Burendian ruins. Makes all my fires burn hotter, but it only works if… well if I actually have fires. Since I can burn anything now, it's suddenly a lot more useful."

Eve opened her mouth to ask why he hadn't told her about it, before frantically shutting it as she realized her **Mana Rush** was still ticking away. She canceled the skill with three hundred Mana to spare.

You have defeated Level 39 Frigid Hellhound: +1320 exp!
You have defeated Level 39 Frigid Hellhound: +1320 exp!
You have defeated Level 38 Frigid Hellhound: +1260 exp!
You have defeated Level 38 Frigid Hellhound: +1260 exp!
You have defeated Level 38 Frigid Hellhound: +1260 exp!
You have defeated Level 37 Frigid Hellhound: +1200 exp!

"Damn, those were worth a lot," Eve commented. "We should've come out here sooner."

"I'm pretty sure we would've died if we'd come out here sooner," Preston replied.

"Don't worry," Alex said, "we can still die as we are."

Preston paused for a moment before changing the subject. "I wonder what hell they came from."

"One of the frozen ones," Eve answered.

"Really. You don't say." Sarcasm dripped from the healer's voice.

A wave of heat washed over the party as they talked, prompting Eve to turn towards her pyromaniac companion. "Um... Wes? The hounds are dead; you can put out the fire now."

He blinked, jerking his gaze away from the growing inferno. "Oh. Right." With a wave of his hand, the flames petered out, leaving a wide circle of charred earth in its place.

"Well it looks like we've managed to burn away our chance at loot," the *Striker* commented, "but at least we earned exp. I got almost an entire level from that, so I'm sure you've all leveled."

An uncharacteristic string of curses echoed through the quiet woods, setting three pairs of eyes staring at the normally professional *Survivor*.

Preston spoke with a gentle tone. "Is—um—is everything okay?"

"Did you not level up?" Eve asked.

"Oh I did," Alex snapped. "I should've leveled up twice. Key word should. Fucking look." Her eyes flashed blue, prompting the others to lean in to see the reflection of her status screen.

Exp: 5243/5244

Eve snorted. Preston clamped a hand over his mouth to mask his snickering. Wes laughed outright.

"That," he managed through loud guffaws and gasps for breath, "has gotta be the shittiest luck I've ever seen."

"One exp out of five thousand," Eve chuckled through the words. "That can't be a coincidence, can it?"

"That's the worst part," the warrior sighed. "It *has* to be.

Exp is all math, scholars determined the formula years ago."

Wes collected himself at the mention of math. "Right right. Take the thirty base exp of these hounds, multiply it by double their level minus your level, and you get..." He inhaled for a moment as he calculated. "You were one thousand, one hundred and seventeen exp towards level thirty-two when we started?"

Eve rolled her eyes. "You don't have to show off. We all know you've got a lot of Int."

He flashed a cocky grin but didn't reply, maintaining his air of superiority as he dove back into his own notifications.

As the only one without level-ups and ability upgrades to distract her, Eve approached the fuming warrior. "You have to admit, it *is* kind of funny."

"Yeah, yeah." Alex sighed. "I know. At least it's just a random level-up. Could you imagine if there was a promotion on the line?"

Eve laughed. "I'd hold off on getting that one exp for as long as I could. Gotta take every chance at a rarer class, you know." She placed a hand on the warrior's shoulder. "Where we're going, that's not gonna happen."

Alex nodded. "If there were eight of those things just wandering around outside, we're bound to see a whole bunch once we find the place."

"Good," Wes joined in as he finally shut his status screen. "We came here for exp, after all. Once we find that dungeon and kill us some more demons, we'll be leveling up like hell."

A chorus of groans rose up in response.

"Come on, that was a good one!"

Eve held her head in her hands. "Alright, Wes. That's enough demon puns for one day."

"Please, we've got a whole dungeon ahead of us." He

winked. "We're just getting started."

Chapter 38

Nightlight

The grove glimmered with silver light, the darkness of night kept at bay despite the thick canopy above. Eve had first watch. Her eyes flicked between the shifting shadows in the distance and the black remains of their campfire, every once in a while jerking to the motion of one of her teammates rolling over in their sleep.

It wasn't until Wes let out a groan that she realized they were, in fact, very much awake.

"Damnit Eve. I'm trying to sleep."

Preston squinted. "It's too *bright*. Can you turn it down?"

She furrowed her brow. "I don't know."

Wes rubbed his eyes, furiously blinking as he tried—and failed—to look directly at her. "Then cover it up? I have a blanket here somewhere…"

Eve sighed, looking down at the brilliant white with which she shone. "I can cover my neck, but I can't do anything about my eyes. I can't exactly keep watch with a blindfold on."

Preston opened his mouth to speak when a sharp tearing sound rang out. Three adventurers turned as one to watch

Alex tie a piece of torn fabric around her own eyes. She muttered *something,* but all Eve managed to catch was the word "idiots." Fair enough.

"Get some sleep," Eve directed the boys. "I'll wake you when I get tired."

Wes nodded as he wrapped an entire blanket around his head. "At least we don't have to worry about anything sneaking up in the dark."

Preston snorted. "And on top of that, all this light means I get a *perfect* view of how ridiculous you look."

The mage's voice came back muffled through the layers of cloth. "You just don't recognize my genius. It's like a built-in pillow!"

Eve rolled her eyes. "Go to sleep."

Less willing than Alex to deface a piece of his clothing, Preston tied two socks together to create his own makeshift sleeping mask before himself retiring. Wes followed suit.

Eve exhaled as the evening dragged on. She yawned, more from boredom than anything else. Hells, she wasn't even tired. If she was going to start staying awake half the night, she'd need to come up with something to actually *do.*

She considered stepping away for a bit of practice, but she didn't want to risk waking the others yet again. Training seemed like a great way to trick them into thinking they were under attack. She shook her head.

Nearly twelve minutes into her watch, Eve was about to start training anyway when a different idea struck. Preston had mentioned reducing the light she emitted; figuring out how sounded like as good a task as any.

She sat up straight, shutting her eyes and crossing her legs in that uncomfortable way the mystics and mages in the old stories always did. She breathed. Truth be told, Eve had absolutely no idea what meditation had to do with Mana, or even how to go about *doing* it. She thought to turn her focus inward, but for the life of her the *Striker* couldn't fathom what that actually meant.

From time to time she peeked, both to check if her glowing had subsided and to maintain some semblance of keeping watch for monsters in the woods. Nothing happened.

Eve sighed. She doubted the glowing was necessary to live. It if were a part of the Mana her body ran on, shouldn't the jagged streaks of light be all over her body instead of just her chest, neck, and eyes? She shook her head.

If she couldn't directly sense the Mana within her, perhaps she was supposed to imagine it. Eve created a figure of herself in her mind's eye, complete with pulsing Mana running through it. She envisioned it reaching out to travel along her skin in the affected areas like so many arteries spreading the brilliant Mana from its source at her heart.

But her real veins weren't on the outside of her chest. They were within.

Eve imagined the Mana withdrawing from the network upon her skin, continuing its circulation where none could see.

As her eyes popped open to check if she'd been successful, she found not the gleaming white of Mana, but the tacky blue of notification.

You have learned the basic skill Mana Manipulation!
Through mediation and understanding of the Mana within your soul, you've taken the first step on the path of magic.

Eve snorted. It was the first basic skill she'd found since learning **Appraise**, and it seemed just as useless. The first step on the path of magic? She already knew four spells, for hells' sake. Sure, they were all modified versions of

Stamina skills that had switched to Mana with her race change, but they were still *spells*.

More interesting to Eve, however, was the mention of her soul in the skill description. She had no Mana in her soul. A quick check confirmed her Spirit stat still rested at a grayed-out zero. Was the skill description wrong? She supposed the description would be accurate for anyone else. Perhaps her new race really was unique.

The *Striker* shook her head, dismissing the message. It wasn't until she noted the still-glimmering state of her upper body that Eve realized her lapse in focus. She closed her eyes and tried again.

Once she finished re-envisioning the Mana retreating from her skin, Eve made a point of keeping the image in her mind as she allowed her eyes to flick open. The shadows loomed.

A grin spread across the *Striker's* face as she held a hand up to her neck, noting the dim illumination that struck it. Not perfect, but better. Unless she missed her guess, the lines would be completely invisible in full daylight. She hoped.

Eve made it three minutes before her concentration failed, and the light returned once more. Still she smiled. At least now she had a skill to practice while the others slumbered.

When at last the first light of dawn pierced the thick canopy, it landed upon a party of four, distinctly human-looking adventurers.

* * *

The cave entrance was almost painfully nondescript.

Where the party had finally left the woods, the "foot" of the mountains was more of a fifty-foot sheer cliff. The vertical wall of limestone left Eve reeling as she looked up to watch the clouds float over it, but at least the geographical feature made their search easy. They only had to walk along it for a few hours to find their destination.

It was more a crack in the towering rock than a proper cavern. Sure, the only cave Eve had ever seen had been the carved arch marking the way to the Burendian Ruin, but she'd always imagined dungeon entrances as grand openings into the deep. They might've missed the open crack were it not for the gust of frigid air it emitted.

Alex gulped as she took the first step in. "This is it!" she called back. "But I'm afraid it's more than just a few rogue demons."

As Eve squeezed in after her, she found the source of Alex's concern.

You have entered the dungeon: Temple of Garaxia! Fight well.

Wes had to turn his body sideways to fit through the narrow entrance. "Does—um—anyone happen to know who Garaxia is?"

Preston took up the rear. "Archdemon of some sort? Do you think he's here?"

"Is Ayla in your cathedral?" Eve asked.

"Right, right," the healer said. "So what's there to worry about?"

"If it's a temple," Alex explained, "there'll be worshippers. I don't think this is a place some wild demons holed up in. They were summoned here."

"Does that change anything?" Eve asked.

"I'd say we need to be careful, but that *should've* been the plan from the moment we left." Alex sighed. "I doubt any cultists we find will be much higher level than the hellhounds we've already fought."

Wes chimed in, "If there's worshippers, do you think they have relics? Sacrificial daggers or golden altars or anything we can sell?"

Eve laughed, "As long as you don't set them all on fire. It's hard to loot a pile of ashes."

"That's enough," Alex quieted them with a harsh whisper. "We don't need to announce our presence to the entire dungeon."

The companions nodded, allowing the conversation to die out as they inched through the narrow passage. A few minutes of silent scraping later, the crack widened out into a proper cave.

Alex shivered as icy air struck her. Preston huddled up to Wes for warmth, the fire mage ever flush with heat to spare.

For her part, though goosebumps popped up along Eve's exposed skin, the chill itself never pierced beyond the surface. She wondered if the extra heat cost her Mana, but the rate at which her supply depleted from regular activity was too inconsistent to properly measure.

Either way, she was more than happy to escape the unpleasantness of the frigid cavern. Apparently temperature regulation was one of those bodily functions made more efficient by the use of Mana. Eve smiled, suppressing the urge to brag about it to Wes. Now wasn't the time for banter.

The web of lines along Eve's skin lit the way, their ethereal glow casting a thousand sparkling dots upon the walls as a layer of frost reflected her light. The party walked together through a cavern of stars, if a particularly cold one.

The imps came from nowhere.

A dozen of the three-foot demonoids seemed to step out of the cavern wall itself, baring their jagged teeth at the intruding adventurers. Their skeletal bodies were made of the same deep blue ice as the hellhounds, their claws just as sharp and their cry just as eerie.

The first frost bolt landed on Alex's shield. The second grazed her arm, but the gash closed up before Eve's eyes.

The *Striker* **Charged!** before there could be a third.

Eve didn't bother with **Fate-al Blow,** the three hundred Strength from dropping thirty Mana into **Mana Rush** more than enough to shatter an imp with a single swing of her morningstar.

She skirted the edge of the battle, keeping to the cavern wall as Alex intercepted the demons' spells and Wes retaliated with magic of his own. Whenever a swipe of the warrior's spear or a burst of mage's fire left an imp separated from its cohort, Eve struck.

There were only three left when the frost bolt hit her.

She'd seen it coming. Hells, she'd been running the beast down as it channeled its spell. What Eve *hadn't* expected was for Wes's growing inferno to suddenly flare up with stifling heat and blinding light.

She was still blinking the dark spots from her vision when the spell struck.

The force behind the flying ice shard sent it right through the thick leather guarding her left thigh. Pain exploded through her as the attack cut deep into the side of her leg. It was enough to send her careening away, backpedaling wildly away from the fray until she collided with the cavern wall.

By the time she recovered her footing, the fight was already over.

You have defeated Level 32 Frostborn Imp: +450 exp!
You have defeated Level 32 Frostborn Imp: +450 exp!
...
You have defeated Level 30 Frostborn Imp: +390 exp!

The twelve imps came to 5040 exp in total, enough to cause two additional notifications to appear in Eve's vision.

Level Up!

Ability Upgraded!
Passive Ability - Mana-hardened
Redirect Mana within your body to reinforce particular areas.

A quick check confirmed the skill still had all the old benefits of the **Battle-hardened** from which it had evolved, so Eve was plenty happy for the upgrade. She wondered if discovering **Mana Manipulation** had influenced the change. Given how similar the description sounded to what she'd done to dim her glowing, it would only make sense.

A fresh wave of pain from her injured leg pulled Eve back to the real world. "Preston, I know you're excited to level up again, but I would really appreciate some healing."

Silence greeted her.

"Preston?"

Wes spoke up, "He was just with…" He trailed off as the blue reflection of a status screen faded from his eyes. He jerked his head back and forth, peering down the passage in both directions. "Shit."

Eve's heart raced, pumping ice through her veins as she called out once again. It was no use.

Preston was gone.

Chapter 39

When in Doubt, Burn the Puzzle

"Check the walls." Cold authority filled Alex's voice, hiding a backdrop of well-controlled fear. "Unless he just started sprinting as soon as the imps appeared, they must've taken him through a secret passage."

Wes practically raced to the nearest wall, running his hands across the frozen surface with the vigor of desperation. Eve joined in as much as she could, limping along on her wounded leg.

"His pack's here!" Wes's shout echoed down the empty cavern. "This must've been where..." He trailed off, abandoning the messenger bag to scan every inch of cave-side above it.

Alex paused in her search to root through Preston's belongings. "Regi's gone too."

"That's something," Eve tried to offer comfort. "At least they're together."

Wes was having none of it. "So we've managed to lose *both* of our most defenseless party members. Great. 'Protect the healer' is rule number gods-damned one."

Alex stood, turning back around to toss a tight-sewn leather pouch across the cave. Eve caught it.

Healing Tincture
Rarity: Uncommon

She swallowed it in a single gulp, wincing as the bitter syrup dripped down her throat. The pain in her leg vanished immediately as the skin knit itself back together. The hole in her armor was another issue. "Good thing he bought these. Though I'm not sure Preston should be the one carrying them. We'd be screwed if he hadn't dropped his pack."

"It's no use." Wes took a step back. "It's solid ice. They must've used frost magic to open it up."

"Shit," Alex cursed under her breath. "This is just like —"

"It's okay," Eve interrupted before Alex could travel too far along that thought. The *Survivor* had made too much progress since full-on panicking at the sight of a dungeon. She needed Alex to keep it together. "If they wanted Preston dead, there'd be a corpse here. We have his potions, and we're all capable adventurers. We can still find him."

"Not if the door only opens for ice mages," Wes said, his shoulders slumping. He pointed down the open tunnel ahead. "For all we know that path goes on for miles before winding up wherever they took him."

Alex rubbed her temples. "Ice melts, Wes."

The *Acolyte* didn't stop to chastise himself for the lapse in thought. He simply raised a hand, and the wall came alight. For Wes, ice burned too.

Hot steam filled the air, shining orange with the bright glow of the magical fire as the walls themselves gave way to the devouring flame. Wes watched the inferno with intensity in his gaze, his eyes glimmering the same flickering hue of the blaze before him.

345

The fire raged.

Eve coughed as ice gave way to stone, and steam to sticky black smoke. "That's enough!"

Still it burned.

"Wes!" she called, placing a hand on the mage's shoulder.

He shook her off, glowering as he nonetheless clenched his fist and quenched the flames. Now only Eve's silver light shined upon the lingering steam and ash and dust, forcing the companions to squint and wait for the haze to settle. When at last it did, a passage revealed itself.

Wes lurched forward, squeezing his shoulders in to fit within the narrow confines of the stone tunnel. Alex stopped him. "I'm first. We do this right or not at all. You can't help Preston if you die to a random frost bolt."

The burly mage scowled but remained silent as he stepped away to allow Alex past.

Eve stooped over to collect Preston's pack as she took up the rear, slinging it over her shoulder to rest beside her own. It would be tricky to ditch both in the event of a fight, but given the tight space in which they traveled, she wouldn't be much use anyway.

Alex set a careful pace down the dark path, regularly holding her ground as Wes prodded her to go faster. The third time she reminded him that survival was more important than haste seemed to quiet his protests.

From her limited vantage at the back of the procession, Eve found the constant stops to carefully check each and every corner of twisting passage a bit unwieldy, but she accepted the need for caution. *She* wouldn't be the one getting bitten if they accidentally walked into a pack of hellhounds.

Though the walls of the secret tunnel were rough stone rather than the sheer ice of the main cavern, they were still cold as all hells. Well, Eve supposed they were cold as one particular hell, but she still wasn't sure which. She was pretty sure the fourth through eighth hells were all frozen, and she *thought* the second might've been as well but couldn't say for certain. She was no theologian.

After three sharp left turns, two gentle rightward bends, and an uncomfortably long staircase down, the passage opened up into a wide chamber. Alex scanned the room for hostiles before lowering her spear and allowing Eve and Wes inside.

The circular cavern, nearly thirty feet across and as many tall, was mostly empty. Three doors blocked off three paths, one of wood, one of stone, and one of steel. Eve didn't need to try their handles to know they were locked—the room's only other feature made her sure of that.

Three square pillars stood in a line at the cavern's center, each no taller than Wes's chin, and each topped with a rectangular block of ice. Much as Eve marveled at their pure edges and crisp corners, it was their contents that drew her gaze.

Three keys sat suspended in the ice, one of wood, one of stone, and one of steel.

"I thought this was a secret passage," Wes said. "What is a gods-damned puzzle room doing here?"

Alex shrugged. "Maybe it's symbolic?"

"It doesn't look like much of a puzzle," Eve commented. "Steel key for the steel door? Unless I'm missing something..."

"It probably has something to do with their scripture; the different materials mean different things." Alex sighed. "Or it's all completely random and the ice is only there to keep non-frost mages out."

"We don't have time for this." Wes stormed up to the wooden door at the cavern's left. "They could've taken Preston down any one of these tunnels." He raised a palm to the oaken planks, setting it alight with **Burning Hand.**

The wood refused to burn.

The flames flared up in a burst of white as Wes threw more Mana into it, but the blaze itself never strayed from the confines of his hand. When at last he ended the spell and pulled away, not even a scorch stained the simple door.

Eve bit her lip to keep herself from laughing; she knew Wes was in no mood for jokes. That didn't stop her. "So you can burn *ice*, but you can't burn some bloody wood?"

"It's gotta be enchanted. I can burn *anything*." Wes turned from the door, heading back to the pillars. "But since you mentioned ice…" He reached for the block holding the steel key.

"Wes, wait," Alex stepped in. "Maybe we should think about this. If it *is* a puzzle room, I don't think blasting it with fire is the intended solution."

"Fuck the intended solution. They have our friend." He cast the **Burning Hand**.

The ice caught fire, spreading steam through the tall cavern as it burned away. Wes grit his teeth, **Fanning the Flames** to speed the process. The room grew hot, the mage fire strong enough to overcome the demonic chill that permeated the dungeon. Flames danced in Wes's eyes as he drove the inferno, set on freeing the key from its frozen prison as soon as possible.

Eve saw the smoke before he did. "Wes, stop!" She dashed across the room, practically shoving the man aside. By the time he finally ended the inferno, it was too late.

Where once had been a key of dark steel was now a malformed lump of melted slag. Wes cursed, releasing a string of increasingly creative expletives as he declared his anger at the gods, the dungeon, his class, and at 'those infernal whispers.'

Eve placed a hand on his shoulder. "It's okay, Wes. It's

okay. For all we know that wasn't even the right way." She fingered her mace. "Let me take a swing."

"Is that a good idea?" Alex asked.

Eve shrugged. "Do you have a better one? I really don't think this is meant as a puzzle—the ice doesn't have anything to do with the different types of door. Assuming it's just there to make people prove they can manipulate demonic ice, I think smashing is probably our best bet."

Alex furrowed her brow in thought before eventually nodding, stepping aside to allow Eve access to the other pillars.

Eve sized up the stone key as she drew her weapon, choosing the target she hoped would prove the most durable. She stepped back.

Activating **Mana Rush** for a hundred Mana per second put her just below thirteen hundred Strength, plenty to break a foot-thick block of ice. With a deep breath and a running start, she swung.

The sound it made was satisfying as all hells. The shattering echoed across the empty cavern, resonating wonderfully as it reached Eve's ears. She smiled. That is, she smiled until she saw the remains of the key on the floor. All dozen pieces of it.

"Shit," she swore, bending over to collect the broken stone. While the teethed tip seemed relatively unharmed, the shaft and rounded end were anything but. At least she had a pile of pebbles for her efforts. Eve lifted the semi-whole end with the intact teeth. "Think this'll still work?"

"Depends," Alex answered. "If you want to jam the lock so nobody can open it and you can't get the key out, then yes, that'll work. If you want to actually open the door…" She shrugged. "No way you'll be able to turn that thing."

Eve cursed again. "Alright. One key left then. Any ideas?"

"Well, we've got two options," the *Survivor* reasoned

aloud. "Either you try and hit it softer, or Wes tries to melt it slower."

Eve watched her status screen as the final seconds of **Mana Rush's** minimum ticked away before she could cancel it. She had to maintain *some* Mana after all. "I could try un-empowered, but my strength boost has gone on cooldown. Will probably take twenty minutes or so to come off."

"I'll do it," Wes said, determination filling his face.

Eve faltered. "Are you sure? Between the fights and the secret passage and the steel key—"

"I was rushing," he snapped, "because we don't have *time*. Every minute could mean the difference between saving Preston or finding a pretty blond corpse on some sacrificial altar."

"The way you stared at those fires didn't look like rushing to me."

Wes swallowed. "I can do this. I'm in control, not my class. I just need..." He exhaled. "I need to focus."

Eve shared a worried look with Alex before quietly nodding. Truth be told, even if they *did* wait for her cooldown, she didn't have much confidence in her ability to shatter the ice. **Mana Rush** only let her change her Strength once—too much and she'd break another key, too little and the ice would hold strong, forcing another cooldown. At least Wes would either succeed or fail quickly. The main tunnel they'd left behind was still open to them.

The fire mage stepped up to the frozen key, holding both hands in the air above the well-carved block. They came alight with a flash, glowing a dim red instead of the sharp white or burning orange they had before.

Eve smiled as the first drop of water struck the floor.

Wes didn't even notice. His eyes were affixed to his **Burning Hands**. They shook as he held them there, drifting down as if to set the block aflame before jerking away as he retook his focus. There was an instability to the gentle blaze as it flared up and died down in random waves, each growing dangerously nearer to touching the ice itself.

Only the bottom teeth of the wooden key were still encased when Wes slipped up. Whether by loss of focus or tiring arms or the chaotic nature of fire itself, a spark leapt from his thumb just as that hand dipped towards the retreating ice. A flame took hold.

Wes let it.

He lowered his hands yet farther, pressing the limits of how much heat he could apply without burning the wooden key. Much as Eve wanted to shout, to insist he slow down and extinguish the growing blaze, Wes pushed forward.

He jerked back with a shout just as the untamed fire consumed the ice. Eve held her breath as she turned to meet his gaze.

A triumphant grin spread across his face as he held aloft his prize, whole and unburnt.

Eve smiled back at him. "You did it!"

"Told you I was in control."

"Um," Alex interrupted, "about that..." She pointed back at the keyless pillar and the growing inferno that now consumed the entire structure. "Let's not burn the dungeon down."

Wes paled. "Right. Sorry. I'll just—" He clenched his fist and fire vanished. "Alright." He brandished the key once more, pointing it towards the wooden door. "Let's get moving."

The women nodded, following him as he crossed the cavern to fit his newly-won key into its respective door. It swung open without so much as a squeak.

As Alex once more took the lead, Eve gave Wes one final

look before following into the dark tunnel.   She grinned. "Well that was the easiest puzzle room I've ever solved."

Wes kept his eyes forward.   There would be no comments of 'you didn't solve shit,' or 'every puzzle is easy when you have a hundred and fifty Intelligence,' or 'when in doubt, burn the puzzle.'   He had other things on his mind.

They could only hope the one door they'd managed to open would lead them back to Preston.

Chapter 40

Burn, Baby, Burn

You have defeated Level 32 Frostborn Imp: +630 exp!
You have defeated Level 32 Frostborn Imp: +630 exp!
...
You have defeated Level 30 Frostborn Imp: +570 exp!
Level Up!

Ability Unlocked!
   Active Ability - Ayla's Ward
   25 Mana/Sec
   The Lady Ayla protects Her faithful. Manifest your love for Her Benevolence into a shield of holy light, perfect for deflecting projectiles.

"Ayla's crooked left tit," Preston cursed as he dismissed the notifications. Gods, his head hurt. He moved to massage his temples and rub his eyes but found his hands refused to budge from behind his back. A few quick test yanks confirmed they were tied together at the wrist. Of course they were.

As the unsightly blue light of his messages faded away, Preston got his first look at his surroundings. They were actually rather pleasant. Plush cushions of velvet and silk protected him from the icy floor, while a series of torches cast comforting heat throughout the enclosure. Indeed, were it not for the row of vertical bars blocking his exit from the small cavern, he might've thought himself a valued guest.

The room outside his cell seemed to be some sort of side chamber, occupied only by a storage cupboard, an empty table of plain wood, and a matching chair. There was an exit on each side of the small room, further driving home the idea that it was more a space for passing through than one for lingering, not that Preston had any choice in the matter.

He swore.

With a quiet sigh, the healer sat up, leaning back against the cold wall. He was just about to begin the unwieldy process of placing a pillow between him and the hard stone with tied-up hands when a voice echoed in from the leftmost path.

"I told you it would work! Adventurers can't resist the promise of exp and loot. All it took was a few dead packs of hellhounds and they came to us."

"That remains to be seen," a snide voice replied, "but if you have indeed snared our prize, Garaxia Herself may soon walk this earth."

The words sent a chill down Preston's spine. Whoever else walked with the man, however, was a bit more enthused.

A chorus of excited chattering broke out before falling dead silent as a dozen robed figures stepped into the chamber. They were all men, as Preston reckoned, though their deep hoods did a bang-up job of obscuring their features. Indeed, between said hoods and the completely nondescript black hue of their garments, Preston could only wonder how they could tell each other apart. Perhaps through their voices?

The snide one—presumably the leader—was the first to speak. "*This* is our virgin *Priestess*? You can't just take a random adventurer and dress him in white robes."

Preston's jaw dropped. "Excuse me?"

A noticeably shorter man at the leader's side spoke up in answer, "Of course not! If your holiness would deign to **Appraise** him..."

Eleven sets of eyes flashed blue as they all used the basic skill. Two gasps and a muttered "by the hells" rang out.

"Now, now," the lead cultist said, "it would appear you've done Her Greatness a great service. We can begin the sacrifice at midnight."

"Begin the what?" Preston interrupted.

'His holiness' smirked at the healer. "The summoning ritual requires the sacrifice of a virgin *Priestess*. Alvin here has been kind enough to provide us with you."

Preston had to stop himself from breaking out laughing at the idea of a dark cultist named Alvin in order to protest another part of the statement. "Yeah—um—I don't think that's going to work out for you. I'm not a virgin."

Alvin grinned. "That's the beauty of it! The scripture calls for a *Priestess* 'untainted by a man's touch.' It doesn't *matter* if you've been with a woman!"

The healer reddened. "Okay, I can't believe I have to say this, but I *have* actua—"

The cult leader cut him off. "Excellent work, Alvin. Her Terribleness will be sure to reward you greatly for your efforts." His voice raised as he addressed the crowd. "Prepare the ritual!" One by one he barked orders to the assembled acolytes before wrapping up with a final, "And Alvin, look after our *Priestess*. You've done well."

Alvin glowed under the praise as his fellows disappeared from the side chamber, followed eventually by the leader himself.

J.P. Valentine

Seconds passed in silence as the *Priestess* and the *Cultist* —an identifier Preston confirmed with a quick **Appraise**— stared each other down. The healer considered explaining to the short man that he very much did *not* fit his demoness's definition of 'virgin,' but the growing smile across Alvin's face gave him pause. He just... looked so *happy*.

Just as Preston weighed telling him now versus waiting a bit to make the demon-worshipers waste their time setting up an incomplete ritual versus desperately hoping they wouldn't kill him anyway if he told the truth, Alvin let out a little cheer.

"I know!" He practically bounced with giddiness. "I'll bake something! What's better than sweets to celebrate such a victory?"

Preston opened his mouth to speak but promptly shut it again as Alvin addressed him, "Wait right here, okay? I'll be back in a bit!" He turned on his heel and scurried from the room, leaving Preston alone once more.

Well that was certainly something, the healer mused. *I guess it takes a certain kind of person to worship a demon.* He wondered why only men had appeared among the cultists. Maybe the women were elsewhere? He shrugged.

Deciding eventually that he may as well get comfy while he waited for the others to rescue him, Preston turned his entire torso to reach for a pillow with his tied-up hands, craning his neck over his shoulder as he clumsily maneuvered. As he finally lifted the velvet cushion, it left behind a pile of feathers and torn fabric, amongst which sat a particular baby drake.

"Reginald! Don't eat the pillows!" he chided the hatchling. "Those aren't..." Preston trailed off, running a finger along the cord which bound his wrists. It was leather. An idea struck. "You must be hungry, huh?" He leaned back, wrapping a hand around the creature. "Why

356

don't you chew on this instead?"

It took more than a little finagling to direct Reginald's head towards the leather strap, but once the rows of teeth in that tiny little maw got to work, there was no stopping them. Preston let out an audible sigh of relief as his hands broke free.

After spending a sufficient amount of time cooing over Reginald for doing such a good job, Preston stashed the hatchling in the sleeve of his robe. He stood, massaging his sore wrists. "Okay, hands untied," he thought aloud, "I guess that only leaves one question." He turned to face the bars of his cell.

"How the hells do I get out of here?"

* * *

Eve was rather less than surprised to find yet more tunnel behind the enchanted wooden door. Sure, she might've hoped for a treasure room or a thrilling combat encounter or to find their missing friend, but she knew well enough such things didn't come so easy. They had just traversed a secret tunnel that jutted off from a larger tunnel—of *course* they had more tunnel ahead of them.

The predictability of it all did little to calm a certain fire mage.

Wes grew more impatient with every passing second, urging the party forward with increasing urgency. Thrice as they progressed down the narrow passage did he accidentally step on Alex's heels, eliciting a sharp glare from the cautious *Survivor*. Eve got the distinct impression that were the cave wide enough to allow it, he would've charged past her in his haste to save Preston.

The *Striker* couldn't help but wonder what Alex thought about his near panic. Wes wasn't exactly doing a good job of hiding his feelings for Preston from her, but Alex seemed not the least bit interested in his behavior. Hells, for all Eve knew, the healer had completely made up his claim that

Alex had 'a thing' for the burly fire mage. *She* certainly hadn't seen any evidence of it.

Either Alex didn't care, was particularly good at hiding it, or was simply too concerned with surviving the dungeon to bring it up now. Eve had no idea which. At least the potential conflict wasn't getting in the way of their survival. She could worry about any disputes—should they occur—once they were all safe.

Preston's bag weighed heavily on Eve's shoulder as she followed her inordinately tall companions down the cold tunnel, lighting the way with her conveniently glowing skin. She hoped whatever the demons had taken him for hadn't happened yet.

"These tunnels are too gods-damned long," Wes complained through gritted teeth. "We could be halfway to Lynthia by now."

Eve snorted. "We're still in the Teeth. We haven't gone down enough to be under the plains."

"Actually," Alex said under her breath, "I don't think we've traveled that far at all. We've taken way more left turns than right ones. We're going in a sort of spiral."

Eve and Wes both gaped.

Alex shook her head and let out a sigh. "You know, for all your levels, you're still insanely green. If you count the turns and the steps between them, you can get a general idea of the layout of a dungeon. We're going a lot to the left, and the number of steps between each turn is getting bigger. It's a spiral. Kind of. There's right turns and other weirdness, but it's *like* a spiral. Wherever we're going, this is the long way."

"Then *hurry up*," Wes groaned.

Alex ignored him.

Eve furrowed her brow. "What about the other tunnels? If we're spiraling out, shouldn't we intersect with them?"

The warrior shrugged. "Maybe they're spiraling too?

Or maybe those doors just lead to rooms instead of passageways? Not that it really matters; this is the only path ahead."

"Still," Eve wondered aloud, "it's a weird layout for a cave. It doesn't seem natural, but why would someone *build* a spiral tunnel like this?"

"It's a temple, remember? Probably has some symbolism to whatever demon they—" Alex stopped in her tracks. "Listen."

A series of quiet scratches and high-pitched whimpers echoed down the path ahead. Eve wrapped a hand around her mace. Alex leveled her spear.

Wes didn't question the careful pace Alex set towards the mysterious noises. He simply readied a spell and followed in silence. His crackling firelight was the first to reach the cavern.

"Shit," Alex cursed as she stepped into the fifty-foot chamber. "They aren't just summoning demons. They're breeding them."

Eve stepped around Wes's oversized form to cast her own silver light upon the room. Other than a clear path towards the exit across from them, every inch of the cavern floor housed either a mewling baby hellhound or the bones and viscera from a former meal. She retched.

The corpse of what could've only been the mother rotted in the room's center, long torn apart by the hungry teeth of its young.

Steel filled Wes's voice. "Wait by the exit. I'll take care of this."

Alex and Eve shared a solemn look before slowly nodding and picking their way across the cavern. Despite their minuscule size and apparent weakness, Eve made a point of keeping her distance from the demonic puppies. Even young as they were, blood already stained their icy teeth.

The fires had already begun by the time Eve reached the exit.

They spread in a circle around their source, devouring stone and bone and flesh alike. Demonspawn cried and whimpered and fled as they could, but the cavern was crowded and the flames quick. The inferno raged, and so too did its master.

The fire mage poured magic into the blaze, urging it to burn higher and hotter and faster just as it in turn converted its fuel into the very energy that powered it. As long as the flames continued to feed, Wes's Mana would never run dry.

As the firestorm reached the cavern's edge and the last of the piteous cries fell silent, Wes turned to rejoin the others at the exit.

Eve watched him approach with awe in her eyes. As he strode through the inferno, untouched by the flames that licked at his ankles, she couldn't help but wonder if they'd simply replaced a frozen hell for a fiery one.

And then he clenched his fist and the flames disappeared and the Wes she knew was there once more. "Come on," he said against a backdrop of char and ash, "we have a friend to save."

Chapter 41

Cultist of the Month

Eve swallowed for the hundredth time that day, futilely hoping the act would somehow aid her sore throat. It never did. "Maybe," she wheezed, "we should stop starting fires inside caves."

Apparently the tunnel through which they walked sloped slightly upward, just enough for the smoke from Wes's stunt with the baby demons to follow them through the depths. Eve was less than enthused.

"Did you have a better idea?" the mage asked. "We couldn't let them grow up to start killing people, and we didn't have time for you to go through and stab them one by one."

Eve exhaled, fighting off a fit of coughs. "I suppose that's the downside of all this Manaheart stuff—I can't explode anymore."

"Right." Wes snorted. "Because *exploding* is always a good option. Didn't you collapse an ancient ruin and nearly kill us all the last time you exploded underground?"

"Hey, that was my *sword* that exploded, not me. Actually, no. It was *your* shitty sword."

"Hold on." Wes held up his hands. "To be fair, it was

Mr. Potts' shitty sword. Except it wasn't even his because it was gods-damned stolen."

"To be *fair*," Eve repeated his words back to him, "I didn't see you complaining when I exploded to kill the giant spider."

Wes countered, "You mean the one I could've killed safely completely on my own if you hadn't run in?"

"Look, the point is, I need a new skill. A thousand Strength doesn't do shit when I can only hit one thing at a time."

Alex stepped in, "That's the whole point of a *Striker*, though: high, single target damage. Daggers and maces are never going to be great against a crowd, just like giant firestorms won't do much damage versus a massive drake."

Eve snapped her fingers. "That's right, Wes *was* pretty useless against the drake."

Alex sighed. "That's not my point. Nobody can be good at everything. We actually have a really balanced team—Wes deals multi-target damage, you do insane things against a single target, I soak up damage, and Preston keeps us all alive."

Wes's shoulders sank. "Except right now. 'Cause we've done a shit job of keeping *Preston* alive."

Eve placed a gentle hand on his arm, all humor draining from her voice. "We'll find him. I promise."

She knew she shouldn't make promises like that, that the words were meaningless comfort from the mouth of one who knew just as little as Wes did. Eve had no idea if they'd find Preston, but Wes needed every bit of hope he could get. She still remembered the words of that guard at Foot's Garrison: "Two things adventurers are good at: drinking and dying."

Eve shuddered. Even as the lingering smoke scraped against her throat, she couldn't truly fault Wes for burning the demons. She understood the need to destroy things right now.

To be entirely honest, she could use a little violence herself.

Fortunately enough, or perhaps unfortunately by any sane person's reasoning, the dungeon was happy to provide.

The labyrinthine tunnel finally came to an end in a grand open hall. As far as Eve could tell from her cursory glance in both directions, theirs was but one of a dozen side doors that met here. She wondered how long it might've taken them to arrive had they not found the secret passage.

As she scanned the chamber, it wasn't the vaulted ceilings or ornate icy columns or even the massive carved-stone door which dominated the right wall that drew Eve's attention. It was the nine-foot humanoid that leaned unmoving against a pillar.

The beast had horns. It had far too many horns. Ayla's tits, it had a lot of horns. While its flesh was the same dark ice as the party's previous foes, the horns themselves were white as bone. The first were a set of thick, curled ram's horns upon the thing's forehead, followed by a stiletto-sharp, more traditionally demonic pair pointing straight from the top of its head.

Eve wondered if the matching sets on the creature's shoulders, elbows, and knees could even be considered horns or if by their position they were simply spikes, but she failed to produce a worthwhile answer. She was too busy staring at how many damned horns this thing had.

Wes couldn't help himself. "That has got to be the hor —"

"Wes," Eve cut him off, "if you say what I think you're about to say, I'll feed you to the demon myself."

He shut his mouth before the pun could escape.

Eve shrugged both hers and Preston's bags from her shoulders. She drew her mace. "Alright. That looks like a single target to me."

"Assuming you can get past the spikes," Alex said, gesturing with her spear, "and the claws."

"It'll be easy if you keep them busy for me."

The warrior sighed. "That *is* my job. Just be careful; you don't have a healer backing you up."

Eve cocked a smile. "Don't you worry; I'm *well* past my falling-on-my-face phase."

Wes rolled his eyes.

With a quick nod of confirmation, Alex leveled her shield and stepped into the hall proper.

Eve skirted behind the pillars, trying to position herself behind the beast as Alex slammed her spear into the cobblestone floor to attract its attention.

It roared. Its flat, featureless face split open to reveal two rows of needle-sharp teeth, each dripping with black ichor. The terrible cry echoed throughout the cavern, vibrating the very air as if the sound alone could paralyze its prey.

It's a good thing Eve was no prey.

The moment the demon turned to approach the tall *Survivor*, Eve **Charged!**

She arced her path around it, keeping out of sight as it lowered its head and raced to ram Alex.

Alex held fast. She planted her feet and braced herself and activated her shield's enchantment to reinforce it with the floor beneath them. The stone offered little in the way of support, resistant as it was to the earth magic, but it was enough.

Whatever abilities the *Survivor* had used in tandem proved enough, as a monstrous thud filled the air. Demon and warrior alike fell back, both dazed by the impact.

Eve had her opening.

Charge! drove her forward as **Mana Rush**ed through her blood, empowering her muscles with arcane energy for the coming exchange. Her heart pounded with every step, keeping time with the breakneck pace she set. As the beast drew near, Eve pulled back her mace for the **Fate-al Blow.**

No amount of horns could stop it.

The crisp sound of shattering ice filled the hall as the mace struck true, passing clean through the abomination's torso—she could reach its head—without issue. It collapsed to the floor in two halves and a heap of melting shards.

You have defeated Level 81 Frosthorn Demon: +5080 exp!

Eve didn't pause to ask around about levels gained or abilities upgraded. She didn't stop to consider the weird similarities between killing first Frostborn Imps and now a Frosthorn Demon. She didn't even wait for her **Charge!** to run out.

She simply dashed back to where she'd left the supplies, dug a Mana potion from Preston's pack, and turned to the massive stone door that could only lead to the main temple.

"So," she said, cognizant of the time pressures before them, "let's get this thing open."

* * *

Alvin spat out his tea. "He actually said that?!"

Preston nodded, a smile crossing his face. "I shit you not, those were his *exact* words." He pointed up at the cultist's agape expression. "That was my reaction too."

The two sat together on the floor of the prison room, exchanging conversation between the petrified-wood bars. Alvin sat comfortably on a cushion Preston had passed through the barrier while the healer sipped on tea kindly provided by the friendly cultist.

"What did you do?"

Preston turned up his palms. "What could I do? I ran the hells out of there and never looked back. Lesson learned: just because you see collars in the window doesn't mean it's a pet store."

Alvin shook his head, his face rapidly approaching the color of a beet as he let out waves of wild laughter. "I can't believe people—" He froze. "The tea cakes!" He shot to his feet, not waiting for a reply as he dashed from the small chamber.

Preston chuckled to himself as he watched the man leave. He rather liked Alvin, though he had to wonder how one such as he had wound up part of a cult. Maybe he had family connections?

He dismissed the thought as Alvin reappeared with a white apron wrapped around his cultist robes, clutching a metal tray with two fluffy oven mittens. The scent alone drove Preston to his feet.

Precisely twenty-four bite-sized pastries lined the sheet, each cut into pristine squares with a flourish of bright pink frosting for decoration. Smell aside, if the treats tasted as good as they looked, Preston might have to kidnap the cultist for his own culinary purposes. He never got a chance to find out.

Three robed figures rushed into the room from the other entrance, their gasps for breath a prelude to the panic in their voices. All three began speaking at once, wasting precious seconds on a jumbled mess of words before one finally took the lead. "Alvin! Have you seen Lord Melithor? We have a problem!"

"We certainly do," a familiar snide voice sounded from behind the kind baker-cultist. The cult leader—presumably Lord Melithor—stepped into the tight room flanked by two others. "What's this I hear about—oh, thank you Alvin." He paused to snatch a tea cake from

Alvin's tray. The room fell terribly silent as he chewed.

The cultists trembled.

He swallowed, venom returning to his voice. "What's this I hear about the nursery?"

"They've—um—they've burned it, your holiness. It's gone."

Alvin gasped. "Not the puppies!"

Melithor cursed. "Without the hellhounds, Garaxia will be without Her army. She won't be pleased." He addressed his frightened underlings, "How did they find the nursery? Which of you idiots forgot to enchant the key to break if they interfered with its casing?"

"It's a wooden key!" a voice protested. "It would've snapped like a twig if they tried to break it free or caught fire if they tried to melt the ice!"

The leader rubbed his temples. "Caught fire? *That's* your excuse? And what, pray tell, happens to ice when it melts?"

"It—um—it turns to water?"

"And how well does wood burn when it's *soaking gods-damned wet?*" he yelled through his teeth.

The cultists cowered before him.

Melithor continued, "You're all useless! Somehow I've managed to gather the least competent group of people to ever summon an archdemon!" He paused, every ounce of cruelty disappearing from his tone. "Not you, Alvin. You're doing a wonderful job and we all appreciate you."

Alvin beamed as a chorus of nods reaffirmed the praise, only to halt as Lord Melithor turned back to his other underlings.

"But the rest of you—useless! Please at least tell me you've completed preparations for the summoning ritual. We're lucky the adventurers took the long way here."

"Yes, your holiness," a quivering voice answered. "We're nearly—"

He cut off as a horrible demonic cry echoed in the distance.

Melithor cursed. "They're at our gods-damned front door. Nearly isn't gonna cut it. Finish the runes, prepare the altar, rein in the imps, whatever still needs to be done. I don't wanna hear excuses, I want you to do your damned jobs."

He reached into his robe, withdrawing a crooked knife of pure obsidian. "If you all fuck this up, I swear to Her Greatness those adventurers won't need to do shit. I'll kill you myself." Six cultists trembled at the violence in his words until he tacked on an extra "Not you, Alvin." The remaining five continued their trembling.

"Go!" he barked, shocking the gathered cultists into action. With a vile grin, Melithor turned to address Alvin with a sudden warmth in his voice. "Prepare the *Priestess*," he ordered before heading off for one of the open tunnels. "It's showtime."

Chapter 42

Showtime

Alvin didn't seem to realize Preston had slipped free of his bindings even as he grabbed the *Priestess* and slung him over his shoulder with surprising *Strength*. Preston struggled, of course.

Having failed to escape the cage, freeing himself from Alvin was his next best bet at avoiding the sacrificial altar. Much as he disliked writhing and kicking and scratching at the kind cultist, he disliked the idea of dying to summon an archdemon even less. The *Priestess* was smart enough to realize that every second he could delay the ritual was another opportunity for his companions to arrive. So he struggled.

Unfortunately, his unimproved eight base *Strength* proved useless against Alvin's ironclad grip. Hells, the cultist didn't even react to Preston's efforts. Whether he was too strong to notice or too polite to comment, Alvin practically skipped down the icy tunnel with the healer in tow.

Preston gave up three minutes in. "How—how are you so strong? I didn't think *Cultist* gave any *Strength*."

"It doesn't," Alvin chirped. "I was a *Blacksmith's*

Apprentice before Lord Melithor found me. Racked up a lot of *Strength* and not much else."

Preston furrowed his brow as he tried and failed to imagine the short-statured baker working a forge. "So how does a trainee blacksmith end up here?"

Alvin's shrug dug into Preston's stomach. "I always hated it. Stuck in a hot smithy all day with a bunch of folks too distracted by the clanging of their hammers to hold a pleasant conversation. I practically jumped at the chance to leave when I found Lord Melithor's pamphlet."

"His... pamphlet? He was recruiting for his evil cult by handing out *pamphlets?*"

"How else would he have done it?" Alvin asked. "It's foolproof, really. No man could gaze upon Garaxia's beauty without becoming enthralled. Of course, the leaflets only had a crude sketch, but even that was enough to sway the hearts of many."

Again with the 'no man,' Preston thought. He opened his mouth to ask about the word choice, or even why he'd yet to see a female cultist, but Alvin beat him to it.

"Oh, here we are!" He stopped short in the middle of a hallway. "I've known brothers of Her cult to stand here and gaze up at Her mural for hours."

Two thoughts crossed Preston's mind as he twisted his neck to look up at the painted wall. The first was that Garaxia was anything but beautiful. Her skin was the same deep blue of the demonic ice, and her face was warped both in rage and by the pair of tusks jutting past her upper lip. The mural depicted her wielding two brutally jagged swords, each stained red with the blood of whoever army she'd been cutting through.

The second thought to pop up in Preston's mind was of understanding. *Welp,* he sighed to himself, *that explains why the cult is all men.*

Garaxia was topless.

As Preston reasoned, either the painter had taken a good number of artistic liberties with the size of her chest, or the demoness herself employed some amount of illusion magic, because there was no way *those* had any place on a field of battle.

"Isn't She magnificent?" Alvin muttered.

"Alvin, *no*," Preston answered. "You could do so much better."

The cultist sighed. "Look, I'm sure Ayla is absolutely lovely, but I couldn't just abandon my friends."

Preston snorted. "'Lovely' isn't a word I would use to describe Ayla, but that's not my point." He shook his head, thinking better of diving into Alvin's love life at that particular moment. He switched tactics. "Are you sure this is the kind of person you want to be? There are more options between *Cultist* and *Blacksmith.*"

"That's the plan!" Alvin grinned. "Lord Melithor says once She's summoned, Garaxia will grant a boon to all who contributed to Her great arrival. I'm going to ask for money to start a tea shop."

Preston blinked. "A tea shop?"

"Yep!"

"There are easier ways to get funding. Why didn't you just... get a loan?" The *Priestess* sighed. "Hells, if you let me go I'll give you the gods-damned silver myself."

"Really? Awww, that's so nice of you! It's not just about me, though. Larry needs to pay his brother's bail, Riley needs to hunt down the basilisk that killed his father, and Andrew needs Her help to locate his missing son. I can't abandon them."

Preston instinctively moved to rub his temples at this headache of a situation, but Alvin's restraining grasp held his arm in place. "You're all gonna die. If my friends don't kill you, some other party will, and that's *if* you survive summoning an archdemon in the first place."

Alvin shrugged. "We can't all be adventurers, and we can't all fight our way to what we want." He looked up at the mural. "We take the opportunities that present themselves. Either they pan out or they don't. At least at the end we can say that we tried."

He turned, leaving the painting behind as he continued on down the frigid hallway.

As Preston's mind raced to find ways to refute the cultist's statement, he found his arguments increasingly hopeless. He could only hope the coming bloodshed wouldn't prove as costly as he feared.

* * *

"All ready?" Urgency filled Wes's voice as he addressed the others.

Eve watched her Mana pool tick up as the potion did its work. "Just about. A few seconds left on my cooldowns, but they'll be up in time to fight."

Alex simply nodded.

"Alright." Eve positioned herself against the cold stone of the massive door. "I open it and Alex steps in first?"

"Is that the best strategy?" the warrior asked. "Pushing open this behemoth won't exactly be subtle, and that's *if* it's even unlocked."

The air glowed orange as Wes's hand came alight. "I'll burn it down if I have to. One way or another, we're going through that door."

"Right, right, subtlety isn't your strong suit," Eve teased. "Maybe there's another secret passage we could—"

She trailed off as a chorus of masculine voices filled the cavern, somehow unmuffled through the thick door. They chanted in a language unknown to the *Striker*, but she didn't need to understand the words to know they didn't mean anything good.

Wes stopped forward. "Time's up."

Eve nodded, bracing herself against the cobblestone

floor.   With a burst of strength and the aid of her **Surefooted** to keep her from sliding, she *shoved*.

The gargantuan, foot-thick door swung open without resistance, slamming into the interior wall with a resounding thud. It was apparently not only unlocked but also enchanted for ease of opening. Whoops.

The chanting came to an abrupt halt as two dozen hooded faces turned to stare at the intruders.

"So much for subtlety." Eve drew her mace.

The ritual chamber itself was octagonal in shape, roughly eighty feet across in all directions. The walls were lined with paintings and tapestries of a half-naked demon woman Eve could only assume was Garaxia, but she had neither the time nor attention to spare judging the tasteless depictions.

A stone table dominated the cavern's center. It rested upon a wide platform, atop which the entire congregation of cultists stood in a circle. Eve had just a moment to note the demonic runes carved into the floor and the familiar *Priestess* tied down to the sacrificial altar before the first frost bolt flew her way.

Alex leapt forward, catching the projectile on her shield. Three more followed.

The room erupted with flame as Wes launched his own barrage in retaliation. It was met with screams of agony. A smile began to spread across the mage's face as his spells did their work, only to falter and fail as an explosion of ice quenched the flames.

The already frigid air turned sharp as the chill spread, forming a layer of frost upon the ground. Twice Wes tried to continue his assault and twice his **Fire Bolts** flickered out before they reached their target.

The cultists didn't let up. Each time Eve made a move to dash from behind the cover of Alex's shield, a frost bolt flew by, sending her back to the *Survivor's* protection.

J.P. Valentine

"Hold fast!" Alex called. "They have to run out of Mana eventually!"

Eve bit her lip, counting the impacts as spell after spell struck the warrior's shield. She waited.

It wasn't a lapse in the onslaught that eventually prompted Eve to leap into action. It was the series of hideous inhuman cries.

She **Charged!**

A whirlwind of frost encircled the dais, obscuring the platform in its own contained blizzard. No wonder Wes's spells had failed. A silhouette stood at the maelstrom's center, his arms held to the sky as he channeled the protective spell. Eve could worry about him later—if he was busy channeling he wasn't stabbing Preston.

Instead, she turned her focus towards the steady stream of figures emerging from the tempest. Eve gripped her mace.

Were it not for the familiar robes they still wore, Eve might've thought them summoned beasts. As it was, whatever metamorphosis they'd undergone had left little humanity behind.

Their skin took on the same deep-blue sheen as the demons, their hands grown to slender claws nearly as long as Eve's entire arm. Pointed horns tore through the tops of their hoods, matched by the viscous maws of needle-sharp teeth that stretched across their faces.

Eve had her work cut out for her.

She picked a target and raced towards it, pulling back her mace for a deadly swing as **Mana Rush**ed through her. She counted down as she approached, waiting for the strike she knew was coming.

Three.

Her heart raced, pumping warmth through her to counteract the frost in the air.

Two.

She held her breath.

One.

She leapt back as the transformed cultist took his swing, her feet sticking well to the frozen floor as **Surefooted** did its job.

Her opponent had no such skill.

The demonic hybrid skidded forward as it lost its balance, its shredded boots unable to find purchase on the slick ice. Eve's mace was ready for it.

You have defeated Level 48 Cultist of Garaxia: +1830 exp!

Eve dismissed the notification, not even bothering to grin as she turned to face her next opponent. Even as Alex swung her spear and even Wes joined the fray wielding **Burning Hand** where **Fire Bolt** had failed, she moved with haste.

They had too many foes left to defeat before they could turn their attention towards the altar and the blizzard protecting it, and the *Striker* could only wonder what was going on within.

* * *

Preston strained against his bindings as he jerked his head back and forth between the only two figures that remained within the confines of the ice storm. Adrenaline more than anything fought off the cold as loose bits of snow and ice pelted his skin.

"Finish the ritual!" Melithor yelled over the howling wind as he maintained his spell. "I'll hold them back as long as I can!"

Alvin gulped, his eyes flicking from his master's impressive figure to Preston's pleading gaze to the jagged knife at Melithor's waist.

"You don't have to do this!" Preston shouted.

"But my friends need—"

"They're dead, Alvin!" the *Priestess* shouted. "Or they will be soon. Your ritual won't even bloody work with me as your sacrifice."

"We should've gagged him," Melithor sneered. "He's just trying to save his own skin. Do it, Alvin, for the glory of Garaxia!"

Alvin gulped. With a shaking hand he reached out to claim the ritual knife.

"If you do this, there's no going back. They'll kill you. You can still surrender. You can still stand down. I won't let them hurt you if I'm still alive to talk to them."

A demonic screech pierced the snowstorm as yet another cultist fell to Eve's mace and Wes's flames.

Alvin jerked his head in the direction of the noise, his eyes glassing over as he stared at the whirling ice. "Larry…"

"You can't save them, but it's not too late to save yourself! You can still have your teashop."

The knife fell to the floor. "I… I had to try."

"And you did! But this won't work. I'm telling you, another opportunity is presenting itself. You just have to take it."

Melithor snapped. "Don't listen to him! You're destined for greatness, Alvin. Now claim it!"

Alvin ran.

The storm parted for him as he dashed through. Preston watched with bated breath as his silhouette separated itself from the chaos of battle, slipping away down a side passage. He smiled.

A string of expressive, if unoriginal, curses escaped the cult leader's mouth as he took a step back. "Useless, cowardly, imbeciles all of them!" He lowered a hand, the whirlwind visibly weakening as he diverted a portion of his attention from its upkeep. "If you want something done right…" He reached for the fallen knife.

It wasn't there.

Between maintaining his defensive spell and cursing out Alvin, Melithor had failed to notice a baby drake in the process of chewing through a certain length of rope—a very specific length of rope, in fact.

Preston surged forward, thrusting with all his measly eight *Strength*. The jagged knife buried itself in Melithor's neck. "Alvin deserves so much better than you," he growled. "Maybe now he'll find it."

He didn't need to read the notification to know Melithor was dead.

The winds died down and the tempest faded as the cult leader collapsed to the stone floor, allowing the faintest glimmer of warmth to return to the frigid air. It echoed through Preston's heart as three familiar faces greeted him.

"Hey guys," he managed, still clutching the bloody dagger, "long time no see."

Chapter 43

Is it Getting Cold in Here or is it Just Me?

Eve managed to keep her eyes on Preston for all of two seconds before he disappeared once more, this time behind two hundred and fifty pounds of fire mage. She had to wait until Wes was good and finished for her own turn to hug the rescued healer.

"Good timing," he eventually said once all the pleasantries of being reunited were complete. "They almost had me there." He rubbed the back of his neck. "Not sure why you chose to take the long way here."

Wes's brow shot up. "The *what?*"

Eve smirked. "Found a secret tunnel, broke some ice, burned some demons, ya know, dungeon stuff."

Preston's face lit up. "Any good loot?"

"Not yet." Eve shrugged. "But there's two dozen dead cultists that have gotta have *something* valuable."

Wes stepped in, his eyes already flashing blue. "Messages first, loot second."

"He's right," Alex said, still grasping her spear and shield. "I'm not letting my guard down until I see a 'dungeon complete' notification."

Eve snorted. "Yeah, *that's* why Wes wants to do

notifications first. It's got nothing to do with how close he is to tier three."

Too distracted by his reading to formulate a witty reply, Wes resorted to the good old rude gesture.

Eve returned one she knew he couldn't see before opening her own blinking messages.

You have defeated Level 48 Cultist of Garaxia: +1830 exp!
You have defeated Level 48 Cultist of Garaxia: +1830 exp!
You have defeated Level 47 Cultist of Garaxia: +1770 exp!
...
You have defeated Level 36 Cultist of Garaxia: +1110 exp!

Twenty-three cultists in all left her with a grand total of 34410 exp. Had she been blessed with the opportunity to have been tasting one of Alvin's delicious tea cakes at that particular moment, she would've spat it out. How had a bunch of cultists gotten so high-level? Why were they worth so much? It seemed too easy.

Eve shrugged internally, deciding ultimately not to look a gift demon in the mouth. She'd take whatever exp she could get.

Level Up!
Level Up!

Ability Upgraded!
  Passive Ability - Surefooted
  Circulate Mana through your feet to adhere to surfaces!

Eve's immediate thought was of climbing walls. She even took a step towards the nearest pillar to see if she could walk up it before realizing the description only mentioned her feet—a vertical wall would *certainly* require the use of her hands as well.

The upgrade was probably targeted more towards icy or moving surfaces. The *Striker* was just fostering ideas of standing upright on the back of a griffin in flight when another concern arose.

Will this work through boots?

Her daggers required physical contact for her to charge them, and Eve wasn't particularly fond of her bare feet coming into physical contact with stuff. Maybe she could find some enchanted boots that would allow Mana through? She sighed. It was another thing she'd need to spend money on.

Ability Unlocked!
Active Ability - Mana Burst
300 Mana
You don't need to be a master spell caster to simply throw Mana at the problem. Unleash a short-range blast of concentrated Mana, dealing magic damage in an area in front of you.

Warning: You have reached the Active Ability cap. Please choose an ability to replace.

Eve was conflicted. She *had* vowed to replace **Fate-al Blow** at the earliest opportunity—both for its cringeworthy name and relative uselessness—but its strength scaling combined with **Mana Rush** was nothing to scoff at.

Beyond even that, **Mana Burst** looked an awful lot like a worse version of her daggers. It had a fixed Mana cost—unlike the enchanted weapons—that had to be paid on cast instead of being stored ahead of time. Then again, the words "area in front of you" *did* spark her interest. Any skill that could hit multiple enemies at once would be useful, short range or otherwise.

Sure, she had Wes for that, but what if they got

separated? It had already happened once in the Burendian ruin, and in all likelihood would happen again *eventually*.

She could, of course, replace a different ability, but they were more important than **Fate-al Blow**. **Charge!** and **Mana Rush** were the core of her kit, and **Jet** had far too many possible uses or future upgrades to even consider replacing. Eve exhaled.

"At least I'm free from the pun," she muttered as she accepted the change. It hurt to lose the ability, but **Mana Rush** alone did insane single-target damage. **Fate-al Blow** was redundant. Being well-rounded was more important.

Eve blinked the blue from her vision as the last of the notifications faded away. It took more than a minute for her eyes to readjust from the bright glow of the status screen back to the dimly lit ritual chamber. When at last they did, she was unsurprised to find Alex already finished with her own messages while Wes still read on.

The disappointed look on Preston's face, however, did elicit a reaction.

"You alright?"

The *Priestess* shrugged. "I didn't get credit for killing the cultists, just Melithor here." He pointed down at the bleeding corpse at his feet. "Got me to level twenty-four."

Eve cringed. He was so close to his next promotion, yet there were no demons left to kill. "No milestones either?"

"No, not for…" He trailed off. "It doesn't matter. I'll get there soon enough."

"Yeah," Alex barked, "once we've actually finished the dungeon. That drops exp, remember?"

"Right!" Eve snapped her fingers. "So how do we finish it? Are there more monsters?"

"Or we need to find the core," Preston said.

"So… back into the tunnels?"

"Well," the healer thought aloud, "if the Burendian ruin was anything to go by, it'll be somewhere fairly central, with a lot of magic, and of import to the theme of the dungeon."

The three turned as one to stare at the stone altar.

Eve was the first to get to it—fifty-four percent higher movement speed had its perks. She stepped over Melithor's body and the carved runes in the floor to reach the rectangular block of stone itself. Sure enough, a head-sized obsidian sphere sat inlaid in its center.

Preston was the first to speak. "So—um—how do we get it out?"

Eve drew her daggers. "Dungeon cores are explosion-resistant, right?"

Alex placed a halting hand on Eve's arm. "Let's not find out. We can either chisel it out or wait for Wes to burn the altar down once he's done with his reading."

Eve sighed, pressing the tips of her daggers into the space between the stone and the core. "Alright, hard way it is. I'm gonna have to completely resharpen these, aren't I?"

Without waiting for a response, she dumped a few points of Mana into **Mana Rush** before getting to work. She had nearly pried the thing free when Wes's voice filled the chamber.

"What are you all standing around for?"

"Dungeon core," Alex explained.

"You finished with your reading, then?" Eve asked.

"Yep," Wes chirped. "Unlocked six classes, but only one of them's worth taking. It's nothing particularly interesting, just the natural continuation of the Devouring Flame line, but it's way better than the other options."

Eve furrowed her brow. "Is that a good idea? You've been getting a bit—I don't want to say crazy, but... flame-happy? Maybe the Devouring Flame isn't worth fucking with."

"I'm fine." A sharpness overcame Wes's voice, his

comment hanging in the air for a moment before he recovered his excitement. "I haven't even told you the best part! *Disciple of the Devouring Flame* is gods-damned *Epic.*"

Alex cursed. "Of course," she muttered more to herself than anyone else. "Of bloody course he gets an *Epic* class at tier 3. Why shouldn't he?"

Eve reacted a bit more positively. "Wes, that's amazing! At this rate, you'll be *Legendary* by level a hundred."

"You—um—" Preston stammered, "you know who else was a *Disciple?*" He pointed down at the former Lord Melithor. "*He* was."

Wes exhaled. "Look, we don't have to decide right now. I'm not taking the promotion until I'm sure we're safe. Who in their right mind would let themselves pass out in the middle of a dungeon?"

Eve and Alex exchanged a sideways glance at that, knowing the *Survivor* had done exactly that in the Burendian ruin.

"You sure?" Eve asked. "You'll miss out on the dungeon completion exp if you don't evolve first."

Wes shrugged. "There'll always be more exp. Besides, I don't want to miss out on the looting!" He made a move for the nearest body, carefully maneuvering around the assorted claws and spikes and horns it had grown in combat. "There's gotta be something worth taking in here somewhere."

Eve rolled her eyes at the typical display of adventurer greed before returning to her task of defacing a religious artifact to claim the dungeon core within. It was a messy process. Chips of stone and dust flew in all directions as she worked, chiseling away at the altar with every strike. It wasn't until she held the foot-thick orb in her hands that the notification appeared.

You have cleared dungeon: Temple of Garaxia: +20000

exp!

Level Up!

Ability Upgraded!
   Active Ability - Jet
   Apply the momentum change to individual body parts!

"Well shit," Eve swore to herself. Just as she gave up **Fate-al Blow**, **Jet** evolved into a sort of replacement. She couldn't really see any use for the change other than to speed up her mace swing, but if she ever needed extra damage, it would certainly do the job. Given the power of **Mana Rush,** she had to wonder if the cooldown would be better spent using **Jet** to maneuver around the battlefield, but the option was nice to have.

It was Preston's turn to read a long list of potential evolutions while the others discussed.

"That was…" Eve said, "a lot more exp than the ruins gave."

Alex shrugged. "It's a higher level dungeon. Now put that thing away and we can move on to these cultists."

Eve nodded, rearranging the contents of her pack to fit the dungeon core inside. By the time she finished, Wes was already leaning over Melithor himself. She watched as he slipped a hand from the cultist's pocket to his own, wondering why he didn't bring up the find to the others. She opened her mouth to ask about it just in time for Preston to step in first.

"Hey guys? Is it getting cold in here, or is it just me?"

Truth be told, Eve had no idea. She certainly didn't *feel* cold, but she hadn't felt cold this entire time.

"It's always been cold," Alex answered from across the room.

Wes sat up, holding a jagged sacrificial dagger in his

hand. "Do you think this is worth anything?"

Eve shrugged. "Probably? If you've got space in your bag for it, you might as well—"

Preston interrupted, "Ayla's tits that's a lot of blood."

The *Striker* peeked around Wes's wide body to peer at the now unplugged knife wound in Melithor's neck. An unnatural amount of crimson gushed from the corpse, flowing along the runes in the floor like so much water through a maze of canals.

Her eyes widened. "That can't be good."

Wes lunged forward, sticking a single finger in one of the rune structures to stymie the flow, too low on Mana to find a more elegant solution. Were it not for the seriousness of the situation or the simple fact every *other* segment of the vast engraving still had blood running through it, Eve might've laughed at the silliness of the display. Instead, she drew her mace.

Alex leapt up to the dais to join them. "What's going on?"

"Their ritual," Wes answered, "I think it's working."

Sure enough, a fingertip wasn't enough to fully disrupt whatever magic drove the spell forward. The blood surged around Wes's makeshift stopper, continuing on to fill out the entire floor's worth of runes.

"So—uh... if sacrificing a virgin *Priestess* summons Garaxia, what happens when you sacrifice a *Disciple* and two dozen *Cultists?*"

None of the four companions were remotely well-versed enough in demonology to actually answer Preston's question. They knew nothing of Mana alignments or soul frequencies or any of the other jargon best kept to scholars.

What they did know, however, was that whether or not they could venture a reasonable guess as to the result of the imminent summoning, they were sure as hell about to find out.

Chapter 44

Prove Your Valor

You have entered the dungeon: Goblin Warren! Fight well.

"Ooh, we get a neat little message and everything." Liam grinned, twirling one of his throwing knives around his fingers. "Fight well."

"I'll show them fighting well," Jason laughed, his chest sticking out as he rested his hands on his waist. Truth be told he looked rather heroic posing like that with his plate armor and the steel sword hanging at his hip, not that Alex would ever admit that.

"You gonna keep peacocking or are we gonna actually clear this place?" she asked.

Priya giggled, covering her mouth with the draping sleeve of her oversized hand-me-down Witch's robe. "Let him have his fun. It's not like we're on a clock or anything."

Liam smirked. "We didn't come here so Jason could show off his shiny new armor. We came to kill some gods-damned goblins."

"Yeah," Alex added, "the longer we waste letting Jason have his fun, the longer I've gotta wait before I can have mine." She planted the butt of her spear in the rocky soil beneath her feet.

"Gotta get that exp somehow."

"Alright, alright." Jason drew his sword, taking the first step down the dark tunnel. *"We'll see if any actually live to get past me."*

"Careful you don't get cocky," Liam teased, executing yet more flashy feats of sleight of hand with his short blades, *"can't kill anything that's already got a knife in its neck."*

Priya rolled her eyes. *"Boys, boys, you're both pretty. Now let's go. You can brag about your kills once you actually have them."*

Alex resisted the temptation to prod at them with her spear, choosing instead to swallow her impatience as the Knight and the Knifesinger took the lead. Her quest said she had to *"prove her valor,"* and she was going to have a hard time doing that if her friends took all the kills. She sighed.

The two men walked abreast as long as they could, but this burrow wasn't built for humans. Ten minutes in, the passage had already constricted enough to force them into single file.

The taller members of the party, specifically Alex and Jason, even had to stoop over to fit beneath the damp earth ceiling. Unable to hold her weapon upright, Alex found herself falling behind her companions in order to avoiding stabbing them in the back as she carried her spear pointed forward. At least she'd be ready for any goblins that somehow managed to get past all three of her friends.

From her limited vantage at the back of the procession, she never had a chance to see the ambush coming.

It wasn't until Priya's horrific shriek filled the cramped tunnel that Alex even knew something was wrong.

Jason collapsed backwards with a heavy thud, his armored form pinning Liam to the ground. With Priya in the way, Alex couldn't see the arrow in his eye or the crimson running down his neck or the emerald glow of Priya's magic desperately trying to stem the bleeding. It did no good. She was a Witch, not a Necromancer.

Liam panicked. Lacking the Strength to move the mass of muscle and armor atop him, the rogue could but flail his blades in the air to try and fend off the coming foes.

Alex's heart raced. She instinctively lurched forward to grant what help she could, but Priya blocked the way. There simply wasn't space in the confines of the warren to allow the Soldier *past.*

Her muscles tensed up. Her breathing quickened.

Priya abandoned her healing, leaning down to help lift the fallen Knight. *She was too late.*

Two kill notifications popped up in Alex's vision as Liam threw what knives he could with his free arm. His efforts ended with a goblin spear through his throat.

The goblins' smaller forms maneuvered deftly through the tunnel, stepping over the bodies to continue their assault. Priya had no way to stop the charge.

Alex ran.

She dropped her spear, letting the weapon fall to the floor rather than try and reverse her grip on it in the confined space. She ran back through the dirt tunnels, through the layer of foliage atop the dungeon's entrance, through the grasslands she'd once thought peaceful. No more.

It wasn't until her Stamina ran out that she collapsed to the soft earth, panic and adrenaline finally giving way to tears. It wasn't supposed to be like this. They were heroes. They were adventurers, slaying monsters and saving lives, each and all destined for greatness.

But here she was, crying alone in an empty field. It wasn't a game. It wasn't a grand adventure to save the world. It wasn't even a worthwhile adversary. A couple of goblins was all it took, and for all her training and all her confidence, there was nothing Alex could've done about it.

The sky glowed red with the setting sun by the time she finally stood.

As Alexandra Reeve took her first steps on the long walk back home, a single thought drove her forward. It kept her going as she fought with the guild to claim what pay she could for the failed dungeon, as she spent her final coin replacing the lost spear, and as her finances forced her to once again sign up at the guild to be paired with a new team.

Next time there'd be something she could do about it.

Next time, she wouldn't run.

* * *

The air itself broke apart. A jagged crack ran from the vaulted ceiling to the stone floor, spewing frost into the ritual chamber. Eve took a step back. "I don't have the Mana for another fight."

Wes nodded in agreement.

Preston snatched his pack off the ground, digging through it in search of the relevant potions. Alex stood at his side, reaching in to withdraw one for herself.

The crack widened.

Eve took a step back, her heel colliding with the stone altar behind her. Shifting silhouettes appeared on the other side of the growing portal, outlines of horns and teeth and claws she'd sooner forget than engage in combat.

The crack widened.

"I don't know about this," Wes said, shouldering his own pack.

The crack widened.

Eve got her first good glimpse of the veritable horde within. They were each over eight feet tall, their flesh a haphazard collection of rough stones bound together by a layer of dark ice. Their eyes glowed blue.

The crack widened.

Level ?? Lithodemon
Level ?? Lithodemon
Level ?? Lithodemon
Level ?? Lithodemon

Four **Appraises** was enough for Eve.

"Run!"

They ran.

Wes was the first to heed her call, picking one from the array of doorways and dashing for it.

Eve lingered for a moment to make sure Alex and Preston made it in after him before following herself. With her supernatural speed, she would always catch up, and there was no point in running ahead. Her efforts would be better spent helping anyone who fell behind.

Wes's staff came alight as they ran, his flames lighting the way through the dark tunnel.

The cavern shook as howls rang out behind them.

Preston stumbled, but Eve was there to support him as he regained his footing. She took the opportunity to look back.

The demons were coming.

They ran on all fours, like the twisted amalgam of man and beast and golem they were. Their icy claws scraped against the stone with every bounding step, forming a dissonant chorus of ice and rock to join their terrible snarls.

Fear welled in the depths of Eve's stomach, not for herself but for her companions. *She* could outrun the high-level demons. Her friends couldn't.

They came in droves. Only three could fit abreast along the tunnel's floor, so the monstrosities found space along the walls and ceiling, digging into the stone as they charged. It painted a horrifying picture as the horde seemed to devour the passage itself.

At least the path ahead held some hope. Its straight and upward slope didn't escape Eve's attention. This tunnel they'd chosen had to lead *somewhere*, and she could only hope that somewhere was outside. She tried not to think about the fact the demons could just follow them out. It wasn't like there was much she could do about it.

Alex had a similar thought.

Eve noticed the warrior lift a leather pouch to her mouth, downing the potion as she continued to run.

The demons drew nearer, their howls more ravenous, their clawing louder.

They weren't going to make it.

Eve's mind raced as she fled, deliberately slowing herself to keep pace with her companions. There had to be *something* she could do. She considered carrying them like she'd once carried Wes, but she had more companions than she had arms. She mentally reread each of her abilities, desperately brainstorming for some combination that could stop the coming horde.

She found none.

The cavern grew brighter as the ethereal white glow of raw Mana filled the air. Eve scowled. She hadn't eaten anything. Hells, with all the running her Mana pool should've been *shrinking*. A quick scan of her status screen confirmed it was.

It took Alex stopping short in the tunnel's center for Eve to realize what was going on.

That was no Stamina potion the *Survivor* had swiped from Preston's supply.

The web of lines along Alex's right hand shone with blinding brilliance as she clutched her spear.

Eve froze. "What are you doing?!"

The Burendian Mana core in the warrior's spear glowed brighter than it ever had. The weapon vibrated with energy as Alex pushed it well beyond its capacity. "You can't outrun them!" she called back.

Eve's heart froze. She ran back to stand at Alex's side. "And you can't fight them!"

The warrior's face hardened, determination sharpening her jaw. "I don't have to."

"Alex, you can't—"

Alex snapped, "I'm not running. Not again." She held up her spear, its enchantments already growing unstable. "Remember the Burendian sentry golem?"

The demons grew closer.

"Alex, no!"

"This isn't just about *us*. How many people will they kill if they get out of here? We have to do *something*."

Eve's stomach sank. "Not this."

Alex swallowed. "I'm not running," she repeated. Her eyes flashed blue as a notification appeared.

Eve knew she'd lost the moment she glimpsed the message's reflection.

Life Quest Complete: Prove Your Valor.

"Alex, I—"

The howls rang louder.

"Run!" Alex barked.

Eve ran.

Her **Haste** carried her away from the lone *Survivor* even as the tears began to fall. She couldn't look back as Alex slammed her spear tip into the stone wall. The weapon snapped.

Eve **Charged** forward as the explosion shook the very ground beneath her. Only **Surefooted** kept her on her feet as the first of the rocks began to fall.

She caught up with Preston first, snatching him off his feet to carry him under her arm. She grabbed Wes in similar fashion moments later.

With a companion under each arm, Eve shot through the cavern, stone and dirt collapsing behind her. The last of the howls fell silent long before the earth finally stilled.

Eve released Wes and Preston with a shaky breath, all three adventurers turning to look back the way they'd come at once. A wall of stone greeted them.

"Did—um—" Preston stammered, "did Alex just…"

"She did." Eve gulped. "Brought the cavern down on top of herself to stop the demons getting out."

"Gods below," Wes cursed. "Do you think she could've —I mean—she's a *Survivor*, right?"

"I don't—I can't imagine she—" Eve sighed. "I don't know, Wes. It doesn't seem likely. I mean…" She trailed off, gesturing to the mass of rubble before them.

"Shit."

"We knew what we were getting into," Eve murmured. "Adventurers are good at two things: drinking and dying."

The guardswoman's words cut through them. They all remembered how she'd directed them to the graveyard upon their arrival at Foot's Garrison. The thought didn't help.

Eve exhaled, fighting back the tightening of her throat. Silence dominated the stale air as she turned her gaze ahead, squinting down the passage ahead. They weren't home yet.

"Wait," she said, "do you guys see that?"

Wes and Preston followed her gesture, nodding along as they confirmed the sight.

There, in the distance, beyond an untellable distance of gloom, a glimmer of autumn sun shined in. However dark and twisted and hopeless their journey there may have been, at least this tunnel in particular had a light at the end.

Chapter 45

The Wrong End

Three adventurers walked together down a dark tunnel, each wrapped deep in their own thoughts as they processed in silent solemnity. Eve kept her face stoic. She could appreciate the irony of the *Survivor* being the first to die, whether or not her companions still held out hope.

Even if Alex had lived through the initial cave-in, no number of survival skills could keep someone alive long trapped beneath a thousand tons of stone. Eve shuddered. She'd rather die outright than slowly suffocate under a mountain of rubble.

She wondered, as they followed the gentle slope up to the distant light of the cave's mouth, what she would do next. Maybe she'd take a break. It'd been some time since she'd been home to Nowherested, and Eve could *certainly* use some of her mother's cocoa right about now.

Continuing as an adventurer would mean heading back to Foot's Garrison, selling the dungeon core and other loot, collecting the measly fee for the job itself, and making the trek all the way to Lynthia to find a new tank. Replacing Alex felt hollow, wrong somehow. Eve swallowed. A break sounded good.

It was shortly after coming to the decision that Eve noticed something off about the light to which they walked. It was unfiltered. There was a purity to the orange glow, a certain crispness devoid of the mottled shadows of a forest canopy.

Eve squinted. "Do you... see any trees?"

"No?" Wes shrugged. "So this exit's in a clearing. Or a bit farther into the mountains. Shouldn't be too difficult to find our way back; south is south, after all."

"Right," Eve said, allowing the conversation to go quiet once more. She *had* known this wasn't the way they'd come in; it was only a question of exactly how far they'd traveled in the maze of passages. She hoped it wasn't too far.

Her concern only grew as they traveled closer and closer to the opening. From her vantage lower in the sloping tunnel, Eve could see no trees, no stone, no features of any kind. Only late afternoon sky filled the mouth ahead. It wasn't until they finally arrived that she realized *why*.

It was gods-damned high.

Or at least, Eve assumed they were high up. The exit spat them out upon a wide stone landing overlooking a sea of clouds. To her left a narrow stairway carved into the rock descended into the mists, but all other directions held only more of the same sheer cliff face.

The clouds themselves weren't quite right. She gazed across not the fluffy white of a spring day nor the gloomy gray of a summer storm, but a dirty pale brown. If she stared too long, they even seemed to pick up a hint of sickly green, a color no self-respecting cloud should *ever* be.

None of the land below revealed itself through the obscuring blanket, leaving Eve to wonder where exactly they'd found themselves.

Preston had an idea.

"Ayla's bloody tits," he cursed to himself.

Wes's face fell. "What's wrong?"

"We're fucked is what's wrong," the *Priestess* replied. "These are the dead fields."

Eve furrowed her brow. "What does that mean?"

"It means we're on the northern side of the gods-damned mountains." Preston's voice shook. "We've come out the wrong end."

"So we'll find a way back over. There's gotta be a pass around here somewhere." Eve gestured down the ragged stairway. "The path seems pretty clear."

"You don't understand," Preston said. "You ever wonder why the adventurer's guild has a tier four working the front desk? Because once you get to the high eighties, your options are either retire or come *here.*"

Eve gulped. "Okay. Okay. Um... alright. So we're lost in a place way higher level than we are. Got it. The good news is you both have class promotions pending."

Wes's eyes lit up. "You know, I'd forgotten about that."

Eve snorted. "No you didn't. You've spent this entire time daydreaming about how cool your *Epic* is gonna be. Your probably dangerous, going-to-drive-you-insane *Epic.*"

"Actually," Preston spoke up, "I think he should take it. We're gonna need all the power we can get. Wes's class driving him mad won't be a problem if none of us survive to make it home anyway."

Eve sighed. "You may be right." She rounded on Wes. "You'd better tell me if the whispers are getting to you."

He held up his hands. "I promise you, I will do my absolute best to avoid, you know, going *insane.*"

"Okay," Eve exhaled. "So we've got our *Disciple of the Devouring Flame.*" She turned towards Preston. "What about you?"

The healer shrugged. "No *Epics,* but I've got a *Rare: Caretaker of Ayla.* Something to do with animals. Thank you, Regi." He reached into his sleeve to caress the baby drake.

Wes snorted. "So you're a veterinarian now?"

"Hey, it beats being a *Priestess.*"

Eve held up two silencing hands. "Alright, you two. Let's just go ahead and accept the upgrades. I'll lookout." She tried not to think about keeping watch over Alex in the Burendian ruin while she'd slept through her promotion to *Survivor.*

Preston nodded, setting out his pack as a pillow as he lay on the hard stone.

Wes lingered for a moment, watching the healer's eyee turn blue and then shut entirely as sleep took him. The mage exhaled. "Do you—um—" he started, "do you still have that chess piece the man of the mists gave you?"

Eve cocked an eyebrow at him as she reached into her pocket to withdraw the ivory knight. "Right here, why?"

"I found this in that cult leader's pocket."

Eve cursed as she gazed upon the item in Wes's hand. A bishop. It was the same snowy white, bore the same simple yet stylized carving, and released the same wafting tendrils of cool fog.

Wes handed it to her. "What does it mean?"

Eve turned the matching chess pieces over in her hand. "I don't know. Either Melithor was another potential recruit, or the man of the mists *intended* me to fight him and find this."

"So it's a test? Maybe you have to find a whole set's worth of pieces?"

"I don't know," she repeated. "Maybe." She shook her head, pocketing the knight and bishop. "I don't think I'd want to work for someone who recruits cultists. Or someone who puts together a bunch of cryptic puzzles for that matter." She shrugged. "We can worry about it later. Mysterious job offers don't mean shit if we all die to some high-level monster."

Wes nodded, stepping around to lie at Preston's side. "We're going to get out of this," he said as his eyes flashed blue with a status screen. "Just you wait."

Eve looked on with soft eyes and a hesitant grin as Wes too fell into a deep slumber. She breathed. The air was fresh on the mountainside, though she suspected that wouldn't last as they descended into the haze below. She'd have to enjoy it while she could.

It was only then, once the rhythmic snores of her companions left Eve in the comfort of solitude, that the tears finally came. She cried for the desperation of their situation. She cried for the wall of stone between her and the comforts of home. She cried for Alex.

The grief struck in waves, each passing with the mirage of solace before crashing against her anew. She'd only known the warrior a few weeks, and never well at that. Still she wept. How could there be joy and hope and laughter anymore? Alex was gone and with her the carefree world they'd all thus far enjoyed. Any one of them could be next.

Eve didn't let herself hold out hope. It was better this way, she told herself, better to face the grief now than to hide behind a bulwark of prayer that the *Survivor* might've done just that. Still she wept.

Only as the hours dragged on and the autumn sun dipped low upon the horizon, did Eve finally look up from her grief to marvel at the painting before her. Yellows and reds and pinks danced through the sky, twirling and blending with an artistry only the heavens could hope to match. The clouds beneath glowed orange with the fading sunlight, as if a sea of flame had come to cleanse the blanket of filth once and for all.

Eve smiled.

It was a weary thing, weak and wet with tears, but in

that moment, it was everything. For all the death and danger and general terribleness her bullshit life quest had set upon her, she could still appreciate the unearthly beauty of a sunset on a clear night.

And then she saw it.

A dark shape darted in and out of the sunlit haze, distant enough to be no more than a silhouette, but large enough to catch her notice from so far away. Eve squinted. Out of some combination of curiosity, boredom, and a need to confirm this place truly was as dangerous as Preston believed, she **Appraised** it.

Her eyes flashed blue and her jaw dropped open. She **Appraised** it again. The result was the same. Eve thought back to all the beasts she'd seen thus far. The drake, the golem, hells, even the *lithodemons* had all displayed with two question marks in place of their level. She reread the unsightly azure screen before her.

Level ??? Ironclaw Griffin

Eve's imagination ran wild as she envisioned what other sorts of monstrosity may lurk beneath the layer of clouds, what manner of beasts even a tier four might fear. She cursed. No matter how she thought and rethought through their situation, a single conclusion bubbled up again and again.

"Preston's right," she muttered to herself, "we *are* fucked."

Status

Evelia Greene
Manaheart
Level 38 Shatterfate Striker
Exp: 12715/25311
Health: 720/720
Stamina: 0/0
Mana: 2850/2850
Constitution: 72
Mana Density: 285
Intelligence: 12
Dexterity: 85
Strength: 108
Spirit: 0

Passive Ability - Haste

A quicker step is the difference between life and death. You run [MND/5]% faster.

Passive Ability - Surefooted

One slip up means death, and you've become familiar with high speeds and difficult terrain. Gain increased traction and stability, especially on moving objects. Circulate mana through your feet to adhere to surfaces!

Passive Ability - Mana-hardened

You've seen your fair share of battle, and your body has adapted for it. Gain increased bone density and resistance to impact injuries. +20% Explosion resistance. +20% Poison Resistance. Redirect mana within your body to reinforce particular areas.

Passive Ability - Ethereal Metabolism

Overcome the inefficiencies of flesh. Mana is the purest form of energy, and your body has learned to use it. Metabolize food directly into Mana. All bodily functions require Mana instead of Stamina.

Active Ability - Charge!
85 Mana

Put those feet to work. Whether ducking in or out of combat, a good Striker needs to do it quickly. Triple your maximum running speed for [MND/5] seconds.

Active Ability - Mana Rush
X Mana/Sec

The strength of a manaheart is determined by the energy that runs through their veins. You've learned to use that to your advantage. Gain [X*MND/20] Strength for the duration.

Active Ability - Mana Burst
300 Mana

You don't need to be a master spell caster to simply throw mana at the problem. Unleash a short-range blast of concentrated mana, dealing magic damage in an area in front of you.

Active Ability - Jet
500 Mana

Momentum is a tool just like any other, and you've learned to wield it.   Massively increase or decrease your personal momentum or that of an individual body part.